Glittering par~~~ ~~~~~~~~

passio~~~

Regency

HIGH-SOCIETY AFFAIRS

They're the talk of the Ton!

Beloved Virago
by Anne Ashley

&

Lord Trenchard's Choice
by Sylvia Andrew

The Regency

HIGH-SOCIETY AFFAIRS

Regency

HIGH-SOCIETY
AFFAIRS

Anne Ashley &
Sylvia Andrew

*M&B™ and M&B™ with the Rose Device
are trademarks of the publisher.*
Harlequin Mills & Boon Limited, Eton House,
18-24 Paradise Road, Richmond, Surrey TW9 1SR

First published in Great Britain in 2003

REGENCY HIGH-SOCIETY AFFAIRS
© Harlequin Books S.A. 2009

The publisher acknowledges the copyright holders of the
individual works as follows:

Beloved Virago © Anne Ashley 2003
Lord Trenchard's Choice © Sylvia Andrew 2003

ISBN: 978 0 263 87553 9

052-0709

*Printed and bound in Spain
by Litografia Rosés S.A., Barcelona*

Beloved Virago

by

Anne Ashley

Anne Ashley was born and educated in Leicester. She lived for a time in Scotland, but now makes her home in the West Country, with two cats, her two sons, and a husband who has a wonderful and very necessary sense of humour. When not pounding away at the keys of her word processor, she likes to relax in her garden, which she has opened to the public on more than one occasion in aid of the village church funds.

Chapter One

January 1815

Despite the vast improvements to many of the roads, the majority of those who could well afford to journey about the land remained unwilling to suffer the discomforts of winter travel unless the trip was totally unavoidable. Consequently Miss Katherine O'Malley had found no difficulty in attaining rooms for herself and her maid the previous afternoon, when a strengthening wind and the threat of snow had persuaded her to veer on the side of caution and seek refuge in a superior posting-house. Fortunately at some point during the night the wind, having changed direction, had eased considerably, and Katherine had woken to discover a landscape prettily laced with only the finest covering of snow and bathed in watery winter sunshine.

After glancing out of the window to view the highly encouraging sight of a carriage bowling along the road, Katherine returned her attention to her companion in time to see a freshly baked roll, liberally covered with jam, being consumed with relish, and succumbed to an imp of pure mischief.

'Most people might be forgiven for supposing that the substantial amount of strawberry preserve with which you manage to coat your bread would succeed in sweetening your disposition, Bridie. But I have known you far too long, and therefore do not hold out much hope.'

The instant she had swallowed the last mouthful, Bridie showed no reluctance in responding in kind. 'And to be sure 'tis a mystery to me how anyone with a tongue sharper than a barber's razor could have the brass-faced nerve to criticise an easygoing soul like myself.'

Reaching for her coffee cup, Katherine silently acknowledged the truth of what her lifelong companion and self-appointed protector had said. Ashamed though she was over this undeniable flaw in her character, the fact of the matter was that she had never been afraid to speak her mind, not even as a child.

Regardless of the fact that in recent years she had attempted to control her occasionally ungovernable temper, she was still sadly inclined on occasions to wound with a cutting barb, and remained impatient of folly. This did not mean, she sincerely hoped, that she had become so intolerant, so self-willed, that she wasn't prepared to listen to the views of others. At least, she amended silently, she would always try to take account of the feelings of that plump and loving female who had taken care of her with such touching devotion for a score of years and more.

'We should be with your aunt and uncle by early afternoon, providing we suffer no further mishap.' Bridie tutted. 'But I'll say it again, Miss Katherine, 'tis plain daft to be gadding about the country at this time of year.'

A tender smile went some way to dimming the teasing

gleam in Katherine's strikingly coloured blue-green eyes. 'You know full well why I was determined to make the trip.' She paused to sample the contents of her cup. 'You didn't truly expect me to forgo the pleasure of celebrating my cousin's engagement, and enjoying the company for a week or so of the only family I have left in the world, simply because of the few discomforts I must be prepared to suffer in travelling at this season of the year?'

'I know you well enough, Miss Kate, to be certain sure that when your mind is set on something there's no reasoning with you, and that you had every intention of attending the party. Though why in the world your cousin couldn't have arranged to become betrothed in the spring, like any sensible girl, when the weather is warmer and law-abiding souls can journey about the land without fear of becoming stranded, I'll never know!'

'It wasn't through choice, as you're very well aware,' Katherine reminded her. 'Caroline's future husband is a soldier. Captain Charlesworth wouldn't be able to obtain leave at the drop of a hat. He still has duties to perform, even though the war with France is now, hopefully, at an end.'

'To be sure, that's true enough,' Bridie acknowledged, before transferring her gaze to the clock in the corner of the private parlour, and rising to her feet. 'And I suppose we ought to be thinking of making a move, if you wish to arrive in plenty of time to have a wee rest before the party. The weather's fine at the moment, but there's no saying it'll remain so. I'll away now to check our overnight bags have been returned to the carriage, and arrange for the post-boys to have the vehicle waiting at the door.'

After nodding assent, Katherine remained for the time it took to put on her bonnet and collect her reticule and gloves from a side table, and then followed her Irish maid's example by going out into the coffee-room, where she discovered only the landlord lurking in the shadows.

Eager to recommence the journey, she wasted no time in settling her bill, and then made her way towards the front entrance, slipping her purse safely back inside her reticule as she did so. Consequently she didn't observe the tall gentleman, swathed in a voluminous grey cloak, entering the inn, and promptly collided with what felt like a solid wall of bone and muscle. Air left her lungs in a rush, and it was only the two long-fingered hands which immediately clasped her upper arms which saved her from reeling from the impact.

'I'm so very sorry, ma'am. I trust you are unhurt?'

The deep voice clearly betrayed concern, and Katherine didn't hesitate to assure him, the instant she had regained her breath, that she had suffered no real harm. 'And it was as much my fault as yours, sir,' she added, graciously accepting her share of the blame, 'for I wasn't attending where I was going.'

The continued clasp of strong hands was oddly reassuring, and strangely reminiscent of a certain someone's touch in the dim and distant past. Katherine raised her head, only to find the breath leaving her body in a faint gasp for a second time as she gazed at the swarthy, wholly masculine features looming above.

For a moment it was as much as she could do to stare into thickly lashed, dark eyes, as she tried ineffectually to capture an elusive memory. She saw them widen fractionally, clearly revealing a hint of appreciation in their warm brown depths, as they calmly began to scan every contour of her face. Although not precisely unaccustomed to receiving admiring glances from members of the opposite sex, she was forced silently to own that there was something both faintly disturbing and remarkably engaging about the directness of this tall gentleman's unwavering gaze.

He seemed reluctant to release her, but after a further unsettling moment he allowed his hands to fall to his sides. 'Are you certain you are all right, ma'am? Perhaps I should summon the landlady. You are a little pale, if I may say so.'

'I am perfectly well,' she assured him swiftly, if not quite truthfully. 'But I thank you for your concern, sir.'

Bemused by the peculiar sensations this enigmatic stranger had somehow managed to evoke, Katherine successfully slipped past him and out into the crisp morning air. Fortunately he made no attempt to detain her further, but she could almost feel those attractive, almond-shaped eyes boring into her back as she hurried across the forecourt to the waiting carriage.

'Why, you look as if you've seen a ghost!' Bridie remarked the instant her young mistress had scrambled into the post-chaise and had begun to make herself comfortable on the seat opposite.

'I feel as if I've just seen one,' she didn't hesitate to admit. 'Did you happen to notice that tall gentleman who entered the inn a few minutes ago?'

'Can't say as I noticed a soul, miss. Why, was it someone you know?'

Katherine frowned in an effort to remember, for there was something there still lurking in the dim recesses of her memory which she just could not capture. 'He seemed oddly familiar, yes. But for the life of me I cannot imagine where I've seen his face before—certainly not in Bath, I feel sure.'

'And was it a handsome one?' Bridie couldn't resist asking, thereby earning herself an impatient glance.

'I wouldn't have described it so, no. He was attractive, certainly, but not what I would call handsome.' Katherine paused to straighten the skirt of her dark blue carriage dress. 'Not that it would have made a ha'p'orth of difference to me if he had been a perfect Adonis.'

'No, I know it wouldn't!' Bridie retorted, with the speed of a striking snake. 'And we both know why, don't we?'

Katherine elected not to answer, and turned her head to stare resolutely out of the window, a clear indication that she considered the conversation at an end. Unfortunately the action didn't prevent her from thinking about her maid's prompt rejoinder.

She didn't suppose for a moment that Bridie had intended to be heartlessly cruel. It was not in the woman's nature. In fact, the opposite was true. Bridie, loving and unfailingly loyal, had always been there to offer comfort and encouragement. Which was possibly just as well, Katherine reflected, for she sometimes felt she would never have survived the many heartaches she had suffered in recent years without the constant support of that occasionally infuriating and frequently overprotective Irish woman.

It was from Bridie, who had been there to witness the event, that Katherine had learned that she had been born during what had been one of the worst storms to hit Ireland in living memory. While the high wind had been battering the country, leaving a trail of devastation in its wake, Charlotte O'Malley had been giving birth to a daughter, a protracted and agonising ordeal that had al-

most brought about her own death and had resulted in
her not being able to have any more children.

Oh, yes, she had indeed been a scourge to those close
to her since the day of her birth, Katherine reflected dis-
mally. Although blissfully unaware of the fact during her
idyllic childhood, she had been forced to accept in recent
years, after the series of tragic events which had struck
her life, that she did indeed bring ill fortune to those for
whom she cared most deeply. Only one person seemed
immune to the lethal Katherine O'Malley curse.

She couldn't prevent a tiny sigh escaping as she instinctively cast a glance at the plump, middle-aged female seated in the opposite corner of the carriage. It
would be foolish to hope that any prospective husband
might be similarly protected, and Katherine certainly had
no intention of burdening her conscience further by encouraging the advances of some poor unsuspecting male.
It was perhaps fortunate, therefore, that her silent resolve
never to marry had not been tested thus far.

During the six years she had lived in Bath, she had
been introduced to numerous very personable gentlemen,
and yet not one had ever succeeded in arousing in her
more than a faint interest. Not once had she ever experienced the pull of mutual attraction... At least, she silently amended, never until today.

She couldn't deny that she had felt oddly drawn to
that tall gentleman back at the inn. His touch had been
strangely reminiscent of her father's—gentle, yet wholly
protective. It was perhaps just as well that their paths
were unlikely ever to cross again, for she very much
feared that the enigmatic stranger might be just the type
of man who would test her resolve to remain a spinster
to its limits.

* * *

By early afternoon, when the hired carriage had pulled up outside her aunt and uncle's charming house in Hampshire, Katherine had succeeded in thrusting the brief encounter with the disturbing stranger from her mind. After being admitted to the house by Meldrew, the very correct manservant, and discovering that both her aunt and cousin were at home, Katherine removed her outdoor garments and, leaving Bridie to take charge of the unpacking, went directly into the comfortable parlour where she discovered the two female members of the Wentworth family happily engaged in their favourite occupation.

Mrs Lavinia Wentworth, raising her head at the opening of the door, betrayed her delight by a warm smile. Setting aside her sewing, she was on her feet in an instant, her arms outstretched in welcome. 'How lovely to see you, my dear!' she announced, after placing a kiss on the face which so closely resembled her dear, departed sister's.

After returning the embrace with equal warmth, Katherine turned to the only other occupant of the room, who betrayed no less delight at her arrival. 'You look blooming, my dear Caro. Captain Charlesworth is a lucky man! I trust everything is in readiness for the party tonight?'

'Yes, indeed,' Caroline assured her. 'Mama and I have been busy all week finalising the arrangements. We are expecting around a hundred guests. And I'm so very glad that you are to be among them. When you failed to arrive yesterday, both Mama and I began to fear that you had changed your mind, and didn't choose to risk making the journey, after all.'

Eyes glinting with unholy amusement, Katherine sat beside her pretty cousin on the sofa. 'My, my! What a feeble creature you must think me! I might be almost three years your senior, Caroline, but I'm not in my dotage quite yet. No, it was merely that a threat of snow yesterday afternoon forced me to take shelter at a posting-house. That, and a desperate need to silence the dragon-lady's continual carping.'

Knowing precisely to whom her niece had referred, Mrs Wentworth could not forbear a smile. Although Katherine had grown into the image of her lovely mother, she had inherited her wonderful dark auburn hair and blue-green eyes, made more striking by dusky brows and lashes, from her Irish father. She certainly favoured her sire in temperament too, for she possessed a fine Irish temper and could be quite outspoken on occasions. 'Bridie has only your best interests at heart, Katherine,' she remarked. 'And I must confess that it has relieved my mind during these past years knowing that she has always been there to care for you.'

Katherine chose not to comment, for although she valued Bridie highly, there had been occasions, most especially in recent months, when she had found her loyal Irish maid's continual cosseting increasingly irritating. So, instead, she changed the subject by enquiring into the whereabouts of Caroline's elder brother. 'Is Peter not here at present?'

'No, he's back at university, although he did spend Christmas with the family,' Caroline enlightened her. 'To be frank, I believe he was relieved to be going. I do not think he quite relished the prospect of having to aid Papa in entertaining the dowagers this evening.'

Katherine cast a glance brimful of wicked amusement in her aunt's direction. 'And does my esteemed uncle look forward to such an onerous duty, I cannot help asking myself?' she remarked, knowing full well that Henry Wentworth, although a most agreeable, warm-hearted gentleman, was not disposed to socialising to any very great extent.

Reaching for the tambour frame once again, Mrs Wentworth could only admire her niece's perspicacity. 'I think it would be more truthful to say that he is resigned to the task expected of him, Katherine. Unless I much mistake the matter, when he rode out a little earlier it was for the sole purpose of calling on a neighbour of ours, Sir Giles Osborne, in order to enlist the baronet's aid.'

His wife's suspicions were uncannily accurate, for Henry Wentworth had set out for Osborne House, and was at that moment enjoying a glass of burgundy in the company of his friend.

'I have already assured you that I shall not fail to attend,' Sir Giles answered in response to the heartfelt request. 'My sister would never let me hear the end of it if we didn't put in an appearance. We shall arrive promptly at eight, and you may rely upon my unfailing support.'

'You're a good friend, Osborne.' Mr Wentworth tugged at his cravat, as though it had suddenly grown uncomfortably tight. 'Don't mind admitting that I'm not relishing the prospect of entertaining a pack of fiendish harridans.'

Sir Giles, a master at concealing both thoughts and emotions, permitted himself a thin smile. 'The Dowager Lady Charlesworth is certainly a formidable matron. It is something of an enigma how she and that apathetic late husband of hers ever managed to produce two such well-balanced, engaging sons. I know you and Lavinia must be delighted with the match. Richard is an agreeable young man and a credit to his regiment.'

Unlike his sister, who enjoyed nothing better than a comfortable coze, Sir Giles only ever indulged in small talk when it was to his benefit to do so. Today, however, he was prepared to exert himself a little more than usual in an attempt to prevent his amiable neighbour from brooding unnecessarily over the ordeal ahead of him.

'I have every faith in that charming wife of yours to be sure that everything will run smoothly this evening.' There was no response, though Mr Wentworth, looking moderately more relaxed, did lean back in the chair and stretch his feet out towards the blazing fire. 'I seem to remember my sister remarking that almost everyone who received an invitation has accepted. And the weather appears to be favouring you thus far.'

'Yes, thank the Lord! At least we haven't had snow, except...' The worried frown returned. 'My wife's niece didn't arrive yesterday as expected. Which makes me wonder whether the rest of the country is so fortunate, and bad weather might be heading our way.'

'Had she far to travel?' Sir Giles enquired, striving to maintain a polite show of concern, even though his interest in the unknown female was zero.

'From Bath. My daughter will be very disappointed if she doesn't arrive. Caroline simply adores her. My wife does too, come to that! Lavinia has been trying to persuade Katherine to make her home with us for the past twelve months, but without success. Still...' he shrugged '...the girl seems happy enough to remain in the house left to her by her great-aunt. And it isn't as if she's a chit straight out of the schoolroom. She'll attain the age of three-and-twenty later this year. And she doesn't reside alone. There's a companion living in the house, and an Irish maid who is devoted to her.'

'Evidently her parents are dead,' Sir Giles remarked, successfully stifling a yawn.

Henry Wentworth confirmed this with a solemn nod of his head. 'Yes, it was all very sad. It so happens that her father was approached by the government to take a cargo of horses out to Portugal in readiness for the arrival of the British expeditionary force in the summer of '08. There was no better man at breeding or handling horses than Liam O'Malley. The craft he was on met up, as previously arranged, with two other vessels that had left England, also carrying urgently needed supplies. They were attacked by the French just off the Bay of Biscay.'

His expression changed, and he suddenly appeared more angry than sad. 'Damn it! Where was the British Navy? Where was that promised protection, that's what I'd like to know? Some damned mix-up at the Admiralty was what we were told! Apparently they had received information stating that the cargo vessels wouldn't be setting sail for another ten days.'

Only for a moment did a speculative gleam flicker in the baronet's steely-grey eyes as he digested these disturbing facts. 'Yes, that does seem strange.'

'Deuced odd!' Mr Wentworth agreed. 'My wife's poor sister never recovered from the shock of losing her husband. She died a few weeks later after contracting a simple chill which went to her chest, and my father-in-law, Colonel Fairchild, went over to Ireland and brought Katherine back to live with him.' Again he shook his head. 'Poor little mite was just beginning to recover from her parents' deaths when the Colonel suffered a fatal heart attack.'

'Indeed, your niece is to be pitied,' Sir Giles acknowledged, whilst momentarily wondering why the name Fairchild should seem vaguely familiar.

'She was in Bath at the time. The old Colonel considered the girl was in dire need of a little polish, as you might say, and packed her off to live with his spinster sister so that she might attend a seminary. The house in Bath now belongs to Katherine, and she's comfortably circumstanced. I can vouch for that, as I'm one of her trustees. Although she cannot touch so much as a penny piece of the money she attained from the sale of her father's sizeable property in Ireland, and the money her grandfather left her in his will, until she attains the age of five-and-twenty, her great-aunt, Augusta Fairchild, ensured that she will live very agreeably until then.'

Once again Sir Giles found his interest in this unknown young woman swiftly waning, and experienced a modicum of relief when his butler unexpectedly entered to announce the arrival of another visitor. He was on his feet in a trice, surprising his neighbour somewhat by betraying a degree of delight when a tall gentleman, his muscular figure swathed in a voluminous grey cloak, came striding purposefully into the book-lined room.

'Ross, my dear boy! This is an unexpected pleasure!'

The new arrival betrayed no similar joy as he shook the baronet's proffered hand, although Mr Wentworth noticed a less hard set to Major Daniel Ross's well-shaped mouth when the visitor was introduced to him.

'Just a flying visit, Osborne,' the Major announced. 'I've a letter here from Cranford, which I undertook to deliver personally as I was making a trip to the capital in order to attend a reunion dinner with some fellow officers and spend some time with a particular friend, and therefore wouldn't be inconvenienced too greatly by the slight detour.'

'Thank you, my dear boy,' Sir Giles responded, as he relieved the Major of the sealed missive and consigned it to the safety of his jacket pocket.

'Cranford? Would that be the Honourable Charles Cranford, a member of Parliament?' Mr Wentworth asked, thereby regaining his neighbour's attention.

'Why, yes,' Sir Giles confirmed. 'Are you acquainted with him?'

'Not personally, no. But I dealt with my late father-in-law's estate after he died, and unless I much mistake the matter it was none other than Charles Cranford who purchased the Colonel's house in Dorset.'

'Ah, yes! You may possibly be right, Wentworth. And that is perhaps why the name Fairchild seemed vaguely familiar to me,' Sir Giles confessed, before casting an enquiring glance in the Major's direction. 'Young Daniel, here, should be able to enlighten us. Also he ought to be able to set your mind at rest over the state of the roads in the west.'

Although betraying mild surprise, the Major didn't hesitate to assure Mr Wentworth that, although there had indeed been a light covering of snow overnight, all the main routes were passable. 'I set out before dawn, and had no trouble whatsoever in reaching Andover, where I ate a late breakfast. And to answer your first query— yes, Charles Cranford did purchase the late Colonel Fairchild's property. My home is situated close by. I knew the Colonel very well.'

'Good Lord! It is a small world, indeed!' Mr Wentworth exclaimed. 'You must be acquainted with my wife Lavinia, the Colonel's younger daughter. Although,' he added, as he saw dark brows draw together above the Major's faintly aquiline nose, 'I expect you were a mere boy when we married and she moved away from the county.'

'I remember that the Colonel had two daughters, sir. But as you remarked, it is a long time since last I set eyes upon either of them.'

'Well, sir, I'm certain my wife would enjoy seeing you again. She retains fond memories of that part of the country. In fact,' he added, as a thought suddenly occurred to him, 'we're holding a party this evening. Why not come along? You'd be most welcome. I know Lavinia would enjoy nothing better than chatting over old times.'

'First, let us see if we cannot persuade him to remain long enough to enjoy a glass of wine,' Sir Giles intervened, sensing that Major Ross was on the point of declining Mr Wentworth's kind invitation.

Quickly finishing off the contents of his own glass, and refusing a second, Mr Wentworth cast a brief glance at the mantel-clock, which clearly informed him that it was time he was heading homewards. 'And I must be on my way. Hope to see you at the party tonight, Major.'

'He genuinely means it, Ross,' Sir Giles assured him, the instant his neighbour had departed. A ghost of a smile once again flickered about his thin lips. 'Not that I suppose for a moment that I could influence your decision one way or the other, but you're most welcome to put up here for the night. It would grant us the opportunity to reminisce pleasurably over old times.'

The Major's dark eyes were brightened by a decidedly cynical gleam, as he accepted the glass of burgundy, and lowered his tall frame into the chair recently vacated by his host's neighbour. 'You will forgive me for saying so, Osborne, but I cannot recall that our dealings were ever precisely enjoyable.'

'You are thinking of that delectable French filly, Justine Baron, I do not doubt.' Sir Giles settled himself in the chair on the opposite side of the hearth, and gazed meditatively down at his glass. 'Undeniably that must rate as my greatest failure. I came so close to catching *him* then.'

'Are you certain that she would have kept to her part of the bargain?' the Major asked, sounding decidedly sceptical, and after a moment the baronet nodded his head.

'I could of course have attained the information I wanted by—er—other means. But in Justine's case I chose to be merciful. She did not become a spy through choice, but because she was forced into it, although she was well paid by her country for her services. There was only one thing Justine loved above money…and that was her sister. We kept to our part of the bargain, and I'm certain in my own mind she would have kept to hers by revealing that British traitor's name, if the devil hadn't discovered where I'd hidden her. I knew even then it had to be one of two people. That belief has not changed. Nor my resolve to unmask the rogue.'

The look in the Major's eyes contained neither sympathy nor encouragement. 'The war is over.'

'It might be for you, Ross,' Sir Giles countered, reaching into his pocket for the letter his companion had kindly taken the trouble to deliver. 'But there are still a few of us remaining who are determined to see justice done.'

He took a moment to apprise himself of the contents of the missive before returning it to the safety of his pocket. 'Cranford writes to inform me that he is organising a party at his home at the beginning of April, and has, it seems, been successful in persuading several—

er—interesting people to attend. Will you be among the guests?'

'Possibly,' the Major answered, clearly unwilling to commit himself.

'By the by, I had heard that you'd sold your commission,' Sir Giles remarked with an abrupt change of subject. 'What will you find to do with yourself now your career in the army is at an end?'

'Look after the property I've neglected for far too long.'

'Ah! So those old, festering wounds have finally healed, have they? I'm glad to hear that you are ready to settle down.'

Daniel stared intently into the baronet's shrewd eyes. 'My God!' he muttered, experiencing a mixture of anger and grudging respect. 'Not much ever escapes you, does it, Osborne?'

Just a hint of smug satisfaction crept into Sir Giles's expression. 'I have endeavoured over the years to ensure that not much ever does. And since you are to attend a reunion dinner you must have brought suitable evening attire.'

'Only my dress uniform,' Daniel disclosed.

'Excellent! Then there's no reason why you shouldn't attend the party tonight.'

Chapter Two

'I think I shall wear the pearls, Bridie,' Katherine decided, after studying her overall appearance in the full-length mirror.

Although Bridie's apron had covered many duties over the years, including those of nursemaid, housekeeper and cook, she was also a very proficient lady's maid, and Katherine was delighted with the more elaborate arrangement of her auburn curls. She was satisfied too with her choice of gown for the special evening ahead. She had wished to look her best for the occasion, and considered the dark green velvet dress suited her very well, its soft folds emphasising the shapely slenderness of her figure, while its colour subtly enhanced the green in her eyes.

'I think we chose wisely when we selected this new gown,' she remarked, seating herself once again at the dressing table in order that Bridie, several inches shorter, might fasten the pearl necklace more easily, while she herself concentrated on securing the matching earrings to her small lobes. 'It makes me appear neither a chit just emerged from the schoolroom, nor yet a female at her last prayers.'

Bridie could not help smiling to herself at this candid admission. Her young mistress was so lacking in conceit that she could never be made to appreciate just how very lovely she was. Blessed with delicate, regular features, and a trim shapely figure, she had little difficulty in igniting a glint of admiration in the vast majority of masculine eyes, even in those not disposed to admire her particular colouring. 'You look lovely, Miss Katherine.'

This sentiment was echoed a few moments later when Mrs Wentworth entered the bedchamber to bear her niece company down to the large salon where the party was to be held. 'Every time I look at you, Katherine, I am struck by the resemblance you bear your dear mother,' she admitted, not reluctant to disclose the thoughts that had passed through her mind shortly after her niece's arrival earlier in the day.

Katherine, her eyes shadowed by a moment's bitter regret, cast a surreptitious glance up at her aunt through the dressing-table mirror. Undeniably her mother had been the far prettier sister. None the less, she might have wished that her mother had possessed some of her younger sibling's strength of character. Her dear aunt, Katherine felt sure, would not wither like an exotic bloom touched by the first frost if—God forbid!—anything should ever happen to her husband. Lavinia Wentworth would fight and survive for the sake of her children.

'And you resemble your maternal grandmother too, now I come to consider the matter,' Mrs Wentworth added. 'Little wonder dear Papa was so very fond of you!'

'And I was very fond of him,' Katherine was not slow to confess. 'My one bitter regret is that we were not

given the opportunity to enjoy each other's company for
a great deal longer.'

'Yes, I too feel that was a pity,' her aunt agreed softly.
'My father, I clearly remember, very much appreciated
modesty in our sex. Surprisingly enough, though, he also
admired intelligent women who were not afraid to voice
their opinions. He would have found much pleasure in
your company, my dear.'

Katherine couldn't prevent a wry smile at this, as she
cast a brief glance in her maid's direction. 'You are the
second person today who has remarked on the fact that
I am not afraid to speak my mind,' she admitted, rising
to her feet, and entwining her arm through her aunt's.
'However, I promise to be on my best behaviour this
evening, and will endeavour to keep a firm hold on my
occasionally ungovernable tongue.'

Katherine then accompanied her highly amused aunt
downstairs to the large salon, there to discover both her
cousin, looking bright-eyed and excited, and her uncle,
noticeably less so, hovering near the door in readiness
to receive their guests.

Captain Richard Charlesworth, accompanied by his
family, and a large party of friends, was the first to arrive, and very soon afterwards Katherine, without quite
knowing how it had come about, found herself seated
beside Caroline's future mother-in-law.

Possibly because she had had experience of dealing
with haughty, opinionated matrons, her great-aunt Augusta having possessed a somewhat vitriolic tongue,
Katherine was disposed to be more amused than annoyed by the Dowager Lady Charlesworth's blunt manner and caustic remarks. Added to which, Katherine was
determined not to do or say anything that might lessen

her sweet-natured cousin's enjoyment of what, quite naturally for Caroline, was a very special occasion. Consequently she bore with great fortitude the dictatorial matron's company for a full twenty minutes, and was even gracious enough to agree to partner the Dowager in a rubber or two of whist later, before cunningly engineering her escape.

'Do not allow my mama to monopolise you, Miss O'Malley,' an amused voice whispered in her ear, and Katherine turned to discover the newly engaged couple standing directly behind her.

Caroline bestowed a look of mild disapproval upon her future husband. 'Now that we are officially betrothed, I think you might be a little less formal with my cousin, Richard.'

'I should be delighted to comply, providing Miss O'Malley has no objection, that is?'

Katherine was not slow to assure him that she had none, for she very much approved of her cousin's future husband, appreciating his gentlemanly and unaffected manners. 'I assume that you two have abandoned your positions by the door in order to lead the first set of country dances.'

'We have indeed,' Caroline confirmed. 'And I had better warn you now that you are unlikely to be sitting by the wall yourself for any length of time. All of Richard's army friends are intent on securing you for a partner.'

'And I dare swear I shall be too weak-willed to refuse,' Katherine responded with more tact than truth, for unlike the majority of her sex she had never been drawn to a gentleman merely because he happened to be sporting a scarlet coat. Nevertheless, she felt obliged to add, as she glanced about the room at the numerous dress

uniforms on display that evening, 'I believe it is grossly
unfair to permit officers to attend parties wearing regimentals. They look so very smart and dashing that they
cast those in plain evening garb quite into the shade.'

'They do indeed,' Caroline agreed, before catching
sight of a new arrival wearing a very striking dark green
uniform of almost exactly the same shade as her cousin's
lovely dress. 'Who is that, Richard? Surely not a cavalry
officer?'

'No, indeed, m'dear. That is the uniform worn by ri-
flemen. Can't say I recognise the fellow, though.' He
appeared genuinely intrigued. 'There's a few minutes
wanting before we need take the floor. If you will both
excuse me, I'll go over and discover who he is.'

'Mama appears very well pleased to see him, at any
rate,' Caroline was not slow to observe, after Richard
had departed. 'He's with Sir Giles Osborne's party. I
wonder who he is? I've certainly never seen him before.'

Katherine cast the merest glance over the distin-
guished, grey-haired baronet and the middle-aged lady
clad in a rather startling orange gown, before focusing
her attention on the well-muscled gentleman sporting the
smart green regimentals. 'Great heavens!' she muttered
as he turned at Richard's approach, and she saw his features clearly for the first time. 'It cannot be…'

Caroline regarded her cousin with slightly raised
brows. 'Are you acquainted with him, Katherine?'

'Yes…no…well, I'm not sure. But I do believe he's
none other than the gentleman I bumped into earlier today when I put up at that posting-house. What a coincidence!'

Once again Katherine found herself teased by that elusive memory annoyingly playing hide-and-seek in the
recesses of her brain, while at the same time experienc-

ing a rather startling surge of pleasure at seeing him
again so unexpectedly. She watched his approach with
keen interest, admiring the fluid way he moved, the way
he seemed to stand out from the other gentlemen present.
Then, for the second time that day, she found herself
gazing up into those attractive dark eyes, which clearly
betrayed recognition.

'It would seem, ma'am, Fate has decreed our paths
should cross again.' The deep voice was no less pleasing
than the warmth of the smile which instantly softened
the harsh contours of a wholly masculine countenance.

Katherine discovered herself automatically placing her
fingers in the hand reaching out to her, just as Richard
said, 'Miss Katherine O'Malley, may I present Major
Daniel Ross, an officer whose courage is admired
throughout the British Army.'

With the name pounding against her temples like so
many torturous hammer blows, Katherine withdrew her
hand so abruptly from the Major's gentle clasp that anyone observing the action might have been forgiven for
supposing that her fingers had just been burned. That
she had been so stupid as not to recognise at once a man
whom she had secretly despised for years added to her
swiftly mounting rage, and it was only the vow she had
made to behave with the utmost propriety throughout the
evening that prevented her from releasing the tumult of
emotions warring inside in a blistering tirade.

With praiseworthy self-control, Katherine quietly excused herself, and sought immediate refuge in the room
allocated for the female guests' private use. Having discovered it blessedly empty, she slumped down on one
of the chairs, her thoughts racing back over the years to
those few short months when she had lived in her grandfather's charming house in Dorsetshire, and had struck

up a close friendship with the daughter of one of his nearest neighbours, Helen Rushton.

Looking back, she now realised that their similar sufferings had been the bond which had drawn them together, swiftly turning friendship into a deep sisterly affection, for Helen's father, serving in his Majesty's Navy, had also perished at sea.

Helen had confided in Katherine from the first. Always eager to share her most private thoughts, she had revealed her rapidly deepening attachment to a young gentleman who, after living abroad for several years, had returned to the area, and who had recently acquired a commission in the army. Every time Captain Daniel Ross had paid a visit to Helen's house, Katherine had been regaled with a detailed account of what he had said and how long he had remained.

Undoubtedly Helen had been totally besotted, and then utterly devastated when she had discovered that Captain Ross, rakishly free with his favours, had been paying numerous visits to a dashing young widow living in the locale. Having to face the fact that she had not been the sole object of the Captain's desire had been a grievous blow from which poor Helen had never been granted the opportunity to recover.

The door quietly opening put an end to these sombre reflections, and Katherine was not unduly surprised to see her cousin slip quietly into the room.

'Are you not feeling quite the thing? Do you wish me to summon Mama, or Bridie?'

The prospect of having her lifelong bodyguard fussing about her like some demented hen was all it took to restore Katherine's equilibrium. 'Whatever for? I'm in no danger of fainting, I assure you. I have merely received a most unpleasant shock, that is all.'

'But what on earth overset you?' Caroline was utterly bewildered and it clearly showed. 'One moment you were looking so radiantly happy to be making the acquaintance of Major Ross, and yet in the next—'

'Kindly do not remind me of my shortcomings!' Katherine interrupted, acutely annoyed with herself, if the truth were known, for betraying such unbecoming delight.

Rising to her feet, she began to pace the floor, a sure sign to those who knew her well that she was doing her utmost to maintain a firm control over herself. She had no desire to cause any unpleasantness during the evening by making her intense dislike of the Major generally known. Nor did she wish to run the risk of joining the ranks of those contemptible gossipmongers who did not scruple to ruin reputations. Yet, at the same time, she felt that Caroline deserved some explanation for her odd behaviour towards the Major.

Raising her eyes, she discovered her cousin regarding her intently, and decided to settle on a compromise. 'You are possibly not aware of it, Caroline, but Major Ross was well acquainted with our grandfather. Whilst I resided in Dorsetshire, he paid several visits to Grandpapa's house—' her smile was twisted '—as well as visiting several others in the area. I discovered that his reputation where our sex is concerned is not precisely stainless. Not to put too fine a point on it, he is nothing more than a callous philanderer who isn't above breaking the odd heart or two,' she finished, anger momentarily overriding her resolve not to slander the Major.

'Good heavens!' Caroline muttered faintly, while taking advantage of the chair conveniently positioned directly behind her. 'Are you certain about that? I do not mean to doubt you,' she hurriedly added, swiftly recognising the telltale glint of annoyance in her cousin's blue-green eyes. 'But you were quite young when you lived with Grandfather. Might you have misunderstood the rumours about him?'

'Yes, I might,' Katherine was forced to concede, though it almost choked her to do so. 'Now is not the time to be discussing this, however. Come, let us return to the party, otherwise that handsome fiancé of yours will justifiably blame me for depriving him of the pleasure of leading you out on to the floor.'

As they re-entered the salon, Katherine was not unduly surprised to discover Captain Charlesworth still bearing the Major company. For her cousin's sake she was prepared to be polite and rejoin the gentlemen for a short while, and then slip quietly away in order to mingle with the other guests, thereby neatly avoiding comment.

Unfortunately, this ideal scheme was foiled at the outset, for no sooner had they arrived back at the gentlemen's sides than the musicians struck up a chord, announcing the commencement of dancing, and Katherine found herself, much to her chagrin, quite alone with the person whom she had stigmatised as the biggest beast in nature for almost six years.

'I trust you are feeling a little better now, ma'am?' he remarked, breaking the short silence that had ensued after the engaged couple's departure. 'If I were a fanciful man I might imagine that it was my sudden appearance which had the power to overset you.'

Suppressing the strong desire to walk away without uttering a word, Katherine forced herself to meet a gaze that she might have supposed contained a deal of genuine concern had she not known better. Heartless philanderers did not worry themselves unduly over the feelings of others, she reminded herself, resolved to be polite but no more.

'Disabuse yourself of that notion, sir. I am not so easily overset.'

Much to her surprise, Katherine saw the Major's eyes narrow fractionally at her cool tone. She might dislike the man intensely, but she was obliged to acknowledge that he was no fool. Unless she much mistook the matter, he sensed the antagonism raging within her and was more than slightly puzzled by it.

It was quite evident that he hadn't recognised her, not even her name. This in itself did not strike her as in any way odd. After all, she mused, transferring her gaze to those taking part in the dance, she had only ever spoken to him once in her life before today.

Her grandfather, Katherine recalled, had retained some rather antiquated views, and even though she had attained the age of sixteen he had considered her a mere child. Consequently she had never been invited to join her grandfather when he had been entertaining guests. None the less, Katherine clearly remembered coming face to face with Captain Ross, as he had been then, just once, when she had happened to be in the stable-yard when he had arrived at the house. It was unlikely, however, that he would remember such an insignificant occasion, when he had taken the trouble to pass the time of day with someone whom he also had undoubtedly considered a mere child.

'Miss Wentworth and Captain Charlesworth make a charming couple, do they not?' he remarked, once again breaking the lengthening silence.

'They do indeed, sir,' she agreed, momentarily forgetting her animosity, as she continued to follow the engaged couple's progress down the floor, noticing in particular the way Caroline smiled lovingly up at her handsome fiancé whenever they came together in the set. 'They are well matched, and very much in love.'

She expected him to say something further, if only to maintain the conversation. When he made no attempt to do so, curiosity got the better of her. She turned back to look at him, and was slightly disconcerted to discover him staring at her intently, before his expression was softened by the winning smile of a practised seducer.

No, she must never lose sight of what he was, she reminded herself. Even so, she was forced silently to concede that, had he truly been a complete stranger, he would have been the very last person she would have stigmatised as a hardened rake. He seemed so earnest, so reliable, the kind of person to whom one instinctively turned in time of trouble. Which just went to show that one should never judge by appearances!

'Do you hail from this part of the country, Miss O'Malley?' he asked, while his eyes flickered momentarily over the arrangement of her curls.

'No, Major. I lived for many years in Ireland. However, I now reside in Bath.'

Having decided that she had now conformed to the rules governing polite behaviour, and could leave Major Ross to his own devices with a clear conscience, Katherine was on the point of excusing herself when the dance came to an end and he forestalled her by requesting her to partner him in the next set.

Those good intentions deserting her completely, Katherine weakened to an imp of pure mischief. With a smile of artificial sweetness curling her lips, she looked him over from head to toe. 'Believe me, Major Daniel Ross, nothing in this world would ever induce me to stand up with you. I have made it a rule only ever to take the floor with those gentlemen sporting scarlet coats.'

Beneath their half-hooded lids, brown eyes began to sparkle with a distinctly menacing gleam. 'That decision, if you'll forgive my saying so, ma'am, betrays a shocking lack of judgement for one with your particular shade of hair.'

Only partially successful in suppressing a squeal of indignation, Katherine could quite cheerfully have boxed his ears, and swung away before the temptation to do so became too great.

Daniel, following her almost flouncing progress across the room with narrowed, assessing eyes, found himself experiencing both annoyance and puzzlement in equal measures. How anyone could be radiant and smiling one moment, then offhand and disdainful the next, treating a fellow as though he were a pariah, he would never know. But there again women, he reminded himself, were a law unto themselves, unpredictable and totally illogical!

He continued to watch her as she headed towards the room set out for cards, certain in his own mind that she would have left him far sooner had the opportunity arisen, and might not have conversed with him at all if she could possibly have avoided doing so. But why? Why had she taken him in such swift dislike?

He shook his head, at a loss to understand the workings of the female mind. When Captain Charlesworth had first brought him over, Miss O'Malley had betrayed clear signs of delight at coming face to face with him again so unexpectedly. He had found that initial reaction so very refreshing. She had made not the least attempt to dissemble, to pretend their paths had never crossed before. Then, quite suddenly, she had grown pale, and a look akin to loathing had flickered momentarily in those striking turquoise eyes before she had slipped quietly away.

Undeniably, Charlesworth and his delightful fiancée had been as mystified as he had himself at such odd behaviour. Yet when Miss Wentworth had returned, her face had worn a decidedly thoughtful expression, as though she were not quite certain about something. But what could she possibly have learned to his discredit during that brief absence? He had never met either young lady until today…or had he?

'Something appears to be troubling you, Major,' a smooth voice remarked, and Daniel discovered Sir Giles hovering at his elbow, looking remarkably well pleased about something.

He was instantly suspicious, for he knew well enough that the man beside him was not quite what he seemed. He had the utmost respect for Sir Giles's acute intellect. None the less, if their association during the past years had taught Daniel anything, then it was not to trust the well-mannered, silver-tongued baronet an inch.

'I swear, Osborne, that you were a cat in some former life. Like the pampered feline who lazes in the most comfortable spot in a room, you appear sublimely content. Yet, it would come as no great surprise to me to discover that you sleep with one eye permanently open.'

Sir Giles's shoulders shook in silent, appreciative laughter. 'Ah yes! Cats—remarkable creatures, are they not? I hold them in the highest regard. Lying quietly in wait to strike when least expected, they do their utmost to rid this world of ours of loathsome vermin.'

Extracting his silver snuffbox, Sir Giles made use of its contents before returning the elegant trinket to his pocket, while all the time his eyes stared through the open doorway leading to the card-room. 'Lavinia Wentworth's niece is a strikingly lovely young woman, do you not agree, Major Ross?'

Daniel followed the direction of the older man's gaze in time to see his former companion taking a seat at the table occupied by a forbidding matron sporting an ugly turban of puce satin. 'I did not realise that Miss O'Malley was related to our hostess,' he admitted, eyes narrowing. 'Then her maternal grandfather was none other than…'

'Colonel Fairchild,' Sir Giles finished for him, when the Major's voice faded. 'I understand that she lived with him for a short time. I thought perhaps you knew her.'

How very interesting! Daniel mused, his mind racing back over the years. Then it was just possible that he had met Miss O'Malley in the dim and distant past, though she must have been little more than a child at the time, for Colonel Fairchild had been dead for a number of years.

'Such glorious hair, do you not agree?' Sir Giles remarked, successfully recapturing his companion's attention. 'I myself have always had a particular weakness for auburn-haired fillies.'

'Oh, you have, have you?' Daniel did not believe a word of it, and wasn't reticent about making his own views clear. 'Well, I certainly have not! The few I've come across during my lifetime have all been devious little firebrands—totally unpredictable and not to be trusted. And Miss O'Malley has certainly not induced me to alter my opinion!'

It had taken Katherine a minute or two only to become aware that those of her fellow guests who were drifting into the card-room were keeping well clear of the table where she and the Dowager Lady Charlesworth now sat. Several wicked possibilities occurred to her for this deliberate avoidance, all of which were most definitely to the formidable Dowager's discredit. She was just beginning to come to the conclusion that it was unlikely that there was anyone among the guests brave enough to challenge Lady Charlesworth, when a shadow fell across the table, and she found herself meeting the steely gaze of the distinguished-looking gentleman who had arrived with the disreputable Major.

'Ah, Osborne!' There was a distinct note of approval in the Dowager's booming voice, which gave Katherine every reason to suppose that the baronet would prove to be a worthy opponent. 'Come to challenge me and my young partner, have you? Well, sit down! Sit down, man! Have you met Miss O'Malley?'

'I understand that you are Mrs Wentworth's niece,' he remarked, after Lady Charlesworth had made the introductions so loudly that Katherine was fairly certain that, had anyone else in the room been ignorant of her identity before, such was no longer the case.

Katherine nodded. 'My mother was her elder sister, sir.'

'I also understand that you reside in Bath.'

'Yes, sir. I have lived there for a number of years.'

'But not alone, I trust,' the Dowager put in, looking faintly disapproving.

It would have afforded Katherine the utmost pleasure to inform the dictatorial lady seated opposite that her domestic arrangements were entirely her own concern, but having given way once to her occasionally volatile temperament, she had no intention of doing so again. It would have afforded her even greater pleasure to be able to say that she did live quite alone. Unfortunately she could not do so.

'No, ma'am,' she admitted. 'My late aunt's former companion still resides with me.'

'Very proper,' the Dowager approved, before turning her attention to Sir Giles and demanding to know if he had secured himself a partner.

'My sister will be joining us, ma'am… Ah! And here she is, ready to do battle.'

It would have been hard to find a less formidable-looking opponent, Katherine decided, as she watched the middle-aged lady, dressed in the startling orange-coloured gown, nervously twisting the strings of her reticule round her fingers as she seated herself at the table.

The baronet's spinster sister put Katherine in mind of the companion whom she had unfortunately inherited from her late aunt. Poor Miss Mountjoy, always eager to please, whilst bracing herself for the inevitable cutting remarks, had always displayed the same degree of nervous tension, whenever in her late employer's presence, as Miss Mary Osborne was betraying now.

Katherine well expected the Dowager, undoubtedly fashioned in the same mould as the late Miss Augusta Fairchild, to utter some blistering remark. Yet, surprisingly enough, apart from sniffing rather pointedly as she cast disapproving eyes over the dazzling orange creation, which clashed alarmingly with her own puce gown, she refrained from comment. Which gave Katherine every reason to suppose that the mouse-like Miss Osborne, though lamentably lacking an eye for fashion, had somehow managed to earn the formidable Dowager's approval.

This certainly proved to be the case, for Miss Osborne was undoubtedly a very skilful card player, and her partner no less so. They easily won the first game, and Katherine found herself having to concentrate very hard, which was no easy matter when she was having to contend with her partner's hard-eyed scrutiny, and the frequent, penetrating steely-grey-eyed glances she found herself receiving from the baronet. None the less, her nerve, though sorely tested, held firm, and she and her partner won the second game, and took the first rubber convincingly with the final game.

'I knew I chose wisely when I selected you for my partner, Miss O'Malley,' Lady Charlesworth boomed approvingly. 'A female who can hold her nerve, eh, Osborne?'

'It would certainly appear so, ma'am,' he answered softly, his eyes once again firmly turned in Katherine's direction. 'Miss O'Malley appears to possess all the necessary requirements… Yes, she might prove to be an excellent choice.'

Chapter Three

'I've been giving some thought to what you disclosed on the evening of my engagement party.'

The surprising admission succeeded in capturing Katherine's attention, and she transferred her gaze from the spot beyond the parlour window, where the morning's continuous rain had succeeded in creating a huge puddle on the terrace, to her cousin, who had been industriously plying her needle for the past half-hour. 'About what?' she prompted.

'About Major Ross.'

The immediate response did not precisely please Katherine. Although his name had never once been mentioned within her hearing since the night of the party, she had been irritated by the number of times he had managed to encroach into her thoughts.

'Before he returned to London Richard happened to mention,' Caroline continued, 'that Wellington himself thought very highly of the Major, and used him on many important missions.'

'His bravery is not in question,' Katherine pointed out, striving not to sound waspish. 'I merely maintain that he is a heartless wretch who cares naught for the feelings of others.'

'I'm not so certain you're right about that,' Caroline argued. Highly complaisant and sweet-natured though she was, she wasn't afraid to voice an opinion if she held strong views on a subject. 'I found myself in his company on more than one occasion during the evening of the party. I have to own, I rather liked him, even though I found his conversation a little—how shall I put it?—forthright. But Richard assured me that seasoned campaigners do tend to be plain-spoken and a little abrupt. And the Major was kind enough to fetch me a cup of fruit punch.'

'Oh, well, that just goes to prove I misjudged him entirely, doesn't it?' Katherine rolled her eyes ceiling-wards. 'Any gentleman who would fetch a lady refreshments must surely be a paragon of all the virtues!'

'Furthermore,' Caroline continued, smiling faintly at this blatant sarcasm, 'Richard did furnish me with one tale about the Major that he'd heard from a fellow officer. Seemingly, appalling atrocities took place after our troops were successful in storming Badajoz. Major Ross, by all accounts, offered his protection to the wife of some French officer. I do not know all the details, you understand, because Richard didn't consider it a suitable topic to discuss in my company. Nevertheless, what he did disclose was sufficient to convince me that any gentleman who would put his life at risk to protect a lady's virtue must be a very honourable man. Which makes me wonder whether what you were told about him years ago was completely true.'

'We do not know for certain that the story of his heroism at Badajoz is true either,' Katherine pointed out.

'You know how these tales are much embellished in the retelling.'

'Mama was talking with him a good deal at the party. We could always ask her if she knows anything about his exploits,' Caroline suggested, just as the door opened, and Mrs Wentworth herself entered the parlour.

Although Katherine had no wish to engage in a discussion about someone whom for years she had been happy to stigmatise as a heartless lecher, her cousin, evidently, was not of a similar mind, for Caroline hardly waited for her mother to settle herself comfortably in a chair, before she asked outright whether she was well acquainted with the gallant Major.

'I wouldn't go so far as to say that, dear,' Mrs Wentworth responded, reaching for her embroidery. 'When I left Dorsetshire to marry your father, Daniel was merely a boy, no more than six or seven, though I do remember his father very well. Edwin Ross was such a charming gentleman, and extremely astute. And Daniel, I feel, has grown into his image in both looks and character.'

Somehow managing to suppress a snort, Katherine made a supreme effort to concentrate on the book lying open on her lap, and ignore the ensuing conversation between mother and daughter. Unfortunately she was only moderately successful, and one interesting disclosure had her and her equally astonished cousin exchanging startled glances.

'I didn't realise that Major Ross was Grandpapa's godson,' she freely admitted.

'Oh, yes, dear,' her aunt confirmed. 'Your grandfather and Edwin Ross had been friends since boyhood, and Daniel was very fond of dear Papa. Papa frequently mentioned in the letters he wrote how much he missed his godson's visits when Daniel went out to India.'

This appeared to capture Caroline's attention in a big way, for she immediately set aside her sewing. 'Major Ross has been to India? Oh, what exciting lives gentlemen lead!'

'I do not know whether Daniel himself found the experience so very rewarding,' her mother countered, 'in view of what took place during his absence.'

Although Katherine doggedly refused to betray further interest, she was not unduly sorry when her cousin demanded to know what precisely had happened during Daniel's travels abroad.

'His father passed away just a year after Daniel had set sail for India. Although his uncle, Sir Joshua Ross, did write promptly, informing him of the tragic news, it quite naturally took some time before the letter reached him. And if that was not bad enough, when the poor boy did eventually return, it was to discover that his childhood sweetheart, Julia Melrose, had married Sir Joshua's son Simon just a few months before.'

'Oh, poor Major Ross!' Caroline exclaimed, and Katherine, much to her surprise, found herself experiencing a twinge of sympathy too, and could not resist asking whether there had ever been anything official between them.

Lavinia Wentworth shook her head. 'I do not believe Julia's parents were averse to a match. Daniel, after all, was the son of a wealthy landowner, and therefore quite eligible. I believe the Melroses considered that it wouldn't hurt to wait a year or two before giving their consent to a marriage. Daniel himself had only just turned twenty when he set sail for India. I suppose he considered it would occupy his time until he could officially ask for Julia's hand.'

Caroline cast a puzzled glance across at her mother.

'But if Julia Melrose was truly in love with Daniel, why on earth did she agree to marry Simon Ross?'

'That I couldn't say, my dear. I do know that Julia, Simon and Daniel had known one another all their lives and had frequently played together as children, but from what I have gleaned over the years from the many friends I still have living in the area, Julia always showed a preference for Daniel's company. Most people, including your grandfather, expected them to tie the knot one day.' She shrugged. 'One can only imagine pressure was brought to bear on Miss Melrose to marry Simon. After all, he was the one who had been destined to hold the title, not Daniel.'

Mrs Wentworth sighed and shook her head. 'Whether the marriage was happy or not, I couldn't say, but it certainly proved fruitful. Julia gave birth to a son some five or six years ago, if I remember correctly. One cannot help but feel saddened that the union was brought to an abrupt end. Simon Ross, sadly, was killed whilst hunting in the Shires.'

'Which leaves the field now open for the Major, as it were,' Katherine remarked, with just a touch of cynicism that made her aunt smile.

'It is certainly a possibility that their love will rekindle,' her aunt acknowledged. 'He has, so I understand, never betrayed the least interest in marrying anyone else, even though his name has been linked with several—er—females over the years.'

Out of the corner of her eye Katherine saw her cousin glance in her direction, as though expecting her, now that the opportunity had arisen, to pass some remark, and she swiftly decided not to disappoint her. 'I clearly remember that, when I resided in Dorsetshire for those few short months, Captain Ross, as he was then, betrayed an interest in a close neighbour of Grandpapa's—Helen Rushton.'

'Helen Rushton?' her aunt echoed, frowning slightly. Then her brow cleared. 'Ah, yes, I remember—Hermione Rushton's girl!' The frown returned. 'Are you positive he was interested in her, Katherine? She must have been a mere child at the time.'

'She was seventeen.'

Mrs Wentworth's expressive brows rose this time. 'Yes, I suppose she must have been. So very sad, her dying so young. I remember Mrs Rushton very well—a sweet woman, but something of a dreamer and not very bright. I recall your grandfather mentioning once that Helen had become very like her mother.'

Until that moment Katherine had never considered that Helen had been very immature for her years. Looking back now, however, she was silently forced to own that her friend had been something of a dreamer and might well have imagined that Daniel Ross had been betraying an interest in her.

Swiftly thrusting this traitorous thought aside, she said, 'I also recall, Aunt, that he was displaying marked attention towards a young widow in the locale.'

'Very likely, my dear. He could only have been twenty-three or -four at the time. I doubt his intentions were serious. Gentlemen rarely are at that age. And you must remember he had suffered a grievous blow over Julia Melrose. When I spoke to him at the party I gained the distinct impression that he is more than ready to settle down now, however. He is quite wealthy, so should have no difficulty in finding himself a wife.'

Caroline's soft brown eyes glowed with a distinctly hopeful look. 'Although it is unlikely that Major Ross will ever inherit the title, it is not impossible that he and his childhood sweetheart might one day find happiness together.'

Whether or not it was because she had never fallen in love herself, or that she simply didn't possess her cousin's romantic streak, Katherine was not sure, but her interest had already swiftly begun to wane. The ex-Major's present romantic inclinations were of absolutely no interest to her. Consequently she experienced no compunction whatsoever in changing the subject by voicing something which was of far more concern to her, if a trifle mundane.

'I sincerely hope the weather improves by tomorrow. I do not relish the prospect of returning all the way to Bath in the pouring rain.'

'I wish you were not going back so soon, Katherine. Cannot Mama and I persuade you to remain a little longer?'

Katherine, smiling fondly at her cousin, shook her head. 'I should dearly love to stay another week or two, Caro, but my conscience will not permit it. I have already left poor Clarissa Mountjoy to her own devices for two weeks.'

'I think it was highly unfair of Aunt Augusta to foist that distinctly foolish female on to you, Katherine,' Lavinia Wentworth announced, with a rare show of annoyance. 'She is engaged as a companion and resides in your home for the sole purpose of ensuring that you, an unmarried female, are suitably chaperoned at all times. Yet I swear it is you who takes care of her. It is a fine duenna indeed who cannot bring herself to travel more than a mile or two because she fears becoming queasy!'

A further fond smile touched Katherine's lips as she looked across at her aunt. 'Believe me, Aunt Lavinia, I am not sorry that Mountjoy is afflicted with travel sickness whenever she steps inside a carriage.' She couldn't prevent a sigh escaping. 'I am forced to admit too that I do find her company excessively tedious, for she is undeniably an extremely foolish woman, but she does try so very hard to please. And I would never go back on the promise I made to Aunt Augusta and turn Mountjoy off. The poor woman put up with Great-aunt Augusta's megrims and ill humours for twenty years. I believe she has earned a little peace and contentment in a house where not too much is expected of her, and she can more or less come and go as she pleases.'

A further sigh escaped Katherine as she finally abandoned her book and set it to one side. 'I must admit, though, as chaperons go, she could never be described as diligent. I cannot say that I would feel in the least sorry if she did decide to leave, and I could employ someone of my own choosing.'

'I doubt there is much chance of that,' her aunt warned. 'I fear, my dear, that you have made the woman's life far too agreeable since Aunt Augusta's death for her to wish to take up another post.'

'You are possibly quite right,' Katherine agreed. 'But there is just a glimmer of hope on the horizon. Mountjoy received a letter from her widowed sister a month ago, inviting her to make her home with her. Needless to say I would be delighted if she does decide to leave, but I am resolved that it must be her decision.'

'You would have no need of a chaperon if you chose to make your home here with us,' her aunt reminded her.

Katherine had wondered how long it would be before the subject was once again raised. Her aunt had asked her on several occasions to make her home in Hampshire, and Katherine had always neatly avoided giving a firm answer. It was not that she felt she would be unhappy living with her aunt and uncle, for she was fond of them both, and adored both her cousins. Nor was she afraid that the little independence she had acquired would be drastically curtailed, for her aunt was such an easygoing soul who would willingly allow her to do more or less as she pleased. No, stupid though it might be, she was afraid to take up permanent residence under this roof; afraid that, as had happened so often in the past, she would bring ill fortune to the household if she were ever to remove here.

'That is certainly true, Aunt,' she agreed, her warm smile concealing quite beautifully those deep-rooted fears that had continued to torment her in recent years. 'But I would never dream of inflicting Mountjoy on you. And even if I should be lucky enough to persuade her to accept her sister's kind offer, there is still Bridie to consider. There is not the remotest possibility that I shall ever be able to persuade that fiendish woman to take up another post. I know I shall be cursed with her company for life! She is the most self-opinionated, domineering creature imaginable! If once she takes up residence here, you'd swiftly find her ruling the roost in the servants' hall, and your own staff leaving your employ.'

Mrs Wentworth frankly laughed. 'Oh, I know Bridie can be a little outspoken on occasions, and is certainly not what one might describe as a conventional domestic, but I for one, as I've mentioned before, have always felt very relieved that she has been there to take care of you, Katherine.'

She looked up as the door opened to see her butler enter the room, carrying a small silver tray. 'Yes, what is it, Meldrew?'

'A letter from Osborne House for Miss O'Malley,

ma'am,' he answered, presenting Katherine with the tray. 'The footman is still here, awaiting a reply, miss.'

Surprised, Katherine removed the missive, which did indeed bear her name in bold, elegantly constructed letters, and broke the seal. 'Good heavens!' she exclaimed, after running her eyes over the few lines. 'I've been invited to take tea with Sir Giles and his sister this afternoon at three o'clock.'

She handed the note across to her aunt. 'Have you anything planned for the afternoon, Aunt Lavinia?'

'As a matter of fact, dear, Lady Charlesworth plans to call. But, in any event,' she added, after scanning the brief missive, 'it would seem the invitation is for you alone.' She did not appear in the least offended, as her next words proved. 'I'm rather relieved. I should not have wished to cause offence to either Sir Giles or his sister by refusing. In the circumstances, however, I feel I must remain here, as I have already assured Lady Charlesworth that her visit will be most welcome.'

Katherine was far from convinced that her aunt's assertion was one hundred per cent true. If her cousin's expression of comical dismay was any indication, poor Caroline certainly wasn't looking forward with any real conviction to her future mother-in-law's proposed visit. Caroline, of course, had little choice in the matter; Katherine, on the other hand, most definitely had. She considered she had more than fulfilled her role as dutiful niece on the night of the engagement party, and had no intention of enduring the formidable Dowager's company for a further lengthy period.

'Would you mind very much, Aunt Lavinia, if I accepted the invitation to take tea with the Osbornes? I rather liked Sir Giles—a highly intelligent man who possesses a rather dry sense of humour.' She chose not to add that she had been less favourably impressed with his sister.

'Of course I do not object, my dear,' her aunt assured her before turning to Meldrew. 'Inform Sir Giles's footman that Miss O'Malley will be delighted to accept.'

'My, my, Katherine! You must have made a favourable impression on our reserved neighbour,' Caroline teased, the instant the butler had withdrawn. 'Sir Giles is not renowned for socialising to any great extent. He generally keeps himself very much to himself when in the country.'

'Oh, I do not think that is strictly true, Caroline,' her mother countered. 'Sir Giles has always been a most genial man. I do not deny that since his wife and his younger son died, he has tended to be less sociable, but that is only to be expected. Furthermore, his work for the government keeps him in London a good deal.'

Caroline frowned a little at this. 'Do you know, Mama, I've never perfectly understood the nature of Sir Giles's work. I do not think even Papa understands precisely what duties Sir Giles performs.'

'Our esteemed neighbour has always been a little vague about it, certainly,' her mother agreed. 'I believe he mentioned once that it was something connected with the War Office. I do happen to know that he numbers among the Regent's close friends. So perhaps one of his duties is to keep our future King abreast of events, though why he should feel the need to spend so much time in the capital now that monster is on Elba, and the war is thankfully at an end, I cannot imagine.'

She frowned as a thought suddenly occurred to her. 'In fact, I understood your father to say that Sir Giles accompanied Major Ross to the capital on the morning after the party.' She shrugged. 'Evidently he must have

returned... At least for Katherine's sake I sincerely hope
he has, otherwise she will find herself having to endure
his far less sensible sister's company for an hour or two.'

It required a monumental effort, but Katherine managed to resist the temptation to declare that if it was a
choice between spending time in the company of Lady
Charlesworth and Sir Giles's sister, she considered Miss
Mary Osborne most definitely the lesser evil!

The Wentworth carriage having been kindly placed at
her disposal, Katherine set off on the short journey to
Osborne House in good time to reach her destination at
the appointed hour. She was looking forward to visiting
the home of the man whose company she had very much
enjoyed on the evening of the party. She was pleased
too that the rain had ceased and the afternoon had been
blessed thus far with brief glimpses of an early February
sun. She was not, however, precisely overjoyed at being
denied the opportunity to make this perfectly respectable
visit unaccompanied.

Bridie had taken it upon herself to follow her out to
the carriage and had plumped herself down on the seat
opposite, that mulish expression Katherine had glimpsed
so often in the past taking possession of the homely features.

Katherine turned her head to stare out of the window,
lest her own expression betray the mingled resentment
and annoyance rippling through her. These were feelings
she had experienced increasingly during these past
twelve months. Augusta Fairchild might have been an
irascible old lady, sharp tongued, and not disposed to
consider the feelings of others, but she had not been
bound by convention, and had allowed Katherine freedom to do more or less as she pleased. Since her aunt's

demise, however, Katherine had discovered that treasured independence, which one might reasonably have expected to increase now that she had become mistress of her own establishment, had been gradually curtailed by the two females whom she employed.

And it was utterly ridiculous! She inwardly fumed, resolved to do something soon about her far from idyllic domestic situation. These past two weeks in Hampshire had, if nothing else, shown her that one attained far more freedom from living in the country. Weather permitting, she had gone for a walk, sometimes accompanied by her cousin Caroline, and sometimes alone. It was true that on the occasion they had visited the local town they had taken the little housemaid with them. Yet Katherine had hardly known the servant was there. Walking a few paces behind, the maid had barely uttered a word, and had merely carried the few purchases both Katherine and Caroline had made back to the carriage.

How different from the life she had led in Bath! Not once since her great-aunt's demise had she visited the fashionable shops without having to suffer Mountjoy's incessant prattling, as she scurried alongside like a timid mouse. Always eager to please, poor Mountjoy more often than not had only succeeded in irritating her so much that Katherine had come perilously close on numerous occasions to releasing her pent-up frustrations by administering a sound box round the ears, and only the promise she had made to her aunt had checked the words of instant dismissal she so longed to utter.

Smothering a sigh, Katherine turned her attention to the woman in the seat opposite. Even if she did manage to resolve the problem of her less than ideal companion, there still remained the even greater dilemma of what to do about the woman who had taken such loving care of her throughout her life. Although she had never been afraid to speak her mind where Bridie was concerned, which had resulted in numerous battles of will over the years, and many harshly spoken words, not for the world would she deliberately hurt the person to whom she was so genuinely attached. Yet somehow she must find a way of convincing Bridie that her one-time charge was no longer in need of leading-strings, but a young, independent woman, quite capable of making her own decisions and, more importantly, of taking care of herself. And there was no better time to embark on this crusade for total independence than right now!

'I cannot imagine why you felt the need to accompany me on this journey,' she remarked in a level tone, determined to deny Bridie the opportunity of accusing her of being in a 'naughty' temper, which she so often did when Katherine had taken her to task over something.

The mulish expression returned to the homely face. 'And who would have taken care of you if I hadn't come along, may I ask?'

'My aunt's groom is more than capable of ensuring that I come to no harm.'

'Pshaw! The great lummox didn't even think to provide you with a few necessary comforts,' Bridie retorted, lovingly tucking the fur-lined rug, which she had carried out to the carriage, more securely about her young mistress's slender legs. 'I promised your sainted mother on her deathbed that I would always look after her little girl. And I shan't go back on my word. Bridie will always be here for you, Miss Kate.'

Oh, dear Lord! Katherine inwardly groaned. Although moved by this touching declaration, she was very well aware that the task ahead of her was going to be far from easy. Yet somehow there had to be a way of convincing Bridie that she was now a capable young woman, and no longer a child in need of constant care and attention.

Determined not to be defeated in her objective, Katherine adopted a different tack, as the coachman drew the well-sprung carriage to a halt before the front entrance of the impressive mansion. 'As you have taken it upon yourself to play nursemaid, you had better accompany me inside. No doubt you will be invited to take tea with the more senior servants.' She paused after alighting to cast a cautionary glance over her shoulder. 'So kindly maintain a guard on that unruly tongue of yours for the duration of our visit.'

Bridie, both surprised and incensed at what she considered to be quite uncalled-for strictures, was denied the opportunity to retaliate by voicing her opinion of her young mistress's frequently caustic utterances by the prompt appearance of the very correct manservant who admitted them to the house.

'Sir Giles is expecting you, Miss O'Malley. If you would kindly step this way?' The butler paused, before leading the way across the chequered hall, to cast a faintly superior glance in Bridie's direction when she appeared about to follow her mistress. 'I shall ensure that your maid receives refreshments below stairs.'

Hardening her heart against the hopeful expression in those loving, dark eyes, Katherine swept past the door the butler held open. Only then did she begin to wonder if she had not been a little foolish in not insisting that Bridie remain with her, when she noticed that the book-lined room's sole occupant was Sir Giles.

Rising immediately from behind the desk, he came forward to take Katherine's hand briefly in his own. 'My dear Miss O'Malley. My sister and I were delighted that you were able to accept our invitation,' he announced, before dismissing his servant with the faintest nod of his head. 'Come, take a seat by the fire.'

A glimmer of amusement flickered in the baronet's grey eyes as Katherine hesitated. 'My dear child, I am old enough to be your father, if not your grandfather. Be assured that my sister will be joining us, once she has returned from her trip to town.'

Feeling rather annoyed with herself for so obviously betraying unease, while at the same time thinking it most strange that Miss Osborne should visit the local town when she had invited a guest to take tea, Katherine seated herself in one of the comfortable chairs by the hearth. It was strange too that the butler had shown her in here. Evidently he had been obeying his master's instructions. But surely it was more usual to invite guests to take tea in the parlour?

After watching her host move across to a small table on which several decanters stood, Katherine glanced about the room. It was a wholly masculine sanctum, which put her in mind of her grandfather's library in that charming house in Dorsetshire, the main difference being that this room had a second door, left slightly ajar, which possibly led to a small ante-room.

'Can I tempt you to a glass of Madeira, my dear?' Again there was a moment's hesitation on her part which drew a brief smile to Sir Giles's lips as he poured out a second glass. 'You came to take tea and yet your host is attempting to ply you with strong liquor. What sinister motive can there be in that? I hear you asking yourself. You are wise to be cautious, child, for this world of ours holds many sinister pitfalls for the unwary. And I did have a specific reason for wishing to see you alone.'

More intrigued than unnerved by this surprising admission, Katherine accepted the glass held out to her, observing as she did so that those shrewd grey eyes, alert and acutely assessing, were regarding her no less keenly than they had on the evening of the engagement party almost two weeks ago.

'You have striking colouring, Miss O'Malley,' he remarked, surprising her still further, as he settled himself in the chair opposite, his gaze never wavering from her face. 'Inherited from your Irish-born father, I should imagine.'

'Yes, sir,' she responded, wondering what he would remark upon next. She was not left to speculate for long.

'I am reliably informed that you and your father were very close. It was a tragedy that he lost his life in the service of his country... But it was a tragedy that was destined to take place long before he had set sail from Ireland.' Sir Giles saw the slender fingers tighten momentarily round the stem of the glass, and a look appear in the turquoise-coloured eyes which was no less penetrating than that in his own. 'Ill fortune played no part in your father's demise. The French had been informed that three vessels loaded with urgent supplies would be setting sail for Portugal on a certain date, and they were lying in wait.'

'How—how did you discover this?' Katherine demanded. The heartache she had suffered when she had first learned of her father's death had never left her, but now a completely different emotion, far stronger than the lingering pain, had swiftly gained supremacy. A despicable traitor had been responsible for the death of her father!

'I make it my business to know, child,' Sir Giles responded, smiling grimly. 'One does not need to don a uniform in order to serve one's country. And not all one's enemies are as visible as those on the field of battle.' The look in his steely-grey eyes grew noticeably harder. 'Napoleon is in exile on Elba. But my war is far from over, and shall not be so until I have unmasked the heartless devil who, during these past years, has been passing information on to the French.'

Taking a moment to refresh himself, Giles continued to regard her steadily over the rim of his glass. 'I shall not insult your intelligence by attempting to suggest that the person I am determined to unmask is the very traitor responsible for tampering with the document sent to the Admiralty requesting an escort for the convoy in which your father was destined to sail. There have been a number of agents working for France during these past years. I have a particular interest in uncovering the identity of just one of them, mainly because I was foolish enough once to underestimate him, and in so doing was responsible, in part, for the death of a young Frenchwoman whose knowledge would have proved invaluable in unmasking a cell of agents working in this country.'

Katherine's gaze remained as steady as her host's. She now knew precisely why Sir Giles, the secret spy-catcher, had invited her here. 'You believe that I might prove useful in helping you achieve your objective?'

'Yes, child, I do. From the moment I first set eyes upon you I was aware of the striking resemblance you bear to the young woman who was murdered whilst under my so-called protection,' he admitted, his voice surprisingly betraying a hint of regret. 'I failed her, and that weighs heavily on my conscience. I have no intention of repeating my error. I shall do everything within my power to minimise the risk, but should you agree to assist me it is as well for you to know at the outset that your life would be in danger.'

Leaning back in his chair, Sir Giles regarded her in silence for a moment. 'Now, before I divulge more, I need to know, Miss O'Malley, whether you are willing to undertake a very great service for your country, which, if successful, might go some way to avenging your father's demise?'

Katherine didn't need to take even a moment to decide, but was somewhat startled, after voicing her desire to help in any way she could, when the door leading to the small ante-room was thrown wide and a sparse man in his early forties, accompanied by a woman of similar age, walked calmly into the room.

'Do not be alarmed, my child,' Sir Giles advised gently. 'I wish you to meet Mr Arthur Ashcroft, and his sister Miss Margaret Ashcroft, two of my most trusted associates. They will play a small but vital part in the plan I am about to outline to you. There is one further key player with whom I must make contact, but that can wait for the time being. What we must do now is put our heads together and come up with some scheme whereby you may leave Bath again, and quite alone, in the very near future without arousing the least suspicion.'

A plump, middle-aged figure suddenly appeared before Katherine's mind's eye. 'That, Sir Giles, might prove more difficult than you imagine!'

Chapter Four

Major Daniel Ross laid his head against the back of the chair, and stretched out his long legs in order to rest his feet upon the fender. His time here in Curzon Street, enjoying the hospitality of his good friend Harry Danvers, must soon come to an end. These past few weeks had proved to be highly pleasurable, and some recompense, he supposed, for the many privations he had perforce to endure in recent years.

Undeniably London had much to offer any bachelor of comfortable means. He would have been the first to admit that he had been content to while away the hours in the company of many of those who, like himself, had known the hardship of life out in the Peninsula. There was no denying too that the highly satisfying association with that delicate vessel, short on brains but infinitely skilful in other ways, had assuaged his physical needs and provided a most pleasurable way of passing several evenings and nights. None the less, a totally idle existence was not for him. It was time he returned to his Dorsetshire acres to put into effect those improvements he planned for his house and lands.

After sampling the contents of his glass, he began to

contemplate a future that would be in stark contrast with his past. Yet he had no regrets about the decision he had taken to sell his commission and leave the army. He believed he was more than ready now to take charge of his inheritance. The love of the land had taken time to come to him, but it was there now. Which was perhaps just as well, he mused, for there was precious little else in his life at the moment upon which he might shower attention and affection, least of all a woman.

A wry smile tugged at one corner of his mouth before he reduced the contents of his glass still further. Although he certainly hadn't lived the life of a monk in recent years, no female had succeeded in capturing his heart since Julia had held a place there in his youth. Even now, after all these years, he could well remember how utterly devastated he had been when he had discovered that his childhood sweetheart, the female whom he had considered so perfect in every way, had betrayed his love and trust by marrying his cousin. Had the bitter experience left him hard and cynical, and disinclined to trust another member of her sex? He could not help wondering. Or was it merely that he had searched in vain for a replica?

A slight frown creased his brow. If that was so, why then had he felt nothing within him stir when, after so many years, he had seen Julia again, a few months ago? He would have expected to feel something more than just a faint twinge of nostalgia for the happy hours they had spent together in their youth. Undeniably, time had been kind to her and she was still very beautiful. Graceful and serene, she remained for him the epitome of womanhood. Not like that damnable little shrew who had crossed his path just a few weeks ago! He inwardly fumed, his frown deepening dramatically as the pleasing image of golden locks and limpid blue eyes was unexpectedly thrust from his mind's eye by a set of quite different features, framed in a riot of deep auburn curls.

He shook his head in a vain attempt to dispel the vision which had too frequently plagued him during his stay in town. That unpredictable little virago typified everything he most despised in her sex! Contrary and sharp-tongued, she was just the type to lash out at a poor, unsuspecting male without the least provocation. Any man who was ever stupid enough even to contemplate taking that ill-mannered minx to wife would deserve all he got! he told himself, wondering why on earth he had been singularly unsuccessful in forgetting her very existence.

The door-knocker echoing in the hall brought these less than charitable musings to an abrupt end, and a minute later his friend's very correct manservant entered to apprise him that he had a visitor. A quick glance in the direction of the mantel-clock informed Daniel that the hour was well advanced. He had an appointment early in the morning, and had no intention of delaying too long before he sought the comfort of his bed.

'Did the caller give a name?' he asked after a moment's deliberation.

'He did not,' a smooth voice answered from the open doorway. 'But he felt certain that our long and—er—not uneventful association would be sufficient to grant him admittance.'

'Oh, you did, did you?' Daniel muttered, before dismissing the servant.

In one lithe movement he rose from the chair and moved towards the decanters. 'So, to what do I owe the pleasure of this unexpected visit? I thought you had returned to Hampshire?'

'I did…briefly,' the caller responded, accepting the glass of wine, before seating himself in one of the chairs by the hearth. He then waited for Daniel to settle himself in the seat opposite before adding, 'But I have been back in town for nearly three weeks.'

Frowning suspiciously, Daniel studied his companion over the rim of his glass, before demanding somewhat abruptly, 'Spit it out, Osborne! Why are you here?'

The baronet's thin lips curled into an appreciative smile. 'Always so delightfully brusque!' he quipped. 'Surprisingly enough, I consider it to be one of your most endearing qualities, my dear fellow. One always knows where one stands with you, Ross.' A faintly menacing gleam hardened his grey eyes. 'You are so refreshingly different from so many of those with whom I have been obliged to associate in recent years.'

'Nobody forced you to take up such work,' Daniel reminded him. 'It was done through choice.'

'Through necessity,' Sir Giles corrected, 'though I cannot deny that I have always displayed a certain aptitude. But my task is not yet complete.'

'But mine is,' Daniel returned, unable to prevent bitterness from edging his voice. 'Years of conflict… thousands dead…and for what?'

'So that we in these islands would continue to speak the King's English, and not French. Which you, of course, do so remarkably well… And that is precisely why I'm here, Major Ross. Once again I find myself in dire need of your undoubted talents. I am here in an attempt to persuade you to take charge of a little commission which has already begun across the Channel.'

'No!' Daniel's response, sharp and uncompromising, cut through the air like a knife as he rose once again to his feet. 'My war's over, Osborne. You cannot order me to go, not this time.'

A sigh escaped the older man as he stared intently at the impassive figure, solid and resolute, now standing before the hearth, staring intently down at the burning coals. 'No, I cannot order you to go, Major,' he concurred. 'But should you agree to do so, you might attain some justice for those many friends who needlessly lost their lives throughout the campaign.'

'Damn you and your spying games, Osborne!' Daniel exploded, unable to quell the bitter resentment and anger which had steadily increased throughout the years of conflict, and continued to fester even now, like some open sore that refused to heal. 'Justice for whom? Curse you!'

Daniel cast a glance over his shoulder in time to see the baronet's bony fingers tighten fractionally about the stem of his glass. 'Whose death are you so determined to avenge—your son's? He was a soldier and, like so many others, was prepared to die for his country. He's just another of those poor wretches who now lie buried in nameless graves scattered throughout Spain and Portugal.' His eyes narrowed. 'Or is it perhaps Justine Baron's demise which continues to prick your conscience?'

Sir Giles held the hard-eyed gaze steadily. 'Yes, I do feel that I owe it to Justine to bring her murderer to book.'

'You owe her nothing, Osborne,' Daniel countered, totally unmoved by the hint of remorse so easily discernible in the baronet's voice. 'She knew the risks she was taking. She and the traitorous devil who has plagued your dreams all these years were two of a kind, and both gained considerable financial rewards from indulging in their despicable trade.'

'Very true,' Sir Giles concurred, the composure for which he was justifiably famed seemingly having been fully restored. 'As I remarked before, Justine loved only one thing more than money—her sister. And it is the young woman who has agreed to pose as the former Mademoiselle Louise Baron who just might, if everything goes according to plan, avenge so many needless deaths.'

'Dear God!' Daniel muttered, his expression clearly disdainful, as he once again sought the comfort of the winged-chair. 'Don't you ever give up? Napoleon is on Elba. It's over at last.'

'Perhaps,' Sir Giles conceded, before his eyes hardened once more. 'And this is why my elusive friend has possibly begun to drop his guard. He may have severed all communication with many of his contacts, and now thinks himself safe. But he is at his most vulnerable. What will his reaction be when I make it known that, during these past months of Napoleon's exile, I have worked tirelessly and have managed to locate the whereabouts of Justine's sister? What if I also make it known that Justine left certain documents in the safekeeping of a lawyer whose identity is known only to the sister, and that the aforementioned sister has every intention of travelling to England in order to retrieve them? What if I were to suggest that the documents might prove interesting reading, and that the girl has agreed to let me study them before she takes her property back to France?'

Sir Giles smiled faintly at Daniel's openly sceptical expression. 'Oh, it will undoubtedly trouble him, Ross. He knew of the existence of this sister. But we managed to get to her first, did we not, my dear friend?' A hint of gratification just for one moment flickered in the baronet's grey eyes. 'I promised Justine that I would never disclose her sibling's whereabouts to another living soul. I also promised that I would never involve her in any of my exploits in the future. And I have kept my word, and shall continue to do so. Justine's old maid, Marie Dubois, is a different matter entirely, however. I did make contact with her, and she is more than willing to help in my attempts to uncover her late mistress's murderer. It is none other than Marie herself who is at present taking care of our delightful little impostor across the Channel.'

Daniel arched one dark brow. '*Our* little impostor?'

'Of course you must go to France in order to accompany your—er—lovely wife to England. Naturally you must not cover your tracks too well, as it were. However, by the time our intended victim has managed to alert his erstwhile associates to the hitherto unforeseen danger to his continued anonymity, I shall have the child safe.'

'As safe as Justine was in your care?' Daniel queried, not slow to remind his visitor of past errors of judgement.

Sir Giles was silent for a moment as he stared down into the contents of his glass once again. 'It will be different this time. Once you have brought the girl safely back to Dover, your part in the plot ceases. You'll be free to return to Dorset, and forget the whole business. Naturally you will receive your share of the reward, if we are successful in uncovering this traitor.'

Again Daniel's lips were curled by a smile of unalloyed contempt. 'Was that the inducement you used to persuade this idiotic female to take part in such a damnably foolhardy escapade—money?'

'No, it was not,' Sir Giles assured him. 'She knows

nothing of the reward. She has her own personal reasons for wishing to see this traitor brought to justice.'

Daniel's bark of derisive laughter echoed round the small salon. 'If she supposes for a moment the man will ever stand trial, she is a gullible little fool!'

Sir Giles's eyes were softened by a flicker of admiration. 'No, she is not a fool, Ross. She's an immensely brave young woman who is very well aware that what she has agreed to do is not without personal risk should things go wrong. The least I can do is try my utmost to ensure nothing does go wrong.' He gazed levelly across at the man for whom he had always had the utmost respect. 'And that is why I need you...someone I can trust implicitly. As you have already pointed out, I cannot order you to go, Major Ross. I can only ask you...one last time...to serve your country.'

Sir Giles made a point of visiting his club early one evening towards the end of the week, and was highly satisfied to discover several very interesting persons present, all seated together at a large table in one corner. Sauntering over, he did not hesitate to avail himself of the only vacant chair, before instructing a waiter to bring him wine.

'I didn't realise you had come up to town, Osborne,' the gentleman seated directly opposite remarked, briefly raising his eyes from the cards in his hand. 'Are you acquainted with young Gifford here, a distant relation I'm sponsoring this Season?'

'No, I've not had the pleasure, Waverley,' he responded, before acknowledging the young gentleman seated beside the portly baron, and receiving a stuttered salutation in response.

'You may not be acquainted with a near neighbour of

mine either,' the gentleman seated on his left put in. 'Sir
Joshua and I travelled up to the capital together a couple
of days ago.'

'We are acquainted, Cranford,' Sir Giles enlightened
him, before turning to the baronet. 'How are you, Ross?
Haven't seen you in town for a number of years. I do
run across your nephew on the odd occasion, though.'

'Ha! Do you, b'gad!' Sir Joshua barked. 'Well, that's
more than I do. Seen the boy only once or twice since
he sold out. You'd think he'd settle down now that he's
left the army, but he's forever gadding about. No repose,
no repose at all!'

His sigh was distinctly mournful. 'Don't get about
much myself now,' Sir Joshua continued in the same
booming voice, which induced several other members,
seated at tables nearby, to frown dourly in his direction.
'Health ain't so good. That's why I took the opportunity
to travel with young Cranford here, when I discovered
he was planning to come up to town. Daughter-in-law
kept plaguing me to consult one of these fancy London
practitioners about my hearing. Complete waste of time.
Stone deaf in my right ear, and my left ain't much better,
so you'll need to speak up a bit.'

As Sir Giles did not relish the prospect of shouting
himself hoarse, he turned once again to the gentleman
on his left. 'By the by, Cranford, I received your letter
inviting me to the party next month. Providing nothing
unforeseen crops up, I should be delighted to attend.'

He received a piercing gaze from the bright blue eyes
of the last member of the party. 'What's likely to stop
you now? Your work's done, Osborne, surely?'

'Yes, Davenham, to all intents and purposes, I suppose it is.'

'Well, what's stopping you, then?' the Viscount persisted. 'We'll all be there. You'll be among friends.'

A ghost of a smile hovered momentarily about Sir Giles's lips. 'I cannot tell you how relieved I am to here you say so, Davenham. Unfortunately, there is just a possibility that my presence will be required in town. I'm not quite certain when she'll be arriving, but I should imagine she has reached Paris by now, and is merely awaiting the arrival of her escort.'

Several brows rose at this. Since the death of his wife, several years before, Sir Giles's name had never been linked with that of any female. 'Don't tell me you've found yourself a French charmer, Osborne!' Lord Waverley exclaimed, laughing heartily. 'I'd like to meet her. She must be something out of the common way if you've gone to the trouble of having her escorted across the Channel.'

'Indeed, she is special.' Sir Giles reached for the wine, which a waiter had deposited on the table a few moments before, and filled his glass. 'She is none other than Justine Baron's sister, the former Mademoiselle Louise Baron.'

Viscount Davenham frowned. 'Should we know her? I can't recall hearing the name before.'

'No?' Sir Giles arched one silver-grey brow. 'Then let me refresh your memory—Justine Baron was a French spy who worked in this country a few years ago. She had a sister living in France, and although the girl was not involved in espionage herself, she mysteriously disappeared around the time of Justine's death. I managed to locate her whereabouts a few months ago, and wrote to her. She sent a very interesting letter back. Now that the war is over, she intends to travel to England to visit Justine's grave. She also informed me that Justine left some papers in the safekeeping of a London notary whose identity is known only to Louise. She has agreed to let me peruse the documents when she has retrieved them. So you can appreciate why I'm so keen to ensure that she arrives here safely, for I'm certain those papers will make enthralling reading. Naturally, she and the person I have engaged to escort her will be travelling under assumed names, posing as man and wife.'

The short silence which followed this astonishing disclosure was broken by Sir Joshua Ross who, gathering together the cards and reshuffling the pack, asked Sir Giles if he wished to be included in the game.

'Why not?' he responded. 'I'm feeling distinctly lucky tonight.'

This proved to be the case, and Sir Giles won several hands in quick succession before four of those assembled, making various excuses, rose from the table, leaving only one gentleman to bear him company.

'Dear me,' he murmured. 'Do you suppose it is my skill at cards or something I said? Surely they weren't all alarmed by my purely fabricated tale?'

'You had me almost believing it myself,' his companion admitted, a gleam of admiration flickering in the depths of his grey eyes. 'You can only hope that your—er—intended victim believed it.'

'I'm not so foolish as to suppose that, my dear fellow. No, he probably doesn't believe it. But he will need to be sure. And that is when I'll have him at last.'

'You know who it is, then?'

'I'm not one-hundred-percent certain, no,' Sir Giles admitted softly, 'but I believe I know. I need proof, though. And I'm relying on my little impostor to provide me with the proof I need.'

His companion's eyes widened fractionally. 'So, you have in truth a young female coming over from France.'

'Oh, yes, my dear. And she is indeed being escorted by...by someone I hold in the highest regard. He'll be across the Channel by now, if everything has gone according to plan, and will have the girl safely back in England before our traitorous friend has alerted his French associates. Undoubtedly at this moment our victim is frantically making arrangements for someone to go over to France. I, on the other hand, am for my bed, so I shall bid you goodnight. Come and dine with me tomorrow evening if you're free.'

Sir Giles remained at his club only for the time it took to collect his outdoor garments and then, declining the hall porter's kind offer to hail a hackney carriage, set out on foot and arrived at his home a short time later, feeling very well pleased with how smoothly events had progressed thus far.

Extracting the key from his pocket, he was on the point of inserting it into the lock, when a carriage pulled up outside the front of his house, and a familiar figure alighted.

'Ashcroft! What the deuce are you doing here?'

Not waiting for a reply, Sir Giles quickly unlocked the door and led the way into the house. He had never encouraged his servants to wait up for him, and the house was as silent as a tomb. Even so, he took the precaution of ushering his unexpected guest into the library and quietly closing the door.

'Don't tell me Ross has arrived in Paris already?' he said, going about the room lighting various candles.

Dishevelled, and looking decidedly weary, his faithful

associate availed himself of one of the chairs. 'He hadn't arrived when I left, sir, no.'

'Your orders were to keep watch over the girl until he did arrive, and then report straight back to me.' Sir Giles noticed that his unexpected visitor was looking deeply troubled. 'What's happened, Ashcroft? Was there some hitch during your journey to Paris?'

'No, sir. Everything went smoothly. It was two days after our arrival in the capital that I first learned of it. I advised Miss O'Malley to return to England at once, but she wouldn't hear of it, sir. She said that we couldn't be sure that the rumour was true, and that if it did turn out to be correct, your uncovering the identity of the traitor was even more necessary.'

'What rumour, Ashcroft?' Sir Giles demanded to know, surprisingly betraying signs of losing his iron self-control.

'You haven't heard then, sir? It will surely be all over London by morning… Napoleon has escaped from Elba and is, as we speak, marching on Paris.' He waited in vain for a response, and then added, 'There will be some, I dare swear, who will attach no importance to the event, believing that Napoleon will prove no threat. But others think differently. Panic has already begun to spread throughout the French capital, especially among foreign visitors, and those who openly welcomed the return of the Bourbon King.'

Ashcroft remained silent as Sir Giles, suddenly grave, went to stand before the hearth, then asked, 'What do you wish me to do, sir—return to Paris and bring the girl back here? She could travel under her own name. No one would pay much attention to an Englishwoman wishing to flee the city. I dare swear hundreds are doing so by now.'

A long silence, then, 'No. You will remain here in town. We must now place our trust in Major Ross. He has never failed me before… Pray God he does not do so this time!'

Katherine stared through the rapidly fading light at the street below her window. There were far fewer carriages and people about on foot now; less signs of the panic which had been steadily increasing during the past days. That, she supposed, was because so many had already fled the city, and many more, so she had been informed, were planning to go.

Had she been foolish to remain? She had asked herself that self-same question dozens of times since Mr Ashcroft's departure two weeks before. Having given it as his opinion that, with the unforeseen turn of events, their mission would of necessity have to be abandoned, he had urged her to accompany him. Yet she had chosen to remain, certain in her own mind that Sir Giles would have wished her to see his plan through to the end if it was at all possible. With every passing day, however, success seemed less likely. Had the person chosen by Sir Giles to escort her back to England arrived at the inn, there might have been a chance of carrying the plan through to a triumphant conclusion. Sadly, now, that seemed highly improbable.

The door behind her opened, and Katherine turned to see the middle-aged woman who had taken care of her since her arrival in France enter the bedchamber. Marie Dubois was not given to smiling much, and she was certainly looking far from happy now. None the less, the ice-cool reserve with which she had treated Katherine at the start of their association had swiftly diminished, and relations between them were now very cordial, each having acquired a deal of respect for the other.

'I have bespoke dinner, Madame Durand,' she announced clearly for the benefit of any inn servant hovering within earshot, 'and have requested yet again that it be served in here.'

Although beginning to feel something of a prisoner, Katherine could well understand her companion's continued caution. Marie never forgot the role she had been requested to play—that of a loyal maid to the wife of a prosperous French merchant. Katherine, on the other hand, was forced to own that she had been less successful in her portrayal of the devoted wife, longing for her husband's return from the south so that they could continue their journey to their home. There had been several occasions when she had failed even to remember that she was supposed to be French, and had reverted to her native tongue without having been aware of it.

There was some excuse for these frequent lapses, she supposed. So much had happened in so short a time that she hardly knew whether she was standing on her head or her heels. From the moment she had agreed to take part in Sir Giles's plot her quiet and faintly tedious existence had been brought to an abrupt end.

She clearly recalled the time she and the baronet had spent together on that early February afternoon, planning how they could spirit her away from Bath, unaccompanied, and without giving rise to the least suspicion.

After having divulged the name of a young woman with whom she had struck up a particular friendship during her time at the seminary, and with whom she had continued to correspond on a regular basis, Katherine had needed to do nothing further except try to carry on as normal. She had returned to Bath the following day as planned, and a week later had received a letter, undoubtedly written in a female hand, inviting her to stay with her friend. Miss Ashcroft, pretending to be her good friend's maiden aunt, had then arrived at the door a few days later, and had announced in a very authoritative tone that, as she would be accompanying Katherine throughout her stay, there would be no need for either a chaperon or a maid, as her own servants were more than capable of catering for both their needs.

Bridie, of course, had not wished to be excluded, but Miss Ashcroft, having been forewarned of Bridie's stubbornness, played the part of a dictatorial maiden aunt quite wonderfully, and had foiled each and every one of Bridie's attempts to be included in the trip.

Katherine had then been escorted to France without delay. In Calais they had been met by yet another player in the game, Marie Dubois. Miss Ashcroft had returned to England, and Katherine, having adopted the guise of a prosperous Frenchman's wife, had travelled on to Paris with Marie and Mr Ashcroft, where all that remained was to await the arrival of her 'husband'.

Everything had proceeded so well up until then, she reflected. Sir Giles had planned everything right down to the last detail. But he could not have foreseen the surprising turn of events that had taken place since her arrival in the French capital, and which, sadly, would ultimately foil his meticulously organised stratagem for uncovering the traitor.

Katherine sighed as she moved away from the window and took a seat at the table, where she had eaten all her meals since her arrival at the inn. 'I think we must now face the fact, Marie, that Sir Giles has possibly been forced to abandon all his well-laid plans. Tomorrow I shall commence the journey back to England.'

'I think that wise,' Marie whispered in English, as she joined her at the table. 'I did not like to tell you this, but whilst I was downstairs earlier there was talk that, even though the King had dispatched troops to intercept him, Napoleon entered Lyons without a shot being fired. He has many supporters in the army. Should they change allegiance…'

'Which makes it all the more imperative that you return to your home,' Katherine announced, knowing what Marie could not bring herself to say. 'If Napoleon does by some miracle manage to reach Paris and take control, then our countries will in all probability once again be at war. I do not wish you to be branded a traitor for protecting an enemy of your country.'

Marie's hard features were softened by a rare smile. 'I do not consider you an enemy, *mademoiselle*. But there are those who might should you remain. You will forgive my saying so, but you could never pass yourself off as a Frenchwoman, *petite*.'

Katherine was forced to acknowledge the truth of this. 'I did inform Sir Giles that my grasp of the Gallic tongue could best be described as adequate, but he insisted that that was of little importance, and that the person he had in mind to escort me back to England would have no difficulty in convincing anyone that he was French.'

The older woman's eyes narrowed speculatively. 'I wonder…?' she murmured.

'Wonder what?' Katherine prompted.

'I wonder if it is the same man who helped me rescue my late mistress's sister four years ago?'

Katherine was not at a complete loss to understand to what Marie was alluding. Before embarking on this exciting escapade, she had learned a little about the woman who had for two years passed on secret information supplied by the British traitor whom Sir Giles was determined to bring to book. More recently she had learned something of Justine Baron's early life from Marie who, Katherine had discovered, had been employed many years before as a maid in the Baron family's home on the outskirts of Paris.

Although not of the aristocracy himself, Justine's father had been a wealthy man who had made the mistake of speaking out against the injustices of the new regime, and in consequence had had his house and lands seized by those in power before he and his wife had been executed. Justine and her younger sister Louise had only just managed to escape with their lives. Spirited away in the dead of night by their devoted servant Marie Dubois, they had been taken to an isolated farm, owned by Marie's brother, deep in the French countryside, where they had remained safely hidden from the French authorities for several years. Unfortunately, by the time she had attained the age of eighteen, Justine had become utterly bored with the bucolic existence and, accompanied by the devoted Marie, had decided to find some means of supporting herself in the capital.

Having been the daughter of wealthy parents, Justine had received a good education, and had had little difficulty in acquiring a position in the establishment of a famous *modiste*. With her striking looks and superb figure, she had been perfect for modelling her employer's latest creations, and it had not been too long before Justine had fallen under the eye of a high-ranking government official. She had willingly become his pampered mistress, and for several years had lived in comparative luxury in a house overlooking the Seine.

During this period in her life, she had continued to visit her young sister regularly. Unlike Justine, Louise had been content to live a quiet life on the farm. Consequently Justine had been happy to leave her there, and had provided for her sister by sending sums of money to Marie's relations at regular intervals.

This act of generosity on Justine's part was to prove her downfall. When the time had come for her to find a new protector, she had chosen unwisely by agreeing to become the mistress of a sinister, shadowy figure who had close links with the man who four years previously had declared himself Emperor.

Her new lover had not been slow to make use of all Justine Baron's talents. By removing Louise from the farm and placing her in a secluded house, where she had become a virtual prisoner, he had attained the means by which he could force Justine to do precisely as he had wished.

Within weeks she had been despatched across the Channel, where she had swiftly found employment in the establishment of a famous Bond Street *modiste*. If the *modiste* had been faintly uneasy about her new employee's ability to obtain silks and laces at a much reduced rate, she had kept her suspicions to herself, and had not asked too many questions concerning Justine's frequent trips to the south coast. Which, of course, had allowed Justine to pass on the secret information obtained from the British traitor.

'I seem to remember you mentioned that you accompanied your mistress to England, Marie,' Katherine remarked as a thought suddenly occurred to her.

'Yes, *mademoiselle*. That was when I learnt to speak your language. We were there for a little over two years.'

'And in all that time you never once saw the man who sold my country's secrets?'

Marie shook her head. 'My mistress did not want me

involved. I cooked and cleaned in the little house we rented, and never went to the shop in Bond Street. It was at the shop, I think, that that devil passed on the information to my mistress, for no one ever came to the house, except Sir Giles on that one occasion.'

Katherine frowned. 'I suppose Sir Giles at some point must have become suspicious of your mistress's activities, Marie, and had her watched. But what I do not understand is why Justine remained in England when she might have given Sir Giles the information he required in return for her safe passage back to France.'

Marie betrayed surprise. 'Why, because of her sister, of course! She had had no contact with Louise in over two years. She was not even permitted to write to her, but she managed after several months to discover where her sister was being held, and wrote to my brother. He was permitted to see Louise on one occasion. He wrote and told us the poor child was treated badly, worked from dawn till dusk, and never allowed out of the house. My mistress was determined to get her little sister away from that dreadful residence, which was no better than a prison, and place her with people whom she trusted to love and care for her.'

'And Sir Giles was willing to offer his aid, providing she told him everything he wished to know,' Katherine remarked, when her companion fell silent. 'How, I wonder, did he manage to effect Louise's escape?'

Marie's harsh features were once again softened by a surprisingly tender smile. 'He did it, *mademoiselle*, by enlisting the aid of a very brave Englishman. I accompanied this man, who was a soldier, I think, over to France. Once he had achieved his objective, I returned with him, eager to impart the good news to my mistress, only to discover...'

'I know, Marie,' Katherine said gently. 'I'm truly sorry that the traitor managed to locate Justine's whereabouts.'

Marie must have believed the sympathy genuine, for she smiled wanly across the table. 'I know my mistress would have kept to her part of the bargain. She would have told him all he needed to know, and that is why, before I returned to France, I promised Sir Giles that if in the future he should ever need my help to catch the devil who murdered my poor mistress, he need only contact me.' She sighed as she gazed down at her work-roughened hands resting in her lap. 'I am a good Frenchwoman, *mademoiselle*. I love my country. But I would do anything to avenge my poor mistress's death. I had great hopes too, for although I never knew the real name of that brave man who rescued little Louise, when I heard the name you were to use, I thought perhaps—'

Marie checked at the knock on the door and rose instantly from the chair to answer it. Supposing it to be the inn servant bringing their food, Katherine did not pay much attention, until she clearly heard Marie exclaim, 'Ah, *monsieur*! So it is you! Now we shall do very well!' Then she raised her head and for a moment was unable to believe the evidence of her own eyes as they focused on the tall figure, swathed in a voluminous grey cloak, peering over Marie's head from the open doorway.

Quite forgetting her role, she was on her feet in an instant. 'What in the name of heaven are you doing here?'

Chapter Five

Marie, looking from one to the other, would have been hard put to it to say which of them appeared more stunned by the other's unexpected presence. Or more angry too, come to that! Blue-green eyes, brightened by a dagger-look, were openly hostile, and there was a definite hint of menace in dark brown orbs too, before the gentleman whom she had been so pleased to see took a step into the room and quietly closed the door.

'It is good to see you again, Marie, after all these years,' he remarked in French, and Katherine, even in her intensely perturbed state, was forced grudgingly to own that anyone might have been forgiven for taking him for a native of France. 'I can only apologise for my late arrival, and trust that you have not found these past days being forced to endure my—er—oh, so charming *wife*'s company, too much of a trial.'

Marie clearly detected the half-smothered squeal as the young woman whose companionship she had found increasingly agreeable swung away to turn her back on the new arrival. 'On the contrary, *monsieur*,' she didn't hesitate to assure him, before she recalled the young lady's one grave failing. 'But I think I ought to warn

you she does have a tendency to forget that she is supposed to be a Frenchwoman.'

'That,' he responded, removing his hat and gloves and
placing them on top of a convenient piece of furniture
nearby, 'isn't all she has a tendency to forget. She is
wont to forget her manners too on occasions.'

Out of the corner of her eye Marie noticed two slender
white hands curl themselves into tight, angry little fists.
She had found her young friend courteous and charming.
None the less, she didn't suppose for a moment that she
had been blessed with that colouring for no reason, and
decided it might be wise to intervene before 'Madame
Durand' was tempted to deal her 'husband' a sound box
round the ears, something which, Marie did not doubt,
her young companion was more than capable of administering if sufficiently roused to anger.

'Have you eaten, *monsieur*? I have ordered dinner, but
it would be no trouble to delay it a little to enable you
to join us.'

'I have already dined,' he answered, his expression
softening noticeably as he removed his gaze from the
silent, slender figure whose taut features were clearly
mirrored in the window and looked down at the older
woman. 'There is no necessity to delay your meal on
my account. I shall perhaps sample a glass or two of
mine host's fine wine before I retire. But first I think it
might be beneficial to have a little private conversation
with my *wife*.'

Marie was inclined to agree. That the two had met
before and were not upon the best of terms was abun-
dantly clear. Therefore, it could certainly do no harm for
them to attempt to settle their differences before they
embarked on their homeward journey, she decided. 'In

that case, sir, I shall return downstairs and attempt to hurry along our dinner.'

The instant Marie had departed, very tactfully closing the door behind her to enable them to clear the air without being overheard by any inn servants about their work, Daniel addressed himself to the woman who for the next few days would play the part of his wife, loving or otherwise. 'Well, this is a surprising turn up, is it not, Miss O'Malley?'

He noted the faint stiffening in the perfectly proportioned, slender frame. All the same, he had no intention of attempting to conceal the fact that he was not best pleased to discover that the female he had endured several days' hardship in order to rescue was none other than the infuriating little madam who, like some pestilential insect, had all too frequently returned to plague him, mentally if not physically, since their last encounter. 'I had been wondering who our mutual friend had managed to persuade to embark on such a ludicrous venture. It goes without saying that I was convinced it had to be someone with more hair than wit!'

'Oh, you were, were you?' Katherine managed to respond in a surprisingly mild tone. Only the glint in her eyes, when at last she turned to face him again, betrayed the fact that she was not as composed as she might wish to appear. 'Well, let me assure you, Major Ross, that, had I known that you were to figure as a key player in Sir Giles's plot, nothing in this world would ever have induced me to take part.'

Daniel studied her in silence as he removed his cloak and tossed it casually upon the bed. 'Ah, yes! I was forgetting your totally unfounded and quite infantile dislike of me. Tell me, Miss O'Malley, is it in an attempt to satisfy some puerile whim that induces you to display antagonism towards virtual strangers?' He could almost hear those small, perfect teeth grinding together, but steadfastly refused to spare her. 'I discovered on the evening of your cousin's engagement party that you were Colonel Fairchild's granddaughter, and that you resided with him for a short time. Would I be correct in thinking that your resentment stems from nothing more significant than my inability to recall that we had perhaps met in the distant past?'

Daniel noticed the strikingly coloured eyes momentarily stray in the direction of the porcelain vessel on top of the washstand. He didn't doubt for a moment that that small hand was just itching to reach out for the handle on the pitcher and then hurl the delicately painted piece of porcelain in his direction. Yet her voice when she spoke remained surprisingly calm and controlled.

'When I resided with my grandfather, we were never formally introduced, Major Ross. I did witness your arrival at the house on several occasions from an upper-floor window, however, and I believe we did once exchange a few words when I happened to be outside and you rode into the stable-yard one day.'

He frowned, endeavouring to remember, but swiftly abandoned the attempt. 'You must forgive me, ma'am, but I fail to recall the incident.'

'It is of no consequence, I assure you. I was little more than a child at the time, and quite naturally evinced no interest in you at all.' The faint twitch at the corner of her mouth was evidence enough that she had enjoyed delivering this mild insult. 'What I find hard to forgive,' she continued, when he refused to comment, 'or forget, for that matter, is that your callous behaviour was in part responsible for the death of my friend.'

For several moments it was as much as he could do

to stop himself from gaping across the room at her in astonishment. He would have been the first to admit that he had killed many during his years in the army, but as far as he was aware he had never been responsible for anyone's death off the field of battle. 'What the devil are you talking about, young woman?' he demanded, not attempting to moderate his language.

'I am referring to Helen Rushton, Major Ross,' she responded, not noticeably cowed by the barking tone. 'She and her widowed mother were close neighbours of yours, were they not? Helen and I became friends when I went to live in Dorsetshire towards the end of '08.'

This time he was more successful in his efforts to remember. 'Ah, yes! I recall her now. She was the daughter of Captain Rushton who died at Trafalgar.' He regarded her in frowning silence for a moment. 'But she was a mere child. She used to go about all the time carrying a rag doll, of all things! And if my memory serves me correctly, she and her mother unfortunately both lost their lives in a minor smallpox outbreak which occurred shortly after I had sailed for Portugal.'

Katherine's chin lifted. 'Helen was seventeen. Unlike her mother, she was young and strong and might well have survived had she not lost her foolish heart to a worthless profligate who gave her every reason to suppose his interests were engaged, only to cast her aside without so much as a second thought.' She paused to raise an accusing finger. 'After your treatment of her, she lost the will to live.'

Once again Daniel regarded her in silence, his expression totally unreadable, then he bridged the distance between them in three giant strides, and before she could do anything to avoid it, had imprisoned her chin in one long-fingered hand.

'And it is this upon which your dislike of me is based—my thoughtful attentions to the daughter of a man I admired, which were obviously totally misconstrued?'

Although Katherine remained stubbornly silent, she found herself unable to hold his openly contemptuous gaze, and lowered her eyes, but not before Daniel had glimpsed the look of mingled doubt and self-reproach she failed to conceal.

He tightened his grasp on the pointed little chin, forcing her head up and giving her no choice but to raise those delicate lids. 'Retain your infantile dislike of me if you will, Miss O'Malley, but if you possess any degree of sense at all you will refrain from permitting your misguided judgement to induce you to behave foolishly during the time we will be forced to endure each other's company.'

The warning was clear, and all the more menacing because it had been delivered in a surprisingly soft voice. 'If we stand the remotest chance of successfully returning to England unscathed, we must work together. Therefore I shall brook no childish acts of defiance on your part.'

Smiling grimly, Daniel watched the play of different emotions flitting over the delicate features before finally releasing his hold on her chin. He wasn't fooled by the seemingly silent acceptance of his dictum. Unless he was gravely mistaken, nothing would have given her greater pleasure than to place a well-aimed kick on his shin, before telling him to go to hell.

He cast a brief glance over the neat arrangement of fiery curls. No, he mused, he would be foolish to suppose that she would always be so quietly submissive. Beneath the quite lovely surface trappings was a determined and spirited young woman who was not lacking intelligence. Unless he much mistook the matter, she had already been forced to accept the fact that she needed his protection in order to return to England.

'I do believe that we are beginning to understand each other at last,' he could not resist adding. 'If you should continue to exert such admirable self-control, I believe we shall deal tolerably well. And now, Miss O'Malley, I shall leave you alone to ponder over the wisdom of what I have said, whilst I repair downstairs for an hour or so.'

With which he swung round on the heels of his decidedly dusty boots and, head held high, strutted from the room, like a combatant leaving the field of battle in the certain knowledge that he was the clear victor.

The instant the door had closed behind him, Katherine closed her eyes, and somehow managed to quell the temptation to reach out for that pitcher whose handle was invitingly close, and hurl it at the exact spot where the Major's arrogant head had been only moments before. How glad she was now that her grandfather had insisted that she spend a year at that superior Bath seminary! One schoolmistress of whom she had been particularly fond had endeavoured to teach her to control her temper, and to consider any forceful display of emotion faintly vulgar. She had certainly needed to heed those excellent teachings during the past few minutes, and attempt to behave in a dignified manner. Whether she would be able to continue to do so during the days ahead was a different matter entirely!

Suddenly feeling incredibly weary, Katherine slumped down on the bed, and began to consider her present predicament. Unpalatable though it was, she had to face the fact that she would, perforce, need to spend a considerable amount of time in the Major's company. Like it or not, she did require his escort to return to England. He had not said as much, but she was acutely aware that she desperately needed him, whereas he did not really need her. It certainly put her at a distinct disadvantage, and she was honest enough to admit that she very much resented the fact.

She very much resented, too, having to acknowledge that he had been right to stigmatise her dislike of him as childish. If the truth were known, her own conscience had begun to prick her over the attitude she had adopted towards him on the night of the engagement party. Yes, he had been right, curse him! Dear Helen had been rather immature in her ways, and, although Katherine had completely forgotten the fact until he had remarked upon it, Helen had frequently been seen in possession of the ragdoll her mother had given to her.

One of Helen's favourite pastimes had been sewing. She would spend hours creating fashionable outfits for that wretched doll which she herself longed to wear. It had created a very odd impression, all the same, to see the toy so often in her hands.

Yes, it was little wonder that Major Ross had looked upon Helen as a mere child, Katherine reflected, experiencing once again a pang of regret for the way she had behaved towards him. She had been grossly at fault to condemn him as heartless. That did not mean, of course, that she could ever bring herself to like him. Arrogant and overbearing, he epitomised everything she most disliked in his sex. Yet somehow she was going to have to learn to tolerate him until her feet were firmly planted once more on British soil.

A light scratch on the door forced her to abandon her unsettling reflections, and Katherine raised her head to see Marie enter. She thought she detected a glimmer of sympathy in the older woman's eyes before Marie turned to the two serving-maids, bearing trays, and instructed them to enter.

Whilst the servants busied themselves placing the various dishes on the small table tucked in one corner of the bedchamber, Marie maintained a flow of inconsequential chatter, remarking that the evening had turned chilly, but that the landlord had predicted a fine day for tomorrow. She had never once forgotten the role she had been instructed to play—that of a devoted and conscientious lady's maid. She was always alert and remarkably astute, which made her obvious regard for Major Daniel Ross all the more puzzling.

Even in her own highly disturbed state, Katherine had realised by Marie's reaction to his unexpected appearance that Major Ross was none other than the man whom Sir Giles had engaged a few years before to effect Louise Baron's escape. What she quite failed to understand, however, was why Marie held the odious creature in such high esteem. It was perhaps understandable why she should retain feelings of gratitude. But she had greeted him like some long-lost friend, for heaven's sake!

Determined to have her curiosity satisfied, Katherine didn't hesitate to broach the subject the instant the servants had completed their tasks and had left them to enjoy their dinner in private.

'Major Daniel Ross.' Marie repeated the name Katherine had just divulged as though it were a benediction. 'Yes, *mademoiselle*. It was indeed he who succeeded in helping little Louise Baron,' she added after a moment's thoughtful silence.

'You evidently hold him in high regard,' Katherine

prompted when Marie turned her attention once again to the food on her plate.

'Indeed, I do, *mademoiselle*.' Marie raised her eyes to gaze at some spot behind her dinner-companion's head. 'His orders were to secure Louise's release. But he put his life at further risk by aiding me to escort her to a place of safety.'

Marie was silent whilst she subjected Katherine to a prolonged, searching stare. Then, seemingly satisfied with what she detected in the delicately featured face, she said, 'I believe I told you that the Baron family was once very wealthy. Monsieur Baron employed a steward, a man who had worked diligently for the family. Some years after her parents were killed, whilst she was residing in Paris, Justine discovered where her late father's steward and his family had fled, and it was in their care Justine wished her sister to be placed. Major Ross, as I have mentioned, ensured that we arrived at our destination safely. We should never have succeeded without him, that I know.'

'And does Louise still reside with the family?' Katherine enquired gently.

Marie nodded. 'With one of them.'

'And is she happy?'

'Oh, yes, *mademoiselle*. Within a short time she married the eldest son, Pierre, and they have now two lovely children. With the money Justine left her sister, Louise and Pierre bought a vineyard, and have prospered. I too live with them,' she added, before her gaunt features were softened by a gentle smile. 'Until you revealed it a short while ago, I never knew the real name of the man to whom we owe so much. I only ever knew him as Antoine Durand.'

Her expression suddenly turning grave, she reached

across the table to clasp Katherine's left hand. 'Set aside your differences, *petite*,' she urged gently. 'Believe me when I tell you that you could do no better than to put yourself in that man's hands. He will guard you well.'

Later, after she had changed into her night-wear, Katherine sat on the edge of the bed, and began absently to pull a brush through her long auburn tresses as she turned over in her mind what Marie had disclosed during dinner.

Yes, she could well appreciate now why the French-woman thought so well of Major Ross. Yet when it had been suggested that she could do no better than to place herself in his care, she could not bring herself to agree. But why?

A bitter smile tugged at one corner of her mouth. Oh, yes, she knew well enough why she had been so willing to blame him for poor Helen's death; why she had been so contented to allow Major Daniel Ross to figure as the villain of the piece all these years. But that, she silently reminded herself, did not explain why now—now, when she had acknowledged how incredibly unjust and foolish she had been—she was still so determined to dislike him, to keep him at a distance.

It could not be denied that he possessed many of those traits she abhorred in his sex. None the less, she had been acquainted with several arrogant and dictatorial gentlemen during her lifetime, her grandfather to name but one, and she had experienced no difficulty whatso-ever in tolerating their peccadilloes. So why was she so set against a more companionable relationship develop-ing between her and the Major? After all, there was ab-solutely no danger at all in just liking someone. It was only when—

'Ahh, what a delightful sight! The dutiful wife remaining awake in order to welcome her lord and master to bed.'

Katherine started so violently that the hairbrush shot out of her hand to land on the wooden floor with a clatter. It was as much as she could do to stare in horrified silence as the smugly smiling Major Ross entered the room and calmly closed the door. Just how long he had been standing there in the doorway, watching her, she had no way of knowing, for she certainly hadn't detected the click of the latch, but she could not fail to hear the grating of the key now as it was turned in the lock.

'What on earth do you imagine you are doing, sir?' she demanded in a voice which had suddenly risen by an octave, making her sound more like a frightened child than the self-possessed young woman she had wished to appear.

'What the devil do you imagine I'm doing, madam wife?' he responded, sounding distinctly bored, as he proceeded to slip the key into the pocket of his tight-fitting breeches. 'I am about to retire.'

For a moment Katherine was too stunned by this almost blasé pronouncement to notice that he was calmly appraising her modest night-attire, from the ties at the base of her throat to where her unshod feet protruded from beneath the hem. Then she detected that unmistakable predatory gleam which she had glimpsed all too often in recent years in many pairs of masculine eyes.

She was on her feet in an instant, almost tripping over the edge of the rug in her haste to scramble into the robe which she had left hanging in the wardrobe. If the sudden smile which pulled at the corners of an attractive mouth was any indication, her actions appeared to have afforded him no little amusement, a circumstance which served to strengthen her resolve to be rid of his unwanted presence without delay.

'I too wish to retire, sir, so I would be obliged if you remove yourself forthwith. Anything you have to say to me can quite easily wait until morning.'

'For once we are in complete agreement, m'dear,' he announced, surprising her somewhat, but the hope that she might be rid of him so easily was swiftly dashed when he plumped himself down on the bed, and began to remove his jacket.

Katherine could only gape in astonished disbelief as cravat and waistcoat were added to the coat which he had flung over the back of the chair, and it was only when he tossed one boot into the corner of the room that the full import of his actions hit her with frightening clarity. 'You do not imagine surely that you are going to sleep in here?'

After removing his other boot and sending it the way of the first, he bent a look of mild surprise in her direction. 'Where the deuce do you suppose I'm going to sleep?'

'Anywhere but in here,' she returned, silently cursing herself for foolishly forgetting to lock the door after Marie had returned to her own room. 'I recall the landlord mentioning only yesterday that the inn is half empty now.'

'Yes, I dare say it is. Most British visitors to this city have made a bolt for the Channel ports. Why do you suppose it took me so long to get here?'

Momentarily diverted by this snippet, she asked, 'Was the journey here so very arduous? I wondered why you were delayed.'

There was more than just a hint of reproach in the glance he cast up at her this time, as though he considered her in some way to blame for the delay. 'I was left kicking my heels in Dover for twenty-four hours because of rough conditions in the Channel.'

He sounded genuinely peeved which, perversely, amused her, though she managed to suppress the wicked smile of satisfaction threatening to curl her lips.

'When I eventually arrived in Calais the *diligence* to Paris was full,' he continued in the same highly disgruntled tone, 'and I had perforce to wait two days before I could manage to acquire a seat in one of those pestilential vehicles, which I might add lost one of its wheels when we had travelled no more than twenty miles from the port. I was then compelled to put up at one of the most uncomfortable hostelries it has ever been my misfortune to enter, was refused a seat on the next coach to Paris on account of its being full, and tooled by the only driver I have ever come across who flatly refused to accept a bribe. Consequently I was obliged in the end to leave most of my belongings at the inn, purchase the landlord's misbegotten gelding, owing to the fact that he wouldn't entertain the notion of hiring it out, and then complete the journey on a horse that could not be induced to go above a sedate trot. So as you can appreciate, my dear, I am somewhat fatigued.'

'Quite understandable,' she was forced to admit, but steadfastly refused to concede more than this.

Now that she had overcome the initial shock at seeing the impertinent rogue walk brazenly into her bedchamber, Katherine found herself experiencing mere irritation at his continued presence, but certainly no fear. Which was most odd in the circumstances, considering that if he was determined to remain she would need to seek the assistance of the landlord and perhaps two burly ostlers in order to have him forcibly removed.

She swiftly decided that maybe a more tactful approach would serve her purpose better. 'All the more reason for you to enjoy a good night's rest in another room. I'm certain the landlord will be only too willing to oblige you.'

He didn't attempt to move, and merely regarded her, much as he had done earlier in the evening, as though she were some irritating and unruly child who was best ignored. Katherine succeeded in controlling her rising ire, even though with every passing second it was becoming more of an effort.

Without considering the wisdom of her actions, she moved towards him, holding out one hand. 'Give me the key at once, Major Ross!' she demanded in a voice which clearly betrayed that she was fast approaching the end of her tether, 'otherwise I shall create such a commotion that I shall rouse the entire inn.'

For a tall, powerfully built man, Daniel could move with lightning speed when he chose, a fact which Katherine was swiftly to discover to her cost. One moment she was standing with her bare feet planted firmly on polished wooden boards, and the next she was lying, supine, on the bed, arms pinned above her head. She was conscious of the stone-hard chest pressed against her breasts, and acutely aware too of the muscular leg clamped over her lower limbs, effortlessly pinioning both to the mattress.

She did not need to see the unholy gleam of satisfaction in the dark eyes staring down at her to know that she was now his prisoner, incapable of escaping. Yet, oddly enough, she felt more indignant than afraid, and thoroughly nettled for so foolishly placing herself in a position whereby she could be so effortlessly seized.

'Release me at once, you loathsome creature,' she or-

dered, stubbornly refusing to concede defeat, 'otherwise
I shall scream my head off!'

The gleam in the dark eyes grew distinctly more om-
inous as he encircled her throat with one shapely hand.
'I could render you senseless in a trice, you provoking
little witch,' he warned, sounding as though he would
not have found the exercise wholly distasteful. 'But perhaps,' he added, his strong teeth flashing in yet another
of those distinctly predatory smiles, 'there is a more effective means of ensuring your silence.'

Katherine watched those dark eyes widen fractionally
as they focused on her mouth. His intent was clear, and
she braced herself for the onslaught. Only for a moment,
though, did she experience the punishing force of masculine lips as they clamped down over hers, successfully
smothering the cry for help which too late rose in her
throat; then his mouth became surprisingly gentle, ex-
erting only sufficient pressure to induce hers to part, and
evoking peculiar sensations which she was ashamed to
own were not altogether unpleasant.

Although acutely aware that it would be altogether a
waste of energy to attempt to free herself, and that she
was completely at his mercy, she was astonished not to
discover an expression of smug satisfaction over his obvious mastery when at last he released her, and hurriedly
rose from the bed. No, amazingly enough, he appeared,
if anything, slightly shaken and not just a little puzzled
too, although his voice when he spoke was as infuriatingly self-assured and dictatorial as before.

'Let that be a lesson to you, young woman, to think
long and hard before you embark on any such foolish
escapades in the future.' He towered above her, arms
folded across his chest, every inch the dominant male.
'It wasn't likely, I'll admit, that Sir Giles would have

placed your well-being in the hands of someone whom he did not wholeheartedly trust,' he freely acknowledged. 'None the less, gentlemen do not always behave as they ought on occasions. Think yourself very lucky that I'm not disposed to ravishing innocent maidens. Nor do my tastes run to bedding sharp-tongued viragos.'

If he expected a show of gratitude for this assurance, he was doomed to disappointment. Katherine was hard put to it not to respond in kind by informing him in no uncertain terms that he was not to her taste either, but wiser counsel prevailed. She therefore contented herself with flashing him a further speaking glance, before rising from the bed and fastening her dressing gown, which at some point during his recent assault upon her had become undone.

'So you have nothing to fear from me, providing you do as you're told,' he continued, swiftly suppressing a smile as turquoise eyes favoured him with a further dagger-edged look. 'Be assured, Miss O'Malley, that I find our present situation as disagreeable as you do. Unfortunately we are supposed to be man and wife, and we have no choice but to maintain the pretence, at least for the duration of our stay in Paris. And married couples, let me remind you, are inclined to share the same room.'

The fact that the maddening creature was absolutely right did nothing to improve her state of mind, and when he calmly slid between the sheets, patting that portion of bed beside him invitingly, as though he expected her to play her part to the full, the tenuous hold she had maintained over her temper finally snapped, and she whisked the top coverlet off the bed.

He neither made the least attempt to stop her from taking it, nor, which was more infuriating still, did he offer to do the gentlemanly thing and suggest that he spend the night in one of the easy chairs by the hearth. He merely bade her an infuriating 'Goodnight,' before slipping further between the sheets.

Muttering under her breath, Katherine went about the airy chamber extinguishing the candles. For all his protestations to the contrary, she strongly suspected that Major Ross was attaining much amusement out of her evident discomfiture in having to share this room with him.

She shook her head, marvelling at her own stupidity. How on earth she could have imagined that there was the remotest possibility of her ever liking him she would never know. Without doubt he was the most maddening, detestable creature it had ever been her misfortune to meet!

Chapter Six

The following morning, when finally she had managed
to prise open her eyelids a fraction, Katherine felt as if
she had taken a punishing tumble from a horse. There
didn't seem to be an inch of her that didn't ache abominably, and her poor back felt as if it might break if she
attempted to move. Discovering bright morning sunlight
surprisingly streaming through the bedchamber window
did little to improve her overall discomfort, and she
swiftly closed her eyes against the sun's smarting rays,
but was prompted to open just one again a moment later
when she clearly detected a strange rasping sound emanating from the general direction of the washstand in
the corner of the room.

'Oh, God!' she groaned, when at last she had brought
that nightmarish figure dragging a razor across its chin
into focus, and her one and only hope that the events of
the evening before had all been some fiendish bad dream
had been wholly dashed.

The muttered exclamation carried, and Daniel paused
in his shaving to stare through the mottled glass on the
washstand at his companion's pained expression. A few
minutes before, whilst still soundly asleep, she had

looked utterly adorable, with those auburn locks in en-chanting disarray framing her lovely face. It was quite evident that her mood had not improved to any signifi-cant degree during the night hours, and he could not in truth say that he was in the least surprised. The winged-chair might be comfortable enough to sit in for an hour or two of an evening, but it hadn't been fashioned to afford its occupant a good night's repose.

He managed with precious little effort to suppress a smile, but was not nearly so successful in ignoring that imp of pure devilment which induced him to say, 'Good morning, sweetheart. I trust you slept well?'

The darts of antipathy discharged from the depths of turquoise-coloured eyes very nearly sent him into whoops of laughter and in grave danger of taking a slice off his chin with the razor. Controlling himself with an effort, he glanced at her again through the mirror before concentrating on his own reflection. She was a terma-gant, right enough, stubborn and headstrong, and not every man's idea of a comfortable companion. Yet, in truth, he could not be sorry that she did possess an abun-dance of spirit, for he very much feared that she would require every ounce of mettle she possessed if they were to come through this venture unscathed.

Deciding to keep these reflections to himself for the time being at least, he concentrated on preparing himself for the day ahead. When at last he had arranged his cravat neatly about his neck, he slipped on his jacket, and turned at last to face her.

'There is sufficient hot water left in the pitcher to cater for your needs,' he remarked, successfully bringing to an end what appeared to be her idle contemplation of the dead ashes in the hearth. 'I'll go downstairs and order breakfast. You'll feel better for having some food inside you.'

His considerate gesture to leave her to undertake her toilette in private did little to alleviate Katherine's disgruntled mood, and she darted yet another vitriolic glare in his direction. 'My spirits are only ever likely to improve, Major Ross, when we part company… permanently.'

His lips twitched. 'Believe me, m'dear, it would afford me the utmost pleasure to oblige you. Unfortunately I'm unable to do so, at least not for several days.' He made to move across to the door, then checked and looked down at her again, a frown between his eyes. 'Let me hear you say something in French. Say anything you like to me.'

How Katherine wished her command of the language was such that she could do precisely that by consigning him comprehensively to the devil! Unfortunately it was not and she had to be satisfied with telling him politely to withdraw immediately, to which his response was to utter a protracted groan and clap a hand over his eyes.

'Dear God! Bath seminary French! Marie was right— you would never pass for a Frenchwoman in a million years!' He removed his hand to bestow a faintly exasperated look upon her. 'None the less, we must strive to maintain the pretence of a happily married French couple as best we can. Meet me downstairs when you're ready. You cannot remain skulking in the bedchamber now that your husband is here to protect you. We'll eat in the coffee-room. But kindly leave all the talking to me.'

'Insufferable oaf!' Katherine couldn't resist muttering the instant he had departed.

'I heard that,' a deep voice informed her from the other side of the door.

Aches and pains instantly forgotten, Katherine flew out of the chair to lock the door. From what sounded suspiciously like a rumble of deep masculine laughter floating down the length of the passageway outside the room, she strongly suspected that his sharp ears had also detected the grating sound of the key turning in the lock. The confounded man had the acute senses of a cat! And could move as silently as a feline too! She would have sworn she had been awake throughout most of that wretchedly uncomfortable night, striving to combat the very natural desire to part company with the Major at the earliest opportunity, and yet in all honesty she could not say she had heard him return the key to the lock.

She turned her attention to her small trunk, which had sat in the corner of the room since her arrival at the inn. Nothing would have afforded her more satisfaction than to begin to re-pack it at this very moment with her belongings, and persuade Marie to accompany her at least as far as Calais. Her wretched conscience, however, simply wouldn't permit her to attempt this course of action. She had pledged to do all she could to help Sir Giles in his endeavours to unmask that British traitor who had eluded him for several years. So she must strive, somehow, to overcome her quite understandable antipathy and collaborate with the Major. Their mission was the important thing, not her disinclination to work with someone whom she found an utter bane, and she must never lose sight of this fact, she reminded herself.

Consequently she swiftly made use of the pitcher's remaining contents, and after dressing herself in one of her modest, high-necked day dresses and arranging her hair in a neat chignon, she made her way down the stairs to the coffee-room, where she discovered the Major seated at the table by the window, staring intently out at the street.

Not surprisingly he detected her light footfall almost at once, and rose from the chair to place his lips lightly on one cheek before Katherine could do anything to avoid the fleeting contact with that much too attractive masculine mouth. She would have derived a deal of pleasure from stamping on one of those large feet encased in boots that since the previous night had received a polish, but as there were several other patrons present she refrained and merely betrayed her resentment of the chaste salute by flashing a speaking glance, which he blithely ignored.

As this was the first time she had eaten downstairs since her arrival at the inn, Katherine gazed about her with interest, and although the Major maintained a flow of conversation to which she only needed to contribute the occasional 'yes' or 'no', she did notice his attention straying as the meal wore on, his keen gaze alternating between a spot beyond the window, quite outside her own field of vision, and a certain area in the coffee-room beyond her left shoulder.

She realised at once that something was not quite to his liking, and was not unduly surprised, after they had both eaten their fill, that he seemed disinclined to linger. 'I fear, my dear, that I must leave you to your own devices this morning,' he remarked in a carrying voice, which the bearded man seated alone at the table nearest the door must surely have heard. 'I have an appointment with my bankers, so I'm afraid we must delay our departure until tomorrow. Annoying, I know, but it cannot be helped.'

Had Katherine not known that the Major was acting the part of the loving, considerate husband, she might

have supposed the smile of gentle warmth he bestowed
upon her as they made their way towards the stairs was
perfectly genuine. 'Why not enjoy a last spending spree
and treat yourself to a new bonnet?' he suggested. 'It
might be some little time before we have a chance to
visit Paris again, my love, so take advantage of a last
browse round the shops.'

After accompanying her back up the stairs, he followed her into the bedchamber, where he remained only
for the time it took to collect his outdoor garments. Then,
without uttering anything further, not even a word of
farewell, he left her, closing the door quietly behind him.

Katherine clearly detected a murmur of voices from
the room adjoining her own, which Marie had occupied
throughout their time at the inn. She could not hear precisely what was being said, and even if she could she
doubted very much whether she would have understood
half of what was being uttered, because the conversation
quite naturally was being conducted in rapid French.
Even so, there certainly seemed an urgency about the
whispered exchanges.

Some few minutes elapsed before she heard a firm
tread along the passageway, and several minutes more
before she saw, from her bedchamber window, Major
Ross leave the inn, and set off at a brisk pace towards
the centre of the city. Almost at once a figure emerged
from one of the doorways on the opposite side of the
street and made off in the same direction. Mere coincidence, or something more sinister? She could not help
wondering.

Her faintly troubled thoughts were interrupted by a
knock on the door, and a moment later Marie entered,
dressed in her outdoor clothes. 'Ah, *madame*!' she announced cheerfully, immediately perceiving Katherine

by the window. 'Your husband has instructed me to bear you company in your quest for a new bonnet. How lucky you are, *madame*, to have such a generous husband and one who, moreover, panders to a lady's every whim.'

Katherine's response to this piece of arrant nonsense was to give vent to an unladylike snort of derision. She couldn't help thinking that poor Marie was allowing those lingering feelings of gratitude to cloud her judgement when it came to assessing Major Ross's true character.

She chose not to argue when it was suggested that it might be wise to don her heavy, fur-lined cloak before venturing out on what promised to be a very mild, almost spring-like day. Nor did she attempt to discover why Marie should consider it essential for her to place all the funds in her possession, enough to purchase a dozen dresses, let alone bonnets, in her reticule before setting off. It was only after they had left the inn, and Marie for once chose to dawdle along the streets, while maintaining an inexhaustible flow of small talk that Katherine began to suspect her companion had a very good reason for behaving in such an uncharacteristic way.

This suspicion was confirmed when, idly glancing in a shop window, she happened to catch sight of the man who, earlier that morning, had been seated alone at a table in the coffee room. His grey hair and beard suggested that he was not in the first flush of youth, and yet his gait was remarkably sprightly, and his hard, dark eyes, she noticed, before he stopped to study the goods on display in another shop window, appeared youthfully clear and direct.

'Marie, am I imagining things, or are we being followed?'

Katherine feared the worst when her companion's fixed smile began to crack. 'Yes, *petite*,' Marie admitted, as they continued their stroll. She did not, however, attempt to quicken her pace. 'Major Ross suspected that there were people watching the inn. But do not be afraid. He is at this very moment organising your removal from the city. All we need do is successfully lose our shadow. And I believe I know how this can be achieved. Endeavour, *petite*, to behave normally, and on no account be tempted to keep checking if he is still behind us.'

Resisting the temptation to glance over her shoulder proved to be more difficult than Katherine might have imagined. Strangely enough, though, she did not feel alarmed; in fact, she felt more intrigued than anything else, wondering how the traitor's henchmen had managed to locate their whereabouts.

Of course she realised that Sir Giles had intended to make it known that he had managed to discover the whereabouts of Justine Baron's sister, and that Louise would be travelling to London under an assumed name. It was also possible that Sir Giles had made it known that the person whom he had engaged to escort Louise to England would be adopting the role of her husband. But what had made them suspect that she might be Justine's sister? Did she truly bear such a strong resemblance to the Baron sisters?

This might possibly be the reason, Katherine supposed. Yet it still did not account for the fact that the traitor's associates had managed to locate her so easily. Paris was littered with inns. It would take some considerable time to visit them all in order to search for their quarry. Had it been pure chance which had prompted them to stumble upon the inn at which she and the Major were putting up?

Marie's unexpected exclamation of delight induced Katherine to abandon her puzzling conjecture for the present, and she turned her attention to the creation in the shop window which appeared to be holding Marie so enraptured. She suspected at once that there was something more to her companion's display of enthusiasm, and so offered no resistance when Marie insisted on entering the premises in order to view the fussily adorned bonnet more closely.

No sooner had they stepped over the threshold to find the establishment surprisingly empty except for one sales assistant than Marie's demeanour changed dramatically. She insisted upon seeing the proprietress, and after a few moments' haranguing the young assistant was persuaded to go in search of her mistress.

Not appearing best pleased at having her daily routine disrupted, the *modiste*, like a fearsome Amazon prepared to do battle, suddenly appeared between the plush red velvet curtains. Surprisingly enough, however, after one startled glance of recognition, she clasped Marie to her ample curves, for all the world as if she were some long-lost bosom friend.

A hurried and whispered exchange swiftly followed, the result of which had Madame throwing up her hands in a despairing gesture, casting a sympathetic glance in Katherine's direction and voicing the fervent hope that all hardhearted males would suffer the torment of eternal perdition.

Although faintly puzzled by this pronouncement, Katherine didn't hesitate to follow the *modiste* when she beckoned imperiously with one podgy, beringed hand. Having once passed between the velvet curtains, she found herself in a dimly lit passageway, from which, she swiftly discovered, one gained access to an enclosed, narrow yard.

Extracting a bunch of keys from the pocket of her severe black gown, Madame unlocked the gate set in the high, stone wall, and then surprised Katherine again somewhat by enveloping her in her plump arms.

'You may place your trust in Madame Pérot, *petite*. I shall send that fool who follows about his business if he should dare to enter my shop,' she announced, before utterly confounding Katherine by adding, 'Now go, *petite*. And God speed! You shall soon be safe in the arms of your lover.'

Before Katherine could gather her wits together sufficiently to demand of Madame precisely what she meant, Marie grasped one of her wrists and, after checking no one was lurking in the alleyway beyond the gate, commenced to lead the way hurriedly along a series of narrow, twisting streets. It was only when they eventually arrived at a much wider thoroughfare, running parallel to the Seine, that Marie slackened her pace.

Finding herself in a part of the city where she had never ventured before, Katherine looked about with interest, but eventually her mind returned to the brief encounter with that larger-than-life *modiste*. That Marie was well acquainted with Madame Pérot was obvious. What wasn't quite so clear was what she had imparted during that hurried and whispered exchange which had taken place in the shop.

Curiosity got the better of her at last and she found herself asking, 'How long have you been acquainted with Madame Pérot, Marie?'

'Do you not recall my mentioning that Justine Baron worked for one of Paris's most fashionable dressmakers, *petite*? That was Madame Pérot. She was fond of Justine.

She admired very much her spirit. After I returned to France, I kept in touch.'

That, of course, explained why Madame Pérot didn't hesitate to offer her aid, Katherine mused. It did not, however, explain Madame's curious parting words. 'What did you tell her about me?'

Marie's harsh features were once again transformed by one of those endearing smiles. 'I told her you were my new mistress, and that you had been very good and kind to me.'

'And?' Katherine prompted, when she surprised a mischievous glint in those world-weary eyes.

'I told her you had fallen deeply in love with the most brave and charming man, but that your papa stubbornly opposed the match. I told her you had been forbidden to leave the house, and had been denied all contact with the man you love, so you had been given no alternative but to agree to an elopement. Unfortunately your papa, guessing what you might do—'

'Stop! Stop!' Katherine beseeched her, both amused and slightly resentful at being cast as one of those idiotic, lovelorn heroines too frequently found between the covers of those books to which her companion, Miss Mountjoy, seemed addicted. 'I believe I can guess the rest.'

Katherine cast the woman beside her a fond smile. Undoubtedly in the normal course of events they would have viewed each other as enemies. Yet Fate had decreed that their paths should cross in exceptional circumstances and, even though their countries were probably in imminent danger of once again being at war, she and Marie had, against all the odds, become friends. How Katherine wished that Marie was in truth her companion,

for she doubted she could ever find one to suit her half
so well.

'You have the most fertile imagination, Marie,' she
could not resist telling her. 'And you are the most convincing liar to boot! I dare swear that Madame Pérot
believed every word of your ridiculous tale!'

'But, *petite*, it was not a complete lie,' Marie protested. 'I am taking you to a gentleman who is both
brave and charming, and you are about to fly with him
far away from Paris.'

This succeeded in wiping the fond smile off Katherine's face. Foolishly, up until that moment, the fact that
it would be impossible to return to the inn simply hadn't
occurred to her. But of course they could not! There was
bound to be someone watching the inn, awaiting their
return.

'Will you be accompanying us?' she asked, clinging
to the faint hope that she might rely on Marie's unfailing
support at least until they reached one of the French
ports, but deep down knowing what the answer would
be even before she detected the slight shake of her
trusted companion's head.

'No, *petite*. Major Ross does not need the added burden of taking care of me too.' She shrugged. 'Besides,
there is no need. I shall be perfectly safe. I know this
city well. I have several friends here and can hide myself
easily enough until I find some means to travel south.'

They turned off the main thoroughfare into yet another of Paris's many side roads to discover a one-horse
gig waiting halfway down the street, and an unmistakable tall figure standing beside the decidedly battered
conveyance.

Katherine felt the touch of fingers on her arm, and
turned to see a look of mingled concern and affection in

grey eyes. 'My task is almost complete, *petite*. But yours has only just begun. Do not allow your dislike of Major Ross to prompt you into foolish actions,' she advised in an urgent whisper. 'Do what he tells you and I have every faith that you will come through this unscathed.'

The advice had been kindly meant, and Katherine refrained from dismissing it out of hand. Even so, she was not prepared to commit herself. 'I have never made a promise which I thought I would be unable to keep, Marie, and I do not intend to begin by doing so now. But be assured that I shall not go out of my way to make difficulties, and shall, as far as possible, attempt to work with Major Ross and not against him.'

Even though Katherine had meant every word, resentment at his behaviour the night before remained and she could not bring herself, when at last they approached him, to acknowledge his presence with more than a cursory nod of the head.

Daniel regarded the frigid set of delicate features for a moment before turning his attention to the older woman. 'As you are late, Marie, I assume that you also were followed.'

'Yes, *monsieur*. It was as you suspected—there were two of them watching the inn. We managed to shake off our shadow, as you evidently did yours.'

'It might not be so easy next time, should they locate us again,' Daniel warned. 'I do not doubt that before too long there will be others scouring the streets of Paris for us. So we must not delay.' He reached for her fingers, and held them briefly. 'You are an old hand at this game, Marie, so you need no advice from me, save to say, God speed. If the outcome of this venture should prove successful, I shall ensure that you are apprised of the fact.'

Daniel refused to linger over protracted farewells, and

gave Katherine only sufficient time to receive a surprisingly warm embrace from the older woman, and then placed his hand under her elbow, giving her no choice but to take her seat in the gig.

'You have evidently found favour in the austere Marie's eyes, Miss O'Malley,' he remarked, after Katherine, peering round the side of the gig, had watched Marie turn and walk back along the narrow street.

'For several days she remained aloof,' she admitted, faintly relieved that he considered it safe enough to converse in their own language. 'Gradually, though, she became more friendly,' she went on, wondering if there was the remotest possibility that their relationship might follow a similar course. She did not hold out much hope, but was determined to keep the hostility which lingered towards him under control. 'I quickly grew very fond of her. She took very good care of me.'

'As I fully intend to do, Miss O'Malley.'

Out of the corner of his eye, Daniel noticed the suspicious glance she cast him, as he turned the gig into a much wider thoroughfare. Yes, she was certainly wary of him, and he was forced silently to own that, after his behaviour last night, perhaps there was good reason for her caution. Undoubtedly she was as innocent now as she had been on the day of her birth, a gently nurtured, chaste young woman. Which made her willingness to involve herself in such a perilous venture all the more mystifying, for he felt sure that she must have been aware from the start that there would be more than just an element of risk involved. From something her aunt had disclosed on the night of the engagement party, he had gained the distinct impression that Miss O'Malley was, if not extremely wealthy, a young woman of comfortable means, so he doubted very much, as Sir Giles himself had intimated, that the prospect of attaining a substantial reward would have played any part in her decision to become involved.

He was intrigued, and was determined to discover precisely what had persuaded her to embark on such an undertaking, but decided not to attempt to satisfy his curiosity at this juncture. Instead, he chose to be brutally frank about their present situation, and could not help but feel a deal of admiration for the calm way she accepted the unpleasant state of affairs.

'Yes, I had already realised that returning to the inn was out of the question,' she admitted, before a slight frown marred the perfection of her forehead. 'I wonder what made them suspect us?'

As Katherine kept her eyes firmly fixed in the direction they were heading, she missed completely the frowning glance he cast the errant curls showing beneath the rim of her fashionable bonnet. 'A pity really,' she went on. 'During my many ventures with Marie about the city during the past couple of weeks, I purchased several items of clothing, one of which was a rather pretty day dress.' Her faint sigh betrayed slight resentment over the garment's loss. Then she shrugged. 'The poor landlord is more out of pocket. We cannot even return to pay him for our food and board.'

'Save your pity, Kate. If I know anything, the old rogue will sell your belongings to recoup his losses.'

'Yes, I expect you're—' She caught herself up abruptly, when at last she had digested fully his every word. 'I cannot recall giving you permission to address me by my given name, Major Ross.' There was no response. If the slight twitch she perceived at the corner of his mouth was any indication, however, it was quite evident that he would take no account at all of her dis-

approval. She had no wish for them to be at odds at this
early stage in the proceedings, and so reluctantly decided
to compromise. 'But if you must resort to making free
with my Christian name, you'll oblige me by calling me
Katherine and not Kate. I only ever permit my personal
maid to address me in that fashion.'

'Why, don't you like it?'

'I much prefer Katherine.'

He didn't attempt to hide his surprise. 'I think Kate's
a pretty name, myself. Besides, it suits you. My name is
Daniel, by the way. People will persist in still calling
me Major, but it's a courtesy title only.'

'I'm aware of that, Major Ross.' She had not meant
to sound quite so frigid, so haughtily formal. Yet it was
as well that he should be made aware at the outset that
she had no intention of allowing a friendlier relationship
to develop between them, she told herself, while at the
same time wondering why, perversely, she should feel
piqued because he made no attempt whatsoever to persuade her to use his given name.

Katherine's thoughts were soon turned in a new direction when she became aware, a few minutes later, that
the road they were using to leave the capital was not the
one by which she had arrived in the city almost three
weeks before.

'We are not making for Calais,' Daniel responded in
answer to her question. 'I would be very surprised if
there were not already people stationed at each of the
major Channel ports awaiting our arrival. Just as I suspect that, now we've been—er—rumbled, as it were,
there will very soon be those posted on every major road
leaving the city on the lookout for us.'

This immediately called to mind her earlier thoughts.
How on earth had they managed to arouse suspicion?

Apart from passing the time of day when venturing out of the inn in order to take a little daily exercise, she and Marie had not fraternised with the other people putting up at that hostelry. Daniel had arrived only yesterday. So when and how had they managed to betray themselves?

He shrugged one broad shoulder when she echoed her puzzling thoughts aloud. 'We don't know what Sir Giles saw fit to reveal. I suspect he would have disclosed enough information into certain receptive ears to ensure that our trail wouldn't be hard to follow. Of course, he hadn't bargained for the surprising turn of events which have overtaken us. By this time he would have expected to have had you safely back in London. The traitor must have viewed Napoleon's escape from Elba as nothing short of a godsend. It has offered him ample time to instigate a search for you.'

'True. But why on earth did those two men watching the inn suspect that I might be Louise Baron? Do I resemble her so closely?'

Brown eyes regarded her quite dispassionately for a moment or two. 'As far as I can remember—yes, there is a certain similarity. And of course you're about the right age. It's quite possible that Justine herself might have disclosed certain facts about her sister to the traitor during the time she worked with him. And you do have red hair.'

'Ah, I see!' Katherine could now appreciate just why Sir Giles had chosen her for the task. 'So Louise has red hair?'

'Yes, and so too did Justine Baron, although, if my memory serves me correctly, theirs was somewhat lighter than yours—more Titian.'

Katherine nodded. 'Red hair frequently runs in families, although it is not always the case.' She was silent for a moment, then revealed her disappointment at the unexpected turn of events by releasing her breath in a despondent sigh. 'Poor Sir Giles. Napoleon's escape couldn't possibly have come at a worse time for him.'

'It couldn't have come at a worse time for us, come to that,' Daniel reminded her, smiling to himself.

Their present situation was anything but rosy, and he suspected the young woman seated beside him knew this very well. It was, he mused, much to her credit that she had accepted the loss of her belongings and this impromptu flight from the capital with a quaint and dignified resignation, and he couldn't help but admire her for this present display of admirable self-control. Whether she would continue to behave in such a commendable manner during the days ahead was another matter entirely. He very much feared that, should the mood take her, she could prove to be a handful, fiery and stubborn. One thing was certain, though, during the next few days he was unlikely to be afflicted by the boredom which, unfortunately, all too frequently plagued him when in the company of most members of her sex for any length of time.

'Ideally I would have preferred to remain at the inn for a few days,' he remarked, surprising her somewhat. 'Those men watching us would in all probability have dropped their guard had we gone about the city displaying a lack of concern. Unfortunately, that was not possible with the Corsican on the loose once more. Last night I learned that Napoleon is not coming up against much resistance as he heads towards the capital. All he needs is to win the support of the army, then I'm afraid…'

'Do you think that is possible?' she prompted when his voice trailed away.

'I very much fear that it is, Miss O'Malley. His soldiers love him.'

'Oh, that wretched little man!' Katherine exclaimed, able to express her feelings more fully now than she had when in Marie's company. 'After all these years of conflict, has he not had enough of war? God forbid that it begins again!'

'Amen to that, m'dear,' he concurred, as they approached the outskirts of the city, and he turned his attention to what was going on about him, watching intently for any suspicious characters loitering by the roadside. He noticed no one, but he refused to be lulled into a false sense of security, for he very much feared that before the end of the day there would be someone, or possibly several, hot on their trail.

Fortunately his companion, continuing to behave with commendable restraint, didn't plague him with questions that he could not or might prefer not to answer. She didn't bore him to tears by trying to maintain a flow of small talk either. In fact, apart from generously praising him for his foresight in providing them with a basket of food, tucked away under the seat, she said very little, not even when they were obliged to stop on several occasions throughout the day in order to rest the horse. Only when, early in the evening, he turned off the main highway into a narrow country lane did she betray an interest in precisely where they were bound.

'Normandy.' Daniel didn't hesitate to enlighten her, and Katherine, in turn, didn't attempt to hide her surprise. 'I have a good friend living there.' His lips curled into a secretive little smile. 'I know I can rely on this person to aid us. Needless to say I do not expect to reach

the town where my friend resides tomorrow, or the day
after, come to that. So, in the meantime, we must make
do as best we can. I'm afraid, though, that you are not
going to find this journey particularly comfortable.'

'Do not concern yourself over me, Major Ross,' Katherine responded, feeling unaccountably resentful because
he no doubt considered her some pampered ninnyhammer who couldn't do without her creature comforts for
a few days. 'I cannot deny that I had not planned to
leave Paris in such a fashion, but I do not hold you in
any way responsible for that. Be assured that I shall do
my utmost not to be a burden, and have no intention of
causing you the least concern.'

She turned her head in time to catch a second rather
secretive little smile playing about his mouth before he
astounded her by admitting, 'You have been causing me
no little concern for quite some time, Miss Katherine
O'Malley.'

Before she could enquire precisely what he had meant,
he changed the subject by informing her that he dared
not risk putting up at an inn that night.

'I do not doubt that there are those already hot on our
trail,' he continued. 'I strongly suspect that they will
begin by searching for us in the inns along the main
road we have just left. Which will buy us a little time,
but not very much, I'm afraid. It will be dark in an hour,
so we must find some form of shelter soon, for I have
no intention of travelling at night and running the risk
of getting us lost.'

It was then that he caught sight of billowing smoke
in the distance, and turned off the road on to a deeply
rutted track. 'There is some form of dwelling just up
ahead, possibly a farm. With any luck there might be a

village nearby. I'll have a scout around and see what I can find.'

Just for a second she thought she glimpsed a flicker of unease in his expression, before he handed her the reins and then jumped to the ground. 'Can you by any chance handle firearms, Miss O'Malley?'

'Yes, Major, I can,' she assured him. 'My father taught me, though not since I lived with my grandfather have I used one.'

Even in the rapidly fading light she could easily detect the glint of amusement in his eyes, and what might have been a hint of respect too. 'In that case I shall leave this in your care,' he announced, delving into the pocket of his cloak and drawing out a pistol. 'Do not hesitate to use it if you feel at all threatened.' There was a flash of white teeth. 'But I would be grateful if you do not mistake me for one of our pursuers. I shall give a low whistle to announce my return, just to be on the safe side.'

It was as much as Katherine could do to suppress an angry retort, and yet the instant he disappeared from view she experienced fear for the very first time since setting out on what she was now beginning to view as a madcap venture. Given the choice, she might not have wished Major Daniel Ross to have been designated her protector. There wasn't a doubt in her mind that he would continue to irk her unbearably during the days ahead. Yet she was forced to own that she experienced a most comfortable feeling of security when he was near, which was singularly lacking now.

She shivered and drew the rug that the Major had had the forethought to supply more closely about her legs. She was already feeling the loss of warmth which that large, muscular frame so close to her own had provided throughout what had been a mercifully dry day. She could only place her faith in the Major to find them some form of shelter, for she certainly didn't relish the prospect of spending a night under the stars.

A rustling sound emanating from the small clump of trees off to her left caught her attention, and she instinctively felt for the pistol which she had placed on the seat beside her. She derived a modicum of comfort from having the lethally formed piece of metal clasped firmly in her hand, but she couldn't deny that it was no substitute for a certain someone's presence.

A further noise reached her ears, then another and another, each sounding much closer and more menacing than the last. She had never been afraid of the dark, not since she was a child, but as dusk arrived, she came perilously close to crying out in relief when at last she detected that low whistle.

No one would have supposed for a moment that she was overjoyed to see him, least of all Daniel himself, when he finally clambered up beside her again, and she demanded to know where he had been and why it had taken him so long to return.

Strong teeth flashed more brilliantly in the dark when he turned his head to bestow a wicked grin upon her. 'Did you miss me, sweetheart?'

'I certainly did not enjoy being on my—' Stopping mid-sentence for the second time that day, Katherine favoured him with an angry look, her eyes flashing no less brilliantly than his smile. 'And don't call me sweetheart, you impudent rogue!'

She could feel that comforting frame shaking with suppressed laughter as he reached for the reins. 'It's a relief to know your spirit hasn't deserted you completely, Miss O'Malley. And I apologise for taking so long, but at least I was successful in my endeavours.

There is a village a couple of miles up the road. So you'll no doubt be relieved to know you shall attain at least a modicum of comfort this night.'

Katherine was beginning to feel so weary after the many hours they had spent travelling that she would have been quite happy to sleep on a dirt floor. Daniel swiftly proved he was able to offer her something more comfortable than that, however, when they reached the outskirts of the village and he drew the gig to a halt outside a blacksmith's premises.

After a swift glance up and down the deserted street to ensure that no one was about, he jumped nimbly down from the gig. Katherine saw him extract something from his pocket, and was rather surprised to see the large wooden door swing wide a few moments later. She succeeded in curbing her curiosity until they were safely inside and Daniel had provided further evidence of his resourcefulness by finding a lamp and lighting it.

'How on earth did you manage to remove that padlock, Major Ross?' she demanded to know, making herself useful by releasing the horse from its harness and leading the gelding into a stall.

After draping a piece of sacking over the one and only grimy window, Daniel satisfied her curiosity by extracting a cunningly fashioned thin piece of metal from the pocket of his jacket which, even in the dim light, she had little difficulty in recognising, for she clearly recalled being shown such an article several years before by a casual labourer who had worked for her father for a very short time.

Although she arched one fine brow, Katherine refrained from comment, and merely turned her attention once again to the gelding who was happily champing away on a substantial pile of hay. 'You are certainly no fiery steed, and definitely not in the first flush of youth, but you did us proud this day, old fellow.'

Daniel noted the affectionate way she both stroked and spoke to the animal. Evidently fear of horses was not one of her weaknesses, even if a dislike of the dark was. 'I'm afraid he and the gig were all I could manage to find in so short a time. I couldn't afford to be choosy.'

'You did very well in the circumstances,' she responded, surprising him somewhat by the mild praise. 'He's certainly strong and healthy, and has been well cared for.'

'Evidently you know something of horseflesh, Miss O'Malley,' he remarked, collecting the basket of food and rug from the gig, before lowering himself on the mound of hay piled in one corner of the stone building. 'We'll finish off the food and then get some sleep. We must be away from here at first light.'

Hunger swiftly overcame her understandable wariness, and Katherine joined him on the pile of hay, reflecting as she did so that this was the first time in her life that she had ever sought refuge in a smithy. She had no cause to complain though, she reminded herself, gazing absently at the fire, the ashes of which still retained sufficient heat to take the chill off the air. The bread and cheese might be simple fare, but it was wholesome, and her surroundings, though hardly palatial, certainly provided sufficient comfort and warmth.

The instant she had consumed the last mouthful of bread, Daniel rose to his knees and began to spread the rug over the hay. 'Come, let us settle ourselves for sleep. As I mentioned earlier, we must be away at first light, before the owner of this establishment turns up for work,' he remarked, before he noticed her staring down at the cover as though it were a hot bed of coals, and best avoided.

His lips twitched. 'What is the matter, sweetheart? Don't you trust me?'

Katherine transferred her gaze to those dark eyes glinting with sheer devilment. 'Let me assure you, Major Ross, that I consider it immensely difficult to trust a man who carries a picklock about his person.'

'Vixen!' he exclaimed, laughing in spite of the fact that he experienced a twinge of resentment because she obviously continued to mistrust him.

But perhaps he had given her reason enough to continue to remain a little aloof, he reminded himself, wrapping his cloak about him and settling himself on the hay at a discreet distance away from the rug. His behaviour towards her the previous night could hardly be described as that of a gentleman, though it had to be said in his defence that she had sorely tried his patience, and badly needed someone to take her in hand. Undoubtedly she had been allowed far too much licence to do and say exactly as she pleased. She wasn't spoilt, precisely, but was certainly accustomed to having her own way. Yet today he had glimpsed certain facets to her character that he couldn't help but admire. Blessedly her tongue did not run on wheels and she betrayed no signs of succumbing to a fit of the vapours if subjected to hardship. All in all, he was beginning to feel that Sir Giles Osborne, the cunning old rogue, had chosen well when he had selected Miss Katherine O'Malley for this venture. She might be an infuriating little madam on occasions, but by heaven she had certainly proved equal to the task thus far!

'I'm sorry, Kate, what did you say?' he asked, suddenly realising that she had spoken.

'I said—what's that noise?'

For a second or two all he could hear was the gelding contentedly champing away on the hay, then he clearly detected a scratching sound somewhere off to his left. 'A rat, I should imagine.'

'Heaven spare us!' he heard her mutter before she edged a little closer. 'And don't call me Kate!'

Daniel's response was merely to blow out the lamp, and then settle himself for sleep.

Chapter Seven

Although uncertain quite what had disturbed him, Daniel was suddenly wide awake and very conscious of something soft lying against him, and something softer still tickling his chin. Even in the dim light of early morning he could clearly see long tendrils of hair stretching across his chest and instinctively raised one hand to twist several of the gently curling strands round one finger; then just as quickly he released them and carefully edged himself away, before his suddenly aroused body tempted him to take further liberties, which at this early stage in their relationship would, he felt sure, be met with fierce resistance. The last thing he desired was for his soundly sleeping companion's understandable wariness to deepen into fear. No, it was her complete trust he must win, then maybe…

Refusing to allow his thoughts to dwell on what hopefully would be the very satisfactory outcome to a closer relationship developing between them, Daniel carefully raised himself on one elbow in order to study the perfect arrangement of delicate features now framed in a tussled mass of fiery curls: the small straight nose, the infinitely kissable and perfectly moulded lips above a determined little chin, which tended to lift so stubbornly on occasions. Undeniably she was a most desirable young woman, beautifully packaged and utterly feminine. Which made her single state rather puzzling, though he strongly suspected that this was entirely through choice.

He detected the slight movement of ridiculously long, curling lashes, and a moment later those striking turquoise orbs were gazing up at him rather wonderingly, before a suspicious frown drew finely arched, dark brows together.

'What on earth do you imagine you are doing hovering over me like some ravenous bird of prey, about to swoop, Major Ross?' she demanded to know.

'Spot on form again, I see.' Shaking his head in disbelief, Daniel rose to his feet. 'How is it possible, I ask myself, for someone to appear so beautifully angelic in sleep and yet possess the tongue of an adder?'

Katherine satisfied herself with flashing him an angry look, which only succeeded in igniting a rumble of masculine laughter. With narrowed eyes, she watched him walk over to the window and remove the piece of sacking. Tongue like an adder, indeed! She inwardly fumed. He had a crass nerve to criticise her when he wasn't above uttering some barbed remark himself! she decided, scrambling to her feet and giving her cloak a vigorous shake.

'You haven't time to concern yourself over your dishevelled state,' Daniel told her bluntly, turning in time to see her attempting to make use of the few pins that remained in her hair. 'We cannot risk being found here by the blacksmith when he arrives. Which, if I know anything, will be quite soon. It's already daybreak.'

Although she prided herself on her appearance, and never set forth unless perfectly groomed, Katherine appreciated that attempting to make herself presentable was hardly important in the circumstances, and merely thrust her reticule into her cloak pocket before swirling the fur-lined garment about her shoulders once more.

'As you appear to have a way with horses, sweet Kate, perhaps you'd be good enough to collect our trusted steed from the stall so that I can hitch him up to the gig?' Daniel requested, and received his second dagger-look of the morning.

'Willingly, Major Ross…and don't call me Kate!'

Grinning wickedly, he occupied himself, while Katherine went to do his bidding, by plumping up the pile of hay to hide all evidence of two people having used it as a bed. With his back towards it, he didn't notice the large wooden door open a fraction. Katherine too was oblivious to the fact that an unkempt rascal was stealthily entering, or that three equally villainous rogues were at their compatriot's heels. The first indication she had that they were no longer alone was when a shot rang out, by which time it was already too late to scream out a warning.

Katherine saw Daniel extract the pistol from his pocket and with unerring accuracy dispose of one of the intruders, before the other three, on him in a trice, knocked him to the ground, raining a barrage of kicks and blows down on him. Hidden by the gelding, Katherine looked wildly about for some weapon, and her frantic gaze swiftly fell upon a solid piece of wood. Without the least concern for her own safety, she joined in the fray, felling one of the attackers with a single blow to the head before anyone knew she was there.

'You damnable coward!' she screamed, delivering such a powerful blow to yet another assailant that he dropped the weapon he had been wielding, and made for the door with all possible speed, screaming in agony as he clutched his right arm.

Showing no mercy, Katherine scooped up the unwieldy firearm and gave chase like some avenging virago out for blood; while Daniel, having by this time managed to rise to his feet, easily disposed of the last attacker with a well-aimed blow to the jaw. He then turned in time to see Katherine, using both hands, striving to level the heavy weapon. Before he could yell out a warning, her finger had squeezed the trigger. There was the most almighty report, and a moment later, appearing dazed and not just a little embarrassed, she was sitting plump in the middle of the village street.

Galvanised, Daniel was beside her in an instant, demanding to know whether she was hurt. 'Only my pride,' she assured him, glancing at where she had dropped the firearm. 'What in the name of heaven is that thing?'

'The Lord only knows! Looks to be something between a blunderbuss and a ''Brown Bess'' to me. A ''Brown Bess'' is a musket,' he explained in response to her questioning look.

He cast her an impatient one in return as he helped her to her feet. 'Don't you know any better than to attempt to handle unfamiliar firearms, young woman?' he demanded sharply, continued anxiety over her well-being making him sound far harsher than he had intended. 'They can be notoriously unpredictable, not to mention downright dangerous. Though it appears,' he added, betraying a hint of admiration in his expression now, as he glanced at the spot directly in front of the inn, where the fourth attacker lay motionless on the ground, with something which Daniel couldn't quite make out lying on the road beside him, 'that you managed to discharge that monstrosity with remarkable accuracy. No mean feat, my darling, believe me!'

He quite failed to notice the swift and faintly sheepish look cast up at him through long lashes, for his attention was captured by a few villagers who had begun to emerge from their houses in order to investigate the commotion. To remain a moment longer would, he knew, be to court more trouble. There was every chance that others in search of them were in the area. Furthermore, he didn't relish the prospect of trying to explain to the French authorities just why they were being pursued across the country by a gang of hired assassins. Consequently he took a firm hold of a slender wrist and, before she knew what was happening, hauled Katherine willy-nilly out of the village towards a large stretch of rising pasture land, dotted with sheep happily grazing.

Katherine perfectly understood the reasons for their hasty departure. She could appreciate too why they could not have delayed in order to harness the horse to the gig. All the same, she felt that she might have been allowed the few seconds it would have taken to collect her bonnet from the blacksmith's barn.

The wind whistling across the open ground caught at her hair, lashing strands across her face. The cowl on her cloak was of precious little use, for unless she kept a firm hold on it the wind whipped it back in a trice. She refrained from complaining, however, for she needed all her breath in order to keep abreast of her companion.

Daniel set a cracking pace, and Katherine found herself almost having to run in order to keep up with that elegant, long-striding gait. Not until they had left the village far behind, and he seemed satisfied that no one was giving chase, did he attempt to walk at a more moderate speed; even so he did not suggest that they rest until quite some time later, when the open landscape had given way to a vast woodland area.

Settling himself on the grass, Daniel leaned his back against the substantial trunk of a conveniently fallen tree. Although he wasn't breathing particularly heavily, after their swiftly executed cross-country flight, Katherine wasn't slow to note that he was looking a little flushed. Initially she didn't give much thought to the unusual ruddy complexion, until she noticed him favouring his left arm, grasping it at frequent intervals beneath the folds of his cloak. Then, as he withdrew his right hand again, she clearly saw the telltale red stains between the long fingers.

'Daniel, you're hurt!'

Forgetting her own insignificant discomforts, she dropped to her knees beside him, and threw back his cloak before he had a chance to stop her. The instant her eyes focused on the charred portion of jacket just below the shoulder, and the dark stain surrounding the hole, she remembered the first shot fired in the barn. She had thought the attacker had missed his target entirely. Clearly he had not.

'Why on earth didn't you say something, you foolish creature!' she scolded.

Daniel assured her that it was nothing, barely a scratch, but made no demur when she insisted that he remove his cloak and jacket, and then his shirt, because the wound was too high up on the arm to reach by merely rolling up the sleeve.

Obligingly, he pulled the linen garment over his head, sending his dark brown hair into disarray. It was by no means the first time Katherine had seen a person of the opposite sex in a state of undress. Many a time when she had lived in Ireland she had seen men remove their shirts on warm summer days before they had attempted to groom one of her father's fine horses. So the sight of dark hair covering a well-muscled chest came as no surprise to her whatsoever. What sent a shock wave rippling through her, however, bringing her almost to the verge of tears, was the clear evidence of past suffering, and unmistakable bravery.

Without conscious thought, she reached out and began to trace the path of the longest scar, which ran from his right shoulder almost down to his pelvis, only to have her fingers swiftly captured in a firm yet gentle clasp.

'What is it, Katherine?' Daniel wasn't slow to detect long lashes moistened by tears barely held in check. 'What has occurred to upset you?'

'I-I feel so very ashamed.' Her voice was little more than a shaky whisper, but there was no mistaking the heartfelt contrition it contained. 'So very ashamed that I ever thought so badly of you; that I foolishly attempted to hold you responsible for dear Helen's death, when I always knew deep down that it wasn't your fault.'

Although she didn't attempt to draw her hand from his, she seemed unwilling, or unable, to meet his gaze, and her complexion had grown worryingly quite ashen. He didn't doubt her sincerity, but was puzzled by the admission. He had been inclined to dismiss her dislike of him as nothing more than a pampered young woman's childish spite. Now that he had come to know her a little better he was certain that that initial judgement had been sadly flawed. She was no foolish ninnyhammer prone to take a pet for no reason. Far more, he now realised, lay behind her former conduct towards him.

'Why were you so determined to dislike me, Katherine?' There was no response. Undeterred, he added,

'Come, do you not think that the man you've treated with such contempt on occasions deserves an explanation?'

This succeeded in drawing her eyes briefly to his, before she turned her attention to his most recent injury. 'Because it was far easier to blame you than myself,' she finally admitted, astonishing him somewhat.

Removing her hand from his at last, Katherine delved into the pocket of her skirt for her handkerchief, and proceeded to dab at the wound, which blessedly was little more than a scratch. 'I'm a scourge, Daniel. Everyone I have ever loved, or cared for deeply, every person with whom I have lived, has died. I tried to convince myself that Helen, at least, might have survived had she not lost the will to do so because she was mooning like a lovesick fool over you. It was grossly unfair of me to try to pin the blame on you. She was far too immature to capture a gentleman's interest. I suspect you were hardly aware of her existence…just as you were hardly aware of mine when I lived with my grandfather for those few short months. How I wish now that I had never resided in Dorsetshire!'

Not knowing quite how to respond, and feeling confused by these startling disclosures, Daniel remained silent as he watched her rise to her feet, and move in that graceful way of hers over to the tiny stream which gurgled its way through the woodland just a few yards from where he sat.

He didn't doubt for a moment that for some obscure reason she was determined to hold herself in some way responsible for the deaths of her grandfather and her friend, and possibly her parents too. He had no idea how Mr and Mrs O'Malley had met their maker, but there was no mystery about Colonel Fairchild's demise, and

Helen Rushton was by no means the only person to suc-
cumb to that outbreak of smallpox. Unless he was mistaken, her mother had perished too. So why was Katherine so determined to blame herself?

Although he would be forced to admit that, as yet, he
didn't know her very well, he wouldn't have supposed
for a moment that she was a young woman prone to
indulging in foolish flights of fancy. So what deep-
rooted fear was persuading her to believe such absolute
nonsense? There was something…there simply had to
be! And he was determined to discover precisely what
that something was.

Deciding not to press her for an explanation quite yet,
and thereby risk damaging the rather sweet rapport
which had surprisingly developed between them, he
changed the subject the instant she returned by remarking that he was relieved to see that the sight of blood
didn't turn her queasy. 'Not that I'm unduly surprised,'
he added, bestowing a look of the utmost respect upon
her, as she began to dab at the slight wound with the
handkerchief which she had soaked in the clear waters
of the stream. 'Any young woman who possesses the
courage to do what you did back there in that village
isn't likely to flinch at the sight of a little blood.'

She cast him a distinctly rueful smile. 'You may as
well know now that I have been cursed with an appalling
temper, Major. I've learned to control it over the
years…well, at least for the most part,' she added, incurably truthful. 'But the sight of those four men setting
about you made me fume. Damnable cowards!'

'And you came to my aid without any thought for
your own safety,' he murmured, experiencing a wealth
of oddly contrasting emotions which left him not quite
knowing whether he wished to kiss or shake her for do-

ing such a foolhardy yet courageous thing. 'Wellington could have done with you out in the Peninsula, my girl. Who did you say taught you to handle firearms, by the way?'

'My father,' she reminded him, before asking if he had a handkerchief about his person.

He delved into the pocket of his breeches and drew out a square of linen, which she promptly pressed over the cleaned wound. 'You're a damned fine shot. You'd have made an excellent rifleman had you been a boy.'

This time he didn't miss the faintly sheepish expression, and was puzzled by it until she announced, 'It's no good. My conscience simply won't permit me to allow you to continue to view me as some sort of wonder woman. I've discovered today that I'm not that good a shot.'

He raised his brows at this. 'You managed to down that rogue who was doing his level best to get away,' he reminded her.

'Yes, and no,' she responded, confounding him still further, before once again casting him a glance from beneath long lashes. 'Did you not notice the inn sign lying in the road?'

'I noticed something, certainly.'

Katherine decided to confess before she had a chance to change her mind. 'Well, the truth of the matter is...I hit the sign, shattering its hinge, and the sign hit him, plump on the head.'

For several moments Daniel regarded her in silence, then he threw back his head and roared with laughter. The woodland area surrounding them resounded with the infectious sound, and Katherine found it impossible not to laugh herself.

'It isn't that funny!' she chided gently, regaining control first. 'I was mortified, I can tell you, when I saw that dratted sign fall. My aim has never been so awry before.'

'I doubt anyone would have stood the remotest chance of hitting his mark with that monstrous weapon,' he assured her, as she rose to her feet and blithely tore a strip off the bottom of her underskirt.

The sight of a neatly turned ankle, swiftly followed by the renewed touch of those gentle fingers on his arm, as she deftly wound the strip of material over his handkerchief, certainly put a further strain on his self-control. Desperate to turn his thoughts in a new direction, he searched about for something, anything, that might take his mind off earthy masculine desires, and his gaze swiftly fell upon her bloodstained handkerchief, lying on the ground.

Reaching for it, and earning himself a stern reprimand in the process for not sitting still, he studied the beautifully embroidered monogram in one corner. 'Is this your stitch-work, Katherine?'

'No. Bridie embroidered it. She was my nursemaid when I was a child,' she explained when he raised an enquiring brow. 'Now she's my personal maid... housekeeper...you name it.'

'What does the "F" stand for?'

A moment's silence, then, 'Fairchild.' She grimaced. 'I've Bridie to thank for that too!' she informed him, her disgruntled tone evidence enough that she wasn't best pleased. 'Apparently she took one look at me and announced that I was the fairest child she'd ever set eyes on. My mother, much struck by this, as it happened to be her maiden name, decided it would be most appropriate, and as Papa had chosen my Christian name he allowed her to have her way.'

'Fairchild,' he echoed. 'Yes, it suits you. It suits you very well.'

Half-suspecting him of mockery, Katherine paused in her tying of the makeshift bandage to cast him a suspicious glance. 'There, that should hold,' she announced, reaching for his shirt. 'Hurry and get dressed. I don't want you taking a chill on top of everything else.'

The garment was stained with blood, but he had no choice but to put it back on. Neither of them had a change of clothes, which, Katherine mused, didn't appear to trouble Daniel to any great extent; but she knew it would begin to irk her unbearably if she was forced to remain in the same garments for any length of time. She wasn't accustomed to going without meals either. Not a morsel of food had passed her lips since the previous evening, and she was now beginning to feel decidedly peckish.

Refraining from bringing this to his attention, she merely seated herself on the fallen tree. Despite the fact that Daniel's injury was, as he had stated himself, only slight, and she didn't suppose any complications would arise as a result of it, he was still looking slightly flushed, so it could do no harm to let him rest for a while.

Evidently he was of a similar mind, for he made himself more comfortable, and very soon afterwards closed his eyes. Katherine sat quietly beside him for a while, content to gaze at their pretty surroundings, which were thankfully betraying clear signs that spring had arrived. Then her stomach elected to remind her quite noisily that she required something to eat, and she decided it was time to do something about it.

Chapter Eight

The glade was pleasantly sheltered from the gusty wind that earlier had gathered strength across the open countryside, hindering their flight from the village. The March sun too was surprisingly warm, and Daniel had found little difficulty in dozing. The slight dizziness that had induced him to rest for a while seemed mercifully to have passed, and he was sufficiently restored now to recommence their cross-country trek to Normandy.

He turned his head, expecting to see his darling companion once again sitting on the trunk of the tree beside him, and was faintly surprised to discover no sign of her. Earlier, when a slight sound had disturbed him, he had opened one eye to catch her slipping quietly away. He had resisted the temptation to call out and ask where she was going. She might be a damnably brave little soul to have come to his aid, he reflected, but he suspected that, for all her innate courage, she would find it acutely embarrassing to admit that she was forced to answer a call of nature.

Women! Smiling to himself, he shook his head. He would never understand them. A jumbled mass of contradictions was what they were. At least, he silently amended, that red-haired little darling most certainly was. One moment snapping a fellow's nose off for absolutely no reason; the next a ministering angel, touchingly concerned and tending to his every need. Yet, for all her contrariness, he could think of no other female of his acquaintance whom he would prefer to have with him on this assignment. Come to that, he could think of no other woman, with the possible exception of his late grandmother, who would have possessed sufficient courage to do what Katherine Fairchild O'Malley had done that morning. Not to put too fine a point on it, she had in all probability saved his life—foolhardy, perhaps, but worthy of the utmost admiration.

And where the deuce had the damnable little firebrand got to? Sitting upright, Daniel consulted his pocket-watch. How much time did it take a female to perform some simple bodily function? She had been gone twenty minutes or more, for heaven's sake!

He rose to his feet and began to scan the surrounding woodland area, his sharp eyes searching for any slight movement that could not be attributed to natural rustling resulting from the wind. All seemed still and silent, except for the singing of birds, and occasional scurrying noises in the undergrowth.

His first instinct was to go in search of her, but wiser counsel prevailed. If she returned to find him gone, he very much feared that she wouldn't hesitate to go wandering off again, looking for him, and get herself hopelessly lost or, worse still, walk straight into the hands of those whom they were trying their utmost to avoid, if indeed she had not done so already.

Concern increased with every passing second, and he had almost reached the point where he felt he had no choice but to search for her, when his sharp ears caught the sound of humming, and a moment later he glimpsed her weaving a path through the trees, appearing as if she hadn't a care in the world.

'Where the hell have you been?' he demanded, resorting to the fierce tone he had adopted when dealing with any foolhardy, raw recruit under his command. She regarded him in mild surprise, but didn't appear unduly chastened which, perversely, only served to stoke the fires of his wrath. 'Haven't you more sense, girl, than to go wandering off by yourself? You might easily have walked straight into the hands of those villains engaged to capture us!'

Intrigued rather than incensed by this display of ill humour, Katherine held the hard-eyed gaze. She strongly suspected that this surprising show of annoyance on his part stemmed from anxiety over her well-being, and she was faintly moved by his evident concern.

'Oh, come now, Major Ross, be reasonable,' she urged gently, in an attempt to placate him. 'How many spies do you suppose there are in France? It was highly unlikely that I would have come across any more.'

'God give me strength!' Daniel clapped a hand over his eyes. 'You don't imagine for a moment that those four villains we encountered back there were spies, do you?'

'Were they not?' Katherine couldn't in all honesty say that she'd given the matter much thought. 'Who were they then, do you suppose?'

'Rogues hired to search for us, you damnable little idiot!' he snapped, which clearly proved that her soothing manner had not achieved the desired result. He removed his hand to glower down at her yet again, as she calmly seated herself on the trunk of the fallen tree. 'Be under no illusions, girl,' he warned. 'Should you fall into their hands, they won't be over-nice in their dealings with you.'

Her shrug of indifference wasn't likely to improve his state of mind, but Katherine was beyond caring. She considered that she'd had reason enough to venture forth on her own. 'Well, I don't suppose it's very likely that any others who might be in search of us would be able to pick me out amongst the throng.'

For a moment it was as much as Daniel could do to stare down at her in open-mouthed astonishment. 'Not be able to…?' Words failed him, but not for very long. 'I've been unfortunate enough to come across several harebrained females in my time, Katherine Fairchild O'Malley, but without doubt you reign supreme! You've a head of hair on you like a flaming hayrick, girl! You stand out like a beacon!'

If there was one subject guaranteed to stir her own uncertain temper, then it was someone passing a disparaging remark about her hair. 'I didn't ask to be cursed with auburn locks, Major Ross!' she flared. 'And might I remind you that had you permitted me the few seconds it would have taken to collect my bonnet, instead of dragging me away in that odiously cavalier fashion, I might have been in a position to keep my cursed tresses well hidden!'

She watched the anger fading from those dark, masculine eyes as he cast them over her hair, which she had managed during her brief venture alone through the French countryside to confine neatly at the nape of her neck by means of a further strip torn from her underskirt.

'I considered that I had a sound reason for wandering off on my own.' From beneath her cloak, she drew out a loaf of bread and a goodly wedge of cheese. 'Though why I bothered to bring them back here to share with you, I cannot imagine,' she added, feeling quite out of charity with him now.

Daniel sat down beside her and, relieving her of the round loaf, proceeded to tear it in half. 'Where did you manage to lay your hands on this delicious fare, may I ask?' he enquired, secretly impressed by this display of self-reliance on her part. 'Is there some village nearby?'

Katherine shook her head. 'Didn't see one. There's a farm in the valley, though, just beyond the wood. The rear door to the main building was wide open. I didn't see anyone about, so I slipped inside and removed these from the kitchen table.'

He bent a look of mock severity upon her. 'That was stealing, my girl. Many in Wellington's army were hanged for less.'

'As I left some coins on the kitchen table, I do not consider I was stealing,' she responded, winning herself a faint smile of approval.

'In that case, I'll forgive you this time. But you're not to go wandering off again by yourself, understand? I can appreciate that there will be occasions when you'll desire a—er—little privacy,' he added delicately. 'As long as I can see the top of your head at all times, I shan't object.'

Katherine didn't pretend to misunderstand and glowered at him, the picture of indignant outrage. 'I'll take leave to inform you, Major, that you're an exceedingly vulgar man. Top of my head, indeed! I've never heard the like before!'

Although he found it impossible to suppress a smile, Daniel managed not to add to her obvious annoyance by laughing outright. 'One tends to forget the social niceties after years of hard campaigning out in the Peninsula, Kate.'

'Then it's high time you began to re-acquire a few, Major. And you can begin by paying me the common courtesy of remembering not to call me Kate.'

Clearly he was not prepared to begin his retraining quite yet, for he merely applied himself to the bread and cheese for several minutes, and then surprised her by remarking, 'For someone who places such store by correct behaviour, I'm rather surprised that you lent yourself to this outrageous scheme.' He studied her in silence for a moment, his gaze penetrating, but not unduly censorious. 'Why did you agree to aid that crafty old reprobate, Sir Giles Osborne?'

Katherine returned that searching gaze, reflecting as she did so that, had he asked her such a thing just twenty-four hours before, she wouldn't have hesitated to tell him to mind his own business. Now, for some obscure reason, she didn't object to his knowing in the least.

She transferred her gaze to the stream a few yards away, which put her forcibly in mind of the one that had rippled its way across her father's Irish acres. 'There were several reasons,' she admitted truthfully. 'The main one, I suppose, was because I wished to avenge in some part the death of Liam Patrick O'Malley.'

'Your father?'

'Yes, Daniel, my father. Had I been a boy I would have been granted the opportunity to do so by enlisting in the army. That, however, was denied me. Sir Giles offered me the opportunity to rectify this...and I didn't need to think twice about it.'

'How did your father die, Katherine?' he asked gently, as he detected the shadow of sadness flickering over the delicate features. 'Was he a soldier?'

She shook her head. 'My father owned a stud in Ire-

Daniel didn't doubt for a moment that it had been Osborne who had suggested that he be chosen so often for those perilous missions behind enemy lines in Spain and Portugal. His command of the French tongue, coupled with a complete disregard for his own safety, had made him a prime choice.

He knew for certain that it had been at Sir Giles's request that he had been sent back to England to effect Louise Baron's escape. He hadn't wished to desert the men under his command, but he'd been given little choice in the matter. The verbal order to do so had come from Wellington himself. His army days were now over, of course, and he wasn't obliged to take orders from anyone. So what the deuce was he doing here now, stuck in the heart of France, once again involved in that unscrupulous baronet's fiendish stratagems?

Daniel glanced briefly at the lovely young woman sitting beside him, who was daintily eating her way through the chunk of crusty bread and portion of cheese. Although his years out in the Peninsula had undoubtedly changed him from a vulnerable young man into a self-possessed, if faintly cynical, ex-army Major, he couldn't find it within himself to be in the least bit sorry that he had allowed that foxy old baronet to persuade him to take part in one last venture for his country, for he was beginning to feel increasingly that it would turn out to be the best decision he had ever taken in his life.

By the time evening had arrived Daniel judged that they had covered a good twenty miles. More importantly, he had discovered a deal more about his delightful companion and the idyllic life she had enjoyed in Ireland. If she had had one fault to find with her childhood, then it had been the lack of companionship of girls her own age. Which, undoubtedly, was the reason why, after suffering the loss of both parents in quick succession, and removing to England to live with her grandfather, she had swiftly struck up such a close friendship with Helen Rushton.

Little wonder the foolish little darling had convinced herself that she was some sort of curse, Daniel reflected, as he at last saw signs of what appeared to be a sizeable habitation just up ahead. It was utter nonsense, of course—a fact that he had every intention of making perfectly plain at the earliest opportunity. The underlying reason for this foolish notion had become increasingly clear to him too—she was determined never to form a deep attachment to another living soul, simply because she was desperate to avoid suffering the searing heartache she had all too frequently experienced in the past.

Sadly it was all so very understandable. Still, it was no way to live one's life. It might take some time, but he would eventually peel away those protective layers in which she had shrouded herself, he thought determinedly, little realising that he had already begun to do so.

As Daniel, ever alert, paused for a moment to cast his eyes up the main street of the small market town they had just entered, Katherine stared up at him, her eyes resting for a moment on the square, powerful jaw, before studying the other strong contours of a face that was certainly not handsome, but full of character and ruggedly attractive. At least she found his physiognomy extremely appealing and, more surprisingly still, she was beginning to find his nature very engaging too.

Strong willed and determined, Daniel certainly possessed the power to annoy her from time to time by uttering some blunt remark. Yet beneath the brusque, no-

nonsense manner was a wealth of tenderness, which manifested itself in quite touching displays of gentlemanly consideration.

More than once throughout the day he had kindly offered a helping hand to clamber over some gate or stile, and on one occasion, much to her intense annoyance, he had gone so far as to toss her over one brawny shoulder, as though she weighed no more than a sack of grain, and had carried her across a wide stream to save her feet and clothing from becoming sodden.

Although still faintly aggrieved at having been manhandled in such an odious fashion, Katherine couldn't deny that, against all the odds, she was genuinely beginning to like and admire this occasionally infuriating man.

'I don't know about you, my little Amazon,' Daniel announced, resorting to one of those many colourful epithets by which he was wont to address her, 'but I'm feeling decidedly weary and in desperate need of sustenance. Are you willing to risk paying a visit to the inn up yonder?'

She didn't need to take even a moment to consider the matter. Not a morsel of food, or a drop of liquid, had passed her lips since the morning, and she wasn't in the least doubtful that she could do full justice to a substantial meal.

'Very well,' he added, after she had given several vigorous nods of assent, 'but you must remain on your guard. And do not forget you're supposed to be a native of this country. So for the Lord's sake don't relapse into English!'

Thus adjured, Katherine was quite content, as they entered the inn, to leave it entirely to Daniel to order their food, and left him to do precisely that whilst she seated herself at the vacant table in the corner of the room, well away from the other patrons who just might overhear her and guess her true nationality.

Fortunately the same would never be suspected of Daniel. She had discovered during the day that he had learned to speak the language fluently from his maternal grandmother, a Frenchwoman of immense character, according to Daniel, whom he had absolutely adored and then missed dreadfully after she had passed away shortly before he had embarked for India.

Apart from these few snippets Katherine had learned next to nothing about him. It wasn't that she had gained the impression that he was disinclined to talk about himself, and therefore out of common courtesy she had not attempted to pry; it was simply that he had seemed interested to learn about her, and she had found herself quite surprisingly divulging far more about her past to Daniel than she had to another living soul.

What an enigma the man was turning out to be! she reflected, gazing across at the spot where he stood deep in conversation with mine host. How she wished now that she had paid more attention to what her aunt Lavinia had disclosed about him, when she had stayed in Hampshire for those two weeks. She frowned in an effort to remember, and vaguely recalled her aunt mentioning something about his returning from India to discover the woman he had loved riveted to his cousin.

Katherine surprisingly found herself experiencing a deal of animosity towards this unknown female. How heartless she must be to have dealt such a crushing blow! Yet, to be fair, the young woman whom Daniel had hoped to marry had hardly been in a position to inform him that she had experienced a change of heart, Katherine reminded herself. A letter would have taken months and months to reach him out there in India. Yet it was all so very sad. Daniel wasn't in the least light-minded, and must have cared for the woman deeply to have wished to marry her. It went without saying that her betrayal must have been a bitter blow. Perhaps, Katherine mused, that was why he had never married, though it had to be said that he didn't appear to be suffering now from the pain of unrequited love. Nevertheless, she didn't suppose for a moment that he was the kind of man to wear his heart on his sleeve.

Although she was keen to discover much more about the man whom, against all the odds, she had begun to regard in a very favourable light, Katherine was aware that this was neither the time nor the place to satisfy her curiosity. Her command of the language was not sufficiently good to conduct an inquisition in French. Besides which, she didn't suppose that Daniel would wish to satisfy her curiosity at a time when his prime concern was to satisfy his hunger. So she merely asked, when he eventually joined her at the table, what had taken him so long and whether the landlord had been unwilling to supply them with a wholesome meal.

Daniel cast her a mocking glance as he handed her a glass of wine and slid into the seat opposite. 'Have you ever known a landlord turn away custom? No, he was more than happy to oblige, once he'd seen the colour of my money. Which reminds me... How much have you about you?'

Katherine delved into the pocket of her cloak, which she had removed and placed on the settle beside her, and without hesitation handed him the bulging purse.

Daniel tossed it in his hand, gauging its contents. 'We've done well today, my little darling,' he remarked, consigning the purse to the safety of his own pocket. 'But we're going to need to cover more miles if we stand the remotest chance of keeping one step ahead of those rogues out searching for us.'

Something in his tone put her immediately on her guard, and Katherine instinctively stared beyond his broad shoulders, taking swift stock of the other patrons. 'Would I be correct in thinking that you do not care for that ill-favoured rascal sitting alone at the corner table?'

Daniel didn't attempt to deny it. 'He appeared to be taking an uncommon interest in you when we first arrived, certainly,' he admitted, casting a frowning glance over her curls. 'Let me know if he leaves, or if someone joins him,' he added, before turning his attention to the innkeeper's wife, who arrived at the table bearing a tray laden with several dishes which exuded the most mouthwatering aromas.

It hadn't been difficult for Katherine to guess what had been passing through his mind when he had subjected her hair to a fleeting glance of irritation. Yet it was hardly her fault that she had been destined to inherit her father's colouring and in consequence was, as Daniel himself had tauntingly pointed out earlier in the day, easily picked out in a crowd.

Successfully suppressing a feeling of pique, she immediately set about the rewarding task of satisfying her hunger. During the time it took to consume a bowl of heart-warming broth, and work her way through a selection of meats and a variety of pasties, she succeeded in blotting from her mind the danger the man seated at the corner table might pose. Unfortunately, she just happened to glance in his direction, as she was about to consume the last mouthful of the most delicious fruit tart she had ever tasted in her life, and the very real possibility that he might indeed be one of those assassins hired to discover their whereabouts returned to cause her no small concern.

'I like to see a female with a healthy appetite.' Daniel approved, as he leaned back in his seat, totally replete himself.

For her part Katherine couldn't help but admire the way he always appeared so composed in the face of possible danger. However, he wasn't quite impervious to their present situation, as his next words proved. 'I think it is high time we were making tracks, don't you?'

He regarded her in silence for a moment, his dark eyes assessing as he contemplated the modesty of a dress now sadly creased and travel-stained, and the arrangement of fiery curls. 'You are by no means the only female in France to possess red hair, and it just might be that our friend over there in the corner admires your colouring. On the other hand, if he isn't an innocent local out enjoying his evening tipple, there's every chance that he'll follow us when we leave. And to be perfectly frank with you, I'd rather not leave a trail of corpses littered across France, clearly indicating in which direction we're heading, if I can possibly avoid it. So let us see if we can persuade him that we're not the pair he's been hired to locate.'

Katherine could find no fault in this course of action, until he calmly asked her to undo the buttons at the neckline of her dress, and release her hair from its restraining band. 'Whatever for?' she demanded, not unreasonably.

'Because you, my little darling, are about to become my doxy.'

He could not have startled her more had he tried, and it plainly showed when she gaped across the width of the table at him, not one hundred per cent certain she could have heard aright. 'I…beg…your…pardon?'

There was just a suspicion of a twitch at one corner of his mouth. 'For the love of God, Kate, don't go all missish on me now!' he ordered in a voice which contained a suspicion of a tremor too. 'I'm only asking you to act the part of a strumpet, not to take up the profession in earnest, for heaven's sake!'

Katherine regarded him in silence for a moment, half wondering if he had taken complete leave of his senses, but very much fearing that he was in deadly earnest. 'I shall take leave to inform you, Major Ross,' she said with careful restraint, 'that I am incapable of attempting such a portrayal. My experience of strumpets, and how they conduct themselves, is non-existent.'

'Fortunately mine isn't,' he countered, with what could best be described as an evil leer, and, reaching out, he tugged the strip of material from her hair, allowing the auburn tresses to tumble about her shoulders. 'All you need do is cling to my arm, and look at me as though you find me as delicious as that fruit tart you've just devoured with such relish.'

Although appalled at the mere suggestion, Katherine swiftly came to the conclusion that masquerading as a woman of easy virtue for a few minutes was a small price to pay in order to attempt to avoid a confrontation with a would-be assassin. Consequently she made no demur when Daniel slipped her arm through his, and proceeded to guide her across the inn towards the door, though she might have wished he had refrained from uttering a rather lewd remark in a carrying voice, the result of which induced several patrons to exchange knowing looks and several others to snicker behind their hands.

As they left the inn, still arm in arm, and began to retrace their steps along the street, Katherine was just beginning to think that the embarrassing little interlude had been entirely worthwhile when she clearly detected the sound of a door opening behind them. Before she knew what was happening, Daniel had her pinned against the stone wall of a house, and was smothering the squeal that rose in her throat by clamping his mouth down hard over hers.

For a few moments Katherine was too stunned by the speed of the assault to appreciate why he was behaving in this brutal and uncharacteristic manner, holding her so tightly that there was no possible hope of escape, and forcing an embrace upon her which was singularly lacking the persuasive tenderness she well remembered him displaying on that memorable night in Paris.

'For the love of God, Kate,' he muttered, dragging his mouth towards her left ear, and grazing her cheek in the process with the rough stubble on his chin, 'don't just stand there like a stock, girl! At least try to pretend you wish to bed me.'

A slight movement in the shadows succeeded in thrusting aside the last barrier of reserve. Reaching up, Katherine entwined her arms about his neck, and thought she detected a flicker of what might well have been surprise in his eyes before she took the initiative and forced his mouth down on hers in a kiss which began as little more than a mere meeting of lips, but which swiftly deepened as she instinctively parted her own, moving them back and forth beneath his. The fact that this was pretence, a mere show of passion for the benefit of inquisitive eyes, rapidly faded from her mind as a highly pleasurable but totally foreign longing began to spread swiftly through her limbs.

Without conscious thought she pressed her body closer until breasts, hips and thighs made contact with strong bone and well-honed muscle. They seemed to meld together so wonderfully, like two halves of a perfect whole, that she couldn't say with any degree of certainty whether the sudden tremor that rippled through her, or the low earthy moan which followed, emanated from her or the man who a moment later brought an abrupt end to the intimate contact by almost wrenching his mouth away.

For several moments his breathing seemed faintly laboured, and there was a flicker of something quite intense in his dark eyes. Then he seemed to collect himself, and took a hurried step away.

'Why, you're a passionate wench, and no mistake!' he announced, his strong teeth flashing in a sportive smile. 'Come, take me to your bed, otherwise I'll have you here and now!'

Like a cruel slap in the face, harsh reality returned with a vengeance, and was no less humiliating than the hearty smack he unexpectedly administered to the seat of her skirt, before linking her arm through his once more. Yet it took Katherine, still plagued by a wealth of unfamiliar sensations, several moments to come to terms with the fact that what had just taken place between them had been a sham, nothing more than mere pretence on his part. How she wished she could say with complete honesty that it had been likewise with her!

Wounded pride and bitter resentment was an explosive mixture. Yet Katherine steadfastly refused to give vent to her emotions and betray the fact that she was foolishly feeling unaccountably hurt by this display of seeming indifference on Daniel's part to that passionate interlude which had just taken place.

It certainly did nothing to improve her state of mind when the sound of a footfall close behind suggested very strongly that her humiliation might all have been in vain, and she was just about to suggest that they should confront the stalker, when Daniel's clasp on her elbow was suddenly increased and she was unexpectedly thrust down a side alley.

'Await me at the far end,' he ordered, releasing his grasp, and although she would have preferred to remain, she found herself automatically obeying the whispered command.

It was by now quite dark and Katherine, almost stumbling over the uneven surface, hurried along the narrow alley, not knowing whether it would offer a means of escape, and not caring very much either. She could not, would not, attempt to save her own skin and leave Daniel to face the threat of danger alone. She stopped and turned, clearly hearing the sounds of a scuffle, swiftly followed by a low groan. Then she almost cried out in relief, her former resentment completely forgotten, when she saw that tall, dependable being emerging from the gloom.

His grim expression, as he paused to slip an evil-looking knife inside the top of his boot, told her all she needed to know. He took no pleasure in taking a human life, of that she felt certain, and to do him justice he had done all he could to avoid the confrontation, so she chose not to ply him with unnecessary questions that would only add to his distress.

'Needless to say we shall be unable to remain in this town overnight.' He sounded quite matter-of-fact, but the flicker of anguish lingering in his eyes was unmistakable. 'I doubt our friend back there came here alone. I very much fear there may be others about the place searching for us. Therefore we must resign ourselves to yet another night without any creature comforts.'

Katherine frankly didn't care where they spent the night. A feeling of well-being, something that she had not experienced for several years, washed over her as they left the town and headed for the open countryside. As long as this man was with her she knew instinctively that she would never come to any harm.

Chapter Nine

Katherine awoke to find herself in unfamiliar surroundings yet again. Having had little choice but to lie on a dirt floor, with a thin pile of leaves beneath her, she had passed possibly the most uncomfortable night of her entire life. Yet she clearly remembered that, when they had quite by chance stumbled upon the woodcutter's rustic shelter, she had been too tired to care where she had bedded down, and had fallen asleep almost from the moment her head had touched the ground.

Easing herself into a sitting position, she glanced about the rough wooden structure, which, boasting three sides only, was open to the elements at the front, and was surprised to discover herself quite alone. She immediately experienced a moment's unease, not because Daniel was no longer propped in the adjacent corner, where he had settled himself the night before, but because she suddenly recalled that he had seemed strangely quiet, subdued almost, after they had left the small market town the evening before.

They had been obliged to walk quite some distance before they had chanced upon this shelter, nestling in the wood. Throughout the lengthy trek Daniel had not uttered above a dozen words. At first she had put his unusually subdued state down to the fact that he had been compelled to put a period to their stalker's existence in order to effect an escape. That, however, could not account for the fact that he had seemed disinclined to be near her, to so much as touch her. Why, not once had he offered a helping hand over the rougher ground, which he had not hesitated to do earlier in the day. Furthermore, when they had finally discovered this shelter, he had settled himself as far away as possible from her, when it would have made more sense to have lain side by side in order to share bodily warmth.

Sweeping her hair back from her face, Katherine stared through the wide opening at the surrounding woodland, wondering now if his odd behaviour was not a means to an end: an attempt to protect himself. Perhaps he had no intention of placing himself in a position whereby he would feel obliged to offer her the protection of his name?

She recalled with embarrassing clarity the passionate interlude outside the inn. She hadn't found kissing him, or holding his strong body next to her own, in the least distasteful. In fact, the opposite was all too embarrassingly true. Perhaps Daniel had sensed this and it had put him on his guard? Perhaps, also, he was afraid that she would expect him to do the honourable thing by marrying her once this venture was over? If so, she would swiftly disabuse him, she decided, experiencing a resurgence of that ever-present fear. She had made up her mind years before that marriage was not for her. She had no intention of ever putting any man's life at risk, especially one of whom she had grown so inordinately fond. It had possibly been a grave mistake on her part to become so friendly with Daniel, though she failed to see how she might have prevented herself from doing so. Nevertheless, it might help to ease his mind a little if she followed his recent example and attempted to remain a little aloof herself from now on.

Hurriedly rising to her feet, Katherine went outside to scan the surrounding woodland more intently, but worryingly could detect no sign of him. Where on earth had he got to? Surely he hadn't left her to fend for herself?

The instant the idea entered her mind, she dismissed it at once, ashamed for having had the mere thought. He would never do such an unchivalrous thing! Heaven only knew he could be the most irritating man on occasions—arrogant, overbearing and downright rude! But Major Daniel Ross was no coward. He was an exceptionally brave man who could be quite touchingly considerate on occasions. So where in the name of heaven had he taken himself off to?

Fortunately Katherine wasn't left worrying unnecessarily for very long. A minute or so later she detected the sound of hoof beats, and turned to see Daniel, astride a large bay and leading a second mount, negotiating a safe passage between the trees.

Instantly forgetting her resolve, she ran to meet him, her expression clearly betraying delight, and it was only as she reached his side that she recalled her resolution. His returning smile was just too spontaneous not to be perfectly genuine, and she couldn't help wondering whether she had merely read too much into his strange behaviour and that his former reserve might have stemmed from nothing more than mere fatigue.

'Well, sweetheart?' Looking very well pleased with himself, Daniel drew the horses to a halt. 'What do you think of our latest acquisitions? Not precisely high-stepping thoroughbreds, but I believe they'll serve their purpose by speeding up our journey.'

'Sturdy and, yes, capable of doing the job,' she announced, after a brief examination of both mounts, where she betrayed once more the knowledge she had gained from her father. 'How on earth did you manage to acquire them?'

'You might not have observed those two men propping up the counter at that inn. I, on the other hand, overheard one of them saying he would be bringing two horses to the market held in the town on Friday, and that there was no need for him to make an early start as he lived in a small village just four miles east of the town. That is why I came this way last night. The village is about half a mile away, just beyond the wood.'

Katherine couldn't help admiring his superb sense of direction. Even at night he never seemed to get himself lost. He was immensely capable, equal to any challenge. Why, not only had he managed to acquire horses, but saddles and bridles too!

When he apologised for not having been able to provide her with a side-saddle, Katherine dismissed it with a wave of her hand. 'Don't give it another thought,' she urged him, easily mounting without assistance. 'I frequently rode astride as a girl, and much preferred it. Unfortunately, when I reached a certain age Mama objected, and I was obliged thereafter to ride like a lady. Believe me, I shall enjoy the experience again.'

It took Daniel a few minutes only to appreciate her skill in the saddle. She was an extremely accomplished horsewoman who handled her mount with ease. 'Your father taught you well, Katherine,' he remarked, not reticent to voice his admiration, but could not resist adding,

'His only fault, I strongly suspect, was a reluctance to beat you often enough.'

Katherine wasn't slow to detect the provocative gleam in dark eyes. 'It might surprise you to know, Major Ross, that my father never once laid a violent hand on me. It might also surprise you to know he never felt that he needed to.' Her smile faded. 'He had a certain way of looking at me whenever I had displeased him, which always made me feel so guilty that I promised never to do it again.'

Anyone of the meanest intelligence couldn't have failed to appreciate how deeply she had cared for her father. But was a desire to avenge his death the only reason why she had agreed to involve herself in Sir Giles Osborne's machinations? Daniel couldn't resist asking.

'Good heavens, no! I did it as much for myself as anything else, I suppose,' she was honest enough to admit. 'I have become increasingly disenchanted with the life I have been leading in Bath. I am feeling increasingly restrained…suffocated, almost.'

Katherine released her breath in a resentful sigh, which matched quite beautifully the fleeting glance she cast him. 'It's all very well for you men. You can come and go as you please, but for a female it is quite different. I have inherited a companion who's a dear person, but faintly scatty, and on occasions something of a trial. And then, of course, there's Bridie, who will insist on treating me just as though I were still a child.'

Although he was smiling, he betrayed genuine sympathy as he said, 'There's one course of action which will enable you to sever those restraining ties. You could wed. Married women enjoy far more freedom.'

'True,' she agreed, 'but I do not consider a desire for freedom reason enough to take the matrimonial plunge, at least not in my case. Besides which,' she added, suddenly remembering her determination to put his mind at rest, 'I am resolved never to marry. Remember, I'm a curse, Daniel. I could never reconcile it with my conscience if I were to shorten any man's life.'

If she had expected this declaration to reassure him, and bring about a return of the wonderful camaraderie that had been surprisingly increasing between them, she was swiftly to discover her mistake.

'Don't talk such rubbish, girl!' he snapped, his expression no less harsh than his tone. 'You're no more a curse than I am. Your parents' deaths were tragic, but had absolutely nothing whatsoever to do with you. And how you can suppose you were responsible for your grandfather's heart attack when you were in Bath at the time beggars belief. And as for your aunt Augusta,' he went on, without granting her the opportunity to edge in a word, 'she was an elderly spinster who died of old age, and would have done so had you lived in the house or not. It is much more likely that you made her last years much happier with your presence.'

His expression, if anything, darkened. 'So I want to hear no more of such foolishness, understand? Otherwise I shan't hesitate to shake some sense into you!'

Stunned by the vehemence of the outburst, it was as much as Katherine could do to watch him steer a path through the last few yards of woodland towards the open countryside. By the time she had gathered her scattered wits together sufficiently to formulate a response, he was already some distance ahead.

She quickly discovered that, although her own mount was both healthy and strong, the gelding possessed a decidedly stubborn streak and was determined to progress at his own pace. Consequently she found herself always trailing those few yards behind, a circumstance which didn't appear to bother Daniel to any great extent, for apart from taking the trouble to inform her that they would stop somewhere for luncheon, and would risk putting up for the night at a village inn, he continued to ride on ahead, and remained in an unusually quiet mood for the remainder of the day.

The following morning, after the sheer joy of sleeping on a horsehair mattress, Katherine awoke feeling wonderfully refreshed. As she swung her feet to the floor, and padded across to the washstand, she couldn't help smiling to herself as she recalled the expressions on the faces of the landlord and landlady when she and Daniel had walked into their inn the previous evening, without an item of baggage between them, and looking travel-stained and altogether dishevelled, just like a couple of vagrants.

Daniel, once again proving himself equal to any situation, and improvising quite beautifully, had explained that they had been set upon by rogues who had deprived them of all their belongings, except for several items of jewellery which his sister had cunningly hidden in the lining of her cloak, and which they had subsequently been forced to sell to purchase mounts in order to get home. From that moment the landlord and landlady's attitudes had changed dramatically and they simply couldn't do enough for the poor, unfortunate siblings.

Katherine would have been the first to admit that she had grown increasingly impatient of her dear Bridie's incessant cosseting in recent months, but she had to own that she had been immensely grateful for the landlady's thoughtful attentions. Not only had the kindly woman provided her with a few basic necessities, including the loan of a night-gown, but she had also taken the trouble to wash and dry all Katherine's clothes. It felt wonderful being attired in freshly laundered garments once more, and no less satisfying being able to brush and arrange one's hair.

Once Katherine had completed this task to her satisfaction, she went downstairs to join Daniel for breakfast. She hadn't seen him since he had accompanied her upstairs as far as her bedchamber door the evening before, where he had informed her, prior to disappearing into the chamber opposite, that he had arranged for her dinner to be brought up on a tray. Just why he had taken it upon himself to organise this she had no way of knowing. Nor had she any idea how he had spent the evening. None the less, one glance was sufficient to convince her that he too had received the landlady's kindly attentions. His linen had been laundered, his coat had been sponged and pressed, and he had made excellent use of mine host's razor. The only thing that hadn't improved, she swiftly discovered, was his morose state of mind, for although he rose to his feet as she joined him at the table, and did not fail to ask if she had slept well, he displayed yet again a marked disinclination to indulge in small talk.

Throughout breakfast and later, after they had set off on the last leg of their journey to Normandy, Katherine racked her brains, trying to think of what might have brought about Daniel's strangely subdued state. She would have been the first to admit that there was much she still had to learn about him, but she wouldn't have thought that he was a man prone to brood unnecessarily. So she could only imagine that he was concerned that there might still be pursuers hot on their trail. It would be foolish to advise him not to worry. Besides which, she clearly recalled her mother saying once that gentlemen would share their troubles only if they wished to do so; if not, they were best left alone to resolve their concerns in their own way, for eventually they would return to normal.

And how right her mother had been! As the morning wore on Daniel began to betray definite signs of shaking off his strangely subdued mood, and by mid-afternoon, as they arrived at the town where his friend resided, his spirits had lifted noticeably.

'Except for crossing the Channel, the most arduous part of our journey, sweetheart, is now over,' he announced, sounding relieved.

'Are we so close to the coast?' Katherine asked, surprised that they had managed to cover so many miles.

'We're about ten miles away. We'll have no difficulty reaching it from here. The problem besetting us now is finding someone to take us across to England. And that is where I'm hoping my friend can help. At the very least we'll be offered a bed for the night.'

The certainty that he could rely on his friend ought to have offered some comfort, and to a certain extent Katherine didn't doubt that it had. So she couldn't quite understand what lay behind the troubled look he cast her before he swiftly turned his mount off the busy main street and into a fashionable thoroughfare, lined with large dwellings set a little way back from the road.

Drawing his horse to a halt in front of the last dwelling but one, he dismounted, and then helped Katherine to do so, before securing their mounts to the railings and leading the way towards the front door. Once again Katherine detected that fleeting look of concern before he raised the polished door-knocker and administered several short, sharp raps. They were forced to kick their heels for several minutes before the summons was eventually answered by a middle-aged woman, built on generous lines, who bore all the appearance of a housekeeper.

Grim-faced, she cast disapproving grey eyes over Daniel, before betraying surprise as she glanced in Katherine's direction. 'Yes, what is it that you want?'

Her openly hostile tone didn't deter Daniel from demanding to see the lady of the house. 'She'll see me,' he interrupted, when the woman attempted to inform him that her mistress did not receive callers at this time of day. 'Have the goodness to inform her that Major Daniel Ross is here and wishes to speak with her immediately.'

It was quite evident that the woman had never set eyes on Daniel before, but she certainly recognised the name, for her demeanour changed immediately, and she became almost reverential as she stood to one side and bade them enter.

'*Madame* usually does her accounts at this time of day, *monsieur*, but I'm sure she will see you. If you'd care to make yourselves comfortable, I'll inform her that you're here.'

Unlike Daniel, Katherine availed herself of one of the gilt chairs positioned against the wall, and looked about with interest. Directly ahead was an ornately carved wooden staircase that swept upwards in a graceful arc, and to the left was a wide archway, surrounded by plasterwork cupids, by which one gained access to a large, crimson-carpeted salon. There were several low tables dotted about the very spacious room, surrounded by numerous chairs and several *chaise-longues*, all of which were upholstered in the same shade of dull yellow velvet. The walls were covered with gilt mirrors and paintings of females in various states of undress, or wearing absolutely nothing at all, between which sconces in the shape of cupids held their candles aloft.

The furnishings were undoubtedly expensive, but far too ornate and faintly vulgar. The strong odour of perfume about the place was a trifle overpowering too, Katherine decided, before the door on her right, through which the housekeeper had disappeared a few minutes before, opened. A moment later a woman of about Daniel's age entered the hall, uttered a squeal of delight, and then cast herself upon his chest, planting full red lips upon his mouth.

After recovering from the shock of witnessing such wanton behaviour in a member of her sex, Katherine felt herself in the grip of an emotion quite foreign to her nature, before anger and acute resentment won control. For almost two days she had been forced to endure the humiliation of being virtually ignored for most of the time. But be damned if she would be overlooked yet again whilst he enjoyed an amorous woman's embrace! she decided, inwardly seething, and drew immediate attention to her presence by clearing her throat quite pointedly.

Large brown eyes, clearly betraying surprise, peered above Daniel's left shoulder. 'But what have we here, *mon cher* Daniel?' the woman enquired in a voice that was both silky smooth and seductively husky.

Suddenly appearing highly embarrassed, Daniel disengaged the slender arms from about his neck and held her away. 'Josephine, may I present Miss O'Malley… Katherine, this is my good friend Madame Carré.'

Katherine swiftly discovered that dark eyes could glint with seductive invitation one moment and become quite disconcertingly direct in the next, when *Madame* looked her over from head to toe, her gaze openly assessing and remarkably astute.

Her full lips curling into a provocative smile, *Madame* then returned her attention to Daniel. 'You naughty, naughty man! What have you been doing that you must bring this girl to me?'

'Not what you might suppose, Josephine,' he hurriedly assured her before she could give voice to further outrageous assumptions. 'But I do require your help. Katherine and I need somewhere to stay tonight. And, more importantly, we need to find someone who'll be willing to take us across to England as swiftly as possible. I shall explain everything to you presently. But first, have you a room where Katherine may go...where she'll be safe and—er—left quite undisturbed?'

A look clearly betraying immediate understanding flickered over the Frenchwoman's expressive features. 'Of course, my friend,' she assured him as she reached for the tiny silver bell on the table by her elbow.

Quite some time later, after having been plied with refreshments, and having experienced the sheer luxury of bathing and washing her hair in rose-scented water, Katherine's opinion of the formidable housekeeper had undergone something of a change. From the moment Madame Carré had instructed her servant to take good care of their unexpected guest, the housekeeper could not possibly have done more to oblige, and was even now taking the trouble to groom the long red hair which she had patiently dried on a fluffy towel.

'Your hair is beautiful, *mademoiselle*,' she remarked, at last setting the brush aside. 'Many women would give much to call it their own.'

Maybe, Katherine mused, smiling up at the surprisingly kindly servant through the dressing-table mirror. She knew, however, of at least one person who didn't hold her auburn mane in the highest regard.

'There will be time for you to rest a while before dinner, *mademoiselle*. I shall return presently to dress your hair and shall bring some suitable garments for you to wear. Your own clothes will be freshly laundered and will be returned to you by morning.'

Surprisingly light on her feet for a woman of her size, the housekeeper went over to the door, her expression clearly troubled as she turned back to add, 'Should you require anything further, please do not hesitate to make use of the bell-pull. But I beg of you, *mademoiselle*, under no circumstances leave this room. The house is large, and I should hate for you to lose yourself.'

Puzzled, Katherine watched the housekeeper withdraw. How on earth was she supposed to take that strange warning? she wondered. Was the woman truly concerned over her safety, or was she perhaps afraid that the unexpected guest might be tempted to purloin the family's silver?

What an odd creature the housekeeper was, to be sure! Bemused, Katherine shook her head, sending her long hair floating about her shoulders like a swathe of silk. It was almost as if the woman had a dual personality, not unlike the house in which she worked. One half totally at variance with the other, Katherine mused, as she gazed with renewed interest about the apartments into which she had been escorted some little time before. In stark contrast with the vibrant colours in the ground-floor salon, the bedchamber was charmingly decorated in subtle shades of primrose and cream. Foolish though it might be, it was hard to believe that she was in the same house.

Rising to her feet, she went over to the window, which offered a view of an enclosed garden. Madame Carré too, like her house and devoted servant, was something of an enigma. Who was she? More importantly, what part had she played—did she continue to play—in Daniel's life? The way she had greeted him in that over-familiar fashion suggested strongly that at some point they had been rather more than mere friends.

The cruelly stabbing thorns of that unfamiliar emotion once again made themselves felt, but Katherine stead-fastly refused not to face the very real possibility that at some period in the past the vivacious Madame Carré had been Daniel's mistress. But if that was the case, what had become of Monsieur Carré? Had there in truth ever been such a person and, if so, where was he now? More importantly, where was Daniel himself? And why had he left her here alone with only strangers?

A blessed surge of anger began to protect her from those wickedly stabbing barbs, and she swung away from the window, as bored with the restricted view as she was with the confines of this bedchamber. But what could she do? Her clothes had been removed for laun-dering, and she had been given the flimsiest of dressing robes to cover her modesty.

Suddenly feeling weary, Katherine glanced across at the four-poster bed, and after a moment's indecision de-cided to avail herself of its comfort. A book lay open on the bedside table, and she decided to make use of that too. Fortunately she could read and understand the French language far better than she could speak it, and was able therefore to follow the story of a pair of star-crossed lovers reasonably well. Eventually, though, the effort of translation became too much, and her eyelids grew increasingly heavy.

* * *

Katherine would have sworn she had dozed for a few minutes only. Be that as it may, when she opened her eyes it was to discover the drapes drawn across the window, the bedchamber bathed in soft candlelight, and to see a pile of clothes neatly placed at the bottom of the bed.

The position of the hands on the mantel-clock confirmed that she had, surprisingly, slept soundly for more than two hours. Hurriedly slipping her feet to the floor, she wasted no time in scrambling into the clothes, which were a perfect fit, and exactly to her taste, except for the slightly immodest neckline on the pretty muslin gown. This minor defect was immediately remedied by the donning of a silk shawl, which she arranged carefully about her shoulders as she crossed to the bell-pull.

She raised her arm, but her reaching fingers were stilled for a second or two by a disquieting sound, somewhere between a scream and a squeal. Then, clasping the velvet cord and tugging sharply, Katherine momentarily wondered what the noise might have been—the wind, whistling about the eaves, or perhaps two cats at odds in the garden? Then she clearly detected the noise again, clearer and more shrill this time, and definitely coming from somewhere inside the house.

Certain that someone must be hurt, and perhaps in need of help, she conveniently forgot the housekeeper's warning and immediately went to investigate. The long passageway outside the room had doors leading off at intervals on both left and right, but she judged the odd cry must have come from behind that single closed door at the very end. Beneath her guiding fingers its key turned easily in the lock and the wooden barrier swung wide to reveal the continuation of the passageway in a dazzling blaze of light, its floor, walls and ceiling dec-

orated in the same garish colours as were to be found in
the main salon below, its atmosphere heavy, too, with
the aroma of cheap perfume.

For a few moments it was as much as Katherine could
do to gape in wonder, in disbelief. It was like suddenly
finding oneself in another world, a totally alien place—
intriguing but unnerving, and undoubtedly littered with
unseen snares primed to entrap the unwary. Faint-hearted
she had never been, and yet some sixth sense kept her
rooted to the spot, as that cautionary little voice in her
head gave clear warning not to venture further.

Prudence won the day and Katherine was on the point
of retracing her steps to find the housekeeper, when a
door suddenly burst open, and a squealing female,
dressed only in a pair of frilly pantalettes, erupted into
the passageway, quickly followed by a balding, middle-
aged man, sporting only a pair of under-breeches, and
brandishing something suspiciously resembling a feather
duster.

As the ribald pair disappeared round the corner of the
passageway, the woman squealing with delight as she
received a thwack with the feather-ended stick across the
buttocks, stark reality hit Katherine with all the force of
a physical blow, and was no less disconcerting than the
fingers which suddenly grasped her arm and hauled her
backwards. The door was then firmly closed and re-
locked and she found herself confronted by the highly
disapproving housekeeper.

'I warned you not to go wandering about, *mademoiselle*!' Her tone was scolding, like that of a governess
reprimanding a disobedient child. 'Come, dinner is almost ready, and I have yet to dress your hair.'

In something of a daze, Katherine allowed herself to
be led back into the bedchamber, and made no demur

when requested to sit before the dressing-table. The housekeeper's demeanour changed the instant she began to set about the task of arranging the auburn curls, and she became once again that very obliging woman who had willingly catered for her unexpected guest's every need. Would that Katherine could summon up one ounce of gratitude now for all the care and attention she'd received!

A house of ill repute! A surge of anger swiftly mastered Katherine's searing sense of shame. It beggared belief that any man purporting to be a gentleman would ever think of housing a virtuous young woman in a brothel, let alone leaving her there to fend for herself. Yet her so-called protector, the unprincipled wretch, had done precisely that!

Like a bottle of warm champagne, vigorously shaken, Katherine was ready to explode. Had Daniel been present she would not have been responsible for her actions. Yet she somehow retained sufficient control and good manners enough to thank the housekeeper for the trouble she had taken over the arrangement of her hair, before obediently following her down to a room on the ground floor where a table had been set for just two persons.

She was conscious of a stab of disappointment only to find Madame Carré present, and did her utmost to convince herself that this was purely the result of being denied the sweet satisfaction of subjecting Major Ross to a blistering tirade.

'Ah, Katherine! I may call you Katherine, may I not?' Madame Carré greeted her with every evidence of delight, before she subjected her guest's attire to a swift scrutiny. 'I see the dress fits you very well. I was sure that it would.'

Until that moment Katherine hadn't given a thought

as to whose apparel she had donned. She was fairly certain that it had not been taken from the wardrobe of the woman who was now patting that portion of the *chaise-longue* beside her invitingly. Blessed with womanly curves, Madame Carré was below average height, and several inches shorter than Katherine. It was quite possible, however, that the flimsy garment belonged to one of those females working in this disgraceful establishment.

Cosseted and protected throughout her life Katherine might have been, but she was not completely ignorant of the ways of the world. She had been aware for quite some time that younger men were wont to seek the company of a certain type of female, and it was not unheard of for a married man to satisfy his carnal desires outside marriage either. She wasn't so bigoted as to condemn those poor unfortunates who, through no fault of their own, were forced to sell themselves in order to survive. Madame Carré, however, didn't appear to be undernourished. And neither had that brazen hussy whom she had seen romping along the passageway been a half-starved waif!

Something in her expression must have betrayed her thoughts, and the fact that she was no longer ignorant of the nature of the establishment in which she had been temporarily housed, for Madame Carré, after a moment's thoughtful silence, lowered her deceptively dreamy brown eyes and smiled wryly.

'Oh, dear,' she muttered. 'My darling Daniel will not be best pleased with his little Josephine when he discovers that you know.'

Major Ross's views on the matter were of absolutely no interest whatsoever to Katherine. After all it was he, the unconscionable wretch, who had brought her here in the first place! she decided, at last availing herself of the invitation to sit beside her hostess on the *chaise-longue*. Outraged though she was, she was still not prepared to allow the housekeeper to be blamed for what had been in effect her own misdeeds, and didn't hesitate to make this point very clear, before casually enquiring the present whereabouts of the man who had plummeted in her estimation.

'After we returned in the carriage, he went into the town to see if he could find a buyer for your horses. I no longer enjoy that form of exercise and have no need for hacks. Furthermore, my stable is not sufficiently large to house them. He said he doubted he would be back in time to join us for dinner. But I am certain we can manage to entertain ourselves well enough without him.' Again there was a suspicion of a wry smile. 'As you might imagine, it is not often that I find myself in the company of such a refined and charming young lady.'

Striving not to allow lingering resentment or prejudice to cloud her judgement, Katherine attempted to view her hostess dispassionately as she watched her rise gracefully to her feet and move across to the table on which several decanters stood.

Madame Carré might not have been universally considered a beauty. Yet, blessed with a riot of dusky curls, a flawless ivory complexion, and a pair of sparkling dark eyes, she was certainly most attractive. She was not short on charm or sportiveness, traits which would undoubtedly appeal to the vast majority of the opposite sex, and for all her provocative smiles and dreamy-eyed glances, she was not lacking in intelligence either.

It was only when she accepted the wine held out to her that Katherine realised that, since entering the room, the conversation had been conducted in English and, intrigued, she didn't hesitate to discover where *Madame* had learned to speak the language so well.

'Josephine, please,' *Madame* insisted before subjecting Katherine to yet another of those swift and acutely penetrating glances. 'My parents were prosperous enough to afford the services of a governess for both my sister and myself.' Once again a flicker of a wry smile tugged at the corners of the full-lipped mouth. 'The dress you are wearing is a present for my widowed sister. I intend to pay her a visit in the not too distant future. Needless to say, I cannot invite her or my little niece to stay here with me, though I do try to help her as much as I can. Her husband died in Spain, and she does not find it easy to manage on the little she makes from taking in sewing. I help as much as I'm allowed, but she is very proud. One day I shall buy my house by the Seine, and invite them to live with me.'

Clearly detecting the slightly sombre, almost wistful, note in her voice, Katherine couldn't help thinking that Madame Carré was not altogether happy with her present situation. So why had she chosen such a profession in the first place when she was more than capable of earning herself a living in some genteel occupation? And where did Monsieur Carré fit into the scheme of things?

'And you, *Madame*…Josephine, have you ever been married?' Katherine found herself asking, curiosity having got the better of her a second time, and she quickly discovered that eyes which could twinkle with a wickedly teasing sparkle could harden in an instant and glint like chips of ice.

'Oh, yes, *petite*. Unfortunately I was once married. Both my sister and I married soldiers, the only difference being my sister chose wisely. My brother-in-law was a charming man, courageous and noble, not unlike your Major Ross in many ways; whereas Henri Carré, although possessing all the outward trappings of a gentleman, was a callous, manipulative blackguard who cared for nothing and no one except himself.'

Josephine's eyes, dimmed by bitter regrets, focused on a spot somewhere on the wall opposite. 'Young and foolish, I was beguiled by a handsome face and the silver tongue of an inveterate gamester. And not a very skilled one at that! It did not take me very long to realise the mistake I had made, but I was too proud to return to my family. When he had gambled away my dowry and our home, I had little choice but to accompany him out to the Peninsula, where I swiftly discovered just how vile and contemptible he could be, when he forced me to retrieve his IOUs from his friends and fellow officers in a way that only a woman can.'

Utterly appalled, Katherine was as powerless to prevent the gasp that rose in her throat from passing her lips as she was to conceal the heartfelt sympathy which sprang into her eyes. Yet surprisingly Josephine raised one hand in a dismissive gesture and, more amazingly still, even managed to smile.

'I do not deserve your pity, *ma chère*. I was too proud to return to seek assistance from my family and admit the mistake I had made. And my pride cost me my self-respect. Nevertheless, it also taught me something too. I know the depths to which men can plummet. But I have also been blessed to experience how honourable and chivalrous some quite exceptional men can be.'

The self-deprecating smile which had clung to her lips suddenly became very tender, as did her whole expression. 'When my husband was killed at Badajoz, it was not a Frenchman who came to my aid, but an English captain.'

Katherine gazed at her companion in dawning wonder, clearly remembering at least part of the conversation she had had with her cousin on that wet February day. So it was true! She had been foolish ever to doubt it.

'Yes, *petite*,' Josephine confirmed, expertly judging her companion's expression. 'It was your Major Ross who saved my life, who spared me the humiliation of being violated by several of Wellington's troops, little realising at the time that suffering painful humiliations was nothing new to me. His noble act very nearly cost him his own life. I remained in the British camp and nursed him back to health.' There was a suspicion of tears in the dark brown eyes as they lowered and focused on the contents of her glass. 'He demanded nothing from me during the time I remained with him. He gave me money so that I might return home and even went so far as to escort me as close as he dared to the French lines.'

She paused for a moment to sample the contents of her glass. 'My return to France was not altogether happy. On reaching Paris I discovered that my mother had died just a few weeks before. I didn't choose to live with my brother and his wife, who I had always considered a shrew, and I refused to be an added burden to my dear sister, whose husband had died at Talavera. So I came here to Normandy to take care of an ailing maiden aunt. She had little money, but she did leave me this house which, after my experiences in Spain, I was more than capable of putting to good use.'

Half an hour earlier Katherine would have found such a bold admission deplorable, but this was no longer the case. Now she could understand perfectly, and felt ashamed of herself for having been so naïvely judgmental as to stigmatise the woman sitting beside her as nothing more than an immoral trollop.

She didn't believe she could feel more conscience-stricken, but she was wrong. Her sense of shame spiralled when Josephine unexpectedly announced, 'Although I would never betray my country, I do not forget my friends. When I first settled here in Normandy I did write a letter to Daniel, which eventually reached him. He paid me an unexpected visit last year, in the summer, before finally returning home. Naturally, after Napoleon's abdication, we assumed the conflict between our two countries had finally come to an end. Sadly, this increasingly seems not to be the case. But I told Daniel once that if ever he should be in need of my help in the future, he had only to contact me.'

Slender fingers reached out to give Katherine's hand a reassuring squeeze. 'He brought you here, *petite*, because he knew you would be safe. And for no other reason.'

As the door opened and a servant entered, bearing a tray, Madame Carré rose to her feet. 'That, I think, should satisfy your curiosity about me. And now, while we eat our dinner, you must satisfy *my* curiosity and tell me all about yourself.'

Chapter Ten

It wasn't until later that night, as she sat once again before the dressing-table mirror, absently pulling the brush through her hair, that Katherine began to appreciate for perhaps the very first time the effect her experiences in France were having on her: changing her attitude to a great extent; forcing her finally to face the fact that, when eventually she did arrive back in England, she simply couldn't pick up the threads and continue that humdrum existence she had been leading in recent months, if she wished to bring even a modicum of contentment back into her life.

She might have been prompted by the purest of motives to agree to this venture. Yet she couldn't deny that she had seized upon the opportunity offered to sever those ties placed upon her by Bath society and its petty restrictions. What eluded her completely was why she had lacked the courage, the self-confidence to do so long before now.

Oh yes, when her aunt had been alive there had been some excuse for remaining in that once very fashionable watering place. Sharp-tongued and frequently contrary her great-aunt Augusta had undoubtedly been, but from the very first she had proved to be excellent company, and they had rubbed along together wonderfully well. Since the elderly lady's demise the previous year, however, the atmosphere in the Camden Street house had been for the most part sombre, alleviated only by those battles of will in which she and Bridie occasionally indulged.

Katherine shook her head, at a complete loss to understand why she had allowed herself to live such a repetitive, boring existence all these months, where all she had seemed to do was make and receive calls from the same circle of people. What on earth had happened to the spirited girl who had ridden at that next-to-nothing pace across the Irish countryside with her father, whose days had been filled from dawn till dusk with excitement and laughter? Oh, she was still there somewhere, hidden beneath that mantle of good manners and respectability which she had been forced to don in order to be accepted into the fringes of the polite world. How she longed to toss the restricting covering aside and just be herself again!

But had she not succeeded in doing precisely that in recent days? a tiny voice queried. Had she not, in fact, begun to reveal glimpses of that occasionally volatile and intrepid Anglo-Irish girl some time before embarking on this trip to France?

The second question, filtering through her mind hard on the heels of the first, induced Katherine to pause in her task of brushing her hair and to stare intently at her reflection, seeing not her own image in the glass but a scene in a crowded salon where she had confronted a tall, broad-shouldered ex-army Major, whose Rifleman-green uniform had set him quite apart from every other gentleman in the room. Dear God in heaven! Was it

possible that she had *him* to thank for helping her to
break through that repressive shroud of ladylike respectability? Or had Major Daniel Ross alone been responsible, without her having been aware of it, for slowly
peeling away those layers of conformity and reserve to
reveal increasing glimpses of the Katherine Fairchild
O'Malley of yore?

A knock on the door interrupted these disquieting reflections. Assuming it must be the housekeeper returning
her freshly laundered garments ready for the morning,
Katherine didn't hesitate to bid enter, and was mildly
disconcerted to discover none other than the subject of
her former disturbing thoughts purposefully entering,
with a pile of clothes held firmly in his large, shapely
hands.

The niggling resentment at his behaviour, his almost
total neglect throughout the entire day, swiftly surfaced,
instantly restoring her composure. She rose to her feet,
so determined to air her grievances that she never gave
a thought to her less than respectable state of dress.

Daniel, on the other hand, was instantly aware that the
borrowed raiment left little to the imagination, and it
took a monumental effort to draw his eyes away from
the clear outlines of perfect feminine curves and oh, so
enticing shadows to inform her that he had brought her
attire for the morning.

Momentarily forgetting her pique, Katherine cast a
brief glance at the neat pile of unfamiliar garments
which he had placed on the chair by the bed. 'Those are
not mine. Am I not to wear my own clothes?'

'No.' An expression of rueful amusement flickered
over his features. 'I acquired these garments especially
for you, on account of the fact that tomorrow you are to
take on a new role—that of my nephew.'

'Really?' Although the smile she cast him could not have been sweeter, it didn't quite disguise the return of the dangerous glint in her eyes. 'Well, let us hope you display a deal more consideration towards your nephew than you did the sister you abandoned in this—this disreputable establishment!'

He held her disdainful gaze levelly, not too pleased himself to discover that she was no longer ignorant of the nature of her surroundings. 'Who told you?' he demanded abruptly.

'No one told me,' she admitted, incurably truthful. 'I discovered it for myself.'

'You mean you went wandering about the place, you infuriating girl!' Hands on hips, he regarded her much as an irate father might an erring child. 'I cannot take my eyes off you even for five minutes without you getting into—'

'Had it been only five minutes,' she interrupted, her voice no less censorious than his own, 'I might possibly have remained ignorant of the fact that you, you unconscionable wretch, had abandoned me in a house of ill repute!'

'Damn it, you little shrew, I did not abandon you!' Sighing, he ran impatient fingers through his hair, clear evidence of a troubled mind. 'I discovered from Josephine, shortly after we arrived here, it's strongly rumoured that Louis XVIII has fled and Napoleon is now back in the capital. If it's true, then I very much fear our country will once again be at war, so it's imperative we get back to England as swiftly as possible. Josephine very kindly agreed to accompany me to the coast, where she made contact with a friend of hers who subsequently agreed to take us back across the Channel tomorrow.'

If this was meant to appease her it fell far short of the

mark, for she had already learned of this earlier from
her hostess during dinner. All the same, Katherine was
fair-minded enough to appreciate fully his reasons for
not wishing her to accompany them. She could not have
been of any use whatsoever, whereas Josephine had
proved of immeasurable help. Furthermore, if there still
happened to be those out scouring the countryside in
search of them, and there was every reason to suppose
that there might be, Daniel wouldn't have wished to put
his good friend's life in jeopardy by being seen in their
joint company. And neither would Katherine herself,
come to that!

Amazingly enough Katherine couldn't help but feel a
deal of respect for a woman who had suffered so much
and yet had managed to withstand all the cruel blows
life had dealt her. Despite the fact that the means by
which Josephine was attempting to build a new life for
herself, whereby one day she would be able to enjoy a
comfortable and quiet existence in a modest house overlooking the Seine, could not but appal any virtuous
young female with the least sensibility, Katherine
couldn't find it within herself to condemn the woman
for making use of the experience which she had been
forced to acquire during her turbulent marriage.

Nevertheless, she retained a deal of resentment towards the being who had seen fit to place her in the
hands of a brothel-keeper, no matter how certain he had
been that the greatest care would be taken of her. Surely
he must have known her every feeling must be outraged?
Or was it, perhaps, that he had considered her so naïve,
such a ninnyhammer, that she would never suspect for
a moment that she had been lodged in a house of ill
repute?

Perversely, this very real possibility annoyed her more

than all the rest, and she began to pace the room, striving to control her rising ire, and resist the very great temptation to hurl the hairbrush still clasped in her hand in the general direction of his head.

Daniel, watching her closely, was not slow to note the tense set of the perfectly proportioned, slender frame, nor the dangerous glint in those gorgeous eyes, before she had turned away to begin her angry pacing. Understandably, she was deeply offended, and not just mildly resentful too at being brought to such a place. But what other choice had been open to him?

Had she but known it, he had suffered the gravest misgivings, and even though his friend had assured him that every care would be taken, and Katherine would be safely placed in that totally private part of the building, where only Josephine's closest friends were ever invited to enter, he hadn't known one moment's peace throughout the entire time he had been away.

'Oh, come now, Kate, be fair,' he urged, in a voice clearly laced with exasperation. He was tired after the many tasks he had been obliged to perform that day. He had not eaten a morsel since breakfast, and if the truth were known he was not in the best possible humour himself. 'It isn't like you to be missish. Do you think I would have brought you to this place if I'd any other choice? I couldn't take you to one of the inns, and risk your being noticed. That hair of yours is an absolute bane on occasions. But at least I've managed to overcome that particular problem for the remainder of our travels. I had the forethought to acquire a hat.'

No response was forthcoming, and he began to grasp at straws. 'Look on the bright side, sweetheart. Your situation could be a devil of a lot worse.'

This pronouncement was sufficient to stop Katherine

in her tracks. She swung round to look directly at him, wondering whether she had misheard or he had taken complete leave of his senses.

'Worse…? Worse!' she echoed, regarding him in a mixture of outrage and disbelief. 'How in the name of heaven, you blockhead, could my situation possibly be any worse? Behind me lurks Napoleon, no doubt amassing an army as we speak. Awaiting me across the Channel is a traitorous wretch bent on putting a period to my very existence. And I'm stuck here in a Normandy brothel with the…with the most notorious rake ever to hail from the county of Dorsetshire!' She raised her eyes ceilingwards, as though seeking divine guidance there. 'Ye gods! How the deuce could my situation possibly be any worse?'

The grasp Daniel had managed to maintain over his mounting exasperation finally snapped. 'You damnable little virago!' he growled back at her, raising clenched fists to the whitewashed plasterwork above his own head. 'I'll teach you to maintain a guard on that viperous tongue of yours if it's the last thing I do!'

Only by the execution of some swift, side-stepping footwork did Katherine neatly avoid the long-fingered hand reaching out to grasp her arm. Daniel proved equally nimble in avoiding the hairbrush that she could no longer resist hurling in his direction a moment later, and which went harmlessly sailing past his left ear to hit the wall, narrowly missing the window. His growling threat of immediate reprisals sounded frighteningly sincere, for all that Katherine could clearly detect a slight tremor in his voice, though whether from laughter or anger she would have been hard pressed to say. And she wasn't about to wait around to find out either!

The room which only minutes before had seemed

wonderfully spacious appeared to have shrunk alarmingly, with the Major looming large and threatening within its walls. Her only means of escape was the door and she didn't waste a precious moment in making a beeline for it. She was within a yard or two of grasping the handle, when her toes became entwined in the hem of the negligée, and only the strong muscular arm that snared her waist saved her from falling. The next moment she was lifted quite off her feet, and before she could so much as cry out in protest, she had been tossed carelessly down on the four-poster bed.

The two hundred pounds of solid bone and muscle that were swiftly lying half on top of her, not to mention the one strong hand effortlessly holding both her wrists captive above her head, made any attempt at escape rather futile. Torn between indignation and amusement, she stared up into dark eyes brightened by a gleam that was no less predatory than the grin which hovered about that shapely mouth only inches above her own.

'Let me go at once, you great ox!' she demanded, nowhere near ready to admit defeat, nor reticent to continue doing battle with the only weapon left to her.

'Certainly, when you've apologised for your appalling behaviour,' he responded, with all the smug satisfaction of someone who knew he had the upper hand.

'My behaviour...?' Incredulity succeeded in stilling her tongue for all of five seconds. 'Fagh! That's rich, coming from you!'

One dark brow quirked. 'Are you going to apologise, young lady?'

'Never!' she avowed, stubborn to the last.

'I was hoping that would be your answer,' he surprised her by announcing before lowering his head, and masterfully preventing the unflattering string of epithets rising in her throat from passing her lips.

The instant his mouth touched hers, Katherine's defences crumpled, and she found surrender far too sweetly satisfying even to contemplate a resumption of hostilities. Something lurking somewhere in the deep recesses of her brain was desperately striving to peal out a warning, but the chime was too indistinct and too swiftly silenced by the demands of a body aroused by that wholly masculine and intensely special touch.

Not one inch of her skin seemed immune to the wealth of sensations prickling through her as he removed his mouth from hers to trail his lips down the length of her neck to explore the hollows at the base of her throat. The instant the grasp about her wrists slackened, she raised her arms and wrapped them about him, eager to acquaint herself with the contours of a strong back and powerful shoulders. The guttural sound that instantly followed was no less satisfying than the demands of the mouth which once again captured hers, or the hand which stole beneath her to hold her so fast against him that her breasts both ached and tingled with pleasure at the hard contact with the large expanse of chest for those few brief seconds before he repeated an action which was rapidly becoming all too frustrating. Releasing her abruptly, Daniel once again proved that he could move with amazing agility for a man of his powerful build and was on his feet within seconds, leaving Katherine, bereft and bewildered, to stare up at him. He returned her gaze for a few moments, his expression wooden, devoid of emotion except perhaps for a trace of what might have been regret, then he swung round on his heels and headed across to the door.

'I'll leave you now to get some sleep.' His voice

sounded so coolly matter of fact that he might have been addressing a complete stranger, not the person with whom he had just shared an all too brief but exquisitely intimate episode. 'There's no need for you to rise early. We do not need to leave here until mid-morning.'

Determined not to give way to tears that could serve no useful purpose, Katherine waited until, without so much as a backward glance or a gentle word of farewell, he strode from the room. Then she lay and stared at the canopy above her head, at a complete loss to understand why he should have called a halt to an occurrence that innate feminine wisdom assured her he had been enjoying every bit as much as she had herself. Yes, he had done so before, she reminded herself, on two quite separate occasions. Somehow, though, this time had been different. For all his threat of reprisals, he had been gentle from the first, swiftly extracting a response that— God forgive her!—was all too swift in coming.

Ashamed though she was to admit to it, she could no longer deny that when in Daniel's arms self-restraint and morality were all too easily forgotten, swept aside by a rapidly increasing yearning demanding fulfilment. Just the touch of his hand had the power to affect her like no other man's had done before. But so it had been from the very first, on that bitterly cold January day, when they had collided with each other in the doorway of that inn and he had prevented her from falling.

How strange that she should recall the incident now; recall too that his touch had put her forcibly in mind of her father's reassuring, protective hold. Yet there had been nothing paternal in the hands which had caressed her so gently not so very long ago, and honesty prompted her to admit that she was glad of it.

Drawing her eyes away from the lace-edged canopy,

she glanced about the tastefully decorated chamber, clearly recalling its owner's parting words after they had dined together. 'You may rest easy tonight, *petite*. This part of the house is entirely private. Be assured too that, although the bed you sleep in is indeed mine, no man has yet been invited to share it with me.'

Although Josephine might have spoken no less than the truth, Katherine was brutally aware that one might well have been sharing it this night if Daniel hadn't possessed the strength to call a halt before their mutual passion had taken them to a point beyond which there was no turning back.

For her sake, and most especially for his, it must never occur again, she thought determinedly, little realising that below, in the room which functioned as both dining and sitting-room, Daniel's feelings on the matter were vastly contrasting and that he was equally determined that it should.

His appetite having deserted him, he had managed to consume very little of the delicious supper the housekeeper had kindly brought to him, and he rose from the table, taking both bottle and glass over to a comfortable chair.

Scant compensation, he mused wryly, studying the bottle for a moment before refilling his glass. All the same, it would need to suffice for the present, though there were times, he was forced to admit, when he wished he might forget that he was born a gentleman. And never more so than tonight!

Yet, deep down he knew he had done the right thing, the only honourable thing, he reflected, leaning back against the soft fabric of the chair. No, he could never have reconciled it with his conscience if he had taken advantage of the situation in which they now found themselves. For all that she could match his passion with her own, she was a highly moral young woman. Furthermore she trusted him. How could he betray that trust, even though he now felt quite certain that she wasn't indifferent to him? When he did make her his own, and he would eventually, it would be on their wedding night and in his own bed, not in a room in a Normandy bawdy house. To have done so would have been to cheapen what he felt for her, and take cruel advantage of her vulnerability, not to mention her innocence.

No, there was not a doubt left in his mind now. Although at the beginning of this venture he might possibly have experienced no more than the desire to take her to his bed, that had swiftly changed. Katherine was the woman with whom he wished to spend the rest of his life. They were so right for each other in every way—almost kindred spirits. But first there was still that one huge barrier which needed to be demolished: somehow he must find a way to rid her of those foolish notions that she had allowed herself to believe in an attempt to protect herself from future hurt. He could not have her fretting unnecessarily, believing the worst every time he might be delayed in returning home, as most assuredly she would, unless he eradicated those fears completely and forced her to face the truth. Now was certainly not the time to make the attempt. Once they were safely back in England, once this foolish escapade was behind them, he would storm the citadel of her fears. In the meantime he must continue to maintain that control over his desires and emotions, which during the past couple of days he had succeeded in doing reasonably well, even though it had meant for the most part attempting to ignore her very existence.

'Ah, *mon cher!*'

Josephine, smiling at him from the doorway, effectively brought his musings to an end, and he even managed to return her smile, as she settled herself on the floor at his feet.

'I shall keep you company for a little moment. You have been up to see Mademoiselle Katherine and have assured yourself that she is well, no?'

Katherine's welfare had been the first thing about which he had enquired on his return to the house. 'Yes,' he muttered, as memory stirred. 'And all I received for my pains was a hairbrush thrown at my head. Damnable little termagant!'

Josephine's gurgle of laughter was infectious, and Daniel found it impossible not to smile too. 'Ah, yes, your Katherine certainly does not lack spirit.'

He stared down for a moment into the large brown eyes twinkling up at him, before transferring his gaze to the contents of his glass. 'What makes you suppose that she is *my* Katherine?'

Full lips curled into a knowing smile. 'If she is not already, then I suspect that it is your intention to make her so. And I am very happy for you, *mon cher*, even if it does mean that I have lost you.'

The small hand resting lightly on his knee did little to ease his frustrations, and brought vividly to mind a very satisfying interlude they had enjoyed the previous year. 'What makes you suppose that you have lost me?' The husky timbre of his voice betrayed clearly enough his mounting desire. 'Katherine as yet has no right to place demands upon me.'

'Her affection and her trust give her the right, my friend,' Josephine countered, before rising to her feet. 'I think you know that I could happily lie with you again. But I shall not. Even a woman in my profession has her pride. I have never yet shared my bed with a man who has left it regretting that he had been there.'

Daniel regarded her in silence for a moment above the rim of his glass. 'And what makes you suppose that I would?'

'Perhaps you would not until you had to face your Katherine again, and saw the hurt in her eyes, for she would know. She is no fool. Unless I am very much mistaken, she already suspects that you and I have found pleasure in each other, but she did not know you then. But she cares for you now. Do not hurt her needlessly. It would be better by far for you to face her with a clear conscience in the morning, so I shall place temptation out of reach.'

With a rueful smile curling his lips, Daniel watched her leave. 'You're a damnably astute woman, Josephine Carré,' he murmured, before returning his attention to the only solace he would receive that night, and finishing off the wine.

Chapter Eleven

'What the hell do you suppose you're doing?'

Katherine, who had been about to make the first judicious snip, almost jumped out of her skin, and was granted only sufficient time to recover from the shock of Daniel's unexpected presence in the room before the scissors were snatched from her fingers.

She had chosen to partake of breakfast in the bedchamber in an attempt to delay the inevitable encounter with him for as long as possible, and had spent no little time pondering over what his attitude towards her might be this morning. She had half-expected him to distance himself, as he had done before, only speaking when it was absolutely necessary, and then in a voice which bordered on the icily polite. At the very least she had anticipated a little reserve in his manner, and yet he was behaving just as though nothing untoward had occurred between them, adopting the same high-handed approach which had not infrequently irked her during their short but highly eventful association. Somehow, though, it made facing him again after the events of last night so very much easier, so she swiftly decided to follow his

lead by revealing her own faint annoyance at his imperious attitude.

'Well, I certainly wasn't about to lop off an ear,' she
responded with thinly veiled sarcasm, while having no
difficulty whatsoever in returning his angry gaze through
the dressing-table mirror. 'And hasn't anyone ever told
you that it is extremely rude to enter a lady's bedchamber without knocking first? Also that it is most impolite
to snatch.

'I don't know why you are glowering at me like a
bear with a sore head,' she went on when she quite failed
to win an apology. 'You informed me that I was to adopt
the role of your nephew. It might have escaped your
notice, but boys don't generally wear their hair halfway
down their backs.'

If anything his expression darkened. 'I cannot imagine
why you are so out-of-all-reason cross,' she continued,
taking little heed of the angry sparkle in his dark eyes.
'I thought you would be pleased that I was willing to
sacrifice my hair for the role. After all, you dislike it
intensely.'

This did at last manage to elicit a response. 'I'd like
to know from where you gleaned that piece of utter nonsense,' he retorted, placing the scissors well out of
harm's way and then reaching for the hairbrush. 'Your
hair must rate as possibly the most beautiful I've ever
seen,' he astounded her by admitting, before making use
of the hairbrush and sweeping the rich auburn locks
gently back from her face, and securing them at the nape
of her neck with a length of ribbon.

It was the total sincerity in his voice that astonished
Katherine as much as anything else, and in an attempt
to hide her confusion she proffered a mild joke. 'You

missed your vocation in life, Major Ross. You would have made an excellent lady's maid.'

'Any more remarks like that, young woman, and I shall apply this hairbrush none too gently to quite a different part of your anatomy,' he threatened, with a swift return to his former domineering manner. 'Which would be no more than you deserve, after hurling the wretched thing at me last night.'

Evidently he was not in the least reticent to allude to the incident, but Katherine wasn't so certain whether the memory of those more tender moments was one that he found difficult to forget, or simply did not wish to do so, for his expression was quite unreadable as he handed her the hat that he had acquired to complete her disguise.

'Yes, very neat,' he approved, after watching her secure her hair beneath the rim, and scrutinising her overall appearance. 'Providing no one looks at you too closely, you'd pass for a lad. Now, if you're ready, we'd best be on our way. Josephine has kindly put her carriage at our disposal. But first, she wishes to make her farewells.'

They discovered both the carriage and its owner awaiting them in the courtyard at the front of the house. None of them chose to linger long over the leave-taking, although Katherine did promise, before finally clambering into the carriage, to visit Paris again when Josephine had acquired her house overlooking the Seine.

'You sounded as if you genuinely meant that,' Daniel remarked as he made himself comfortable in the seat opposite, and they commenced the last stage of their journey through France.

'I did,' she assured him. 'Although I might not wholeheartedly approve of the way Madame Carré earns a living, I cannot help but admire her spirit and determination. What she was forced to endure during her marriage would have destroyed a lesser woman.'

'Possibly,' he agreed.

'Furthermore, it does not necessarily follow that, just because she runs a bawdy house, she need participate in any of the activities that take place beneath its roof. In fact, I gained the distinct impression last night that she spends most of her evenings entertaining guests in the card-room, though I do not suppose for a moment that she would refuse to be—er—private with a gentleman if he should appeal to her.'

Thankful now that he had spent the night alone on the couch, Daniel was able to return that penetrating turquoise-eyed gaze. No, Katherine was certainly no fool, he mused. She possibly did suspect that he and Josephine had enjoyed a closer relationship at one time. But that had taken place in the past, long before he had met her. How he conducted himself from now on was all that need concern her.

Katherine was not slow to note his look of smug satisfaction. 'Why are you smiling? Have I a smudge on my nose?'

'No, but it might be better if you had. You make a damnable pretty boy, my darling,' he informed her before, much to her intense surprise, he leaned back against the squabs and closed his eyes.

'Heavens above! Surely you don't propose to sleep?'

The indignant tone brought a further smile to his lips. 'You might have enjoyed a good night's repose. But I most certainly did not. I spent the whole night with my legs dangling over the end of that confounded *chaise-longue* in the parlour. And damnably uncomfortable it was too!'

Katherine hurriedly turned her head away to stare out

of the window, thereby concealing an expression of un-
bridled satisfaction. It ought not to matter a whit to her
where he had spent the night, but it did, and she couldn't
deny the intense pleasure it gave her knowing that he
had spent the night alone.

By the time Madame Carré's coachman had set them
down in the centre of a small habitation on the coast,
and they had visited several of the inns in a vain attempt
to find the man who was supposed to be taking them
across the Channel, Katherine's feelings towards Daniel
were far less charitable. He had been highly critical over
her behaviour from the moment she had stepped down
from the carriage and she was fast coming to the end of
her tether.

'I have not got a mincing walk. I'll have you know
that I have frequently been complimented on the elegance of my carriage. And I do not simper like an idiot,
either!'

'But you're speaking in English again, you infuriating
little baggage!' he snapped, grasping her elbow, thereby
forcing her to halt in the middle of the street. 'Go and
await me on the quayside! And here...' delving into his
pocket he handed her a few coins '...go buy yourself a
pasty from the street hawker we just passed. If anyone
should attempt to hold you in conversation you can start
munching it, then with any luck they won't take too
much notice of your deplorable accent.'

Satisfying herself with casting him a dagger-look,
Katherine did as bidden, buying a pie before settling
herself on the wall by the quay. Although the afternoon
was dry and reasonably sunny, there was a stiff breeze
coming off the sea, and it wasn't too long before she
began to feel decidedly chilled. The rough woollen cloak

he had purchased for her was nowhere near as warm as the totally feminine, fur-lined garment she had been forced to leave behind at Josephine's house.

But of course the wretched man wouldn't have considered that, not when he's no doubt swigging down wine or brandy in some comfortable inn! she thought angrily, following the progress of a boat leaving the small harbour, before her attention was captured by a troupe of acrobats performing wondrous feats as they progressed along the street. So enthralled did she become that she didn't even notice a tall figure positioning himself on the wall beside her.

'You've been well entertained during my absence, I see,' that unmistakable voice remarked, thereby alerting Katherine to Daniel's presence at last. 'You'll no doubt be pleased to hear I was successful in my search, and we'll soon be leaving these shores.'

Katherine watched him glance about him. Ever vigilant, he was always on the lookout for any possible danger. 'You sound relieved,' she remarked, before taking a further bite out of her pie. 'Do you suppose there are people here searching for us?'

'Unlikely. But I shan't be completely easy in my mind until we've set foot again on English soil. Ah! And here's the very person who'll be making that eventuality possible.'

Katherine raised her eyes to see a man of about Daniel's age and build bearing down upon them. The breeze caught his long blond hair, whipping it back to reveal a face which was both bronzed and handsome. He nodded at Daniel before turning his striking blue eyes in her direction. Then he smiled faintly.

'Your nephew, *monsieur*, is ready to leave? Let us hope that—er—he is a good sailor, *hein*?' He raised his eyes and glanced out to sea. 'The wind is getting up. I fear the crossing will not be a smooth one,' he warned, before returning his gaze to Daniel, who was now looking decidedly thoughtful. 'I ask no questions, *monsieur*. I have been paid well to take you. Come, my boat is moored a little further along the quay, and my men are ready to set sail.'

'How on earth did you manage to pay him, Daniel?' Katherine whispered, as they followed the man whom she imagined pirates of old would have strongly resembled. 'Surely the money I gave you was not sufficient?'

'It is Josephine we must thank for his services,' Daniel didn't hesitate to reveal. 'He is a—er—close friend of hers. Even so, she was forced to dig deep into her purse before he would agree to her request.' His worried frown grew more pronounced. 'I do not doubt that he'll keep to his part of the bargain. But what does concern me is that he has already guessed your sex. Stay close by me, Kate.'

She hardly required the warning. It was an effort, but she did just manage to resist the temptation to cling again to that reassuring hand, once Daniel had helped her negotiate the narrow gangplank, and her feet were safely planted on the wooden deck. All the same, she followed him like an adoring puppy to the stern of the boat, where she settled herself as near as she dared beside him on a thick coil of rope, well away from those members of the crew who resembled nothing so much as a band of cut-throats as they continued about their duties.

Katherine experienced a tiny thrill of excitement as the vessel began to move away from the quayside. Unfortunately the pleasure was short-lived, for no sooner had they left the calm waters of the small harbour behind

them than she realised that the captain's warning of a
rough crossing had not been in jest. The wind grew very
much stronger, and it wasn't long before she began to
feel a little queasy at the constant rolling of the boat.

At first she tried to ignore the feeling of nausea, reminding herself that she had travelled by water on numerous occasions when, as a child, she had made frequent visits to England, and had never suffered any ill
effects. Furthermore, when she had travelled over to
France on the packet just a few short weeks before she
had felt perfectly comfortable. None the less, she was
eventually forced to face the fact that she wasn't going
to be all right this time. Her head had started to throb,
and she was beginning to feel hot and sticky, even with
the chill wind full in her face.

'What's the matter?' Daniel had not been slow to note
that she had become increasingly withdrawn. 'Do you
feel unwell?'

She saw little point in trying to deny it. 'Yes, terrible.
In fact, I think—'

She got no further, and made a frantic dive for the
side of the boat, hanging her head over, while at the
same time striving to keep a hold on her hat. Daniel was
beside her in an instant, his firm clasp on her shoulders
steadying her, before promptly handing her his handkerchief.

'Oh, you poor darling,' she thought she heard him
mutter, as he very gently guided her back to their makeshift seat. 'Wait there. I'll not be a moment.'

Through streaming eyes, Katherine watched him making his way with amazing agility along the rolling deck
to where the captain stood issuing instructions to his
crew. She saw those striking blue orbs turn in her direction, before she closed her own in an attempt to stem

the flow of tears rolling down her face. She felt so ashamed for succumbing to a feminine weakness that she had always despised, but she just didn't seem able to stop herself. She felt as helpless as a baby, and couldn't even summon enough strength to shake off the hand which suddenly grasped her arm just above the elbow, urging her to rise, when all she wanted was to be left alone to curl up and die.

'Come,' Daniel coaxed, when she managed to put up a feeble show of resistance at being led across the deck. He would willingly have carried her had he not needed one free hand to steady himself and prevent them both from stumbling. The Channel seemed to be growing rougher with every passing minute, but he somehow managed to maintain his balance and succeeded in getting them both down the few wooden stairs which led to the captain's private quarters, without either coming to grief.

Once safely inside the cabin, Daniel wasted no time in removing Katherine's outer garments. Which was perhaps just as well, for no sooner had he helped her on to the narrow cot-bed than he found himself having to snatch up a bowl.

'You'll feel better soon,' he tried to assure her, once she had made use of the receptacle, though he was far from certain himself. She looked deathly pale, even though her forehead felt clammy to the touch, but there was little more he could do for her except bathe her face with the fresh water he had discovered in a bottle, and then cover her with a blanket.

He very much feared that she wasn't over the worst quite yet, and his prediction proved all too accurate. Unfortunately he wasn't quick enough with the bowl the second time, and Katherine succeeded in badly soiling the front of her shirt.

It took him a few moments only to come to a decision. The captain, although undoubtedly a rogue of the highest order, had been generous enough to put his cabin and its contents at their disposal. Consequently Daniel didn't hesitate to rifle through a large chest, and take out a clean shirt. Whether Katherine felt too weak to put up any resistance, or simply in the throes of sleep was unaware of what he was doing, Daniel wasn't quite sure. However, she didn't attempt to open her eyes or voice any protest when he peeled the shirt over her head, gently sponged her body and then hurriedly dressed her in the clean linen.

He then wasted not a moment in taking himself back up on deck in order to empty the two bowls over the side, and to take some deep steadying breaths, before seating himself on the coiled rope and marvelling at his powers of restraint. He was certainly no stranger to feminine charms, but he couldn't recall setting eyes on a female form more perfect than that.

With a decidedly rueful grin on his lips, he gazed beyond the starboard side of the boat into the darkness. He could only hope that when she discovered what he had done, which assuredly she would, she would understand that his actions had been prompted by the purest motives, though he could not deny that it had been difficult to resist the temptation to look his fill.

'Your young friend is feeling better, I trust?'

Daniel raised his eyes in time to catch a roguish grin on their captain's lips. He had guessed at once, when Josephine had introduced them the previous evening, precisely in which profession her friend was engaged. A smuggler and out-and-out scoundrel the man might be, but he wasn't lacking sympathy, and he was certainly no fool.

'It didn't take you very long to guess my companion's a female,' he remarked as the captain appeared inclined to linger.

He received a shout of laughter in response. 'I am a Frenchman, *monsieur*. You no doubt had your reasons for attempting to conceal her sex. But she is far too enchanting to be a boy.'

Lovelier than you imagine, Daniel mused, as the tantalising image of that perfect, naked torso appeared before his mind's eye to torment him.

'I've been paid well by our mutual friend to take you across to England. I've always made a practice of minding my own business. It is safer that way.' The captain raised his blond head to stare out across the sea. 'The wind is dropping. We've made good time. You shall see your homeland again at dawn.'

Relieved by this assurance, Daniel settled himself more comfortably on the coil of rope. 'You do not envisage having any difficulty in landing us at the location requested?'

'I know your coastline as well as I know my own,' the captain assured him. 'And I'm a master at avoiding your patrolling vessels. No, I do not envisage any trouble. Why do you not go below and get some rest? You shall not be disturbed.'

A further rueful smile tugged at the corners of Daniel's mouth. 'I think it might be wise if I remain on deck, I thank you. I'm in need of a little air.' He chose not to add that he knew his limitations. He was a man, after all, and he didn't wish to be tempted into doing something of which afterwards he might well feel very ashamed.

* * *

Katherine opened her eyes to see the lamp suspended above her head swinging to and fro and, uttering a groan, quickly shut them again. She had hoped it might all have been some diabolical nightmare; that she could not possibly hear the creaking of timbers or be rocking to and fro as though she were in a cradle, but it was all too real. She was still on board that wretched vessel!

'Ha! So you're awake, are you? Good! It saves me the trouble of having to rouse you.'

Katherine forced just one eye open this time to see Daniel, appearing disgustingly hale and hearty, negotiating the last few narrow steps down to the cabin. 'No, I'm not awake. Go away!' she snapped pettishly, as a vague memory of his being here not very long ago and pouring something fiery down her throat filtered through her mind. 'I'm not having any more of that wretched draught you gave me.'

'It was brandy, young woman. And it wouldn't hurt to take a drop more. You must get up,' he announced with what she considered a callous lack of sympathy. 'The rowboat is already over the side, and two members of the crew are waiting to row us ashore.'

His last disclosure possessed the magical effect of some powerful restorative, and Katherine sat up, swinging her feet to the floor. 'Do you mean we're back in England?'

'Not quite, but we very soon shall be,' he assured her, helping her to don both hat and jacket, before swirling the cloak about her shoulders. Then, taking a firm clasp of her wrist, he led the way up on deck, where the captain stood waiting to help her over the side.

Daniel offered to toss her over his shoulder and carry her down the rope-ladder; a suggestion which she instantly declined. Her legs might still feel slightly wobbly and she certainly wasn't fully restored, but she had no intention of suffering the indignity of being handled in such a fashion with the captain and his crew looking on, though she was thankful when Daniel insisted on descending first.

Although they seemed a fair distance away from the shore, Katherine was amazed, once she had managed to scramble into the rowing-boat, just how quickly they reached the beach. The relief of stepping on to dry land almost restored her spirits completely.

'Where in the name of heaven are we precisely?' she asked, after watching the two sailors head back towards their vessel.

'We're on the Dorset coast.'

For a moment she thought she must have misheard. 'What possessed you to have us set down here? How do you propose we reach London…? Walk?'

'I'm not taking you to London. I've funds enough remaining to get us safely to my home, which is about twenty miles from here, where I'll be able to keep an eye on you.'

Puzzled, Katherine joined him on the huge rock a little further up the beach, where he had settled himself. 'I do not perfectly understand, Daniel. Sir Giles wished me to travel to the capital.'

'I know what that old rogue wanted, Kate. But I have no intention of placing you in his hands. I'll send him word that we're back safely, once I've reached home. But until I know precisely what he intends to do, I'm not letting you out of my sight.'

Arrogantly dictatorial his decision might have been, but it engendered such a warm feeling of contentment deep inside as she turned her head to see the rugged lines of his profile now set in hard determination.

What a complex mass of amazing contradictions Major Daniel Ross had turned out to be! she mused. He still did, and possibly always would, annoy her intensely on occasions. Yet there had been times during these past days when she had felt very moved by his displays of attention and thoughtful concern for her well-being. Although she thankfully retained few memories of that wretched sea voyage, she did recall quite clearly how he had helped her down to the privacy of the cabin, and had covered her with a blanket. She recalled too with humiliating clarity the way he had held the basin for her when she had been so helpless in the throes of nausea.

Her smile was distinctly tender. 'I have yet to thank you for taking such care of me last night, Daniel,' she said softly. 'It must have been no less a disagreeable time for you than it was for me.'

'I have enjoyed vastly more pleasurable experiences, certainly,' he conceded.

An understatement if ever there was one! Katherine mused, with a tiny shake of her head, still at a loss to understand why she should have succumbed to the malady. 'It really is most odd. I've never suffered from seasickness before. I can only imagine it must have been that pasty I ate.'

'Possibly,' he returned vaguely, as he raised his eyes to scan the cliff face, which Katherine privately hoped he had no intention of asking her to attempt to negotiate. 'If you feel sufficiently recovered now, I should like to begin the last stage of our journey. I have every intention of reaching Rosslair before nightfall.'

'Rosslare?' Katherine gaped up at him in astonishment as he rose to tower above her. 'But that's in Ireland, Daniel! Why in the name of heaven do you want to go there?'

Once again a wry smile clung to his attractive mouth as he helped her to her feet. 'Yes, I suppose I should have known from the very first,' he remarked somewhat enigmatically, just as a gust of wind sent several auburn curls whipping across her face. 'Rosslair is the name of my home, Katherine,' he enlightened her, as he reached out one hand to capture the errant strands and confine them beneath the hat once more. 'The spelling is different. It is a coincidence, all the same, that I should be taking to my Rosslair a half-Irish girl.'

The fleeting touch of those fingers brushing against her cheek was no less disturbing than the look of tenderness Katherine couldn't fail to perceive in his dark brown eyes. For several entranced moments she found it impossible to draw her gaze away. It was almost as if something tangible were binding them together, making each such an integral part of the other that they were becoming inseparable, becoming one. Then the spell was broken by a further gust of wind off the sea that caught at her cloak, sending it billowing about her. She grasped at the folds in an attempt to keep it about her shoulders, and her attention was captured by the long length of fine lawn almost reaching down to her knees.

Frowning slightly, she began to tuck the shirt front beneath the waistband of her trousers. The garment seemed much longer, and baggier than the one she had been wearing the day before. 'Daniel, this isn't the shirt you purchased for me, is it?'

He hurriedly turned away, but not before Katherine had detected the look of comical dismay which took possession of his features. Eyes narrowing suspiciously, she followed him towards the mass of large rocks which lined the base of the cliff. 'Daniel, where did this shirt come from?'

'You have our free-trading friend the captain to thank for your clean linen, Kate. You soiled your own shirt, and he was kind enough to give you one of his.'

'Free-trader?' Katherine swooped down on this interesting snippet. 'Do you mean he's a smuggler? I should have guessed,' she went on when he nodded. 'I thought it a strange fishing vessel. And I certainly didn't detect the aroma of fish.'

'No, but you'd have detected the aroma of brandy quickly enough if you'd been more yourself,' he responded, thereby returning her thoughts to the borrowed raiment, and inducing a frown.

'It's odd, but I cannot recall being given the shirt.'

There was no response.

'It's odd that I cannot recall putting it on, either.' Again there was no response. Furthermore he had suddenly quickened his pace, determined, it seemed, to remain just that short distance ahead—or determined to bring the conversation to an end. A horrendous possibility suddenly occurred to her. 'Daniel! I demand to know at once how I come to be wearing this garment!'

He stopped and swung round so abruptly that Katherine almost cannoned into him. 'All right, if you're so set on knowing... I changed it for you, as you were incapable of doing it yourself,' he admitted. 'Now, does that satisfy you?'

She could feel the searing heat slowly rising from the base of her throat. 'But-but...I'm not wearing anything beneath,' she squealed, cheeks now aflame.

'I'm well aware of that, strangely enough,' he admitted, before neatly avoiding the small fist which swung in a wide arc towards his left ear.

It wasn't so much the bold admission itself that had instantly replaced the searing humiliation with anger as the provocative gleam which had sprung into his brown eyes. 'Ooh, you—you lecherous wretch!' she screeched, frustration at missing her target only adding to her wrath. 'I trusted you! How could you have taken advantage of me in such a despicable way?'

Half-amused, half-exasperated, Daniel followed as she swung away and began to stride up the beach, her slender frame held rigid with indignation. He could quite understand her mortification and anger, though he found it difficult to maintain his countenance when she swiped his hand away as he reached out to assist her over the rocks.

'All I did was try to make you more comfortable, Kate,' he ventured gently.

'Kindly do not speak to me!'

'My actions stemmed from the purest of motives,' he assured her, sublimely ignoring the request.

The earnest admission won him a brief, considering glance. 'Maybe so,' she conceded in a tight little voice still throbbing with anger.

'Come, be fair, Kate!' he urged, determined to bring her out of her sulky mood, which was so unlike her. She might be a feisty little wench on occasions, hot-tempered and occasionally wilful, but sullenness was not in her nature. 'After all, it was no more than you did to me when I received that slight wound the other day.'

'That, Major Ross, was totally different, and you know it!' she countered, clearly unwilling to be pacified. 'You were fully aware of what I was doing the whole time. Furthermore, I don't suppose for a moment that I'm the first female to have glimpsed you in a half-naked state. Whereas you are most certainly the first man ever to have seen me.'

He hardly needed this assurance, but the totally honest

admission gave him a wonderful feeling of satisfaction all the same. 'No, I don't suppose I am the first, Kate. I expect your father was,' he teased gently, and she swung round, tiny fists clenched.

'Ooh, you really are asking to get your ears boxed!'

'If it will help you recover from your fit of the sullens, then go ahead,' he invited, screwing up his eyes in anticipation of the blow that never came. Consequently he risked opening just one again a moment later in time to catch the faintest of twitches at one corner of that delectable mouth.

'This conversation is becoming ridiculous,' Katherine announced, turning away in time to hide the smile that she seemed incapable of suppressing.

'Wrong,' he countered. 'This conversation was ridiculous from the first. So I would suggest that, instead of wasting our breath in fruitless argument, we channel our energy into something far more worthwhile—namely, getting off this beach.'

She couldn't help but agree with this. 'And do you happen to know of some way off this rock-fall, without having to get our feet wet?'

'There's a path up the cliff a little further along. My cousin Simon and I occasionally played here when we were boys.'

Memory stirred. Katherine was almost sure that the cousin to whom he had just referred was none other than the man who had married his childhood sweetheart. Consequently she tactfully refrained from comment. She had no desire for him to discover that she had already learned something of his past from her aunt. If he wished to confide in her he would do so, she decided, asking instead if they were close to any towns or villages.

'There's a sizeable habitation about three miles away,

where I'm certain we'll have no trouble in acquiring a mount. We'll be able to get something to eat there, if nothing else.'

She cast him an impatient glance. 'If you possess any sensibility at all, Major Ross, you will kindly not mention food to me, especially after what I've suffered.'

His shout of laughter might have held a callous ring, but his voice did not lack sympathy. 'I can understand your sentiments, my little love, but food is precisely what you do need, if only to maintain your strength. I'm determined to complete the last leg of our journey, for I have every intention of sleeping in my own bed tonight!'

Chapter Twelve

Rosslair was bathed in warm afternoon sunshine when Katherine caught her first glimpse of the greystone manor house, set in the gently rolling countryside she well remembered. It was a truly handsome building, not large by some standards, but undeniably the home of a gentleman of comfortable means.

As Daniel urged the weary mount into the courtyard at the back of the house, the sound of hooves on cobblestones brought a stocky individual of average height from one of the numerous outbuildings, which lined the yard on three of its sides. His craggy features were instantly softened by a broad smile of welcome, as his clear blue gaze rested upon the man about whose waist Katherine had clung for the past few hours, and a moment later her ears were assailed by an unmistakable accent.

'To be sure now, I were only saying to Janet this very morn she were worrying herself to no purpose, and that you'd return safe and sound in your own good time. And that happy I am to be proved—'

He checked as his gaze fell upon the delicately featured face peering at him round one broad shoulder.

'Now what have we here, Major, sir? Not another lad to help about the place, I'm thinking.' He peered more closely as Daniel assisted the slender figure behind him to the ground before dismounting himself. ''Tis not a lad at all, I'm thinking.'

'There's no fooling you, Sean McGann,' Daniel announced, before making Katherine known to the man who had served him loyally throughout the hard-fought campaign in the Peninsula.

'O'Malley?' Positively beaming with delight, the ex-sergeant grasped the slender fingers held out to him. 'Now, there's a fine Irish name for you!'

'And with a fine Irish temper to match,' Daniel assured him, much to his loyal henchman's intense amusement. 'Come into the house when you've taken care of the horse, McGann,' he added before leading the way into his home by way of the rear entrance.

In the large farmhouse-style kitchen he discovered his elderly housekeeper, seated at the table, busily occupied in repairing a rent in a sheet. After one brief glance to see who had entered her private domain, she rose to her feet and came rushing forward, with quite amazing speed for someone of her advanced years, to clasp as much of Daniel as she could encompass in her arms.

There was clearly a bond of affection between them that put Katherine in mind of her own relationship with Bridie. It was not unusual for loyal, elderly retainers to be given far more licence, so it came as no surprise to hear the housekeeper administer a scold when Daniel lifted her quite off her feet a moment later in order to plant a smacking kiss on one lined cheek.

Katherine's only partially suppressed chuckle instantly alerted the housekeeper to her presence. She glanced enquiringly up at her master, before subjecting the stranger to a rather prolonged stare which grew increasingly disapproving.

Daniel immediately relinquished his hold, before reaching out one hand to remove the floppy, misshapen hat, and allow those gorgeous auburn locks to fall about slender shoulders. If anything his housekeeper's expression became even more dour and she sniffed quite pointedly.

'You can take that disapproving look off your face, Janet Browning!' he ordered sternly.

Her only response was to sniff again.

'It might interest you to know that it was none other than Miss O'Malley who was responsible for my recent absence from home.'

'Ha!' Grey eyes subjected the figure indecently clad in masculine attire to a further reproachful glare. 'I don't doubt it!'

'I do not think your position is improving, Daniel,' Katherine remarked, *sotto voce*, disposed to be more amused than anything else by the servant's quite evident misconceptions.

He was inclined to agree, although he wasn't slow to note his housekeeper's faintly puzzled expression at the unmistakable refinement in Katherine's voice. 'Yes, Janet. Miss O'Malley is unquestionably a lady of virtue. And it is for this very reason that you are to take very good care of her. I shall explain everything more fully to you presently. In the meantime, I want you to find her something suitable to wear.'

'Well, that I don't object to doing,' she didn't hesitate to assure him, 'though why a lady should be parading round in breeches, I cannot imagine!'

'Because, you inquisitive old besom, for her own

safety she has been masquerading as my nephew for the last couple of days.'

Janet tutted. 'It appears to me, Master Daniel, that you've been indulging in mischief again. You always were one for getting into scrapes.'

Katherine couldn't help laughing softly at Daniel's look of exasperation. It seemed that they both suffered the same problems—servants who persisted in treating them as though they were still irresponsible, mischievous children who should be kept in leading-strings.

'Oh, that is nothing, Mrs Browning. I've figured as his wife and his sister,' she enlightened her. 'In fact, I've reached the point where I've forgotten just who I really am.'

'But I haven't, Katherine,' Daniel assured her gently, and with such a wealth of tenderness in his eyes that Janet hardly recognised the being whom she had known from the day of his birth. 'Tomorrow you must swiftly accustom yourself to yet another role—that of my cousin, Louise Durand, whom I have brought over from France, and to whom Janet shall act as chaperon.'

'In that case, sir,' his loyal servant announced, 'I'll begin my duties at once by ensuring the young lady is made comfortable in your grandmother's old room.'

Having her hand captured in a surprisingly firm grasp, Katherine had little choice but to accompany the house-keeper up a rather handsome wooden staircase to the upper floor. If the servant still retained doubts about her respectability she certainly kept these reservations to herself, and by the time Katherine had helped to put clean sheets on the bed, and had returned to the kitchen to fill a pitcher with hot water herself, the housekeeper was positively beaming with approval and evincing every sign of being very pleased at having another female residing under the roof.

Once Katherine had returned to the bedchamber, she took stock of her surroundings, while making herself appear more respectable by donning clothes which, she suspected, had once belonged to Daniel's mother. The furniture, elegant and well made, was undoubtedly French in design, and had more than likely belonged to the former occupant of the room. Although the primrose bed-hangings and the drapes at the window were slightly faded, as was the delicately patterned wallpaper, it was a pleasant bedchamber, tastefully decorated and comfortable, and Katherine was more than happy to make use of it for the duration of her stay.

Not that she had been given much choice in the matter, she reminded herself, as she began arranging her hair in a simple style by making use of the combs, brushes and pins which most likely had also belonged to the room's former occupant. Daniel, in his usual high-handed fashion, had insisted that she remain in his house until such time as Sir Giles could be apprised of their return. She didn't object in the least, but she was determined, for the duration of her stay, not to be idle. That part of her life was now well and truly over. She was resolved not to spend the years ahead living an unproductive existence where she had nothing better to do with her time than indulge in fruitless socialising with that large circle of people in Bath with whom she had very little in common.

Once satisfied with the arrangement of her hair, Katherine did not delay in returning to the large kitchen, where she discovered both Janet and McGann companionably seated at the table. She would dearly have loved to see over the whole house, but decided that that could wait until later, and that it was more important for her to become better acquainted with the two people whom she strongly suspected had come to mean far more to Daniel than mere servants.

'No, please do not get up,' she adjured them as they both made to rise. 'Would you mind very much if I joined you?'

Her polite manner instantly won her a further warm look of approval from the housekeeper, though the glint easily discernible in masculine eyes stemmed, Katherine strongly suspected, from something quite different. It was no difficult matter to induce them both to talk about the master of the house who, she quickly discovered, was upstairs in his bedchamber, changing his attire.

It swiftly became apparent that both held him in the highest esteem. Janet, who had come to work in the house shortly after Daniel's father, Edwin Ross, had purchased the property some forty years before, had been present at Daniel's birth. She had been present too on that sad day, two years later, when his lovely mother had died after giving birth to a stillborn child, and had remained throughout those years when his grandmother, a woman of immense character, who had escaped from France with her daughter at the time of the Terror, had taken charge of the house and Daniel's upbringing.

'I have to say that the house has never been the same these past ten years, not since his grandmother passed away,' Janet admitted solemnly. 'It's been a sad and lonely place, nothing like the happy home it once was.'

'But surely you didn't remain here alone whilst Major Ross was away in Spain?' Katherine, somewhat surprised, was prompted to ask. The house might not be on the scale of even a small mansion, but it was far too large for just one servant to maintain, and one who, moreover, was definitely not in her first flush of youth. 'Surely there are other servants here to help you?'

'Well, there's McGann here now, and a stable lad who does the heavy lifting. Then there's Mr Prentiss, who's been the land manager for many years. He always sends men over to the house to see to repairs and chop logs for the fires.'

'But isn't there any other female employed here to help you with the general household chores?' Katherine persisted, and was appalled when Janet shook her head. 'That really is too bad of Daniel! This house is too big for only one person to manage.'

'Now, there's a considerate soul!' Janet beamed. 'It would take a female to appreciate the work a woman has to do. And I cannot deny I could do with some help about the place now that Master Daniel has returned. I do have one of the village girls come up once a week to help clean the place. But when the master was away fighting in Spain, and most of the rooms in holland covers, there weren't really any need for extra permanent help. I did intend to mention the matter at the beginning of the year, but then the master upped and spent some time in London, and was back only a few days before he went off again.'

'Well, don't you worry, Janet. I shall ensure the matter is brought to his attention before I leave here,' Katherine promised. 'It's unthinkable that you should be expected to manage the house by yourself. I wonder that your master didn't see to matters long before now.'

'He's had other things to think about in recent years,' McGann put in, not hesitating to come to the Major's defence. 'I don't think his thoughts dwelled too often on his home back here when he were out in Spain.'

'Understandably not,' Katherine responded, striving to be fair. 'Have you known the Major long?'

'Six year, or thereabouts. I were his batman and sergeant, Miss Katherine. He were a Captain when we first met. Won his majority after Badajoz. And no one deserved it more!'

'I'm sure you're right,' Katherine agreed softly, her mind's eye having no difficulty in conjuring up an image of those telltale scars. 'You were no doubt involved in many battles together.'

'That we were, Miss Katherine, and all of them hard-fought,' McGann confirmed, needing little encouragement to reminisce. 'The ''grasshoppers'' were always the ones picked to go out on skirmishes.'

'Grasshoppers?' Katherine echoed, bemused.

'Ahh, bless you, miss! That's what the Frogs called us on account of our green uniforms, but they had a grudging respect for us too, I reckon. The 95th had some of the best shots in the army. And there were none better with a Baker rifle than the Major. To be sure we've been in some tough spots, me and the Major. Talavera was one of the worst. I thought at one point we'd be singing with the angels before that battle was over.'

Katherine's eyes glinted with unholy amusement. 'Or in the Major's case possibly crying, ''Hell, it's hot!'''

'I heard that, young woman!'

Whilst her companions dissolved into laughter, Katherine swung round in the chair to discover Daniel framed in the open doorway. 'Oh, are you here?' she remarked, totally unmoved by his unexpected appearance. 'Well, you know what they say about eavesdroppers, don't you, Daniel?'

'I'll give you eavesdroppers, you impertinent baggage!' he threatened, though the unmistakable flicker of affection in his eyes didn't go unnoticed by any one of those seated at the table.

Janet exchanged a swift glance with McGann before hurriedly rising to her feet. 'Well, I haven't time to sit about gossiping all day. I've the dinner to prepare.'

'And I shall help,' Katherine informed her, rising also and catching a look of distinct disapproval taking possession of Daniel's features.

'I cannot imagine why you're glowering at me in that objectionable way,' she told him, instantly proving to one and all that she wasn't in the least in awe of the master of the house. 'Janet cannot possibly be expected to manage everything, especially not with a guest staying here. And as I'm not completely useless in a kitchen, I see no earthly reason why I shouldn't lend a hand. So if you'll kindly remove yourself from under our feet, and take McGann with you, Janet and I shall make a start on dinner.'

Although muttering under his breath, Daniel departed as requested, and went into the large sitting-room, McGann, chuckling wickedly, at his heels. 'It's all very well for you to laugh,' Daniel remonstrated, once he had the door firmly closed behind them, 'but I'd sooner be asked to manage a company of raw recruits than be responsible for that unruly little madam!'

'She's a spirited little filly, and no mistake. But nothing you can't handle, I'm thinking.'

Daniel refrained from comment, and merely invited his companion to take a seat before explaining precisely why Katherine was a guest in his house. 'So you can now appreciate why I need you to make contact with Sir Giles Osborne without delay,' he went on to say, once he had regaled his ex-sergeant with a reasonably detailed account of his recent exploits on the other side of the

Channel. 'With any luck you'll find him at his country home in Hampshire. Unfortunately, with the very real possibility of renewed conflict with France, he might well be in the capital. In which case you must go on to London with the letter I'm about to write. You are to hand it to Sir Giles personally, McGann, and await further instructions. In no circumstances are you to leave it with a servant or a secretary.'

'Understood, sir.'

By the time McGann was on the point of departure, Katherine had taken Janet into her confidence. Her explanation had taken somewhat longer, for she had found herself having to disclose the reason why a gently bred young woman should wish to embark on such a hazardous venture in the first place.

'But do you not enjoy living in Bath, miss?' Janet asked in some surprise, when Katherine had quite openly admitted that she had become increasingly dissatisfied with the life she had been leading in recent months. 'I've never been there myself, but I've been told it's an elegant place.'

'It isn't as fashionable as it once was,' Katherine responded, raising her head in time to see Daniel's trusted henchman riding out of the yard. 'There's no denying, though, that it's a pleasant place to live, and one is never short of company.' She shrugged. 'I suppose though, Janet, I'm a country girl at heart. I spent the first sixteen years of my life in Ireland, living in a house not unlike this one. Then, after both my parents died, I came here to Dorsetshire to live with my grandfather, Colonel Fairchild.'

Janet only just succeeded retaining her grasp on the bowl she was holding. 'You're Colonel Fairchild's granddaughter…? Then your mother must have been Miss Charlotte Fairchild.'

Fixing her short-sighted eyes on the figure busily working at the table, Janet scrutinised the delicate features. 'Yes…yes, I can see the resemblance now. I remember your dear mother well, Miss Katherine. She were a lovely-looking young woman, with a nature to match.'

'Yes.' Katherine sighed. 'I sometimes wish I were more like her in some ways. She was always so placid, so controlled, whereas I—'

'Tend to be a little volatile on occasions, and act without thinking,' Daniel finished for her, having entered the kitchen in time to catch the last fragments of conversation. 'I'm pleased to see that you two are becoming better acquainted,' he remarked, blithely ignoring the lethal darts emanating from a pair of turquoise-coloured eyes.

'Yes, I've been hearing an account of your recent doings.' Janet tutted, a clear indication that she did not wholeheartedly approve. 'When are you going to stop all this gallivanting about, Master Daniel, and settle down? You ain't a boy no longer. It's high time you began to think about the future and take responsibility for this fine place of yours.'

'I have every intention of doing precisely that,' he assured her before turning to Katherine who was unable to judge whether he was truly in earnest. 'Your explaining the situation to Janet has saved me the trouble of doing so. Much of what will happen next depends upon Sir Giles's response to my letter. I've sent McGann off to Hampshire to apprise him of your arrival in England.'

Katherine nodded. 'It's highly likely that he will want me to travel to London. In the meantime, Janet,' she added, turning to her, 'it would seem that you will be forced to put up with my presence here.'

'That'll be no hardship at all, miss,' she answered, and this time there was no doubting the sincerity of the assurance. 'What bothers me is what I'm to call you.'

'No need for you to trouble yourself unduly over that,' Daniel put in, seating himself on the edge of the table, where Katherine was busily engaged in making pastry. 'We shall put our heads together over dinner and work out some tale which will satisfy the curious. Until word gets about that I'm home, I doubt we'll be plagued with many callers at the house. In the meantime, I would suggest you continue to call our guest Miss Katherine.' His lips twitched very slightly. 'But under no circumstances call her Kate. She only allows me to address her in such a fashion.'

Katherine's look of exasperation only succeeded in making him chuckle. 'Just because I became fagged to death requesting you not to do so, does not necessarily mean I now approve. My father always maintained that you could lead a mule to water, but you could never force it to drink.'

'Horse,' Daniel corrected.

'Mule is more appropriate in this instance,' she countered, which resulted in the kitchen resounding with the housekeeper's appreciative chuckles.

'Oh, I think I'm going to enjoy having you here, Miss Katherine!' Janet declared, much to her master's intense relief, for he knew better than most that his housekeeper did not take an immediate liking to everyone.

'That might well be so, but I am going to deprive you of her company for the next half an hour or so by taking her on a guided tour of the house and gardens—if she would care to accompany me, that is?'

Seemingly Katherine didn't need asking twice, and Janet, watching them leave, caught sight of them a moment later, walking side by side across the yard.

Moving across to the window, she continued to study their progress as they headed towards the gate leading to the garden in which her master's grandmother had loved to work, and which was now sadly overgrown. But it could so easily be put to rights, she mused, a spark of hope igniting. The next few days would give her a clearer indication if her young master had been in earnest, and had made up his mind to settle down at last. Yet already she was forced to own that there had been a change in him. He seemed very relaxed and happy, something which he had not been for such a very long time. And there was that in his eyes when they rested upon that auburn-haired girl…

'We'll trust, Master Daniel, that word of your return doesn't get about too quickly,' she muttered, a worried frown dimming the hopeful glimmer in her eyes, 'otherwise you might receive a visitor to the house I for one would certainly prefer not to see.'

Chapter Thirteen

Katherine found it no difficult matter to settle down to country life at Rosslair. In fact, she loved it, and within a very short time had established a routine whereby she would help Janet in the kitchen for part of the day and spend the afternoons, weather permitting, in the garden. Daniel might frown dourly whenever he saw her down on her knees, doing battle with a particularly trouble-some weed, but even he was forced to concede, before his first week back home had drawn to a close, that there was a noticeable improvement to the look of the rose garden.

The master of the house always made a point of re-turning home to bear her company during mealtimes. Breakfast and luncheon were always eaten in the kitchen, where Janet would join them to make the oc-casions very enjoyable. Nevertheless Katherine always looked forward to the evening meal when she and Daniel ate alone together in the privacy of the large front par-lour, which also functioned as a dining-room.

Undoubtedly the parlour was Katherine's favourite room in the house. There was always a welcoming fire burning in the huge grate by which she and Daniel would sit together in the evenings, sometimes talking; sometimes in companionable silence: Daniel reading a book while she continued to make the new parlour curtains Daniel's grandmother had begun more than a decade before, and which she and Janet had come upon quite by chance in one of the trunks in the attic, whilst they had been searching for garments suitable for Katherine to wear.

Having been forced to don the late Mrs Ross's clothes was the one slight blot in what for Katherine had been a rewarding and very happy first week at Rosslair. The novelty of parading round in garments worn by ladies a quarter of a century before having swiftly dwindled, she longed to dress in her own fashionable clothes again. Unfortunately there had been no word from Sir Giles Osborne, and she had seen no sign of McGann either.

'You don't appear in the best of spirits this morning, sweetheart,' Daniel remarked, after consuming a substantial pile of ham and eggs, and glancing up to catch Katherine's pensive expression.'

'Oh, I'm all right,' she assured him, having no intention of burdening him with her rather insignificant concerns.

He had been very busy since their arrival at his home. Every day he had ridden out with his land manager, discussing ways to improve the yield from the vast acreage of farmland that Mr Prentiss had maintained well during his master's long absence from home.

'No, you're not,' Daniel countered, betraying that keen perception which Katherine sometimes found faintly unnerving. Increasingly she was beginning to suspect that she would never be able to keep anything secret from him, at least not for long.

'Oh, very well,' she relented. 'If you must know, I'm

not quite happy that we've received no word from Sir Giles.'

'Ah! But we have,' he surprised her by announcing. 'McGann arrived back late last night, after you'd gone to bed. I'm to receive further instructions in due course. In the meantime, Sir Giles wants you to stay here and not attempt to journey to London.'

Katherine didn't object to remaining at Rosslair in the least. If the truth were known, she was beginning to dread the thought of having to leave the place. There remained the problem, however, of her attire. 'I do not suppose Sir Giles mentioned anything about forwarding my clothes, did he? I left a trunk full of them in his care for when I should arrive in the capital.'

'Afraid not. And McGann certainly didn't bring anything back with him, except Sir Giles's letter.'

'Oh, confound it!'

Daniel appeared mildly surprised by the unexpected show of annoyance, but Janet perfectly understood, and suggested that a trip to the local market town was all that was required.

'You're sure to find something suitable,' Janet added. 'At the very least you can purchase some lengths of material which we can make up into dresses.'

'What's wrong with what she's wearing now?' Daniel asked, displaying all the tact of the typical male who paid scant attention to fashionable female apparel. 'I rather like her in those clothes. It's a pleasure to see a female clad in garments that emphasise a trim waist. And in its proper place too!'

Katherine's pained expression drew a chortle of laughter from Janet, a sound frequently heard reverberating round the kitchen in recent days. 'You might like them, but I happen to prefer the prevailing mode,' she countered. 'How can I possibly continue to go about looking like a leftover from the last century?'

Daniel's winning smile swiftly crushed her slight feeling of pique. 'All right, sweetheart. I'll take you into town in the gig. We can stop on the way at Lord Kilbride's residence. Prentiss told me yesterday that Kilbride's eldest son is being forced to sell his light travelling carriage and a pair of horses in order to pay gaming debts. We've not had a decent carriage here since I parted with Grandmother's aged landau some years ago. You pop upstairs and put on a cloak and bonnet, whilst I hitch up the horse to the gig.'

Katherine didn't need telling twice. Hurriedly finishing off the last mouthful of buttered roll, she hurried up the stairs to don the wide-brimmed straw bonnet that she had worn during the afternoons when working in the garden, and collect the rough woollen cloak that Daniel had purchased for her in France. Then she returned speedily to the kitchen to discover only Janet there, busily clearing away the breakfast dishes.

'I'll give you a hand until Daniel is ready to leave,' Katherine offered, and was a little surprised not to receive one of the housekeeper's grateful smiles in response.

'No need for you to be troubling yourself, Miss Katherine,' she eventually managed to squeeze past tightly compressed lips, clearly betraying disapproval. 'He'll be some time yet, I expect. He has a visitor.'

'Oh?' Katherine was mildly surprised. 'I didn't hear the door-knocker.'

'You wouldn't have. She arrived when the master was about to cross the yard to harness old Jonas to the gig. He took her into the front parlour. You'd best go through, miss, and let him know you're ready to leave.'

'Oh, no. I couldn't do that, Janet. It will not hurt to wait until his visitor has left.'

'You'd best go through in any case, miss, and make yourself known,' Janet persisted, determined, it seemed, to have her way. 'You can't go hiding yourself away every time someone calls at the house. And it's my belief this one will not be a rare visitor now that the master's returned.' She gave vent to an unladylike snort. 'Though how in the world she found out beats me. The master ain't ridden off his land since he's been back, as far as I'm aware.'

Clearly the housekeeper, for whatever reason, wished to have the kitchen to herself. And perhaps Janet was right, Katherine mused, for unless she wished to skulk away in corners for the duration of her stay in this house, she was bound to come into contact with Daniel's friends and neighbours sooner or later.

She hovered for a moment, uncertain, then made her way towards the parlour to discover the door slightly ajar. Once again she found herself hesitating, debating whether to knock or merely enter, and decided to compromise by pushing open the door and remaining on the threshold.

The pang of envy Katherine experienced at first sight of the female clad in a very stylish, dark blue riding habit was quickly swept aside by the sudden eruption of a far stronger emotion that left her feeling slightly numbed and reluctant to believe the evidence of her own eyes, as she gazed upon the intimate little tableau: the woman with her hands pressed lightly against Daniel's chest; he with his long fingers clasped about slender wrists. So locked was their gaze that they seemed oblivious to the sights and sounds about them, having eyes only for each other.

Then, as though sensing they were no longer alone, Daniel turned his head towards the door and Katherine wasn't certain whether it was a flicker of relief or embarrassment she detected in those dark eyes of his, or perhaps a mixture of both. He certainly didn't seem totally displeased to see her, for he immediately released his hold on his visitor and came smilingly forward.

'Your arrival is most opportune, Cousin Louise,' he told her, his eyes now clearly darting a warning, which Katherine perfectly understood. 'I should like to make you known to one of my oldest friends,' he added, taking such a firm grasp of one wrist that she had little choice but to accompany him into the room to make the visitor's acquaintance.

Katherine guessed, even before Daniel made her known to the woman regarding her with keen interest, that the visitor was none other than the female he had once hoped to marry. It was not at all difficult to understand why he had wished to wed her either, for Julia Ross was undoubtedly one of the most beautiful women Katherine had ever set eyes on. From the perfect arrangement of soft blonde curls to daintily shod feet, she was the epitome of lovely femininity. If there was a slight fault then perhaps it was a mouth that was fractionally too wide. Even so, it was difficult to imagine that the most hardened male could have withstood the allure of the thickly lashed, cornflower-blue eyes.

Beneath the crop of lustrous curls, fine brows rose in surprise. 'Your cousin, Daniel?' She did not attempt to hide her astonishment. 'I didn't realise you had any cousins.'

'Several in France, Julia,' he confirmed. 'Have you forgotten my mother was a Frenchwoman?'

Full lips curled into an easy smile. 'Of course, how very foolish of me!'

Katherine then found her outstretched fingers clasped briefly, while her own features were scrutinised. 'I quite fail to perceive any resemblance between you and your cousin, though, Daniel.'

'There wasn't a great deal between Simon and me,' he reminded her, quick as a flash, before inviting her to sit down. 'Besides which, Louise and I are only distantly related.'

He then recaptured Katherine's wrist, once again giving her little option but to sit beside him on the sofa. Not that she objected in the least to this cavalier treatment. She was quite prepared, for the time being at least, to play the part of his docile little cousin, and more than happy to follow his lead.

'I went over to France to bring my cousin to England,' Daniel enlightened his visitor, after watching the corn-flower-blue eyes flicker momentarily over Katherine's attire. 'You must be aware by now of the unfortunate events taking place across the Channel. It was utter chaos at the ports. Unfortunately, all Louise's baggage went missing, and she is having to wear some of my mother's old clothes.'

There was undeniably a flicker of sympathy in the blue eyes now, but Daniel was not slow to note that it didn't quite disguise the suspicion which continued to lurk there. 'Louise's elder sister married an Englishman, a soldier, shortly after our troops entered Paris last year. Once they had settled in England, it had been their intention to send for Louise. Unfortunately she hasn't heard from them for several months. I called upon her when I was in Paris, and assured her that she could always contact me if she were ever in need of my help.'

Katherine was quite amazed at the wonderful tale Daniel was concocting, but decided, having already wearied of her docile role, that it was high time she added something to the conversation. 'My brother-in-law, he has a house in Der—Derb— Bah! What is the place called, Daniel? My English, *madame*, it is not good, you understand,' she added, turning to Mrs Ross and raising both hands in a helpless little gesture. 'My big cousin I find is a boar, and orders me always to speak the English now.'

A soft gurgle of laughter rose in the air. 'I believe you mean bear, my dear,' Julia offered helpfully.

'Do I?' Katherine turned her head on one side, as though considering this, while masterfully suppressing a chuckle of her own at the darkling look she received from the man beside her. 'Perhaps you are right, *madame*.'

'As you have probably gathered by now, Julia, my young cousin has a somewhat perverse, Gallic sense of humour. Which,' he added, smiling sardonically, 'I'm inclined to believe she'll moderate before too long, especially if she knows what's good for her.'

'You see what I mean, *madame*?' Katherine was beginning to enjoy herself hugely, safe in the knowledge that Daniel could do little in retaliation whilst his guest remained. 'He is a brute, no? Ever since the day he came over to collect me from Paris he has bullied me unmercifully. I yearn to be with my own people again!'

'I'm certain you do,' the visitor agreed, sounding genuinely sympathetic. 'Have you had any success in locating their whereabouts, Daniel?'

'No, not yet, and possibly shan't for some considerable time,' he answered with a certain grim satisfaction. 'So my cousin must reconcile herself to remaining with me. In the meantime, Julia, I must see what I can do about replenishing at least part of her wardrobe. I have promised to take her into town this morning. In fact, I was on the point of hitching up the gig when you arrived.'

If she was offended by Daniel's obvious wish to bring her visit to an end, she betrayed no sign of it, and rose at once to her feet. 'What a pity I have called at such an inconvenient time!' She paused for a moment to slide her slender fingers into a pair of leather gloves. 'I was hoping to persuade you to escort me back to the Hall. Your uncle unfortunately suffered a further mild bout of gout recently, and is feeling a little depressed. But no matter. Perhaps you might ride over to pay us a visit some other time?'

Although uncertain whether it was the promise he had made to escort her into the local town that held Daniel mute, or there was some other reason why he seemed faintly reluctant to escort the lady he had once hoped to marry back to her home, Katherine didn't hesitate to assure him that she was quite willing to await his return, if he did wish to pay a visit to his uncle.

Mrs Ross was quite obviously delighted by the generosity of this unselfish gesture. Daniel's reaction was not so easy to judge, for he betrayed neither enthusiasm nor disappointment before he escorted his visitor out of the room, merely saying that he would return as soon as he could.

There was no mistaking Janet's feeling on the matter when Katherine rejoined her in the kitchen a few minutes later in time to see Daniel riding out of the stable-yard with his beautiful companion beside him.

'Now why on earth is he going off with her? I thought he was supposed to be taking you in to town?'

'I assured him I didn't object to delaying my shopping trip if he wished to escort Mrs Ross back to her home.'

'Well, I could have wished you hadn't, miss.'

'But why, Janet?' Katherine was at a loss to understand the housekeeper's obvious displeasure. 'After all, an hour or two makes no difference. Besides which, Mrs Ross informed Daniel that his uncle is wishful to see him.'

'Ha!' Janet scoffed. 'A likely story!'

More than just mildly curious, Katherine joined the housekeeper at the table. 'What are you saying, Janet? Is there some bad feeling between Daniel and his uncle?'

'Oh, no, miss. I weren't meaning that. They're fond of each other, right enough. Both Sir Joshua and Mr Edwin were very close and their sons were destined to be the same, more like brothers than cousins.'

Setting aside her sewing, Janet relapsed into a reminiscent mood. 'I have to say I was very fond of Master Simon myself. He were a good-natured boy. I have to say too, it was always Master Daniel who was responsible for getting them into a scrape. Forever into mischief he was. Still...' she sighed '...if his father had spent more time with him when he was a boy, he might have been more settled.'

'Were they not close?' Katherine asked gently.

'Oh, the old master loved him right enough. But after the mistress died there's no denying he withdrew into himself and concentrated all his efforts on improving his house and lands. It was a blessing Master Daniel's grandmother was here. She doted on him.'

'Whenever he has spoken of her it has always been with deep affection,' Katherine remarked.

'Oh, yes, miss, there was a real bond between them. But it's small wonder the young master grew restless, and showed little interest in the place. Perhaps if his father had spent more time with him, it might have been different.'

Katherine frowned at this. 'He seems contented here now, Janet. He was talking only the other evening of his plans to improve the land, and his intention of extending the house by adding a separate dining room and a library, and two extra bedchambers.'

'Oh, the love of the place has come to him, miss,' Janet agreed. 'But there was a time when I thought it might never do so. Years ago, when it was suggested that the young master should see something of the world and go out to India to work for the company Mr Edwin had a small share in, I thought it were no bad thing. His grandmother had passed away the year before, and he seemed more unsettled than ever.' She shook her head sadly. 'When I waved him off in the carriage, I never imagined the poor boy would be returning to an empty house…and everything.'

'You mean to discover the girl he loved had married his cousin during his absence,' Katherine remarked, not in the least reticent to reveal that she knew something of Daniel's history to Janet. 'My aunt Lavinia told me a little of his past.'

It seemed so strange, Katherine mused, clearly recalling that cold morning in early February, when she had sat with her aunt and cousin in the parlour, that her aunt's disclosures had had little effect upon her then, save a moderate feeling of sympathy towards the man whom she had so foolishly maligned. How differently she felt now! Daniel had come to mean so much to her… Perhaps more than she cared to admit.

Swiftly thrusting this disturbing reflection aside, she said, 'If my memory serves me correctly, my aunt seemed to suppose that pressure might have been brought to bear upon Julia to marry Daniel's cousin?'

'Pshaw!' Janet dismissed this with a wave of one hand. 'I heard that tale myself, and never believed a word of it! The Melroses doted on their daughter. They may have wished her to wait a year or two before becoming engaged to Master Daniel, and I cannot say I ever blamed them for that. She were only seventeen and he only just turned twenty when he set sail for India. But I don't believe for a moment they forced her into marriage with Master Simon. No, I reckon she just fancied becoming Lady Julia Ross when the old man died and Master Simon came into the title. There's no denying that some say that Sir Joshua served his nephew a bad turn by blessing the match, and that at least he ought to have insisted the wedding be delayed until after his nephew had returned.'

But not you, Katherine thought, but said, 'I imagine that Simon must have been very much in love with Julia.'

'Oh, yes, miss. He loved her right enough. And although Master Daniel might have bore him and his uncle some ill will when he came home from India, that's no longer the case, and he was genuinely sorry to hear of his cousin's death in that riding accident two years back.'

'Am I right in thinking that Julia has a son?' Katherine asked, as a further fleeting memory returned.

'Yes, and he's a nice little boy. Just like his father used to be!' Her smile was replaced by a look of concern. 'And like his father before him, he's proving to be a weak and sickly child, so I've heard. The good Lord knows, miss, I wouldn't want misfortune to befall the boy. Because if he died, then you know who would eventually inherit the title. Not that he has any desire to do so, mind you.'

Before that moment Katherine had given the matter no thought. 'Of course, Daniel would then come into the title!'

'Aye, miss. And if I'm right and it were the wish to become Lady Julia Ross that prompted her to marry Simon, if something does happen to her son, there's only one way she's ever going to achieve her ambition.'

'And you're very much afraid that Daniel might fall prey to the beautiful Julia's charms again, aren't you, Janet?'

'He'd be a fool if he did, miss. And Master Daniel's no fool.'

'Yet, the fact must be faced that in all these years he hasn't met anyone else he wished to marry,' Katherine responded, and then found herself the recipient of a prolonged and contemplative stare which was more than just faintly unnerving. 'What is it, Janet? Have I said something to upset you?'

'Oh, no, miss. I were merely wool-gathering, as you might say.'

'In that case, I shall leave you to do so in peace,' Katherine announced, rising from the table. 'I think I shall occupy my time until Daniel returns by continuing the weeding in the rose garden.'

As she made her way round to the side of the house, Katherine was glad of the protection she obtained from the old fashioned, wide-brimmed straw bonnet, for the day was bright and for early spring the sun's rays were remarkably strong. She swiftly found it necessary to discard her cloak, tossing it down on the grass close by, but surprisingly enough she soon grew tired of the task she normally attained great enjoyment from performing, and found her mind all too frequently returning to the conversation she had had with Janet.

Rising up from her knees, she went through the wicket-gate that granted access to a large meadow and, without paying too much attention to which direction she took, made her way across the wide area of grassland to yet another large field that Daniel had mentioned he had every intention of putting to the plough. After skirting several more fields, which also formed part of Daniel's land, she found herself entering a very familiar woodland area.

Suddenly realising she had walked much further than she had intended, Katherine decided it might prove beneficial to rest for a while before attempting the homeward trek, and promptly discovered a conveniently fallen tree, ideal for the purpose.

How odd that she should have come this way, she mused, gazing about the woodland which she and Helen Rushton had frequently explored during those few short months when she had resided with her grandfather. She had been contented then, living with her grandfather. But nowhere near as contented as she had been during these past few days living at Rosslair.

The thought, unbidden, came so naturally, so effortlessly that any attempt to persuade herself that it was quite otherwise, that it was merely living in the country again which had made her so blissfully happy, would have been fruitless. She might succeed in fooling others but not herself. She loved Rosslair.... But nowhere near as much as she had by imperceptible degrees come to love its master. There was little point in not facing the simple truth that it was Daniel's reappearance in her life which had resulted in her present wholly satisfied state of mind. But it was a situation that could not...must not continue for very much longer.

Oh, dear God! Why had it taken so long to realise that she had fallen desperately in love with the infuriatingly overbearing, adorable man? She had known right from that very first moment, when they had collided in the inn doorway, and the touch of his hands had left her with such a feeling of well-being, that there was something very singular about him. There was some excuse, she supposed, for not having appreciated just how strong the spark of attraction had been back then, on that bitterly cold day in January. But she ought to have realised long before leaving France that her feelings towards him had gone far beyond that of deep respect and friendship. At the very least she ought to have recognised that first uncomfortable pang of jealousy, when she had witnessed him receiving Josephine Carré's welcoming embrace. And she had experienced it yet again earlier, when she had caught him holding the great love of his life.

Oh, but what could she do? Even if Janet was right, and Julia was totally unworthy of him, there was nothing she could do to prevent a marriage taking place between Daniel and his old love. Shackled by fears that refused to leave her, she couldn't fight to win him...dared not. At least with Julia he might be blessed to live a long and contented life; whereas...

Burying her face in her hands, Katherine refused to give way to tears that might help to relieve the heartache for a while but which could never hope to bring lasting relief to a mind that would be forever tortured with what might have been possible if she had not been such a curse. There would be time enough to weep when she returned to Bath. She would have years to dwell on the happiness she would undoubtedly have attained had it been possible for her to become Mrs Daniel Ross. Life without him would be desolate, have little meaning, but better that than be forced to live with the knowledge that she had been responsible for any mishap befalling him.

The sooner she left Rosslair the better, she reflected, hating the mere thought but accepting there was no alternative. In the meantime she must take great care to behave towards him as she had always done. It could only spell complete disaster if he ever suspected that her feelings for him went any deeper than those of mere…of mere sisterly affection, she told herself, before she suddenly contemplated the dreadful possibility that Daniel, discerning demon that he was, had perhaps already guessed the true state of her heart long before she had herself.

The sound of high-pitched squeals succeeded in penetrating the heart-rending reflections, and a moment later Katherine removed her hands to see something rolling along the ground towards her. She bent to retrieve the object at her feet, and then clearly heard a breathless little voice announce, 'It went this way, Papa.'

A moment later a boy of about seven came scampering through the undergrowth, stopping dead in his tracks when he glimpsed her standing there, blocking the path. 'Would this be what you're looking for?' she asked, holding out the ball, which, after a moment's hesitation, he removed from her outstretched hand.

'Yes, thank you, ma'am,' he answered, before turning his head at the sound of his father's voice. 'I'm over here, Papa!'

A fair-haired gentleman, whom Katherine judged to be five or six years older than Daniel, came striding along the woodland track towards them. He betrayed surprise at first catching sight of her, then his gaze as he drew steadily closer grew very much more intense, his clear grey eyes finally coming to rest on the fiery curls clearly showing beneath her bonnet.

'This lady found my ball, Papa.'

The gentleman glanced down to cast a reassuring smile at his son before his gaze returned to Katherine, once again studying her intently before remarking, 'You are a stranger in these parts, ma'am?'

Only just in time did Katherine remember her role. '*Oui, monsieur.* I am staying for a short time with my cousin, Major Ross.'

The boy's eyes, so very like his father's in both colour and shape, stared up at her, puzzlement clearly discernible in their depths. 'Why are you speaking in that funny way?'

Katherine could quite cheerfully have boxed his ears for noticing that she had not spoken with a marked French accent when she had first addressed him. Fortunately his father did the next best thing by reminding him of his manners. 'James, that is not at all polite. This young lady, unless I much mistake the matter, has recently come from France and is a—er—native of that country.' He reached for Katherine's hand. 'Permit me to introduce myself, *mademoiselle*. My name is Cranford...Charles Cranford. And this young imp is my son James.'

'I am pleased to make your acquaintance, *monsieur*. And you too, James. My name is Louise Durand.'

Katherine had by now guessed that the gentleman with the piercing gaze was none other than the present owner of the house in which her grandfather had once resided, and thought it behoved her to apologise for trespassing on his land.

'Do not give it another thought, *mademoiselle*. The middle of the wood forms the boundary between your cousin's property and mine, but we do not quibble, and are both quite happy to permit the other to walk freely across the entire area.'

His reassuring smile went some way to soften his probing gaze. 'You have walked a goodly distance, *mademoiselle*. Can I not persuade you to come up to the house and partake of some refreshments? My wife would be delighted to make your acquaintance.'

Katherine hesitated. She knew she ought to return to Rosslair without delay, but the invitation to set foot inside her grandfather's old house to see how much it had changed since she had resided there was just too tempting to refuse. Besides which, it would grant her the opportunity to marshal all her resources before coming face to face with Daniel again, for the days ahead would undoubtedly prove the greatest challenge she had ever faced in her life.

Chapter Fourteen

Daniel arrived back at his home shortly before noon. He had remained at the Hall far longer than he had intended, mainly because Julia had seemed reluctant to allow him to take his leave, and had insisted on taking him up to the nursery to see her son. That part of the visit had unquestionably proved to be the most enjoyable. Young Geoffrey was the image of his father in both looks and nature. He was a charming boy, and it had been a pleasure to pass half an hour or so sitting on the nursery floor, keeping him entertained by playing with his toy soldiers.

If only the rest of his visit had passed so agreeably! he mused, dismounting and leaving his horse in the care of the stable-lad. He was forced to admit that by the time he had ridden over to the Hall he had surprisingly wearied of Julia's company. He had found her stilted conversation tiresome in the extreme and her evident curiosity about Katherine, quite frankly, distasteful.

Trying to converse with his uncle, whose hearing had become increasingly impaired since attaining middle age, had not proved particularly satisfying either. Yet he would far rather have preferred to remain in the library, forced to shout his every utterance, than be dragged into the parlour to spend a further half-hour with Julia and her mother who, since becoming a widow four years before, had taken up residence with her daughter at the Hall.

He had not set eyes on Eleanor Melrose since before he had embarked for India, and he had been shocked at the changes he had perceived in her. Although she had never been what one might describe as a vivacious, out-going female, she had seemed a mere shadow of her former self, painfully lachrymose and decidedly jaded.

He well remembered that she was a woman who had always set great store by good manners and correct be-haviour at all times; strict codes of conduct that she had instilled in her sole offspring from an early age. Daniel could well imagine that when Julia's looks began to fade, which undoubtedly they would in time, she would turn into a mirror image of her woebegone mother.

Dear Lord! What a lucky escape he had had when Julia decided to marry his cousin, Daniel reflected, shak-ing his head in wonder as he strode across the yard to-wards the house. Looking back, it was hard to imagine that he had been so set on marrying her himself once, and had been utterly heartbroken when he had discov-ered that she had chosen Simon instead.

One must put it down to the folly of youth, he sup-posed. Thank heavens he had acquired some sound com-mon sense during the intervening years! He and Julia simply wouldn't have suited. He was far too outspoken and brusque for her delicate sensibilities. He needed a female who would not dissolve into floods of tears each time he raised his voice above a whisper and one who, moreover, was not afraid to stand up to him. And thank the Lord he'd found the very little virago for him!

Entering his home by way of the rear entrance, Daniel went striding into the kitchen to discover, much to his surprise, only his housekeeper present, for Katherine had made a point, since her arrival at Rosslair, of always helping Janet prepare both luncheon and dinner.

'Where's Kate?'

'She went out into the garden shortly after you left with Mrs Ross,' she answered, giving the broth a stir. 'I must say, sir, she has worked hard on those rose-beds since she's been here. She's green fingers like your dear grandmother, and no mistake! You can see the difference she's made already.'

'Mmm,' Daniel murmured, running impatient fingers through his thick, slightly waving brown hair, as he experienced a pang of conscience. 'I suppose I ought to be thinking of employing a full-time gardener and general handyman. I can't expect McGann to cope with everything.'

'Now there's a considerate soul for you, Janet!' McGann announced, entering the kitchen, with a pile of logs for the stove, in time to catch his master's final remark.

'If the truth be known, I was thinking more of Katherine than you,' Daniel enlightened him. 'I don't want her working her fingers to the bone attempting to get the garden in order.'

'She enjoys herself out there, sir,' Janet assured him. 'Besides, she ain't one to be idle. If she didn't work in the garden, she'd be doing something else.'

Janet smiled to herself as she detected her master's low growl of disapproval before he went stalking out. She turned in time to see him pass the window, heading in the direction of the garden, and was a little startled when he returned a minute or so later, carrying Katherine's cloak, and looking decidedly grim.

'She isn't there. Are you certain she didn't come back into the house?'

'She might have done,' Janet conceded. 'I'll go and check.'

'No, I'll do it!' Daniel responded curtly, leaving Janet now in little doubt as to his frame of mind.

She exchanged a concerned glance with McGann as she heard her master's raised voice calling Katherine's name filtering through from the hall. 'Dear Lord, I hope nothing has happened. The master did say to keep an eye on her.'

'Yes, damn it!' Daniel snarled, returning to the kitchen. 'So why the hell didn't you?'

'Easy, sir. Easy,' McGann soothed. He had seen the Major rant and rage at raw recruits who had done something foolhardy, but he had never heard him speak so sharply to Janet before. 'There's no saying that Miss Katherine didn't just take it into her head to go off for a wee walk, the day being so nice an' all. You can't expect Janet to watch her every moment.'

'It's all right, McGann.' Although touched by this staunch show of support, Janet was not in the least offended by her master's harsh reprimand. In fact, if it had not been for the qualms she was now experiencing herself over Katherine's well-being, she would have given vent to a whoop of pure joy, for she was more than willing to make allowances for the understandable concern of a man very much in love. 'The master is right. I ought to have kept a better watch over her. I'm sorry, sir.'

Daniel's anger instantly ebbed. 'No, Janet, it is I who ought to apologise.' He placed his arm briefly about her thin shoulders, almost bringing tears to her eyes with the smile he cast down at her. 'I'll leave you to make a thorough search of the house and gardens. McGann, you come with me. We'll search the surrounding countryside. There's no saying that what you suspect is true—the damnable little idiot might well have taken it into her head to go off by herself. I'll skin her alive when I find her!'

Janet was more successful in suppressing a chuckle than McGann who, shoulders shaking, followed the Major out to the yard. But an hour later, when all three reassembled in the kitchen, there wasn't so much as a semblance of a smile on anyone's face, least of all on Daniel's.

He paused in his worried pacing. 'Where the deuce could she have gone? She doesn't know anyone hereabouts now, so she wouldn't have taken it into her head to go visiting the neighbours.'

'Well, I've been thinking about that, sir.' Janet raised troubled eyes to his. 'You don't suppose she had a fancy to visit her grandfather's old place, do you?'

'But that's four miles away, Janet.'

'Not if you cut across the fields, it isn't,' she countered. 'It'd be no more than an hour's stroll.'

After silently conceding that it might be worthwhile checking this out, Daniel asked, 'Do you happen to know if the Cranfords are in residence, Janet?'

'I'm certain Mrs Cranford is there. Her husband has been away in London for the past few weeks, so I understand. He might be back now, though. It's the party next week... Or had you forgotten?'

'I've better things to think about than parties, Janet,' he responded testily, just as a carriage, which seemed vaguely familiar, entered the yard, and a moment later none other than the person whose absence was causing him no little concern alighted from it.

The immense relief Daniel experienced at seeing her completely unharmed was swiftly tempered by a surge of irritation as he watched her trip lightly towards the house, swinging her bonnet to and fro by its ribbons and smiling brightly, just as though she hadn't a care in the world. Her cheerful greeting as she entered the kitchen, swiftly followed by the laughingly uttered hope that she hadn't kept them all waiting for luncheon, only resulted in fuelling his rapidly mounting wrath.

'Where the hell have you been?'

The bellowed demand, humiliatingly clear and belittling, echoed round the large room, leaving no one in any doubt, least of all Katherine, as to his mood. Hands on hips, and now glowering like some ferocious creature about to pounce on its hapless prey, Daniel betrayed no signs of the anguish he had been experiencing only minutes before.

'Kindly do not adopt that dictatorial tone with me, sir,' Katherine told him, chin lifting as she turned to face him squarely. 'When you have managed to regain control of your temper, I shall be only too happy to enlighten you. In the meantime, I shall be in the parlour.' And so saying, she turned on her heels and headed for the door, leaving Daniel almost gaping at her retreating form in astonishment.

He recovered soon enough. 'Did you hear that?' he demanded of neither of his remaining listeners in particular, both of whom were having the utmost difficulty in suppressing smiles at his expression of outrage. 'You come back here at once, you damnable little shrew!' he yelled, striding purposefully across to the door himself.

'I haven't finished with you yet…no, not by a long chalk!'

His threat fell on deaf ears, even though his firm, stalking footsteps did not. Katherine, well aware that he was right behind her, continued to walk calmly into the parlour, and across to the chest in the corner of the large room in order to collect the curtain that she had been sewing the evening before.

She experienced a strange mixture of annoyance and relief. Although she refused to be addressed in such a fashion, and had no intention of tamely kowtowing to such dictatorial behaviour, his intolerable outburst had, she was forced silently to own, made it so very much easier to face him again; had made it a simple matter not to reveal those feelings which she must now strive to keep well hidden from those all too perceptive brown eyes.

'If you have followed me in here to continue bellowing like a bull, I think it best you leave,' she told him, determined to maintain her self-control.

'Damn it, woman!' His knuckles clearly showed white as he grasped the door. 'Who's master here?'

'No one is disputing your authority, Daniel,' Katherine responded, before calmly settling herself in one of the chairs by the hearth. 'My position under this roof, however, evidently is in need of some clarification. I am not your chattel, sir, and I shall not tolerate being spoken to in such a fashion, most especially in front of servants. If you envisage that this will put an undue strain upon you, then I think it best I remove forthwith to the local inn.'

For answer he slammed the door closed, and went stalking over to the decanters. Katherine heard the chink of glass, and could almost feel those brown orbs firing angry darts into the back of her head.

Swiftly suppressing a smile, she concentrated for a moment on threading her needle. 'I can appreciate that we all give vent to our emotions from time to time. And I am no exception.'

'Ha! An understatement if ever there was one!'

She ignored the muttered interruption. 'Even so, unlike you, I do attempt to maintain some control, whereas the rein you hold over your temper possesses no more strength than this sewing yarn.'

A sigh of pure exasperation floated across to the hearth. 'If my outburst…my very understandable outburst, I might add, offended your delicate sensibilities, then you must appreciate that I have not spent the past few years making polite conversation in fashionable drawing-rooms.'

'That is patently obvious,' she swiftly returned, attaining a deal of wicked satisfaction in pointing this out. 'If, however, you have any desire to be included in polite society, you must swiftly acquire at least a few basic manners. Which reminds me, Mrs Cranford hasn't received a reply yet to the invitation she sent you, and particularly requested me to remind you of the party being held at her house next week.'

The hand raising the glass to Daniel's lips checked for a moment. 'So you did go over to your grandfather's old house.'

'Yes,' she admitted. 'I didn't intend to walk so far. I had hoped to be back before you returned.' Out of the corner of her eye, she saw him lower his tall frame into a nearby chair. His expression betrayed clearly enough that he remained in no good humour, but at least he was

no longer looking as black as thunder. 'Did you enjoy
your visit to your uncle?'

The heavy frown descended once more. 'No, damn it,
I did not! My uncle's as deaf as a post. And I cannot
abide insipid female conversation.' He paused to sample
the contents of his glass. Which evidently had a soothing
effect on his temper, for he sounded far more composed
as he added, 'I quite enjoyed the time I spent with the
boy, though.'

Katherine raised her head at this. 'Your late cousin's
son?' Receiving only a nod in response she added, 'Janet
seems to think he's something of a sickly child.'

'Rubbish! Julia fusses too much.' Disapproval was
clearly back in his voice. 'There's nothing wrong with
little Geoffrey. He's a stout little fellow who'll no doubt
live to a ripe old age... At least, I sincerely hope he
does. I have no desire to step into his shoes.'

Katherine did not doubt the truth of this. She knew
Daniel well enough to be sure that possessing a title
would mean little to him. She also realised now that
whatever feelings he still retained for Julia Ross love did
not number among them, and could not help feeling that
it might have been better, at least for her sake, if it had,
for he couldn't have made it clearer by his attitude over
her recent absence that he was not indifferent to her.

'Well, if it's any consolation,' she remarked, swiftly
channelling her thoughts in a new direction, 'I came
away from my visit with mixed feelings too. I thought
Mrs Cranford most charming. She insisted I return here
in their carriage, and she also invited me to the party
next week.' She frowned slightly. 'I'm not too sure
about her husband, though. I found his regard faintly
unnerving.'

Daniel studied her for a moment over the rim of his glass. 'In what way?'

'Oh, I don't know. He just kept staring at me. It made me feel a little uncomfortable,' she admitted, just as the door opened, and Janet entered to inform them that a Mr Ashcroft had arrived and was wishful to see them.

'Ashcroft...?' Daniel's brows snapped together again. 'Never heard of the fellow! Probably here trying to sell me something. Tell him to take himself off!'

'No, wait!' Katherine, placing her sewing to one side, didn't hesitate to countermand the order. 'If it's the person I think it is, I most certainly wish to see him. Ask him to come in, Janet.'

When Daniel watched the slight, middle-aged man, who bore all the appearance of a downtrodden and over-worked lawyer's clerk, enter a few moments later, he thought his suspicions were correct, until Katherine darted forward to clasp the man's bony fingers.

'Oh, it is you, Mr Ashcroft! How happy I am to see that you arrived back safely.'

'And I you, Miss O'Malley,' he assured her, before darting a wary glance at the tall figure who now stood staring frowningly down at him from a position in front of the hearth.

'Are you acquainted with Major Ross, sir?' Katherine enquired, drawing the diffident, middle-aged man forward.

'No, I've not had the pleasure,' he admitted, extending a nervous hand in the direction of the tall man who continued to regard him with faintly hostile eyes. 'But I've heard a great deal about you, sir, from Sir Giles.'

'Ha! Have you, by gad!'

Mr Ashcroft not surprisingly appeared faintly un-nerved by the gruff response, and so Katherine hurriedly intervened. 'Do not pay Major Ross any mind, dear sir. He's in a bad humour, but will recover presently, I assure you.'

Ignoring Daniel's muttered oath, Katherine invited their visitor to take a seat. 'Can I offer you some refreshment? A glass of wine, perhaps?'

'No, thank you, dear young lady. And I must not stay. I came here only to pass on a message from Sir Giles.' Mr Ashcroft risked a fleeting look up at Daniel once again, before fixing his gaze on Katherine's far more amiable countenance. 'You are to stay here with Major Ross, and attend the party Mr and Mrs Cranford are holding on Friday next. I am to pay a brief visit to Mr Cranford as soon as I leave here to apprise him of the situation. Unfortunately he had left London before news of your safe arrival reached us.'

'Ah!' Katherine exclaimed, enlightenment dawning. 'So Sir Giles and Mr Cranford are engaged in the same work, are they?'

'Er—in a manner of speaking, yes, miss,' he admitted, casting yet a further tentative glance in the general direction of the hearth. 'Sir Giles has every intention of making your presence known in the—er—right quarter, as you might say, at the appropriate time, and has taken the precaution of sending two of his best men down here to look after you.'

Betraying great fortitude, he then turned his attention to Daniel. 'Sir Giles wishes me to assure you, sir, that the young lady will be in no danger. You are to make use of the two men who travelled with me from the capital in any capacity you think fit. There will be others arriving soon in the locale, and my sister and I shall ourselves be putting up at the local inn. Needless to say, there must be no contact between us once I leave here.'

'Evidently Sir Giles expects the traitor to act as soon as he knows of Katherine's safe arrival,' Daniel remarked, after tossing the remaining contents of his glass down his throat.

'Sir Giles knows how to play the game, sir. He's refining every detail at this very moment. The men he's sent down are merely a precaution, sir, nothing more,' Mr Ashcroft didn't hesitate to assure him. 'Sir Giles knew you'd expect nothing less. The traitor will be given insufficient time to act before next Friday. He'll need to make contact with his associates. But Sir Giles is convinced that if an attempt to…to abduct Miss O'Malley will be made, it will occur on the day of the party, perhaps even at the event itself. Time is not on the traitor's side, sir. He must prevent Sir Giles from escorting Miss O'Malley to London.'

Daniel appeared decidedly grim, and Katherine was experiencing certain misgivings now that all the scheming and planning were showing signs of achieving a result, but steadfastly refused to betray her feelings of unease. 'Then we must all be patient and wait for events to unfold.'

'Believe me when I tell you, Miss O'Malley, that your safety is Sir Giles's main concern,' he reiterated. 'Try as best you can to continue as normal.' Mr Ashcroft made to leave, but then bethought himself of something else. 'By the by, I've brought your trunk of clothes from London, miss. I'll instruct the two men I'm leaving here to carry it into the house for you.'

'Oh, you darling man!' Katherine darted forward to place a kiss on Mr Ashcroft's thin cheek, which had the effect of sending him quite pink with pleasure before he took his leave.

Daniel, unable to suppress a smile, went over to the

decanters to replenish his glass. 'How typical of a woman! At a time like this the only thing that concerns you is clothes.'

'But of course! It will be sheer bliss to don my own garments again. Besides which, Daniel, you know yourself we've nothing to worry about for the next few days.'

'Possibly not,' he conceded. 'At least now I've no qualms about sending a note to my uncle accepting his invitation to accompany him to the local market town to view some livestock next Friday morning. And those two men will certainly come in handy about the place. For a start, I shall set one to work in the garden to keep a permanent eye on you and make sure you don't take it into your head to go wandering off again.'

'Do so, by all means. I shall enjoy the company,' she assured him, refusing to become nettled. 'It's just a pity Sir Giles didn't think to send us a female.'

Daniel raised his brows in surprise. 'Not necessary. Janet can keep an eye on you whilst you're indoors.'

'And how typical of a man!' Katherine parried, casting him a look of exasperation before reaching for the door-handle. 'Janet has far too much to do to watch me all day. It's high time, Daniel Ross, that you sorted out your domestic situation. Janet is in desperate need of help about the place. The sooner this house has a mistress to take charge the better!'

Smiling tenderly, Daniel gazed down into his glass. 'It has already acquired the only one it will ever have whilst I remain master here,' he murmured, the instant Katherine had departed, closing the door quietly behind her.

Chapter Fifteen

'Can I not persuade you to step into the house for a glass of burgundy before you set off home, my boy?' Sir Joshua's invitation was heard even by the footman who emerged from the house in order to assist his master to alight from the carriage.

Daniel hesitated. The visit to the market town had proved surprisingly enjoyable. Not only had he been impressed by the high standard of farm stock offered for sale, but he had come upon a number of neighbours whom he had not seen in a very long time, and had received several invitations to dine. He was eager to return to Rosslair and tell Katherine about the trip, but decided that that could wait a while longer. Sir Joshua didn't socialise to any great extent these days, his hearing having become an increasing handicap, and Daniel had gained the distinct impression that his uncle pined for a little masculine company from time to time.

'That sounds a fine idea,' he responded, accompanying him into the house. 'But I can't stay for too long. There are matters I must attend to back home. And there's the party at the Cranfords' place this evening, remember?'

'Going to be a large affair, by all accounts,' Sir Joshua remarked, before his attention was claimed by his butler who informed him that he had a visitor awaiting him in the parlour.

Although his hearing might be sadly impaired, there was absolutely nothing amiss with his mental faculties, as he proved when he entered the comfortable room, and recognised at once the fashionably attired young gentleman whom his daughter-in-law had been entertaining during his absence.

'Why, it's young George Gifford, ain't it?' he announced loudly, as his unexpected visitor rose from the chair to shake his outstretched hand. 'Some relation of Lord Waverley's, if my memory serves me correctly.'

'Y-yes, that's r-right, sir,' he responded, casting a penetrating glance beyond his host's left shoulder at the spot where Daniel stood.

'Are you acquainted with my nephew, Major Ross?'

'N-no, I've not had the p-pleasure, Sir Joshua.'

Daniel's eyes narrowed as the dandified sprig took his outstretched hand in a surprisingly firm clasp. 'We have never been introduced, Mr Gifford, but I feel certain that I've seen you somewhere before.'

'Quite p-possibly, sir. I've been s-staying in London with Lord Waverley for the p-past few weeks. Perhaps it was there.'

'No, I do not think so,' Daniel countered, accepting the glass of wine Julia held out to him. 'I haven't been in the capital for several weeks.'

'No, been gadding about across the Channel, would you believe?' Sir Joshua put in, seating himself in his favourite chair and staring owlishly up at his nephew, who had positioned himself by the hearth. 'And what's this Julia has been telling me about you bringing back a young female relation of yours?'

Daniel saw Julia's eyes turn swiftly in his direction, but it was the sudden arresting look he perceived in Mr Gifford's dark orbs as the young man resumed his seat which momentarily captured his attention. 'Yes, dear Louise is still with me, I'm delighted to say. I'm escorting her to the party tonight, as it happens.'

'Look forward to meeting the gel,' Sir Joshua declared, before sampling his wine. 'Can't recall your ever mentioning her before, though.'

'No?' Daniel shrugged. 'Well, as I believe I explained to Julia, Louise and I are only distantly related. My grandmother did have a few relations who, like herself, managed to escape the Terror.'

'Damned fine woman, your grandmother,' Sir Joshua announced. 'I was fond of her.'

Daniel's expression softened noticeably. 'I'm certain you will like Louise Durand when you meet her, sir. She is very like my grandmother in many ways.'

'But not in looks. That you must own,' Julia, much to Daniel's annoyance, was not reticent to point out. 'Why, she has flaming red hair!'

Plainly she remained sceptical about the kinship, and Daniel, although continuing to gaze across at his uncle, was conscious of her staring fixedly in his direction, as though expecting him to explain the precise relationship. He found himself experiencing a resurgence of the irritation he had felt when he had accompanied her back to the Hall earlier in the week. Even had he wished to do so he could not at this juncture reveal Katherine's true identity, but he experienced no reluctance whatsoever in revealing the depths of his feelings towards her.

'Her similarity to my grandmother is in character, not

looks. She is quite simply a breath of fresh air. Her mere presence under the roof has turned my house into a home. I could never be content if she remained away from Rosslair for any length of time.'

Unlike his daughter-in-law, who looked as though she had just received a sharp slap across the face, Sir Joshua positively beamed with delight. 'Well, if that's the way of it, my boy, I sincerely do look forward to meeting the girl!' He then returned his attention to his unexpected guest, who was staring thoughtfully down into the contents of his glass, and asked him where he was putting up.

'W-with the C-cranfords, sir,' he answered with a start, as though he had been locked in a world of his own. 'Set out y-yesterday evening. I-I've never been in this part of the world b-before, and wished to see s-something of the countryside. My c-cousin should be arriving any time now.'

'Is Waverley coming down?' Sir Joshua appeared mildly surprised. 'I would have thought, with all this business flaring up again across the Channel, he would have remained in the capital.' He frowned as he continued to stare across at his young visitor. 'Isn't your cousin connected in some way with the War Office? Or am I thinking of someone else?'

'He w-was once, sir, I believe. So too was Viscount Davenham. And he intends to be at the party tonight. Sir Giles Osborne also means to attend, so I've heard.'

'Good gad!' Sir Joshua's bushy, greying brows rose this time. 'If that's the case they can't be taking recent events very seriously.'

'That I c-couldn't say.' Quickly finishing off his wine, Mr Gifford rose to his feet. 'I'd b-better be getting back now, sir. Thought I'd just call to see you as I was in the area, and I l-look forward to seeing you again at the p-party tonight.'

'Are you well acquainted with him, Uncle?' Daniel asked, after Julia, still appearing rather shaken, accompanied Mr Gifford from the room.

Sir Joshua shook his head. 'Met him only once before, when I travelled up to town with Cranford last month and we dined together at our club. Waverley was there. He introduced us.'

Daniel could not rid himself of the suspicion that he had seen the young man somewhere before, and began to experience a decidedly uneasy feeling. There was just something artificial about him. His stuttering speech made him appear nervy, and his fashionable attire slightly dandified, but there was no timidity about the directness of his gaze. 'Was Sir Giles Osborne at the club that night, by any chance?'

'Why, I do believe he was, yes! And Lord Davenham too. We all sat at the same table, playing cards. Are you acquainted with him?'

Daniel's eyes narrowed speculatively. His uncle had travelled to London with Cranford round about the time he himself had set forth on his journey to France. Could it possibly have been that night at the club that Sir Giles had told his totally fabricated tale about Justine leaving certain documents in the hands of a lawyer? It was certainly a possibility, and if he had, then it was reasonable to assume that he suspected someone seated at that table of being the traitor.

Cranford and Sir Joshua were certainly out of the reckoning. Sir Joshua had never had any connection with the War Office. Furthermore, Sir Giles would never have selected Daniel himself to aid him if he had suspected for a moment that Sir Joshua was a traitor. Their relationship was just too close. Gifford at twenty-three, or four at most, was too young to be the traitor, although he could well be in league now with the man Sir Giles was determined to unearth. So that just left Davenham and Waverley, both of whom had had some connection with the War Office, and both of whom had been at White's on that particular night. More disturbing still was that both men were to be among the guests at the Cranfords' party that evening.

'I'm not acquainted with either Davenham or Waverley,' Daniel admitted. 'But I do know Sir Giles.'

'Ah, yes. Now you mention it, I do believe Osborne remarked upon the fact,' Sir Joshua disclosed, before his frown returned. 'Deuced odd that young Gifford should put himself to the trouble of paying me a visit on so brief an acquaintance, especially as he didn't seem inclined to remain very long after we'd returned, don't you agree?'

'Perhaps he didn't wish to outstay his welcome,' Daniel responded, staring intently at an imaginary spot on the carpet. Or maybe he discovered what he came here to find out, he added silently to himself.

That evening, while she busied herself getting ready for the party, Katherine succeeded in maintaining a flow of light-hearted conversation with Janet who, showing no little expertise, was arranging those striking auburn locks in a more elaborate style for the occasion. Yet beneath the carefree exterior Katherine felt as if she were being ripped in two. She knew her stay at Rosslair was rapidly drawing to an end, and she found the mere thought of leaving excruciating, while at the same time she knew it was for the best, for she was not made of iron, and sooner or later she would buckle under the strain of striving to keep her feelings towards the master of the house well hidden.

She was under no illusions that this evening would prove to be the greatest trial of all, for not only must she continue behaving like some fond sister towards Daniel, she must also adopt the role which Sir Giles expected her to play: a double burden, but one she refused to attempt to postpone. So, after taking one last look at her overall appearance in the full length mirror, she picked up her shawl, and left the room.

She discovered Daniel awaiting her in the hall. Although he possessed some fine clothes, he hadn't taken the trouble to acquire any fashionable evening apparel since his return to England the previous year. Consequently he had chosen to don, of all things, the Rifleman-green dress uniform he had worn on the occasion of her cousin's engagement party, which she found a faintly poignant coincidence, for she had chosen to wear none other than the gown she had worn on that particular occasion.

Daniel turned as he detected her light footfall on the stairs, and smiled wryly as he cast appreciative eyes over her faultless appearance. 'I have seen you wearing some charming dresses during these past days, Kate, but I think that particular gown will always retain a very special place in my memory long after it has been consigned to the rag box.'

She didn't pretend to misunderstand. 'Yes, it is somewhat ironic, is it not, that we should have chosen to dress in these particular garments this evening?' She came to stand before him, her eyes gently teasing as she stared up at those ruggedly attractive features. 'I hope it isn't an omen and we end the evening by being at outs with each other.'

She had intended the remark as a joke, but it was clear that he wasn't amused. 'You do not have to go through with this, Kate. It isn't too late to change your mind. No one would think any less of you if you did cry off.'

One would have needed to be deaf not to have detected the note of deep concern in his voice, and blind not to see the worry etched in each rugged contour of that beloved face, which would remain imprinted in her memory until her last breath.

He had been in a strangely subdued mood since he arrived home early in the afternoon, after his visit to the market town. He had openly admitted to enjoying the visit, and yet something had occurred to trouble him during his absence from home. 'I should,' she countered softly. 'I would be a liar if I said I wasn't a little apprehensive. But you know that Mr Ashcroft assured us both that I will be guarded throughout the entire evening.'

The troubled expression remained. Clearly he was unconvinced, but Katherine had more faith. 'Sir Giles has done everything humanly possible to ensure my safety thus far, Daniel,' she reminded him. 'He could not have provided me with a better protector than you. If our roles were reversed, I know that you would see this thing through to the end.'

He didn't attempt to deny it, and yet she sensed that he was suppressing the strong desire to sweep her up in his arms, carry her back up the stairs and lock her in her room. He was more than capable of doing it, too! Surprisingly, though, all he did was merely raise his hands and take a gentle hold of her upper arms. 'Then I would ask only one thing. At the risk of receiving a second rebuff, my precious virago, will you dance with me this evening?'

For several moments Katherine was obliged to grasp

her bottom lip between her teeth to stop it from trembling, as a surge of conflicting emotions, not least of which was a searing sense of shame, came perilously close to crushing the praiseworthy self-control she had managed to exert over herself during these past days. Only the tenuous thread of determination she still managed to retain enabled her to meet the tender gaze of the man she had once so naïvely held in such foolish contempt.

Raising her own hands, she placed them on the shoulders of the black-braided dark green jacket that suited him so well. 'I would be so very honoured to stand up with you tonight...my grasshopper.'

For one heart-stopping moment she thought he might kiss her, and feared she could never summon up enough will to resist if he tried. Fortunately her reserves of resolve were not further depleted, for McGann, forcing them to part, came striding into the hall to inform them that the carriage was ready and waiting at the door.

'I wish you'd let me come with you, sir,' he remarked with a hopeful glance in his master's direction.

'No, McGann.' Daniel's voice brooked no argument. 'Those two bodyguards Sir Giles sent have proved reliable. They will provide sufficient protection for the journey. Besides, I want you to keep watch here, to look after Janet, just in case we should receive an unwanted visitor.'

Mention of the housekeeper thankfully enabled Katherine to turn her thoughts in a new direction, as it brought forcibly to mind a conversation she had had with Janet earlier in the day, and prevented her from dwelling on the fact, as she went outside to the waiting carriage, that in all probability she would never again set foot in the house which she had come perilously close to treating as her very own home.

'Janet wishes to retire, Daniel,' she enlightened him, as the carriage began to move out of the yard. 'Apparently your father promised her one of the cottages he had constructed on his land,' she went on when he made no comment.

'If she said my father promised her that, then I for one do not doubt it,' he eventually remarked, appearing more subdued than ever.

'I can appreciate your reluctance in parting with her,' she responded softly, understanding his feelings perfectly. 'Good housekeepers are hard to find, and Janet is a treasure. But you must take her wishes into consideration. She's no longer young and the work is too much for her.'

'Yes, you're right, of course,' he agreed. 'Do you happen to know of anyone suitable who could fill her shoes?'

Oh, yes—she knew of someone, sure enough. She knew of the ideal replacement. But not for the world would she ever part with her dear Bridie, not even for him. Besides, she had the feeling that she was going to need that unfailingly loyal Irish woman's loving support during the weeks, months, maybe even years ahead.

'You must be aware by now, Kate, that I value your opinion,' Daniel prompted, when the view from the window appeared to have captured her interest. 'I wouldn't have dreamt of purchasing this comfortable carriage and team of fine horses if I hadn't received your full approval.'

'Liar,' she said softly, while praying her resolve, which was weakening with every passing second, did not crumple completely. 'You had made up your mind to purchase this fine turnout the instant you set your eyes upon it. And you'll manage to acquire a housekeeper without any help from me, too.' You are going to have to do so, she added silently.

Blessedly the journey to her grandfather's old house was soon accomplished, and Katherine was able, with a reasonable degree of success, to concentrate her thoughts on the vital role she had been entrusted to play that night.

No sooner had they been greeted by their host and hostess than Sir Giles Osborne approached them, appearing remarkably composed. 'Well, *mes enfants*, all goes well, I think,' he purred silkily.

'And it had better continue to do so,' Daniel muttered at his most grim, the effect of which was to bring one of those rare smiles to the taciturn baronet's thin-lipped mouth.

'I do not doubt that my days on this earth would be well and truly numbered if, indeed, it does not prove to be the case,' Sir Giles parried before instructing Daniel to go away and mix with his friends and neighbours. 'You may safely leave your so charming cousin in my care.

'Well, how goes it with you, Mademoiselle Durand?' he enquired, when Daniel, much to Katherine's surprise, did as bidden. 'I trust you didn't find the journey from France too—er—fatiguing, child?'

'It was certainly memorable,' she answered, refusing to divulge more of what for her would undoubtedly prove to be the happiest period in her life.

Sir Giles's eyes glinted with a flicker of amusement. 'Knowing the good Major as I do, I do not doubt it,' he murmured. 'Your ordeal, however, will not last for much longer. I have every expectation that an attempt to abduct you will take place this evening. Have no fear, child. Even as we speak, your every movement is being closely monitored by my people. We have not much time,' he went on hurriedly, 'for unless I much mistake the matter there is a certain young gentleman about to request you to dance with him. Do so. Refuse the company of no one. You may safely even promenade in the garden, for I have several men stationed outside. When the attempt comes, do not put up the least resistance. Be assured you will not be in unfriendly hands for long.'

Although Sir Giles had sounded supremely confident, Katherine experienced a moment's disquiet as she stepped out on to the dance floor. Undoubtedly the traitor was here in the room, watching her every move, studying her features to see if indeed she did bear some resemblance to the young Frenchwoman whose life he had not hesitated to extinguish four years before. It went without saying that he would as readily put a period to hers also.

Resisting the temptation to gaze about her at the fashionably attired gentlemen lining the walls, Katherine did her best to maintain her role by speaking in a marked French accent to the diffident young man who had asked her to dance. So determined was she to adhere to Sir Giles's instructions that she refused none of the gallants who subsequently requested her as a partner and, when the evening was almost half over, even went so far as to step outside with a dashing young cavalry officer in a scarlet coat to take an exploratory stroll about that section of the garden which had been illuminated for the occasion by brightly coloured lanterns.

Thankfully nothing untoward occurred even then. Unfortunately the relief she experienced was short-lived, for the first person she glimpsed on returning to the salon was Daniel, heading purposefully towards her to claim her hand for the supper-dance.

All at once she felt as if all eyes instantly turned in their direction as they took to the floor. She was being incredibly foolish, of course, she told herself, and even if it was true, it was possibly owing to the fact that they made a striking couple in their corresponding dark green attire. Sadly she was not so successful in thrusting from her mind the realisation that this was the first and possibly the last time she would ever stand up with the man who would always possess her heart.

Forced yet again to call upon those rapidly depleting reserves of resolve, she somehow managed a semblance of a smile as Daniel began to swirl her about the dance-floor with remarkable grace for a man of his size.

'You never cease to amaze me, my big cousin,' she announced, maintaining quite beautifully the false accent. 'Where on earth did you learn to dance so well? On the battlefields out in the Peninsula, I suppose?'

Clearly he noticed nothing false in the teasing manner, for he did not hesitate to respond in kind. 'Naturally. One needs to be nimble of foot to dodge bullets.'

Although the foolish response was spoken lightly enough, she could not fail to detect the underlying tension in him. 'Have you received further instructions from Sir Giles?'

'Yes, damn his eyes! I've been told to keep away from you as much as possible.'

'Then perhaps we ought not to be dancing now.'

'Yes, we should,' he countered, his tone becoming increasingly clipped. 'And I've told the old rogue that I've every intention of escorting you in to supper.'

Knowing him as she did, Katherine didn't suppose for

a moment that he had been unduly polite when he had made his intentions perfectly plain. 'Sir Giles knows what he's about, Daniel. You cannot deny that he's shrewd. He did not say as much, but I gained the distinct impression that the man he's after is indeed among the guests this evening.'

'Oh, yes, he's here right enough, my angel,' Daniel confirmed, after neatly avoiding a collision with the dashing young officer who had escorted Katherine outside a short time before, and who was now twirling his partner about the room with far more zest than grace. 'And, unless I much mistake the matter, that devil Osborne now knows precisely who he is too. He's certainly not been idle during these past weeks.'

'Admit it, Daniel!' she prompted. 'You've a grudging respect for the man.'

'Ha!' he scoffed. 'I'd sooner trust a snake!' He saw the hint of scepticism in the turquoise eyes gazing up at him, and relented. 'He knows his business—I'll give him that. And he's taken every precaution to ensure your safety. If I wasn't firmly convinced of it, you wouldn't be here now.'

Daniel cast a brief glance over at one corner of the room, where their host stood conversing with several of his guests. 'Cranford, as we both know, is in the old demon's confidence. It wouldn't surprise me to discover that he's being groomed to step into Osborne's shoes when the time comes for Sir Giles to retire. And Cranford, I noticed, has engaged extra staff for this occasion.'

Until that moment Katherine had not paid too much attention to the three footmen moving about the room, bearing trays of champagne. 'Then I've truly nothing to worry about. But I'd dearly love to know who the traitor is.'

'I'm afraid I cannot help you there,' Daniel admitted. 'Cranford may know, but I doubt too many others are in Sir Giles's confidence. I'm certainly not. But you can bet your sweet life our traitor is among the pot-bellied peerage here tonight, high up on the social ladder. That, I suspect, is why Osborne is so keen to catch him here, in this quiet backwater, where there will be few witnesses to the event. It goes without saying that if Osborne is successful, the whole business will be hushed up. That is how these people work. The traitor's identity will never become generally known.'

Katherine considered that, for someone who belonged to the landed gentry, Daniel betrayed precious little respect for his own class. 'If what you surmise is true, then perhaps it behoves me to attempt to encourage those middle-aged roués present to partner me in a dance.'

'Don't be so naïve, girl!' he scolded, clearly annoyed that she would even contemplate doing such a thing. 'It will avail you nothing if you tried,' he went on in a milder tone. 'You don't suppose for a moment the villain would risk exposure by attempting anything himself, do you? No, he'll have others here who will do his dirty work for him if he suspects you do indeed pose a threat, and that you might well prove to be none other than Justine Baron's sister.'

As no attempt had been made to abduct her thus far Katherine could not help thinking that the traitor had not been duped, and didn't know whether to feel relieved or disappointed to think that all Sir Giles's planning and that eventful flight from the French capital had been in vain. All the same, she could never feel sorry she had been involved in the venture, even though she very much feared that to her dying day she would be tortured by bittersweet memories of the man who was now swirling her so expertly round the room.

As the dance drew to an end Katherine, desperately striving not to dwell on what undoubtedly would be her barren future, allowed Daniel to lead her across the hall into the dining-room, where a large number of guests had already gathered to enjoy the delicious supper.

She might have wished that he had not chosen to join his uncle's party, whom she had noticed were the last guests to arrive, for although she did take an instant liking to Sir Joshua, she was under sufficient strain already to maintain the pretence of light-heartedness, without having to cope with his probing questions into the exact relationship between his nephew and herself. Like Daniel, she found Mrs Melrose's polite utterances rather insipid. Worse still was Julia's faintly cool reception. Having experienced the noxious emotion herself, Katherine could now recognise jealousy without difficulty when she saw it. Evidently Daniel's former love now viewed her as a rival. How little the woman knew!

Fortunately Katherine was not forced to endure the ordeal for too long, for no sooner had several couples begun to drift back to the large salon than the gentleman who had first claimed her for his partner appeared at her side again, with a stuttered reminder that she had promised him a second dance.

She couldn't recall doing any such thing; nor could she even remember the young gentleman's name. Nevertheless she did not think twice about returning with him to the salon, where couples were already taking up positions for a set of country dances.

'You must forgive me, *monsieur*, but I have been introduced to so many people this evening that I am having a little difficulty in recalling your name.'

'G-Gifford, ma'am…George G-Gifford. I-I'm here with the gentleman who is to s-sponsor me during the f-forthcoming Season.'

Katherine couldn't imagine that the event would turn out to be an overwhelming success, given the young man's evident shyness and painful stutter. It wasn't that he was ill-looking. In fact, some women might consider him quite handsome, and yet she couldn't help thinking that the hard, dark eyes seemed oddly at variance with the boyish good looks and diffident manner.

Just as the musicians struck up a chord, Katherine noticed Daniel enter the room, with Julia clinging possessively to his arm. She noticed him staring fixedly in her direction, with an almost frozen look on his face, as though he had just received a severe shock. She did her utmost to thrust his odd expression from her mind and concentrate on her own partner, managing with a reasonable amount of success to converse with him whenever they came together in the set. At least Mr Gifford proved to be a graceful dancer, so it came as something of a surprise when he managed to step on the hem of her gown, just as the dance was drawing to a close.

'Oh, I am so s-sorry, *mademoiselle*. I have torn y-your gown. W-will you permit me to escort you to the ladies' withdrawing-room? S-so clumsy of me.'

Katherine assured him that there was no need to put himself to the trouble, and that she could find her own way without assistance to the bedchamber their hostess had set aside for the purpose. She discovered him at her side all the same, when she slipped out into the deserted hall. It was then that she sensed the unassuming young gentleman was not quite what he seemed, the split second before his fingers grasped her arm just above the elbow, and she was propelled with considerable force towards the room which had once functioned as her grandfather's library.

Although her every instinct urged her in those first heart-stopping moments to reach out for the vase on a nearby table and bring it down hard on Mr Gifford's head, or at the very least let out a scream for help, she paid heed to Sir Giles's warning and didn't attempt to put up even a token resistance. Naturally it came as no surprise, after Mr Gifford had flung wide the door, and had almost thrust her into the darkened room, to discover a burly figure lurking in the shadows, ready with lengths of rope and a gag which he proceeded to put to immediate use.

'You know what to do.' There was no hint of a stutter in Mr Gifford's voice now, and his features were hardened by a look of pure malice, a look Katherine felt certain she had seen on someone's face in the not too distant past.

That was it! she suddenly realised. That was precisely what Daniel had been attempting to convey a few minutes before. He had, she felt certain, suddenly recognised Gifford. But from where? Where had they run across him? She turned her head, but before she had a chance to study his malevolent expression more closely, a hood was thrust over her head.

Tossed over a brawny shoulder, she was then carried from the house by way of the glass-panelled door which her grandfather had had installed to allow more light into the room and to grant swift access to the garden. Unfortunately this section of garden was quite separate from that part which had been lit so prettily for the occasion, and was not visible from the windows of the salon where the party was taking place. It was only a matter of a few yards, she clearly remembered, before one reached the shrubbery, beyond which ran a narrow lane, wide enough for a carriage.

Her perilous situation suddenly hit her with frightening clarity. Throughout her flight from France she had never experienced real fear, simply because Daniel had been with her. But he wasn't with her now. Bound and gagged, she was as helpless as a new-born babe and couldn't possibly escape without help. If Sir Giles's well laid plans went wrong, and her captor succeeded in getting her away unseen, then her situation was dire indeed.

She was not unduly surprised when her abductor made directly for the shrubbery. Nor was she astonished to detect the chinking of a harness a minute or two later before she was bundled none too gently on to the floor of a carriage. She felt it sway slightly, as though he was attempting to enter. Sounds of a scuffle quickly followed, a sickening thud and a groan. Then the vehicle swayed again as someone succeeded in entering this time.

Her companion did not attempt to move or speak until the equipage had turned on to the main road, then hands slid beneath her arms, lifting her on to the seat, and the bonds securing her wrists and ankles were swiftly removed. The gentleness of her companion's actions was enough to convince her that she was now perfectly safe, undoubtedly under the protection of one of Sir Giles's own people, and yet with the best will in the world she could not stop her hand from trembling as she pulled off the hood and removed the gag. Then she found herself gaping like a half-wit, for her rescuer was none other than Mr Ashcroft.

'Are you all right, my dear?' he enquired. 'I trust the blackguard wasn't too rough with you.'

'I was urged by Sir Giles not to put up a struggle,

which was possibly why I came through the ordeal relatively unscathed,' she admitted, rubbing the circulation back into her sore wrists. 'Though if I'm honest, I'd be forced to admit that it went against the grain somewhat for me not to attempt to put up at least a token resistance.'

'I'm glad you did not. You're in no danger now,' Mr Ashcroft assured her gently. 'We've had men scouting the area for days. Earlier in the evening, when this carriage was spotted drawing up in the lane, we felt certain that an attempt would be made tonight to abduct you by way of the side entrance. You were never in any real danger. Needless to say one of our own people is now tooling this vehicle. The original driver and the scoundrel who carried you from the house have been taken into custody. The rest we can safely leave to Sir Giles.'

A hundred questions sprang into Katherine's mind, but she found herself asking only one. 'Where are you taking me—back to Rosslair?'

'We are to make a brief stop at the inn in order to collect my sister. Until Sir Giles has located the whereabouts of every member of the spy network, you are to remain safely hidden,' Mr Ashcroft responded. 'It is better that you do not return to Major Ross's home.'

'Yes,' Katherine agreed hollowly, 'it would be much safer...for all concerned...if I did not return there.'

Chapter Sixteen

'This is utterly insupportable!' Daniel declared, after examining the several letters McGann had collected that morning from the receiving office, and discovering no word yet again from either Katherine or Sir Giles. 'I would far rather face a French column on the field of battle than endure this intolerable waiting a moment longer!'

'Oh, dear. The Major's blood's up,' McGann whispered, joining Janet at the table. 'Very bad sign, that. You mark my words, there'll be trouble afore long.'

'Shush,' she hissed, before turning her attention back to her master, who had begun to pace up and down, which he was inclined to do whenever angry or upset. 'But, sir, you know what Sir Giles said, when he came here on the morning after the party to collect Miss Katherine's belongings,' she reminded him in an attempt to soothe his evidently mounting ire.

Although she had never perfectly understood the precise nature of the work in which Katherine and her master had been engaged, Janet did know that they had been involved in something very secret on behalf of the government. 'The good gentleman did say that Miss Katherine was in safe hands and would remain so until the business be cleared up completely.'

'But it's been over a month, Janet,' Daniel pointed out, not in the least mollified. 'I should have heard something by now.' He resumed his restless pacing. 'That old fox is hiding something. I sense it. And if I discover one hair of my darling girl's beautiful head has been harmed, I'll take the greatest pleasure in breaking every bone in Osborne's body!'

'Oh, dear. He means it an' all,' McGann confirmed, *sotto voce*.

'It's all my fault, of course,' Daniel continued, ignoring the interruption. 'I should never have agreed to Osborne taking her away from here.' He paused yet again in his perambulations to run impatient fingers through his hair. 'Furthermore I should have declared myself when we were in France. But no, I foolishly decided to do the gentlemanly thing and not put more pressure on her by making her feel uncomfortable.'

Janet cast McGann a secretive little smile. 'We know well enough how fond you are of her, sir.'

'Fond…? Ha! A most inappropriate word, Janet! I'm damnably sure I cannot live without her… At least I'll never be wholly content unless she's by my side.'

Daniel joined them at the table, his expression softening marginally. 'She's a brave little soul. She saved my life, you know?'

It was plain that they did not know. McGann recovered from the shock first. 'Well, to be sure, 'tis no more than you'd expect. The girl's got good Irish blood flowing through her veins, so she has.'

'She's Anglo-Irish, McGann,' Daniel reminded him softly. 'And what's more, she's mine.'

He rose again abruptly, resolve etched in each rugged

contour of his face. 'And by God, she's coming home, back here where she belongs!'

Although Katherine clearly heard the click of the door and then the familiar footfall on the carpet, she continued to stare through the bedchamber window at the view upon which she had absently gazed too often during these past few weeks, and one which she would have had the utmost difficulty in describing if asked to do so.

Daily she was becoming increasingly uninterested in the sights and sounds about her, and although she remained powerless to fight off the debilitating lethargy that continued to hold her firmly in its grasp, at least she retained innate good manners enough to accept the fact that she could not remain as a guest in Sir Giles Osborne's house for very much longer.

'Bridie, I believe it's time we were thinking of returning to Bath,' she announced, in a voice which distinctly lacked any vestige of enthusiasm. 'Perhaps Sir Giles will be kind enough to put his travelling carriage at our disposal. If not, we must make arrangements to hire a post-chaise.'

Bridie regarded her young mistress in silence, at a complete loss to know what to do for the best. She had helped Katherine through many heartbreaking periods, but she had never seen her young mistress more desolate than this.

Contracting influenza from Sir Giles's sister had naturally not helped the situation. Nevertheless, Bridie had known the instant she had set foot inside the house that Katherine was not herself. Her young mistress might have succeeded in concealing her bouts of weeping from Sir Giles and Miss Mary Osborne, but she herself had easily detected the telltale signs and had guessed the truth even before she had heard Katherine call out that certain someone's name in her sleep.

She knew, perhaps better than anyone else, just how steadfastly determined Katherine had been during the past years not to become too attached to another living soul in an attempt to protect herself from further searing hurt. She also knew that a very special gentleman had succeeded in breaking down those defences, and that at some point during their six-week separation her young mistress had fallen deeply in love.

She regarded the slender figure staring resolutely out of the window in some concern. If this show of total apathy was the result of her young mistress's love not being returned, then Bridie did not doubt that Katherine would eventually begin to mend. She very much feared, though, that the opposite was true, and that Major Daniel Ross was every bit as much in love with Katherine as she was with him.

Placing the jug of lemonade down on the table, she noticed the contents of the breakfast tray, which she had brought up earlier, were virtually untouched. 'Would you be looking at that now! You've hardly eaten a mouthful,' she scolded gently. 'How you suppose you'll have strength enough to make the journey back to Bath, the good Lord only knows! Why, there's more fat in Cook's dripping-tray than there is on you now, Miss Kate.'

'I wasn't hungry. I'll no doubt eat a bite for luncheon. Do not fuss so, Bridie.'

'You'll need to eat more than a bite to put the weight back on,' she returned sharply, but knew that it would avail her nothing to pursue the matter, and in her young mistress's present state badgering her was likely to do more harm than good. 'Well, at least when you do return to Bath you won't be plagued with Miss Mountjoy's company for too long. She said she'd remain in the house until you'd returned. But it's my belief she's made up her mind to live with her sister.'

Even this piece of encouraging news failed to elicit a reaction, so Bridie didn't waste her breath in further conversation. Instead, she picked up the tray and was about to leave, when the sound of a thunderous hammering filtered into the room. 'Now, who do you suppose that might be, pounding on a gentleman's front door in such an ill-bred fashion?'

Once again receiving no response, Bridie went out in time to see a tall figure, dressed in riding garb, step into the hall. The butler evidently recognised him, for the high-ranking servant went immediately into the library. Before she had descended the staircase, the visitor was being shown into the book-lined room, and the butler was closing the door, but not before Bridie heard a deep, attractive voice, both clear and carrying, demand, 'Where is she, Osborne? What have you done with my darling girl?'

Sir Giles, who had immediately risen from his favourite chair by the hearth, certainly didn't appear in the least discomposed by his visitor's blunt manner and decidedly hostile expression. 'My dear Ross! What a pleasure it is to see you! Just a passing visit, I imagine. Can I offer you some refreshment…? A glass of burgundy, perhaps?'

'Be careful, Osborne,' Daniel warned with dangerous restraint. 'My patience is by no stretch of the imagination limitless.'

'No, forbearance was never your strong suit, was it, my dear boy?' Sir Giles swiftly raised one bony, long-fingered hand in a gesture of surrender. 'All right....all right! Miss O'Malley is here.'

'Then why the devil didn't you let me know?' Daniel demanded, relieved but not one iota appeased. 'You promised you would once the business was completely cleared up. And you cannot tell me you haven't caught every last one of 'em by now.' The curl to his lip betrayed his contempt. 'I saw that damned piece in the newspaper: *It is with the deepest regret that we announce the deaths of The Right Hon. Lord W——y and his cousin Mr George G——d. Their bodies were discovered after an intensive search, et cetera et cetera—* Ha!' Daniel scoffed. 'By the time you'd finished prising information out of them, there's no way on God's earth you could have let them stand trial!'

'That, my dear boy, as you well know, is never an option,' Sir Giles reminded him. 'Believe it or not, it is a part of my work that I do not enjoy. But it is better for all concerned, most especially the innocent members of their immediate families, that the misdeeds of certain high-ranking gentlemen never become common knowledge. And the Government would be hard pressed to withstand further scandal at the present time.

'But you did not come here to discuss the unsavoury aspects of my work,' Sir Giles continued, after refreshing himself from the contents of his glass. 'Miss O'Malley is indeed here, and in no danger now that we have every member of the spy ring safely under lock and key—at least those few who still remain alive,' he amended, as he noted the sceptical arch of one dark brow. 'Unfortunately she has not been well. She was kind enough, whilst I was away in London, to help nurse my sister through a bout of influenza, and for her pains contracted the illness herself.'

Grey eyes never wavered from Daniel's face. 'The poor child has been quite poorly, and has been keeping to her bedchamber. I shall, however, enquire whether it is possible for you to see her.'

Sir Giles then summoned his butler and requested him to locate the whereabouts of Katherine's maid. 'What think you of the events taking place across the Channel?' he asked, the instant his servant had withdrawn to carry out his instructions. 'The allied armies, as you are undoubtedly aware, are amassing in Belgium. Will you be joining them, I wonder?'

He received no response and smiled grimly. 'No, I thought not. You, no doubt, will have far more important matters of a personal nature to attend to. Dear me.' His shoulders shook in silent laughter. 'I never thought to play Cupid. Please do not hesitate to call upon me if you think I can be of further assistance. My brother-in-law is, I might remind you, a bishop and, as it happens, is paying us a visit at the end of the week. It would be no difficult matter to obtain a special licence. And it goes without saying that you are most welcome to put up here and await his arrival.'

Before Daniel was offered the opportunity to respond to this piece of rank impertinence, the door behind him opened and he turned to see a plump, middle-aged woman enter. He watched her cast an enquiring glance in Sir Giles's direction before fixing her dark eyes on his physiognomy.

'It's Bridie, isn't it? I've heard much about you.'

'Holy Mary, Mother of God!' she exclaimed, reaching out and surprising him somewhat by capturing one of his hands in both of hers. 'So 'tis yourself, Major Ross! May heaven be praised! If you hadn't come for her, sir, I think I'd have fetched you myself.'

Daniel was suddenly filled with foreboding. 'Good gad! Is she so ill, then?'

''Tis not the influenza,' Bridie hurriedly assured him, tears moistening her eyes now. 'But she's suffering, sir…suffering something cruel.'

Daniel was not slow to understand what the devoted Irishwoman was trying to tell him, and cursed himself silently for every kind of a fool for remaining away from Katherine for so long.

He had been certain for some little time that she was not indifferent to him; and even though she had done her level best to keep her feelings well hidden whilst she had remained at his home, he had been granted the dearest wish of his heart on the evening of the Cranfords' party, when she had just for one unguarded moment betrayed the true state of her own by addressing him as 'my grasshopper'. Since then, of course, she had been granted ample time to fret herself unnecessarily over those old foolish fears, which he most definitely would never have permitted her to do if she had remained with him at Rosslair.

He suddenly found himself experiencing more anger than sympathy. 'Is she, by gad!' There was no mistaking the determined set to his square, powerful jaw. 'Well, we'll soon put a stop to that!'

'One may always rely on Major Ross,' Sir Giles remarked, not quite steadily, as he watched Daniel stride purposefully across the room to the table on which several fine wines were kept in sparkling crystal decanters. 'I have done so on several occasions. And have always found him equal to any task.'

Daniel, choosing not to comment on this tribute from a man whose respect was not easily won, selected the decanter containing the claret and picked up two glasses,

before remarking, 'I might consider holding you to one
or two of your former impertinent suggestions, Osborne.
But first, I shall accept your offer of refreshment and
will relieve you of this fine wine. I dare swear my darling girl has had nothing fit to drink for some appreciable
time.'

'There's freshly made lemonade on the bedside table,
sir,' Bridie did not hesitate to assure him. 'I placed it
there myself this very morn.'

'I need say no more,' was Daniel's response before
he went out, leaving the library resounding with Sir
Giles's appreciative masculine laughter.

'Which is her room, Bridie?' he asked, as the maid
scurried after him across the hall, looking if possible
both hopeful and worried.

'Second on the right at the top of the stairs, sir. But
I think I ought to go up and inform Miss Katherine that
you wish to see her.'

'And I had made up my mind that you were a sensible
woman.' Daniel paused as he reached the bottom of the
stairs to cast the loyal maid a mild look of reproach.
'Don't disappoint me, Bridie. One never reveals one's
plan of campaign to the enemy. A swift, unexpected attack more often than not brings victory.'

His smile, both warm and reassuring, swept away the
last of her doubts. 'Have no fear, Bridie. She'll come
about. I'll see to that.'

Assuming it to be Bridie who had entered the room
without knocking, Katherine continued to stare out of
the window. It was only after it had occurred to her as
odd that her normally loquacious maid was unusually
quiet that she abandoned her idle contemplation of the

Hampshire countryside and turned her head to look across the room.

For several moments she refused to believe the evidence of her own eyes. Firmly convinced that, tormented by bittersweet memories, her tortured mind had successfully conjured up his image, she blinked several times in an attempt to dispel the vision, but it stubbornly refused to disappear and, worse, it was now moving slowly towards her.

If the truth were known, Daniel was as much shocked by her appearance as she evidently was by his own. Clearly she had lost weight and looked so pale and drawn that it came as no surprise that she swayed slightly when she attempted to rise, and was obliged to grasp the back of the *chaise-longue* for support.

He was beside her in an instant, depositing decanter and glasses on a low table, before cradling her protectively against him. 'Oh, my darling girl. Whatever have they done to you?' he murmured, placing his lips gently to one corner of her mouth.

It was several moments before Katherine could regain sufficient wits about her to put up even a token struggle, but it was enough. Daniel released her immediately and, after seating himself, drew her gently down beside him.

Determined not to give way this time to the tears which nowadays were never far from the surface, Katherine delved into the pocket of her dressing gown and drew out her handkerchief. 'This really is too bad of you,' she managed in a shaky whisper, before using the lace-edged piece of fine lawn to good effect. 'What do they mean by allowing you to enter my bedchamber quite unannounced?'

'I'd like to know what they mean by allowing you to get into this state!' he countered, at his most grim. 'Osborne promised faithfully to take every care of you. And yet here you are looking fagged to death!'

For all that her thoughts were in turmoil, Katherine couldn't help smiling at this. He was nothing if not brutally frank. Furthermore, he was speaking no less than the truth. Her mirror had told her earlier that morning that she was definitely not looking her best, though whether it was the loss of weight or the lace cap that neatly confined her hair of which he thoroughly disapproved was difficult to judge.

'You mustn't blame Sir Giles, Daniel,' she told him, speedily coming to the baronet's defence. 'He instructed that I be brought here for my own safety. He wasn't to know his sister Mary had succumbed to a bout of influenza during his absence. I helped nurse her, with the result that I unfortunately contracted the malady myself, which has left me feeling very low.'

One dark brow rose in a sceptical arch, evidence enough that he was not convinced that her recent illness was wholly responsible for her present rather haggard appearance. So Katherine decided it might be wise to turn his thoughts in a new direction by asking if he'd seen the report in the newspaper about the death of a certain peer of the realm and his distant cousin.

'Ha!' he scoffed. 'Yes, I read it, right enough. Fatally attacked by a lawless gang, my eye!'

He was plainly disgusted by the whole unsavoury business, and Katherine could easily appreciate why. Daniel was a soldier, and an honourable man. He would not consider killing someone on the field of battle as murder. However he would certainly look upon what had happened to the traitor and his accomplices as precisely that.

On the few occasions Sir Giles had visited her since

his return to the house the week before, he had not once attempted to enlighten her on what had taken place after she had been whisked away on the night of the Cranfords' party. As his work was secret, she had refrained from asking questions, but experienced no such qualms where Daniel was concerned.

'Nothing very spectacular,' he responded, and she thought for a moment she was destined to remain in ignorance, but then he added, 'I saw you go off with Gifford, of course, and guessed at once.'

Katherine frowned as memory stirred. 'When you returned to the salon that night with Julia, you were looking across at me most strangely,' she reminded him. 'Am I right in thinking that you recognised Gifford from somewhere?'

'Clever girl! Yes, I did. I saw him earlier in the day at my uncle's house, and was firmly convinced I'd seen him somewhere before, but it wasn't until I saw him standing behind you, about to take up his position in the dance, that I realised just where I'd seen him. Evidently Waverley chose him as his envoy and Gifford went over to France. With their contacts, Gifford had no difficulty in reaching Paris, and arrived there before me. Undoubtedly he was just one of many scouring the inns for a red-haired female. He was the man seated behind you at the table in the coffee room on the morning we were forced to flee the city. His grey wig and beard proved a reasonable disguise, but it was those hard, dark eyes of his that gave him away.'

'He was the one who followed Marie and myself that morning. I remember thinking at the time that there was something odd about him,' she divulged, before asking what happened after she failed to return to the salon on the night of the party.

'Your continued absence quite naturally was remarked upon. Several of the guests had already begun to take their leave, and when you couldn't be located anywhere in the house, Gifford casually divulged that you had complained of a headache. Cranford then suggested that you had in all probability not wished to cause a fuss and had begged a ride back to Rosslair in a neighbour's carriage. I quite naturally left shortly afterwards, but not before I had received Cranford's assurance that you were unharmed and were being taken to a place of safety.

'I was forced to be content with that until the following morning, when Sir Giles paid me a visit. Although he flatly refused to disclose where you were being housed, he did reveal that the traitor and his young accomplice, Gifford, both of whom had been invited to stay overnight with the Cranfords, had been taken into custody. Seemingly, the following morning, the other guests were led to believe that the two men had made an early start in order to be back in London by nightfall. And no one was any the wiser, until the deaths were reported in the newspapers. By which time Sir Giles had extracted all the information he required from the traitor and his cousin.'

He did not need to go into details, for Katherine could guess that the means adopted to attain such information was nothing short of torture. She sighed. 'It is indeed an unsavoury business, Daniel. All the same, I cannot regret my involvement. Besides which, I have learned a salutary lesson—one should never accept people at face value.'

She watched one dark brow rise questioningly, and smiled. 'I do not know what your opinion might be of Sir Giles's sister, but I suspect Miss Mary Osborne is far from the dithering creature she appears to be. I should have realised that at my cousin's engagement party, when I discovered how intelligently she played the game of whist. When I arrived here she was indeed feeling poorly, but she betrayed no surprise at all at my unexpected arrival, and I have since learned from Bridie that Miss Osborne has been putting it about that I came to Hampshire to stay with my aunt and uncle, completely forgetting they had taken Caroline to the capital in order to purchase her bride clothes, and that Miss Osborne was happily putting me up here until my relations returned. Yes, I strongly suspect she knows precisely the nature of the work her brother undertakes on behalf of the government, and is of immense help to him on occasions.'

'Yes, you may be right, my little love,' he responded, as he reached for the decanter. 'But I could have wished the confounded woman had not passed her ailment on to you. Here, drink this. It will put some colour back into your cheeks. It's high time I took you in hand once more.'

Casting him a decidedly wary glance, Katherine accepted the glass of wine, and obediently took a sip, before announcing, 'I have decided to return to Bath at the end of the week.'

'Oh, you have, have you…? Well, you're not!' He was at his most dictatorial. 'You are returning to Rosslair with me when I consider you fit enough to travel. We'll take Bridie with us. She'll make an ideal replacement for Janet, don't you agree?'

After taking a further fortifying sip of the fine wine, Katherine placed the glass down on the table and rose to her feet. 'No, Daniel, I shall not be returning to Rosslair,' she told him in a voice that was remarkably controlled considering she could quite easily have burst into tears.

Surprisingly receiving no response, though acutely aware those dark eyes never wavered from her direction, she walked slowly over to the window, and once again fixed her gaze on that all too familiar view. 'It is better that I return to Bath.'

'Better for whom?' he parried. 'Certainly not for me. I want the woman I love by my side.'

Katherine closed her eyes. Would that she could obliterate the pain which never left her as easily as she could blot out that vista! Had his declaration of love come as a complete surprise, it might have been easier to bear, but in her heart of hearts she had known for quite some time the depths of his feelings for her.

She had been offered ample opportunity during these past wretched weeks to think about their short but eventful association. Once she had set aside her infantile dislike, her feelings towards him had swiftly deepened. His had too, she realised that now. On those few occasions when he had kissed her, he might so easily have taken advantage of her innocence and taken his lovemaking so very much further. Perhaps if he had, the heartbreaking stance she was being forced to take now would not have been necessary.

'I love you too, Daniel,' she forced herself to admit, even though each word rasped painfully against the sides of her throat. 'And that is precisely why I cannot marry and live with you at Rosslair. I just couldn't bear it if anything ever happened to you because of me.'

Tossing the contents of his glass down his throat, Daniel rose to his feet. The catch in her voice had been hard to withstand, and he was torn between the desire to take her in his arms and soothe away those foolish fears and the violent urge to shake her until her teeth rattled for forcing herself to believe such errant nonsense in the first place. He remained, however, resolutely standing those few feet away, knowing that whatever he said now could well determine his future happiness.

'It is hard to imagine that a woman who could endure so much hardship without a word of complaint, a woman who goes headlong into a fray in order to help a fellow human being without a thought for her own safety, could be such a spineless, snivelling little coward.'

This brought her head round as he knew it would, and for a moment he thought he detected just a glimmer of that determined spirit flicker in those gorgeous turquoise eyes. Then she appeared merely bemused, uncertain.

'I-I don't know what you mean, Daniel.'

'Oh, yes, you do,' he countered, resolved not to spare her. 'You may have succeeded in convincing yourself you're some kind of nemesis, but you'll not succeed in fooling me. It's nonsense and you know it. What you are, though, Katherine, is a damnable little coward! What you're so desperately afraid of is losing someone else you love. But it hasn't stopped you falling in love, has it?' he continued, determined to make her face the truth. 'I can understand your wishing to protect yourself from possible future grief, and make allowances for it. But what I find totally unforgivable is that not only are you prepared to throw away your own future happiness, you are heartlessly prepared to sacrifice mine.'

'No, Daniel, that isn't true!' she cried. 'Nothing in this world means more to me than you do. You'll meet someone else…I know you will.'

'Perhaps,' he conceded, turning and thereby concealing his expression of delight. He knew that fear of suffering again the pain of loss had brought her to this pretty pass, but he believed that her love for him would succeed in setting her free. Victory was at hand. It was time to play his trump card! 'But I'm not prepared to wait around for her to cross my path.'

Katherine, watching him through a haze of barely suppressed tears walk slowly towards the door, suddenly experienced blind panic. There was just something too decisive in that elegant stride of his. 'Daniel, where are you going? Back…back to Rosslair?'

Schooling his features, he checked and turned back to look at her. 'Oh, no, my dear. When you were there the house felt—for the first time since my grandmother died—like a home. It's cheerless without you.'

Katherine swallowed in an attempt to ease the painful ache in her throat enough to ask, 'Then-then, where are you going?'

'Unless I much mistake the matter a battle will take place in Belgium in the not too distant future, which will settle these past years of conflict one way or the other. I no longer have my commission, but I'm certain Wellington will find something for me to do.'

'No!' she screamed, and for all that she was far from well, she succeeded in reaching the door before him, and pressed her back firmly against it, barring his exit. 'It's madness! No one would expect it of you. You've done more than enough for our country.' The determined sparkle was back in her eyes in full measure as she curled her slender fingers into fists and began to pummel his chest. 'I won't let you go…I won't!…I won't!'

Reaching out, Daniel swiftly put a stop to the assault upon him by lifting her effortlessly high in the air, his fingers easily spanning the slender waist. 'Understand this, Miss Katherine Fairchild O'Malley, there is only one way you are going to succeed in stopping me.'

Although he was smiling almost triumphantly now, there could be no mistaking the hard determination in his eyes, and Katherine found her own resolution swiftly crumbling.

'Then may God forgive me,' she said softly, wrapping her arms about his neck. 'But I can't...I won't let you go.'

Marie Dubois sat outside the farmhouse, enjoying the pleasant September sun. On her knee Louise's youngest child was sleeping soundly, and she too could quite happily have dozed if the peace and quiet had not been rudely interrupted by the sudden arrival of a boisterous three-year-old boy and a very pretty lady with red-gold hair.

'Did we disturb you, Marie?'

'Not at all, Louise,' she lied. 'You have not been long in town.'

'No, we accomplished all the marketing very quickly.'

'And we even have a letter here for you,' a deep voice behind her remarked, and Marie turned to see Louise's handsome husband framed in the doorway, his expression betraying faint disapproval as he handed her the missive. 'Three letters from England in less than a year. I'm beginning to think we have a collaborator in our midst.'

'Do not tease her, Pierre,' his wife scolded gently. 'You know the last letter was from an acquaintance in England who wrote to inform her that Justine's murderer had been apprehended and had at last paid for his crime.'

Marie merely smiled as she broke the seal to find a second letter neatly folded inside the first. Both Pierre and Louise knew that she had played a part in attempting to bring Justine's murderer to justice, but they knew none of the details. Nor did they know that her previous letters had been written by Sir Giles Osborne. There were certain facts which Marie was sensible enough never to reveal. She could not, however, hide her joy when she read the signature on this most recent correspondence, and uttered a tiny exclamation, after reading the second letter written in a neat, stylish hand.

'Not bad news, I trust?' Louise ventured, when she saw tears spring to her faithful Marie's grey eyes.

'No, you may read them,' Marie answered, handing over both sheets, and then watching as her former charge's forehead puckered.

'But who is this Major Daniel Ross, Marie? And how come you to know him? He is a soldier, is he not?'

'There, what did I tell you!' her husband put in. 'A traitor in our midst!'

Marie cast him an impatient glance. 'You know that is not true. Besides, the war between our two countries is finally over. England is no longer our enemy.'

'Maybe not,' Pierre agreed, no longer smiling. 'But the wounds have yet to heal. I lost two brothers in Spain, remember?'

'And many Englishmen were killed too,' Marie reminded him, before turning to Louise. 'Major Daniel Ross is none other than the gentleman who rescued you from that evil place, Louise, and brought us here.'

'But-but he was a Frenchman. I shall never forget Antoine Durand. I shall never be able to thank him enough for what he did.'

'Nor I,' Pierre put in. 'I shall be forever in his debt.'

'Then you shall both be forever in the debt of an Englishman,' Marie informed them, experiencing a degree of wicked satisfaction at their astonished expressions. 'His mother, I understand, was French. That is why he is able to speak our language so well. But Major Ross is an Englishman, a brave man who fought in Wellington's Army in the Peninsula. He writes to tell me that he is now married, and living happily in Dorsetshire.'

'This second letter, Marie, it is written in English,' Louise reminded her. 'My English is not so good, and I do not understand it too well. But is it not from Major Ross's wife? How came you to know her?'

'Yes.' Marie's smile was gentle as she took back the letter. 'It is indeed from Katherine. I shall translate for you.

'*My dearest Marie*, she writes. *We parted so swiftly that I hardly had time to say goodbye to you. I do not intend to do so now, because it is my dearest wish that you, Louise, and her family will visit us here in England next year. At the moment we are in disorder at Rosslair, with the builders invading the house, but the extension should be completed within a very few weeks, so there will be plenty of room to put you all up, hopefully in the spring.*

I am very much enjoying married life, Marie. My devoted Bridie is now housekeeper here, and very content with her new status, and her predecessor is happily enjoying retirement in one of the cottages Daniel's father had built many years ago.

Earlier this month we travelled to Hampshire to attend my cousin's wedding. Like so many, her husband, Captain Charlesworth, was injured at Waterloo, but thankfully not badly. Daniel was not involved in that carnage. I stopped him from going by marrying him last May, and he, in turn, has freed me from the shackles of my foolish fears.

I shall explain all when I see you, dear Marie. Please do say that you will visit us. The English countryside is so very pretty in the spring. I should dearly love you to see it. Affectionately yours, Katherine.'

Louise cast her husband a puzzled glance. 'But who is this Katherine, Marie? Did you meet her in Paris when you were there earlier this year?'

'Yes. And it is largely thanks to Katherine that your sister's murderer was finally called to account for his crime. I shall tell you all about her presently. But first, I wish to know whether you will accompany me to England, for I have every intention of paying Major and Mrs Ross a visit next year.'

Louise cast a hopeful glance in her husband's direction. 'We cannot allow her to undertake the journey alone, Pierre. And I should very much like to embrace the woman who avenged the death of my dear sister.'

He was silent for a moment, then he said, 'And I should very much like to shake the hand of the man who made it possible for me to marry Justine Baron's sister.'

Consequently they set out on their visit to Dorsetshire in the spring of the following year, and could not have planned their trip better, for they arrived at Rosslair in time to celebrate the birth of Liam Edwin Ross.

*　*　*　*　*

Lord Trenchard's Choice

by

Sylvia Andrew

Sylvia Andrew has an Honours Degree in Modern Languages from University College, London and, before ending up as Vice-Principal of a large comprehensive sixth-form college, taught English for foreigners in Switzerland, Cambridge and in Compton Park, an international finishing school for young ladies which was housed in a beautiful country mansion leased from the Devonshire family. The house and grounds have provided inspiration for several settings in her novels. She and her husband Simon now live in a small market town in the west of England, which is full of the Georgian architecture which they both love. And just a few miles from their home is the marvellous Dorset Jurassic Coast World Heritage Site. In 2000 Sylvia wrote a historical celebration of the town's splendid fifteenth-century parish church in a millennium *son et lumière*, which was a great success.

She and Simon belong to the Georgian Group, the National Trust and English Heritage, all of which help them to satisfy their love of historic houses and wonderful landscapes. Simon lectures all over the place on architecture and wild orchids, while Sylvia tries to do nothing, and usually fails, since she is heavily involved in the local museum. She just can't keep away from old maps, newspapers, photographs and census returns! Her other passion is theatre performances of Shakespeare. She and Simon have one married daughter, whom they visit quite often, and a very precious grandson called Joe.

Chapter One

Brussels, June 1815

It had been another cloudless day in Brussels, and though the sun was now disappearing behind the Hotel de Ville the air was still warm. There had been more military activity than usual during the day, and rumours were beginning to fly round that the long-awaited confrontation between Napoleon and the Duke of Wellington was not far off. But neither the heat nor the rumours seemed to affect the two officers striding confidently across the Grand' Place in the direction of the Rue de la Blanchisserie.

It was clear to the informed where they were heading. Tonight the Duchess of Richmond was giving what promised to be the most brilliant ball of the season, and, far from being dressed for action in the field, the men crossing the Grand' Place were in full-dress uniform, one in scarlet, one in blue, with much silver and gold lace on their coats. They both wore beautifully fitting pantaloons and carried spotlessly white gloves. The more dashing of the two sported the fur-trimmed pelisse of a Hussar.

Though the good people of Brussels were well used to the sight of the military in their town, this pair attracted many an admiring glance, especially from the female half of the population. They were about the same age, both bronzed, both tall, their close-fitting uniforms revealing lithe, athletic figures, full of grace and power. One, a Major, was not handsome exactly, but there was something very attractive about him in spite of his undoubted air of command. But it was his companion, a Captain in the Hussars, who attracted most interest from the ladies. He was the better looking of the two, with classical features and hair that was so dark a brown as to be almost black. He, too, had an air of confident authority, but there were intriguing lines of laughter round his eyes and mouth, and, as the ladies who caught his eye noticed, he also had a delightful smile and lazily appreciative dark blue eyes.

The two men were talking with the ease of old friendship, and their laughter rang out as they left the square and turned into one of the small side streets which surrounded it.

'So your mind is made up, Adam? This campaign is to be your last?' The Hussar's voice was deep with a touch of a drawl about it. 'I can hardly believe it after all these years.'

Adam Calthorpe spoke quite firmly. 'You may do so, Ivo. I'm needed in England. The Calthorpe estate has been badly neglected for some years, and there's a lot to be done.'

Ivo Trenchard shook his head. 'All the same, it's difficult to imagine Adam Calthorpe of the Fighting Fifty-Second settling down to a quiet life in Somerset.'

'I assure you I shall enjoy it!'

'I suppose you intend to marry, too!' Ivo's voice was so pessimistic that Adam laughed again.

'Why shouldn't I? After all these years of racketing about Europe, what could be better than settling down to a time of quiet with a gentle, home-loving girl? No turmoil, no argument, just a comfortable, orderly life.'

'Well, I wish you luck—if that's what you really want.'

'Why don't you do the same? Once Napoleon's been beaten there's bound to be years of peace. Life in the Army won't be very interesting. What about finding a wife and settling down, too?'

Ivo Trenchard stopped and stared at his friend. 'Adam! Are you quite mad? You know my views on women!'

'I thought you liked them?'

'I do! But not to marry. That's the last thing I want from them!'

'But—'

Ivo ignored the interruption. 'Look, Adam, if you wish to marry, that's your affair. But it wouldn't do for me.'

'Why not?'

'My dear fellow, I hope you are not going to deny that I have some experience of the fair sex?'

'I wouldn't dream of denying it, Ivo,' his friend assured him. 'No one could.'

'Well then, over the years I have come to the sad conclusion that there are only two kinds of women— lively ones with whom one flirts, and boring ones with whom one doesn't. The boring ones make better wives, but they aren't exactly amusing.'

Adam was moved to protest. 'You have to be wrong,

Ivo! My chances of happiness seem pretty small if you're not.'

'I suppose there might be a few exceptions. Let's hope you find one, though it don't seem likely to me!'

'You underestimate me. But what's wrong with a lively wife?'

'Look around you! I'll wager last month's pay that for every beautiful woman happy to be in her husband's company at the ball tonight, there'll be five on the arm of an elderly bore whose only attraction is that he's rich!'

'You're being very harsh!'

'It's true! And Society encourages it. The whole object of a woman's existence is to marry well. The idea is drummed into them from their cradle, and they can be quite ruthless in their quest. Believe me, I know.' For a moment Ivo looked grim. Then he shrugged his shoulders and went on, 'But once a suitable husband is found and the knot safely tied, *then* they look to enjoy themselves. Take it from me, Adam. For most women marriage is a commercial proposition. Loyalty, love, respect play very small parts in it.'

Adam turned a troubled face to his friend. 'I haven't heard you talk like this before. You used not to be so cynical.'

'No? Well, if I am now I have my reasons…which we won't go into at this moment. I intend to enjoy myself tonight. You needn't look so concerned, Adam! I'm not entirely lost—you must have noticed that I leave happily married women severely alone, for example, though I can't say I've noticed many.'

'But the others you regard as fair game? You'll never find a wife that way.'

'You know, I'm really worried about you—you'll

soon be recommending that I turn my attentions to some insipid débutante with a view to matrimony. I swear, I'd rather die. No, I find women such as Arabella Lester, for example, or Heloise Leiken far more to my taste. Charming women, both of them, but I doubt they very often think of their husbands when they are with me.'

'I suppose Madame de Menkelen is another such?' Adam asked.

Ivo looked at him with a grin. 'You don't miss much, do you? Isabelle de Menkelen and I hardly know each other…yet.'

'I'm sure that will change—if Boney gives you time.'

'It doesn't matter if he doesn't,' said Ivo shrugging his shoulders. 'Making love is only one of the two exciting activities in this life. A good campaign is just as much fun.'

'Let's hope I'm more fortunate in my choice of a wife,' said Adam with a smile.

'Choice, choice! What do you mean by choice? Granted that a man is looking for happiness, not wealth, in his marriage, what sensible basis does he have for choosing his partner for life—for the *rest* of his life? No, no, Adam, the only real choice is between marrying or not marrying. Once a man has decided to take a wife, happiness is a matter of chance, not choice!'

'You're making a great deal out of nothing, Ivo. I refuse to believe it will be as hard as you say to find the sort of wife I want. I'm not looking for excitement or passionate love—just a peaceful, unproblematic existence with a reasonable woman.'

'You'll die of boredom within the month!'

'I don't think so.' He looked up at the tall mansion in front of them. 'I believe we're here. The music sounds excellent, but then the Richmonds always provide the best.'

As soon as they went in they were taken straight to a small room on the upper floor. Colonel Ancroft was waiting there for them.

'Good! Tom Payne and the others are already here. The team is complete.'

'Is there any more news, sir?' asked Adam.

'Yes, and it's bad, I'm afraid. The French crossed the Sambre in force early this morning. The Prussians have been under attack all day and it looks as if Charleroi will fall, if it hasn't already done so, indeed. The Army will be in action before dawn. As soon as the Duke and his aides have prepared the orders you'll be required to deliver them.'

'Are we to wait here with you, sir?' Ivo asked.

'On no account! You are to deploy yourselves among the Duchess's guests, doing your best to quell any anxieties. Wellington will arrive before long, and meanwhile he wishes the ball to continue and the guests to be kept reassured. We don't want any panic.' He dismissed them with a nod. 'I'll keep you informed. Off you go, and look as if you are enjoying yourselves!'

'Well, I don't know about you, Adam, but I *shall* enjoy myself!' said Lord Trenchard casting an experienced eye over the gaily dressed company gathered in the Duchess's ballroom. 'And if the ladies need reassuring, I'm the man to do it!'

An hour later Ivo bent over one of the loveliest women in the room and offered her his arm. 'I'm sorry you're feeling the heat, madame. May I suggest we take a turn in the Duchess's garden? It might be cooler outside, though I doubt it. Brussels must be due for a storm quite soon.'

The lady gave him a grateful look from huge brown eyes. 'I should like that, Lord Trenchard.'

As they made their way to the long windows, Ivo could see some of the more stiff-necked guests casting disapproving glances at him. They hadn't yet forgotten the scandal over his recent involvement with the Countess Leiken, but this didn't disturb him. Disapproval usually had the effect of making him behave even more outrageously, and Heloise Leiken had been worth every frown. Beautiful, witty, and enchantingly willing, she had kept him amused for weeks until her husband had appeared on the scene and borne her off to the family estate some miles out of Brussels. He wondered when Menkelen was due to return.

Once outside, Madame de Menkelen smiled up at him. 'I find this most agreeable,' she said.

As Ivo looked down at her his blood stirred. She really was *very* beautiful. 'So it is,' he replied, taking her hand and kissing it. 'Shall we walk to the end of the *allée*?'

The ensuing half-hour spent wandering through the warm, scented air was pleasurable, but Ivo was not unduly disappointed when Madame announced that she wished to return to the ballroom. More exciting things were afoot. He escorted her back, then excused himself and called in on Colonel Ancroft. There was nothing new there. He looked round for Adam, but couldn't see him. With a sigh Ivo joined the throng once again, but, though no one could have guessed it from his demeanour as he danced with one lady, reassured another and laughed a third out of her fears, his heart was not really in what he was doing. After a while he could tolerate it no longer and wandered into the garden again, this time alone. Adam was over on the other side, deep in conversation with Tom Payne, but Ivo avoided them both and stood in the shelter of a tree, smoking one of the small cigarillos he had brought from Spain. He needed to think. For whatever reason he was in a most unaccustomed state of dissatisfaction.

Was it the thought of the coming battle that was unsettling him? Or was it perhaps Adam's talk of marriage, of settling down?

Ivo allowed his mind to wander. For years he had lived life to the full, loving the comradeship, the danger, the exhilaration of fighting the French among the narrow clefts and valleys of the mountains along the Portuguese border, or under a sun beating down on the harsh Spanish landscape. He and Adam Calthorpe had grown close over the years in Spain, sharing the excitements, the narrow escapes, the adventures when the French got too near for comfort. And there had been adventures, too, of a different, more pleasant sort, when he had learned to appreciate the talents, if not the virtues, of the ladies of Spain and Portugal...

It had been much the same here in Belgium, except that the interval of inaction had been longer. Perhaps it had been too long, and now the endless round of concerts, rout parties, fête-champêtres and balls, which had given Brussels the most brilliant season it had ever seen, had suddenly lost its flavour. Even the pursuit of beauties like Isabelle de Menkelen had lost its zest.

Ivo shifted restlessly. Adam had accused him of being too cynical. Was he right? Perhaps. His experience with members of the fair sex had not led him to form a very high opinion of them. After his first youthful escapades he had learned to be cautious in his approach to eligible young ladies. There were one or two mantraps among them, such as Charlotte Gurney, but most of them were silly creatures, too easily smitten with a handsome face, an ability to dance well, a talent for turning a pretty compliment, especially when they came wrapped in a uniform! On the whole, he preferred to seek out the company of sophisticated women of the world, who knew the rules, taking pleasure, as he did, in light-hearted *affaires*, and making no demands other than to be amused. He had been spoilt, of course, but most of his liaisons ended amicably. His conscience was seldom troubled. There were no broken hearts. Indeed, the more he learned of the ladies of Society, the less inclined he was to believe they had any hearts to lose. If that was being cynical, then Adam was right.

But this was not what was causing this feeling of restlessness....

Ivo grimaced. Why was he so reluctant to admit it, even to himself? The real cause of his unrest was, of course, the rift with his father. They had had their differences in the past, but this would be the first time he had ever gone into battle while they were still so completely estranged. Five months. Five months since they had spoken to each other in anything like amity. For all the distractions of Brussels the memory of that catastrophic day in January was still strong. And the prospect of the battle, the possibility that he might not survive, had revived his regret, his bitter sense of injustice. Why had his father not believed him?

A skirl of bagpipes came from the ballroom as men of the Highland regiments came in to entertain the Duchess's guests. But Ivo didn't hear them. The garden, the music, the ball, faded away as he re-lived the events of the past five months, starting with a fateful day at the beginning of January. Who could have imagined that a harmless visit to an old servant in the neighbouring village would have such disastrous consequences…?

Sudiham Castle, January 1815

Ivo Trenchard cut down the dead bracken and brambles which were blocking his path and swore. It had seemed a good idea to take the short cut back to Sudiham through the woods, but somewhere or other he had missed the way and now he was having to fight through thick undergrowth to the drive which led to the house. He shouldn't have stayed so long with old Ben, but it had been impossible to get away sooner. Ben was now bedridden and loved to talk of his time as head groom at Sudiham, of teaching Ivo to ride when he was barely big enough to sit on a horse. But now, unless Ivo managed to find his way soon through this damned wood, he would be late for the game of billiards he had promised his father.

He was frowning as he hacked at a particularly vicious branch. It was time he went back to London. Christmas had been enjoyable, but five weeks of Lord Veryan's company was enough. Much as he loved his father, he had forgotten how autocratic the old fellow could be. Their life together had been a succession of arguments ever since Ivo had been old enough to hold an opinion of his own. He had survived a good few battles in his time, culminating in one that lasted for weeks when he insisted on joining the Army. He had never regretted it. The Army had been good to him, and life at home would undoubtedly have become unbearable. He wondered how Peregrine, his younger brother, had stood it for so long. But then Perry was different. Perry hated scenes, and would always give in rather than risk his father's displeasure.

Lord Veryan's latest whim, that Ivo should now sell out of the Army and marry Charlotte Gurney, was absurd, but the notion had been pursued with an insistence which Ivo found irritating. There were undoubtedly advantages in such a match from his father's point of view. Sir George Gurney was his oldest friend, and Charlotte was Gurney's only child. And the closer tie that marriage to Ivo would bring was not the only consideration. Though not exactly wealthy, the Gurneys owned some of the best farmland in the district. The Gurney heiress would bring many rich pastures into Sudiham's domain.

Charlotte was pretty enough, if you liked rosy cheeks and prominent blue eyes, but her manners and behaviour filled Ivo with disgust. A well-developed girl of eighteen, she had already made it embarrassingly plain that she was more than ready to marry him. Ivo had been forced to explain to her, in a very difficult fifteen minutes, that there was no question of his doing what she and his father wished. The ensuing tantrum had revealed a side to Miss Gurney's character which had exceeded his worst expectations. Ivo shuddered now at the memory...

He hacked at one more branch and saw that he had at last reached one of the rides which led through the wood to the back of Sudiham. Ahead of him was a rundown cottage, which he remembered from his earlier days. He would be home in half an hour. But as he drew close he stopped. The cottage had been uninhabited for years, but the flickering light of a fire was coming through the window. A tramp? A gipsy? Ben had said there were a few about. He slowly drew nearer. 'Is anyone there?' he called.

There were sounds of frantic activity inside. Ivo strode up to the door, and gave it a push. It was locked. Now seriously worried, he put his shoulder to it and after a few heaves it gave way. He burst in. The cottage was a primitive affair, with one main room and a small kitchen built out at the back. The windows were filthy, and little daylight penetrated the room. But a fire was burning merrily enough in the hearth, on the floor were several cushions, and, to his amazement, Charlotte Gurney was standing half-hidden in the doorway leading to the kitchen. She must have been startled at his sudden entry, but she was not, as he would have expected, looking frightened... Guilty, perhaps, but not frightened. Her hat was on the floor beside her and she was clutching her cape together. She looked poised for flight.

'Charlotte!' Ivo exclaimed. 'What the devil are you doing here?'

'I...I...' She looked quickly into the kitchen, then shut the door, picked up her hat, and came reluctantly forward. Then she gave him a brilliant smile and heaved an exaggerated sigh of relief. 'Oh, I had such a fright!' she said. 'I thought I heard someone in the kitchen, but there's no one there. And then you burst in... I'm so glad it's you, Ivo. I was sure you were a robber or a thief. I was quite prepared to be murdered!' She gave a nervous little laugh.

'But why are you here? This is no place for you!'

'I know.'

'So what are you doing?'

'Er... The thing is...the thing is, Ivo I...was out for a ride, as a matter of fact, and...and my horse bolted. I managed to land safely, but I didn't know where I was...until I found this cottage. Then it started to rain, so...so I took shelter inside.'

'And you lit a fire?'

'The fire? Oh...yes! Yes! I was cold.'

What a liar Charlotte Gurney was, thought Ivo dispassionately. 'What were you going to do if I hadn't come?'

Her eyes opened wide. 'Once I was warm again I was going to walk to Sudiham, of course! What else could I do?'

'And your groom? Why isn't he here?'

'He...he went after the horse. I expect he's still looking for her.' She drew herself up, and demanded defiantly, 'Ivo, why are you asking me all these questions? Don't you believe me?'

Ivo was quite certain that Charlotte Gurney was lying her pretty head off, but he wasn't prepared to enter into an argument. The sooner he could extricate himself from this potentially dangerous situation the better. However, he had to see that the girl got home safely.

'Put your hat on,' he said. 'And fasten your cape properly. It's cold outside. I'll escort you to Sudiham, and get you taken home in the carriage.'

'Oh, thank you!' she said, as she did as he had told her. 'Whatever would I have done without you?'

Ivo didn't bother to reply to this, but said briefly, 'Sit down there on the window seat while I make certain the fire is out before we leave. You can hold my coat.' He passed his coat to her and started to rake out the hearth.

Before he had finished, however, sounds of a fresh arrival came from outside.

He got up and went to the door, and his heart sank when he saw his father and Sir George Gurney just pulling up their horses outside. They dismounted, then turned and looked at him in astonishment.

'Ivo!' exclaimed his father. 'I thought you'd be at

home. I was sure I was going to be late for our game! What are you doing here? In your shirtsleeves, too! The cottage has been deserted for years—what the devil is going on?'

'Damme, I'll swear he's got a girl in there, Rupert!' said Sir George with a laugh. 'The young dog! Let's have a look at her, Ivo! Is she pretty?'

'No!' said Ivo desperately. 'You're wrong! I...I just...saw firelight through the window, and came to investigate. Some tramp must have spent the night here. I took my coat off because I was working to damp down the fire.'

A crash came from inside the cottage. The two older men shook their heads at Ivo and laughed again. 'Brave try, my boy! Come on! Let's see this beauty!'

Ivo faced the inevitable. He shrugged his shoulders and stood aside as they pushed their way past him into the cottage. He had done his best to protect Charlotte from her father's anger, but he was not going to lie for her. He stood in silence as they stopped short in the doorway. They gazed at Charlotte in horror.

'Charlotte! What the—what's this?' There was a short silence while Sir George gave the room a swift, all-seeing glance, then he turned back to Ivo, his face purple with rage. 'You *damned* scoundrel, sir! You *villain*!'

'What the devil do you mean, Sir George? What have I d—?' Ivo took a step forward, then broke off as Charlotte came into view. When he had last seen her she was putting on her hat and fastening her cape. But now both were on the floor. Her hair was dishevelled, and she was half-turned away from them, apparently buttoning up her dress. He turned to his father.

'Don't believe what you see, sir!' he said angrily. 'I found her here only a few minutes ago. Just before you came she was fully dressed and ready for me to escort her to Sudiham. She's done this deliberately. *Don't let her fool you!*'

'*What?*' roared Sir George. 'Can I believe my ears? You *coward,* sir! You damned ungentlemanly *coward*! Do you hope to defend yourself with a tale like that? To save your own skin at the expense of my daughter? You're a disgrace to your name, sir! A *disgrace*!'

'You'll soon eat those words, Sir George!' Ivo turned to Charlotte and said forcibly, 'Tell them, Charlotte! Tell them the truth! I only came in to look at the fire. I found you here alone less than ten minutes ago!'

The girl had been watching the exchanges between Ivo and her father in silence, but now she gave a cry and clutched the window frame. 'It's no use, Ivo,' she cried. 'Don't you see? We are discovered!'

'Stop talking such theatrical rubbish, you little vixen, and tell the truth!'

'Oh, how could you?' she exclaimed with emotion. 'How could you say such things to me, call me such names! I am telling the truth, you cannot deny it! Oh…oh…oh, I thought you loved me! But I see it all now—you think as little of me as you do the rest of your amours!' She burst into tears and ran to her father. 'Oh, Papa, forgive me!' she cried. 'You must forgive me! I knew I was doing wrong, but I loved him so much! He pressed me so hard to meet him here and in the end I gave in. I've been so wicked, Papa! But I never thought he would cast me aside so quickly… Oh, how cruelly I am being punished! Oh, Papa!' She collapsed into her father's arms.

'She's fainted! The poor child! You see to her, Gurney, while I send one of the grooms for help. Take my coat,' said Lord Veryan.

'Charlotte already has mine,' said Ivo. 'I gave it to her to hold when I tackled the fire.'

Lord Veryan looked disgusted. He went over and handed his own coat to Sir George, who tenderly arranged it over Charlotte on the window seat. Then Lord Veryan picked up Ivo's coat, which had fallen to the floor, and threw it at his son. 'Take it!' he said harshly. 'The poor girl doesn't need your coat. What she needs from you is a little honesty. And amends! Honourable amends!'

Ivo abandoned his attempts to convince anyone, and leant against the wall, arms folded, observing Charlotte's performance with cynical appreciation. She may not be honest, but by God she was quick! And ruthless. She was making a lot of capital out of this little escapade. There might perhaps be a touch of revenge in it for his frank rejection of her a few weeks ago, but there was more to it than that. Charlotte was playing for higher stakes—if she couldn't *tempt* the son of the richest man in the neighbourhood to marry her, then she would try to see that he was *forced* into it. He was damned if he would let her succeed, but he foresaw a highly unpleasant time ahead of him.

Lord Veryan gave his son another basilisk stare, then went out. He called the groom over, told him there had been an accident and sent him to fetch a carriage from Sudiham as quickly as possible. As he came back in, he said to Ivo, 'You needn't think you are getting away with this, sir. We shall discuss your behaviour when that poor girl is safely bestowed. Then will be the time to decide what is to be done.'

'It's clear what is to be done!' shouted Sir George. 'The villain must marry her!'

Ivo was pale, but showed no other signs of disturbance. He ignored Sir George and said steadily to his father, 'I shall be at your service whenever you are ready, Father, but I have nothing to add to what I've already told you.' With that he turned to go.

Charlotte's eyes fluttered open. She tried to struggle to her feet, but fell back with a little cry. Stretching out her hand in a pathetic gesture, she whispered, 'Don't leave me, Ivo! Not like this! Not after all the things you said to me... What we have been to each other...' Her eyes closed again.

Sir George looked over his daughter's head at Ivo. 'I'll horsewhip you for this, Trenchard, by God I will!' he said fiercely. 'You've played your games around the neighbourhood for years, but you're not going to seduce *my* daughter without paying for it!'

'I did not seduce your daughter, Sir George,' Ivo said, somewhat white around the lips, but still steady.

Lord Veryan erupted into rage. 'That's *enough*, sir!' he shouted. 'I refuse to listen to any more of your lies! It's clear what has been going on, and I'll make you marry the girl, if it's the last thing I do!'

It had been impossible for Ivo to stay at Sudiham after the scene in the cottage. Though he swore he was innocent he was simply not believed. His past reputation in the neighbourhood for success with the ladies now served him ill. When Charlotte 'recovered' enough to talk, she stuck to her story, swearing that Ivo had persuaded her to meet him by promising to marry her. The two fathers ignored the fact that Ivo's light-hearted flirtations in the past had been conducted largely in the open, and never with the young daughters of decent families. They preferred instead to believe every syllable uttered by a sobbing Charlotte.

However, in spite of the fierce pressure put on him, Ivo categorically refused to marry the girl. He repeated his story and swore it was the truth—he had visited Ben, lost his way, and had ended up investigating the light of a fire inside the empty cottage. But he had to agree that there had been no sign of anyone else. He could not blame them for refusing to believe the tale of a bolting horse and a search for shelter from the rain. He hadn't believed it himself—especially after the horse was found neatly tethered in the trees behind the house. No drop of rain had fallen that morning, either. And who had lit the fire? Not Charlotte.

Charlotte Gurney had obviously arranged to meet someone at that cottage, and both fathers were convinced that this was Ivo. He was tried and condemned by the two of them as a dishonourable liar who had shamelessly seduced the daughter of his father's oldest friend, and then disowned her.

So Lord Veryan lost both his old friend and his elder son on the same day. In the face of Ivo's refusal to 'do the right thing', Sir George rode away from Sudiham, swearing he would never enter its gates again. If he hadn't been desperate to save his daughter's reputation, he would have denounced Ivo as a villain to the world at large.

As soon as he had gone, Lord Veryan, nearly speechless with rage and humiliation, banished Ivo from Sudiham, forbidding him to return until he was prepared to confess the truth, and make suitable amends.

Ivo was not surprised at Charlotte Gurney's behaviour. He had known that women, even a girl as young as Charlotte, could be unscrupulous in their pursuit of profitable marriages, and he would have said himself that her manipulation of the evidence against him was nothing less than brilliant.

But he was deeply, bitterly, resentful that his father, whom he loved, who had brought him up to be honourable and truthful, who in spite of their many disagreements had apparently always admired and respected his son, had so easily believed her lies. He had left Sudiham immediately, suffering from a severe attack of injured pride and outrage at his father's lack of faith.

Then in March news came of Napoleon's escape from Elba, and war seemed inevitable. Ivo knew that he would soon be recalled for duty. He had swallowed resentment and pride, and decided to seek reconciliation with his father. But when he arrived, far from giving him an opportunity to make his peace, Lord Veryan still refused to see him, not even allowing him to set foot in his home.

Shocked, sick and angry, Ivo had decided to seek temporary lodging with his aunt, Lady Frances Danby, who lived some fifteen miles from Sudiham in a village called Lyne St Michael. On the way he spent a miserable night at an inn, eating little and attempting to drown his sorrows in particularly vile brandy. He woke up the next morning with a massive hangover, almost wishing he had died in the night. The inn was no place to linger, so he set off doggedly, every movement a penance, on the road to Lyne. At some point he must have left the high road by mistake, and was forced to follow a bridle path that seemed to lead in the right direction. The path was unfrequented and for a while Ivo rode along peacefully enough, almost grateful that he had left the noise of the high road behind him. But then misfortune struck again.

His horse cast a shoe about three-quarters of the way along the path.

Ivo cursed the day he was born, dismounted gingerly and tied the animal to a tree while he considered the situation. The bridle path followed the contour of a fairly steep slope, and below him he could hear the sound of running water. The wish to cool his aching head was overpowering and step by step, with frequent pauses for recuperation, he slowly made his way down...

Chapter Two

Lyne St Michael, March 1815

The stream splashed and sparkled in the spring sunshine, and as Ivo approached the dancing light dazzled him. He could hardly believe his eyes when he saw a superb horse standing on a patch of grass nearby, a bay, with glossy coat and powerful flanks. A thoroughbred if ever he saw one. Amazed, he slowly drew near. It was saddled, but there was no sign of a rider. Had he been thrown? The horse seemed calm enough, but looked as if it would have plenty of spirit if roused. He stretched out a hand…

'You leave him alone, do you hear? Move away from my horse!'

The voice rang out, high and clear. Ivo winced as the sound sent his head throbbing again, and slowly turned. The next moment headache, heartache, everything was forgotten as he stared into the muzzle of a pistol, which was pointing directly at his head, not ten paces away. It was in the hands of a boy who couldn't be more than eleven or twelve. Ivo shuddered as a chill ran down his spine. Guns in the hands of children could be fatal, and this boy looked angry enough to shoot him.

'You scum!' the boy went on, without moving. 'I suppose you meant to sell Star at Taunton, along with all the others you've stolen.'

Ivo found his voice. 'You're making a mistake,' he said, taking a step to the side. The pistol followed him inexorably. He swallowed. 'I'm no horse thief.'

'What were you doing, then?' asked the boy, clearly not believing him.

'I...I saw the horse. I wondered if its rider was...was lost,' Ivo said. This sounded feeble, even to him. What the devil was wrong with him? He cleared his throat and tried a charming smile. 'Forgive me for asking,' he said, 'but... are you used to guns? They're chancy things—especially your sort. You realise that if you fired it you might well injure Star? As well as me.'

Unimpressed by the charm, the boy nodded. 'You're right!' he said. 'Move over!'

'Well, no, I won't do that,' said Ivo apologetically. 'Staying put seems to be my best chance of survival at the moment. Why don't you put that thing down? I'm not a thief, I assure you. You could even consider me respectable, though I know I don't look it at the moment. My name is Trenchard, and I'm on my way to visit Lady Frances Danby. I'm her nephew.'

'Lady Frances!' Disconcerted, the boy took a step back, caught his heel in the root of one of the trees and stumbled. As he struggled to keep his balance the gun went off. For a moment all was confusion as the horse reared and bolted, and the boy staggered, then fell. Ivo, relieved to find himself unharmed, leapt forward. He snatched up the pistol and threw it out of reach. Then he knelt down by the boy.

'Are you all right?' he asked.

'Of all the stupid, bone-headed things to do...' said the boy in disgust as he sat up. 'Yes, I'm all right. I never really meant to shoot, you know. I just wanted to frighten you.'

'Believe me, you did, young man,' said Ivo grimly. 'You frightened me half to death. And now I'm going to give you your just deserts.' He rose, took hold of the boy's collar and hauled him up. 'Bend over!'

'No! You can't! You mustn't!' In a panic the boy broke loose, and took off. Incensed, Ivo forgot his bad head and gave chase. He caught the young imp before he had gone very far and brought him down, but even then the boy didn't give up, wriggling like an eel and kicking hard in a frantic effort to escape. They rolled over the ground, the boy locked in Ivo's arms until he was held firmly down with Ivo sprawled on top of him. There was a moment's shocked silence, then the struggle was suddenly cut short. Ivo released his prisoner and leapt to his feet.

'You're a girl!' he exclaimed in horror.

The girl scrambled up and, hastily tucking in her shirt and fastening her jacket, she snapped out, 'What if I am? What does it matter whether I'm a boy or a girl?' She fastened the last button and then looked up at Ivo defiantly. 'Whatever *I* am, *you*, sir, are a bully and no gentleman, to take your temper out on someone so much smaller than yourself.'

'Of all the cool customers...!' Ivo was practically speechless with shock and anger. 'You deserve worse than anything I could do to you! What the hell do you think you're doing, masquerading as a boy? It's bad enough that anyone of your size carries a pistol at all, but a *girl*!'

'Don't you talk like that! I can handle a gun better than any boy!' the girl flashed back.

'Oh, yes, I could see that,' said Ivo with heavy sarcasm. 'You're a real expert, a proper nonpareil! You do realise, I suppose, that you damned near killed one of us? Not to mention your horse.'

'Star! Oh goodness, Star!' The girl looked round frantically and then gave a piercing whistle, which did nothing to improve Ivo's pounding head. He watched in grim silence as the horse came slowly back into the clearing, and the girl wheedled it into coming to her. She tethered it to the tree nearby, then went over to pick up the pistol. Ivo pulled himself together and was there before her. He held it away from her.

'Oh, no! You can't have this again before I've checked it.'

'Give it to me!' She made a grab for it.

'I can see I'll have to do something about you, you little madam!' Ivo hauled her without ceremony over to the tree and used the remaining length of the tether to tie her to it. 'Stay there till I've finished!'

Ignoring her shouts of rage, he examined the gun. It was a beautifully made duelling pistol, slightly old-fashioned, but by no means a toy. Ivo wondered what on earth the child had been doing with it. He made sure it was safe, and then went back to the tree and released both girl and horse.

'Here!' He presented her with the gun.

She looked at him in surprise. 'I thought you were going to keep it!' she said.

'I was tempted. But I don't steal guns any more than I steal horses. You'd better take it back. I expect it's quite valuable. Your father might well want to know where his best pistol has gone.'

'It's not my father's. It's mine.'

'Really?'

'You needn't sound so sceptical. It *is* mine. And I do know how to use it. It's just that I was surprised. You're Lady Frances's nephew?'

'As I said, yes.'

'Danby Lodge is three miles from here. What are you doing off the road, roaming over our land?'

Ivo realised with amazement that this impertinent chit was actually cross-examining him! But he replied equably, 'My horse has cast a shoe. I left him up on the bridle path. Where's the nearest smithy?'

'Follow the path for another mile or so. It will bring you into the village. The smithy is at the near end of it. Hold Star while I mount, will you! He's still nervous.'

Ivo's sense of humour began to take hold. Amused at her imperious tone, he helped her to mount. Then as she clicked her tongue at the horse, and prepared to leave, he realised that he didn't know anything about her.

'Wait!' he called. 'Who are you? What are you doing carrying that pistol? Does your family know what you get up to?'

'You'll have to find that out for yourself, won't you? Bye!' She dug her heels in, and horse and girl disappeared at a fast trot.

Ivo watched her go. In spite of his condition he had a strong inclination to laugh. For years he had faced Napoleon's armies without a qualm. He had had some close shaves in his time, but never before had he been so afraid as he had been just a few minutes before. It had taken a chit less than half his age and much less than half his weight to put a genuine fear of death into him! And all in a quiet English valley within twenty miles of his home! What would the rest of the regiment say if they knew? He could hardly put forward a hangover as a valid excuse.

When he told his aunt about the incident, she said amid much laughter, 'You've just met my goddaughter, Jossie. What a girl she is! Poor thing.'

'What do you mean? She looked happy enough to me.'

'Oh, she's happy enough. For the moment. But you're surely not suggesting that it's normal for a grown girl to be racketing about the countryside, dressed as a boy, threatening strangers with a gun, are you?'

'Well, no, not really. How has it come about?'

'She's the only child of a monstrously selfish father. When Gerard Morley didn't have the boy he wanted, he decided to bring Jossie up as a substitute son. It is a most unnatural life for a girl, but she adores him and spends most of her time and energy trying to be the boy he desired. I've done my best to help the girl, but there's not much I can do! Major Morley allows no one to interfere.'

'What about her mother? Has she nothing to say?'

Lady Frances shook her head. 'Lucinda Morley died not long after I left London and came to live here. I had known her parents for years, and was delighted when I was asked to be Jossie's godmother, but I can't claim to have done much for her. Her father and I have never liked one another. He believes I tried to put Lucinda off from marrying him, and he's right. I did. It's a pity I wasn't more successful. Now, of course, Jossie is growing up, but she has no idea how to behave. What sort of wife she'll make for Peter Radstock I cannot imagine.'

'Wife? She's just a child!'

'She is very nearly sixteen.'

'I would have thought her about twelve!'

'No, she's almost sixteen, and it won't be long before she is married. It's been known for years that she and Peter would be wed as soon as he is of age. The two estates neighbour one another.'

'Ah, I see!'

'You needn't talk in that odiously cynical tone, Ivo. It don't become you! And there isn't the slightest need for it. If it had been a marriage of convenience I would have done more to stop it. But Jossie and Peter have been inseparable ever since she could escape from her nurses to play with him. They would have no eyes for anyone else, I assure you. And marriage to Peter Radstock would at least mean that Jossie would be free of her father.'

She gave him a piercing look. 'But that's enough about Jossie for the moment. Tell me why you are so out of sorts. Is that pig-headed brother of mine the reason? I take it that you wouldn't be here if Rupert had seen sense at last?'

'What do you mean, Aunt Frances?'

She shook her head at him. 'You needn't try to keep me in the dark. I already knew about the quarrel with your father, but I've now learned the reason behind it.'

Ivo frowned. 'Who told you? Not my father.'

'He won't even hear your name mentioned! No, it was Perry.'

'Perry!' Ivo frowned. 'I am surprised. He ought not to have done it. The aim was to keep it—'

'In the family? Am I not family? But you needn't think ill of your brother—he didn't volunteer the information.'

'I don't suppose he did,' said Ivo with a slight smile.

'I could never keep anything from you myself, once you had made up your mind to know it.'

'Well, then, I guessed some of it and he told me the rest. As you know, I have never liked Charlotte Gurney. A sly little minx, if ever I saw one. So what has your father said or done now to make you so down-hearted?'

'Nothing. He still won't see me.'

She shook her head again. 'I can't account for it. I know that the evidence against you was pretty damning—'

'I didn't seduce Charlotte Gurney, Aunt Frances,' Ivo said in an even tone.

'Oh, I know that, my boy. You always had an eye for a pretty face, but you were never a liar. But why can't *Rupert* see that? He has always been obstinate, but this passes my understanding. *Why* won't he listen to you?' She shook her head in puzzlement. After a moment's reflection she asked, 'What about Perry? Can't *he* do anything? Did you manage to see *him*?'

'Perry met me at the door. He advised me to wait until he could have a word with my father. Then he came back to tell me that it was no use. Father refused even to see me.' Ivo got up, and his aunt eyed him anxiously as he got up and walked restlessly round the room. 'It's no use asking Perry to do anything, Aunt Frances. He would never tackle my father about any controversial matter, especially not one as explosive as this. No, his advice is to carry on playing a waiting game, to give my father more time.' Ivo uttered a harsh laugh. 'I told him that the way things were going in Europe there might not *be* any more time.'

'You think there'll be a fight?'

'Of course there will. The Allies can't let Boney escape from Elba and march around Europe, without doing something about it. They'll have to attack him. And it will be a fight to remember, Aunt Frances. Wellington against Napoleon.'

'We're not talking about a boxing match, Ivo!' Lady Frances said tartly. 'You might well get yourself killed!'

'Do you think my father would mind? Perry would make just as good a successor.'

'You know you don't mean that!' said Lady Frances severely. 'Rupert thinks the world of you. He just won't admit it at the moment. Perry is clever enough, but he hasn't half your character! You take care of yourself, Ivo! And when you come back—I say *when*, you notice—we must put a stop to this ridiculous matter...'

Brussels, June 1815

Sounds of cheering and loud applause brought Ivo back to the present and the garden of the Richmonds' house in Brussels. The Highlanders had finished their reels and strathspeys and were now marching out of the ballroom. Dancing would soon begin again.

Ivo threw away his cigarillo with a gesture of impatience. Nothing was more useless than regretting the past! He looked round. Adam and Tom Payne had vanished. They had probably gone inside to join the Colonel, and it was time he did the same. Unless he was very much mistaken, the present situation was about to change dramatically. This ball was likely to prove the last Brussels would see for some time. From what the Colonel had said, the French had already begun their attack just a few miles to the south.

But one thing was certain. If he survived the battle that would surely follow, he must make an even more determined effort to heal the breach with his father.

* * *

Not much more than twenty-four hours after Adam and Ivo had crossed the Grand' Place on their way to the Duchess of Richmond's ball, the French had taken the Allies by surprise and the Hussars had been required to cover Wellington's retreat from Quatre Bras. And the day after that, the final battle had been fought near the village of Waterloo. It had been fierce, long and bitter and in it Ivo had lost some of his best friends, including Tom Payne. Colonel Ancroft had been wounded, but survived and stayed with his men to the end. Adam and Ivo had escaped unscathed, apart from a number of cuts and scratches, but, along with most of their comrades, they had been left with a desire never to fight another such battle. Victory, when it had come, was welcome, but the cost had been almost too high.

Wellington had lost so many of his most experienced Staff Officers in the battle that those who had been left were expected to accompany their Commander-in-Chief to Paris. It would be almost three-quarters of a year before Ivo could get back to Somerset.

In the meantime he had written both to his father and to Lady Frances. There had been no response from Sudiham, but his aunt had kept him posted of events there. *'I have noticed before,'* she wrote in one of her letters, *'that elderly gentlemen can get some kind of fixed maggot in their brain, and no one can persuade them that they are wrong. I have never known your father so immovable. He still absolutely refuses even to mention your name, and Perry tells me that any efforts he makes on your behalf only meet with what amounts to an apoplectic fit. But do not despair. Rupert will have to see reason sooner or later. It will not do for his heir to be so totally excluded from the estates. Perry does what he can, but he is, when all is said and done, merely a*

*younger son. He always looks so miserable nowadays. I
thought at one time he was interested in Charlotte Gurney, but she never visits Sudiham now, of course.*

'*Jossie Morley's exploits continue to arouse disapproval, delight and pity in equal measure in the neighbourhood. It all depends on who is talking of her…*'

The letter continued, but it was the first paragraph that
gave Ivo food for thought. His aunt might have a somewhat cavalier manner, but he would trust her judgement
before that of many others. If she thought his brother
had at one time been interested in Charlotte, then the
probability was that it was true. Could the man Charlotte
had gone to the cottage to meet have been *Perry*?

Ivo had never given the question of Charlotte's real
lover much thought. For months he had deliberately put
Sudiham and all its affairs out of his mind, and he was
really not very interested in her amours once he had
successfully fended off her father's demands to marry
her. What had hurt was his own father's attitude. The
rest of the world could have believed Charlotte Gurney's
every word, condemned him to perdition and back, and
he would not have given a damn…if only his father had
trusted him. That was the pain he had attempted to forget
in Brussels.

But now the excitements of the war and the conse-
quent negotiations in Paris were finished with, and Ivo
was back in London with time and leisure to think. His
father's silence since he had been turned away from Sudiham the previous March, the fact that he had not written, even after Waterloo, was proof that the rift between
them was too deep to be mended easily. Perhaps a
straightforward reconciliation would never be possible?
Hurtful though it was, Ivo's word was not enough. In

the end Lord Veryan might have to be convinced of the truth by some other means.

Could Perry have been Charlotte's lover? The fact that he had run away would be in character. Peregrine had always run away when danger threatened. But he surely *couldn't* have stood by without saying a word when Ivo was so unjustly accused and punished... Perry was weak, but not vicious. On the other hand, unless Charlotte was enjoying an affair with a groom or a stable boy, who else could it have been?

Ivo at first dismissed his suspicions as unworthy. Though Perry was nearly six years younger, and first school, then Ivo's service abroad, had kept the brothers apart, they had got on as well as most. And in their childhood he had done quite a lot to protect Perry from the worst of their father's rages. Ivo reminded himself that Perry had certainly tried to help since his banishment from Sudiham... But the small, suspicious voice inside him pointed out that Perry's help had not been very effective. Indeed, if his aunt's letter was anything to go by, the situation was as bad now as it had been in the beginning—if not worse.

The small voice gradually got louder. In between returning to England, conducting his affairs in London, signing off from his regiment and enjoying life in the capital again, he found himself debating how to establish the truth. He was quite certain on one point. He would never again announce himself at Sudiham without preparing the ground beforehand. His aunt's house in Lyne St Michael was only fifteen miles from there. When he next went down to Somerset, he would stay with her at Danby Lodge, and take time to assess the situation before trying once again to see his father.

* * *

Ivo put away his unpleasant preoccupations for a while when Adam Calthorpe came to London for a few weeks in March. They spent a good many hours enjoying the clubs and amusements of the capital, and frequently visited Colonel Ancroft, who was convalescing with some Army friends. They talked of Adam's plans for Calthorpe, and at one point Ivo asked his friend whether he had yet found a suitable lady to be his 'pretty little wife'.

'Not yet, but it's early days,' said Adam.

'Er…did Tom Payne's sister like the silks you asked me to bring from Paris for her? Weren't you going to give them to her for Christmas?' asked Ivo casually.

'You needn't look like that, my dear fellow. Tom Payne's sister is as far from my ideal as it is possible to be!'

'I see. Didn't I hear that she and your mother had been in London with you just a week or two ago? And that she's at present living with your mother at Bridge House?'

'Yes, dammit! But you can blame my mother for that. She thinks Kate a wonderful girl. In fact, she has this ridiculous notion that Kate would make me an excellent wife. She's quite mad, of course!'

'Really?'

'Yes, really!' said Adam emphatically. 'The sooner I can see Kate Payne safely married to someone else the better. Look, why don't you spend a night with us in Bridge House on your way to Somerset? You can meet Kate and see for yourself what I mean. In fact, we could travel to Dorking together. I want to take a mare down with me…' Adam paused.

'Well?'

Looking slightly embarrassed Adam said, 'Well…it's

for Kate.' Then, as Ivo burst into laughter, he went on,
'Ivo! I've told you! Kate Payne is a headstrong terma-
gant. She insists on riding a hulking great horse that
belonged to Tom, and one day she will kill herself on
it. I've been forced to look out for a more suitable mount
for her, just to save her neck. And my conscience. After
all, I did promise Tom I'd see she was safe. But there
is no, *absolutely no*, significance in it! I tell you, all you
have to do is to meet the girl—you'll soon see what I
mean!'

They left London together and Ivo spent the night at
Dorking with the Calthorpes as Adam had suggested. He
found Kate Payne enchanting, a delightful exception to
his view of women in general. In other circumstances he
might have been tempted to seek a closer acquaintance
with her. But he decided against it. For one thing he was
not in the market for marriage, and Kate was not the sort
of girl one would offer anything else. For another, he
found himself in complete agreement with Mrs Calthorpe. Kate Payne would make the perfect wife for his
friend, though perhaps not exactly the 'pretty little thing'
that Adam had planned for!

Ivo set off for Somerset after his night at Bridge
House with some reluctance. For the past few months
he had managed to put the situation at Sudiham to the
back of his mind, but now he must face it. He desperately hoped that his suspicions of Perry were unjust. If
Charlotte Gurney's lover did turn out to be his younger
brother, then the problem was even trickier than he had
ever imagined.

Chapter Three

Somerset, 1816

Lady Frances gave Ivo a warm welcome, but she had little to offer him by way of comfort. She had been making a few enquiries of her own, but, though her circle of acquaintances in the county was vast and her gift for gathering information considerable, she had not learned anything to help him. Lord Veryan, who had disowned his own son on Charlotte Gurney's behalf, would have been astonished at what his neighbours thought of her. More than a few were privately of the opinion that the girl was sly, if not downright deceitful. But even so there was no hint of any lover. Charlotte's name was not even speculatively coupled with any young man in the district.

It was no surprise to Ivo when, with her usual bluntness, Lady Frances said, 'It's Perry, isn't it? It has to be. There isn't anyone else.'

Ivo nodded. 'I'm afraid so,' he said with a sigh.

'So what are you going to do about it?'

'I wish I knew!'

'I should have thought it was obvious. You must tax

Peregrine with it, and if he is the man, then Rupert should know!'

'I'm not the one to tell my father, Aunt Frances. And nor are you.'

'But, Ivo—'

'Peregrine will probably tell me the truth if I challenge him, but I can't see him confessing it to my father. He's too frightened of him.'

'He's a grown man!'

'You think that makes a difference?' Ivo got up and walked restlessly round the room. 'Perry suffered a lot when he was younger. He was such a delicate, nervous child—'

'Your mama's baby. I know. And she was always far too protective of him.'

'Perhaps she was. That was certainly my father's view. He wanted both his sons to be robust young versions of himself. And when Mama died he was determined to toughen Perry up. He went about it in quite the wrong way, of course. Perry got so frightened of him that he would do anything, even lie and cheat, to avoid his displeasure! I often felt very sorry for my younger brother, Aunt Frances, and so would you have. I even sometimes took the blame for something Perry had done just to protect him. Father's wrath didn't frighten me— my shoulders were broad enough to take it. But I'm not sure now that I did Perry a service.'

'You didn't! Perry should have been made to face things long ago, before he caused any real harm. Now look what has happened!' She sat in silence for a moment, then she said, 'Ivo, if Perry was so in fear of Rupert, why did he never leave home?'

'I did once suggest to him that he should get away, as I did. The Army would never have done for him, but my father might have agreed to let him take over the management of our estate in Derbyshire. But Perry wouldn't even consider it, and now I think I know why.'

'Charlotte,' his aunt said.

'Yes. I believe he's been fond of her for a long time.' Ivo stopped and shook his head. 'He's a fool! Why didn't he make an offer for her? Sir George is...*was* one of my father's oldest friends. There was no need for the secrecy.'

'My dear boy, do be realistic! Perry is a younger son. Sir George is as hardheaded as the next man, and from what I've heard his daughter is just like him. I doubt very much that either of them would have considered your brother a suitable match—not for one moment. Certainly not while you were alive, and Perry unlikely to succeed to the title. And now that you have left the army and are back safe and sound, it's even less likely.'

Ivo thought for a moment. Then he said with determination, 'I can't betray Perry to my father. I won't!'

'Then what *are* you going to do? Remain an exile?'

Ivo looked at his aunt sombrely. There was another silence, then he said, 'You'll have to excuse me, I'm going out for a ride. I need to think.'

Lady Frances nodded sympathetically. Then she called after him, 'See if you can find Jossie Morley!'

'Jossie Morley? The girl with the gun? Why on earth should I do that?'

'She's a fascinating child, and I'd like you to know her better. This would be a good opportunity. Peter Radstock and his parents are spending several days in Bath, so Jossie will be on her own. Bring her back with you.'

'I hope she's improved since we last met.'

'She may have grown a little.' His aunt twinkled at him. 'Though I doubt enough in the right places. You might still not be able to tell her at sight from a boy. And she's as madcap as ever.'

Ivo sighed. 'Where shall I find her? At home?'

'Good Lord, no! Jossie is never in when she can be out.'

'I rather wanted to be alone myself...'

'Try to see Jossie,' his aunt urged. 'I have a suspicion that that child is going to need a friend or two soon.'

'What does that mean?'

'I just have a feeling... Never mind. Do your thinking, then go and find Jossie.'

Ivo went back to the valley where he had encountered Jossie Morley the year before. There was no sign of her there, but he went down once again to the stream and sat on a rock beside it. He could think here as well as anywhere. It was a sheltered spot, and the spring sunshine was warm on his back. The burbling of the stream provided a pleasant background to his musing...

But his thoughts were not agreeable. He couldn't see Perry confessing anything at all to his father. Ivo sighed. He would not betray Perry, whatever his aunt said. And, in that case, his only hope, a forlorn one, was that Lord Veryan should eventually see Charlotte in her true colours for himself. How long would that take?

He sat for a few minutes longer, but then gradually became aware of a dog's excited barking and the sound of voices. His curiosity was aroused, and he went further down the valley to investigate. As he had half-expected, he found Jossie Morley. She was on her horse, swearing at a villainous-looking gipsy who was standing just a few feet away, holding a cudgel high in the air. At Jossie's side was a large hound, snarling and growling, its lips drawn back to show wicked fangs. Even as Ivo looked, Jossie gave the word and the dog leapt forward to attack. The gipsy hesitated, then dropped the cudgel and fled for his life into the woods behind him. The dog would have given enthusiastic chase, but when Jossie gave a short imperative whistle, he came back to sit down beside her, staring into the wood, every nerve alert. She jumped off the horse, then knelt down a few paces away. She didn't hear her dog's low growl, as Ivo approached. All her attention was on a fox which lay panting in front of her, its leg caught in the jaws of a cruel trap. She stretched out her hand…

'Don't do that!' exclaimed Ivo. 'Don't go near it!'

Jossie gave a startled cry, snatched up the cudgel and turned round, ready to defend herself. The dog stood up, bristling, but to Ivo's relief she recognised him.

'Oh! It's only you!' she said, dropping the cudgel and ordering the dog to lie down. She turned back to the fox again. 'I'll be careful,' she said. 'But I can't just leave him here. He'll die.'

'It'll die anyway,' said Ivo. 'Look at that leg. The kindest thing would be to put the animal out of its misery.'

'No! Some of them do survive, I've seen them. Besides, it's surely better for him to die in his own place, not cruelly held here.' She stretched out her hand to the trap.

Ivo took a stride forward and pushed the girl out of the way, not particularly gently. 'I said don't touch that animal!' he said sharply. 'It's mad with pain and fright, and quite certain to bite you. Here, let me see!'

Holding Jossie back with one hand he examined the trap, keeping well clear of the animal's frantically snapping jaws. The trap was a simple one, and the leg was not as severely damaged as he had first thought. He took out his pocket knife, a dangerous-looking thing he had acquired in Spain, and stretched out to release the fox. Jossie leapt forward.

'Leave it alone! I've told you, you mustn't kill it!' she cried and jerked his arm back. Ivo lost his balance and, though he managed to spring the trap, he couldn't keep his hand out of reach of the fox. The animal sank its teeth into him, and then, as he shook it off with a curse, it leapt away into the trees more nimbly than one would have thought possible.

Ivo looked down at his hand, then regarded his companion. 'You don't give up, do you?' he said grimly. 'If you can't shoot me, or bludgeon me, you'll poison me instead. God knows what diseases that fox is carrying!'

'Pooh! That's not much! It's hardly broken the skin! Go and bathe it in the stream and it'll be fine.'

'Only if you promise not to try to drown me,' said Ivo sourly. He went to the stream and squatted beside it. Holding out his hand, he went on, 'Look at this! Hardly broken the skin, you say? I'm covered in blood, dammit!' He dipped his hand in the water and gave a gasp at its unexpected iciness. Jossie regarded him disparagingly.

'You're making an awful fuss about nothing. I thought you'd been in the Army?'

Lord Trenchard, former Captain of Hussars, survivor of so many campaigns that he had given up counting, fresh from Waterloo, and proud of his reputation as a noted and dashing soldier in the field, rose to his full height, ready to give this impertinent brat a piece of his mind. Then, as he gazed down at the scornful figure before him, still looking like the naughty little boy he had first thought her, the absurdity of the situation struck him, and he burst into laughter.

'You are…unique, Jossie Morley,' he gasped. 'I can honestly say I have never before met anyone quite like you.' He wrapped his handkerchief round his hand and added, 'I still think I had better get this hand cleaned up properly, however. Are you coming?'

'Who told you my name?' she asked, not moving.

'My aunt. She likes you, I cannot imagine why. She asked me to bring you back to visit her. Can you come?'

'Yes, I'd like to. Peter's gone to Bath with his family and I'm on my own. I've nothing else to do.'

'And that might have been better put,' said Ivo. 'Has no one ever taught you any manners?' The pain in his hand was now intense, and he perhaps spoke more sharply than he intended. She flushed painfully and bit her lip.

'Oh, I didn't mean… Yes, it must have sounded very rude. Forgive me! I'm very pleased your aunt has asked me.' She gazed at him anxiously, and Ivo nodded, touched at her instant contrition. What a curious mixture the girl was! One minute an ill-mannered brat, dressed in boy's clothes and behaving like one, the next a sensitive young girl, ashamed of her clumsiness. It was obvious that no one who was interested in her future position in society had ever paid Jossie Morley much attention. She was entirely without artifice, completely untrained, rather like a neglected rose tree—thorny, undisciplined, with little sign of its potential beauty and sweetness… Ivo brought himself up short. What an absurd flight of fancy! The bite from the fox must be making him light-headed. 'Good,' he said. 'My horse is on the bridle path. Come on.'

She collected her horse and they walked up the hill together. She went on, 'I'm sorry about what I said. I *like* Lady Frances, I really do! It's just…well, I was a bit miserable. I suppose I'd hoped the Radstocks would take me with them to Bath. After all, I'll be one of the family once Peter comes of age, and that's only just over a year away. They ought to have taken me, I think. Don't you?'

Ivo imagined the effect Jossie Morley would have on the staid citizens of Bath and fully sympathised with Lady Radstock's failure to invite her. However, Jossie looked so cast down that he said, 'You would have liked to go? I'm surprised—you don't strike me as a girl who is interested in town life.'

'I'm not! But Lady Radstock is always saying that she wished I was…more ladylike. And how can I learn if I never go anywhere?'

Ivo didn't reply. They had reached the bridle path and, after helping Jossie up, he concentrated on mounting his own horse without revealing the trouble his hand was giving him. He was damned if he would expose himself to any more accusations of weakness!

They rode in silence for a while. Then, when Ivo had got his breath back, he said, 'So it's all fixed, is it? You're to marry this Radstock fellow and live happily ever after?'

'Oh, yes!' said Jossie, completely unconscious of any irony in Ivo's voice. 'That's what we've always said we would do. I can't imagine a future without Peter—and he feels exactly the same.' She turned to him, her face full of animation. 'I'm so lucky, Lord Trenchard. I've had the best of fathers, and later I shall have the best of husbands.'

'I shall look forward to meeting this Peter of yours,' said Ivo.

'Oh, you'd like him!' said Jossie. 'Everyone does. It's funny—we get into all the same scrapes together, but people just laugh at Peter, whereas they look prune-faced at me. It's because I'm really a girl, I suppose.'

'Yet you do your best not to look like one?'

'That's because of Papa. I'm his only child and he wanted a boy. I was a great disappointment to him. I still am, I suppose, though I do my best to behave the way he wants. Don't tell him about that fox, will you? He regards them as pests—and they are! He'd have killed it. He would be very annoyed with me for being so weak.' She sighed. 'There are some things I just cannot bring myself to do, even to please Papa!'

Ivo found he was beginning to dislike the girl's 'best of fathers', but he didn't comment. Instead he said, 'Tell me why you're called Jossie. It's a curious name for a girl.'

'Why do you go on so about my being a girl? I wish you would not—I don't like it! Jossie is short for Joscelin, and yes, it's a boy's name. It belonged to one of Papa's ancestors, Joscelin de Morlaix. The boys in Papa's family have been called after him for hundreds of years. And I'm the last of the Morleys. That's...that's why I'm such a disappointment. And now I'd like not to say any more about it, if you don't mind.'

She spoke with determination, and they rode on in silence. Ivo looked at her. She must have grown a little in the year since they had last met, but it was still difficult to imagine her as a girl, and even more difficult to think of her as nearly seventeen. She still had the straight gaze of a child, and her voice remained uncompromisingly direct. At the moment her face was half-hidden from him by a tousle of short dark curls, rather like those of the gipsy she had chased away a short while before. Indeed, altogether she had something of the air of a gipsy, though the breeches and jacket she wore were of

excellent cut and quality. Her horse too was a very handsome creature, but though he obviously had plenty of
spirit she had him well under control. There must be
more strength than Ivo would have thought in those slender wrists.

What sort of father was it who called his only daughter by a boy's name, dressed her in boy's clothing, had
apparently brought her up to be as like a boy as possible,
giving her a pistol, a powerful thoroughbred to ride and
a fearsome dog for company? What sort of father demanded that she disregard the gentler side of her nature
and was angry with her when she failed?

Ivo studied the girl. What he could see of her face
was as contradictory as the rest of her. There was a hint
of severity in her profile, with its straight nose, short,
disciplined upper lip and firm chin. But the line of her
jaw was delicately drawn and her lower lip full and vulnerable. The potential was there for great beauty. He
wondered what colour her eyes were…

'You're staring!' Jossie said. 'What's wrong?'

'Er…nothing,' said Ivo, most unusually at a loss for
words. 'I'm sorry. Shall we move a little faster? My aunt
will be expecting us.'

'Well, I don't see how she can be,' said Jossie. 'She
couldn't be sure you would find me as easily as you
did.'

Ivo drew a deep breath. 'No,' he said firmly. 'Are you
always as logical? But perhaps you should know that
she always has tea at four o'clock. Don't you want some
tea?'

'With muffins? Rather!' Jossie dug her heels in and
the bay moved into a trot. Ivo followed suit. He would
rather have died than mention that the jolting movement
was doing no good at all to his injured hand.

* * *

Lady Frances was delighted to see them both, but exclaimed when she saw Ivo's hand. As he removed the handkerchief they could see it was an angry red and very swollen.

'I shall send for Dr Hargreaves immediately!' she said. 'Jossie, go and tidy yourself up while I see to Lord Trenchard. How on earth did you do this, Ivo?'

Ivo's eyes met those of Jossie. He winked. 'A fox was quicker than I was,' he said. 'But it's nothing, really.'

'It looks awful,' said Jossie, gazing in horror at the mess of his hand. 'I'm sorry. I didn't realise...'

'Don't say another word! I'm near to tears as it is, and any sympathy from you would completely overset me!' said Ivo solemnly. 'We Hussars are babies at heart, you know.'

'Ivo! What on earth are you talking about?' said his aunt, looking bewildered. 'I think you must be delirious. Go and bathe that hand, while I send John Coachman for the surgeon.'

In the days that followed Ivo was hard put to it to maintain his sense of humour. The hand was badly infected and the fox's teeth had crushed two of the bones. It took all of Dr Hargreaves's skill to put it right. Fortunately Ivo's splendid physique served him well. The infection did not spread, and after a week the only serious cause of dissatisfaction was that he still had to keep it held up in a sling, unable to use it for anything strenuous. Boredom would have been his chief enemy but for the fact that Jossie was apparently suffering from a severe fit of conscience. That, combined with the Radstocks' decision to stay longer in Bath, meant that she spent a great deal of her time at Danby Lodge, doing her best to keep Ivo entertained during his convalescence. She demanded to hear about his campaigns in Spain and Portugal, and was eager to learn everything about Wellington. She made him draw out a plan of the field at Waterloo, and was scornful when he couldn't remember every detail.

'I thought it was the Ninety-Fifth who were in the sandpit by La Haye Sainte?' she said once. 'And how could Grouchy have been over there? He was well to the east. You mean Ney, don't you? Really Ivo, I'd have thought you'd know that!'

'I do, I do! I simply got confused. After all, I was just fighting in the damned battle, not designing it for posterity! And who gave you leave to call me Ivo?'

'Well, I can't keep on calling you Lord Trenchard. It's too stuffy. Especially when you owe me so much money.'

Ivo had seldom found himself laughing more often. Jossie was a constant source of amusement, sharp as a pin, full of fun and imagination and always ready with her own particular, original point of view. Her father, probably for his own amusement, had taught her to play piquet and several other games of chance and she was a surprisingly accomplished gamester. They played by the hour. Ivo himself was no mean player, but, at the moment, he was in her debt to the tune of four thousand three hundred and twenty-three guineas. Imaginary stakes, of course, but he still found it galling, and was as eager as any addict to win them back.

They played chess, too, and here Ivo came into his own. She had only played before with Peter Radstock, and was apparently unused to an opponent who thought more than a few moves ahead. Ivo enjoyed watching her as she hung over the board, a frown of concentration on her mobile face, biting her lower lip or touching the upper one with the tip of her tongue. He began to wait for the gleam in her eye when she thought she had him, the expression of disgust when she was caught out, or the crow of triumph when she succeeded. One thing was clear. Jossie Morley was keenly competitive, and a fast learner. The more they played, the greater the effort required to beat her. Ivo made the effort. In chess at least he was not going to be beaten by a mere child, however bright!

A child was how he thought of her. She was so unlike any female he had ever known, so direct, so without artifice, that he simply could not think of her as a young woman. She had a closer resemblance to some of the junior ensigns he had known in the army, except that she was quicker and bolder than any of them. And much, much more impudent. His wider experience, the fact that he was more than ten years older than she was, counted for nothing with Jossie Morley. She very quickly saw through any attempt to cozen or charm her and treated it with laughter or scorn. The way to win her respect was to out-think her at chess, or beat her at piquet, and the secret of holding her serious attention was not to pay compliments but to talk of his life in the Army. She listened eagerly to this, obviously storing up snippets of information with which to amuse her father.

This, of course, was why Jossie remained so immune to the charm which had made Ivo famous all over Europe. She had two idols, her father and Peter Radstock, and the rest of the world hardly existed except in relation to them. The contradictions in her nature were more evident in this than anywhere else, and Ivo found it almost incredible that a girl who was otherwise so sceptical should be so blindly, so uncritically partisan. Her chief aim in life seemed to be to earn her father's approval, to make up to him for the regrettable fact that she was a girl. Her chief happiness was to roam the countryside with Peter Radstock, behaving like the boy Major Morley had wanted. If her father was pleased with their escapades the rest of the county could disapprove to its heart's content, Jossie didn't care.

She was as insouciant about the future. She knew what it was to be, had known for as long as she could remember. She would marry Peter Radstock and live with him in the countryside they both knew so well. Ivo came to see that Jossie had a deep love and understanding of the land, its people, its wild life, its trees and plants. She had no desire to live anywhere else, to see anything of the world outside.

'London?' she replied in answer to a question he put to her. 'Of course I haven't seen London! Nor have I any desire to. I think I would suffocate in a great city such as that—no fresh air, no greenery, all those restrictions and artificialities. And what should I find to amuse me in London?'

'Jossie Morley, how can you possibly dismiss one of the great cities of the world with all its treasures, its beauties, in such a cavalier fashion? I never thought to find you such a narrow-minded little country bumpkin!'

Jossie jumped up, scattering the chess pieces over the floor. 'I'd rather be a country bumpkin than a…a pasteboard fashion plate, talking with a plum in its mouth, and thinking of nothing but the tying of a cravat, or the set of a sleeve! At least Peter and I are *real*, and we shall lead *real* lives!'

'Is that how you think of me?' asked Ivo in some amusement. 'A pasteboard fashion plate?'

'Oh, you're all right. I suppose it's because you've been in the Army. But you should see the young *gentle-*

men round here when they've spent a few weeks acquiring town bronze in the ''Village'' as they call it! Five minutes in their company and Peter and I can hardly speak for laughing! They are ridiculous with their huge collars and elaborate cravats. And the girls are worse, fluttering their fans and their eyelashes, mincing along in silly sandals and frilled skirts. Do you know, Ivo, some of the girls think themselves *failures* because they haven't acquired a Viscount or a Duke, or even just a rich man, in their first season? It wouldn't have mattered what he was like or how old he was—the important thing was to have captured someone eligible. How can they *bring* themselves to take part in such a cold-hearted arrangement? How can they contemplate sharing their lives with a man they have only met three or four times, someone whose only virtue is that he has a title, or wealth?'

Ivo nodded. Jossie's words were an uncanny echo of what he had often thought himself. She swept on, 'Perhaps I am a country bumpkin. If those are London values, then I prefer country ones. When I marry Peter I shall marry someone I have known all my life. I know him as well as I know myself. He and I are friends! We always have been and we always will be.'

'Do you...*love* him?' Ivo asked.

'Well, of course I do! Haven't I just been saying so?'

Ivo didn't answer. He wasn't sure what to say. Jossie's feelings for Peter were obviously deep, a part of her passionate love for her home, her land. They might well be enough for a long and happy marriage, and he sincerely hoped they would. But, though it might not seem so to her, friendship was far from being the whole story in matters of the heart. There was another, potentially more problematic, side to love, and he doubted that she was even aware it existed. What would happen when she encountered physical attraction, desire, the reality of marriage? How would that affect her feelings for Peter Radstock? Ivo took himself in hand. It was none of his business. In any case, how the devil could he even mention such matters to this unawakened child? It was out of the question.

Nevertheless, as time went on, he grew more concerned for her. Her vision of her future seemed to him to be dangerously unrealistic, more a child's view of life, a storybook world in which none of the characters changed or matured like real human beings, but carried on exactly the same forever. He knew neither of her idols as yet, except through what he had heard from his aunt and Jossie herself, but he doubted that any man in the world was worthy of such complete, such unquestioning admiration and devotion.

He saw no reason to change his mind when he did eventually make the acquaintance of the two men in Jossie's life.

Chapter Four

Jossie arrived one day at Danby Lodge in a gig. 'I must just take a piece of harness to the smith,' she said, 'and then I'll come back to fetch you.'

'To fetch us? Where?'

'Papa wishes to meet you.'

Ivo looked at the gig. 'There isn't room for all of us in that thing,' he said.

Jossie looked uncomfortable. 'Just the two of us. Papa didn't mention Lady Frances.'

Ivo frowned and began, 'In that case, I'm afraid—'

'Do go, Ivo!' urged his aunt. She turned to Jossie. 'Don't look so worried, Jossie. Lord Trenchard will come. You take whatever it is to the smith and call back here. I'll make sure he's ready.'

As soon as Jossie had driven off Ivo turned to his aunt, ready to argue. She laughed at him. 'You needn't say a word! I'm not at all offended, and I want you to go. Major Morley would never willingly invite me to see him. I've told you before, he and I are not exactly the best of friends.'

'Then why should I accept his somewhat peremptory summons?'

'For Jossie's sake. And because it would be an interesting experience. I find him a most unpleasant man, but I suppose he has some excuse for it. He was a very able soldier, until his career was cut short. Since then, his life has held nothing but disappointments—in his own eyes, at least.'

'What happened?'

'He was badly wounded years ago, and has been something of an invalid ever since. Lucinda was expecting a baby at the time, and he hoped desperately that it would be a boy. There…there wouldn't be any more children. That's why it was such a bitter disappointment when the child turned out to be a girl. He has a great sense of family pride, and she is the last of the line.'

'I see. When did Mrs Morley die?'

'When Jossie was three. But if you're thinking that she might have had a restraining effect on the Major, then you're wrong. She would never have denied him anything, and he is a self-indulgent autocrat. There, I've been most unkind about one of my neighbours, and I don't regret it a bit. I may be sorry for the man, but I cannot forgive what he has done to Jossie…'

'The child seems happy enough.'

'She's not a child any more!' his aunt said impatiently. 'That's what worries me. The signs are that before very long she will turn into an intelligent and beautiful woman. She's bright enough already. How will she feel when she wakes up to the fact that her two idols have feet of clay?'

'I had already decided that they couldn't possibly be as perfect as she thinks them—but feet of clay, Aunt Frances? Aren't you being a touch harsh?'

'I shan't say any more. I've wrecked enough reputations for one day. Go and visit Major Morley and draw your own conclusions.'

When Ivo first met Jossie's father he was favourably surprised. The Major was sitting in a study furnished for comfort rather than style. Though he was surrounded by books and dogs, there was a sense of severe discipline and order in the room. A large fire was burning in the open fireplace, and on a table close to the Major's chair were a chess set, and a tray of drinks and glasses. The Major got up as Ivo approached and limped towards him.

'There you are, Trenchard! Come in, come in and sit down. I'm delighted to meet you. What'll you have? Jossie, give Lord Trenchard something to drink, there's a good fellow. Then lose yourself. Come back in half an hour.'

Jossie obediently, and expertly, poured out wine for Ivo and brandy for her father, then quietly withdrew, leaving the two men to themselves.

They surveyed each other. Major Morley was in his early fifties, but he was still a handsome man with carefully brushed iron-grey hair and spruce moustaches. His linen was spotlessly white, his coat of a military cut, and he wore pale buff breeches with boots polished to a high gloss. The hand holding the glass of brandy was well formed and well cared for. The Major was obviously a man who took pains with his appearance—unlike his daughter.

'So, Trenchard! Jossie tells me you fought at Waterloo? Cavalry. What was your regiment?'

'The Seventh Hussars, Major.'

'*Hussars!* What sort of soldier is that? New-fangled nonsense! There weren't any…*Hussars* in my day. We were happy to be called Dragoons, none of your fancy foreign names.'

'I fancy we both *fought* much the same, sir' said Ivo mildly. 'Cavalry tactics haven't changed all that much…'

'Tactics! I could tell you a thing or two about tactics. Why, in '97…'

Over the next twenty minutes Ivo changed his mind about Major Morley. His manner was civilised enough, but what he said proved him an opinionated bore, vain, unwilling to give credit to anyone else but himself. He had read the accounts of the battle of Waterloo, and had formed his own opinion of how it should have been fought. Ivo's version of the action was of no interest to him and he gave only grudging admiration to Wellington's performance.

'Arthur Wellesley made his name in India, of course. It was easy enough out there. And once you've got a reputation, those idiots at the Horse Guards think you can't go wrong!'

Ivo reminded his host of Wellington's many battles with the Horse Guards, not all of them ending in victory, and finished by saying firmly, 'He's a very great soldier, sir. His tactics against the French in the Peninsula were brilliant—and I doubt anyone else could have carried the day at Waterloo.'

He didn't convince the Major, who shook his head and said sourly, 'Well, I have my own view on that, but I won't argue with you. It's natural you would be prejudiced in his favour. What d'y think of Jossie?'

The sudden change of subject took Ivo by surprise. 'I…I like her.'

'Not after her y'self, are you?'

Ivo's voice was cold as he said, 'I regard Jossie as a delightful child. No more.'

'Don't stiffen up on me. You have a bit of a reputation, Trenchard. Just wanted to make sure it don't affect my family.'

Ivo suppressed a spurt of fury and said calmly, 'I am surprised you should think that possible, Major. Jossie might well one day be a very beautiful woman, but at the moment you have seen to it that she is too much of a boy to be in danger.'

In a voice of suppressed anger his host said, 'A boy! Ay, that's what she should have been, not a damned girl!'

Then, perhaps sensing Ivo's disapproval of this outburst, he added more calmly, 'Jossie's a splendid chap, a first-rate shot and up to as many tricks as any lad. But that's just what she ain't, dammit!'

'I think you could be proud of her, all the same,' Ivo said somewhat coolly.

'I am, I am! As far as I can be. And if she marries Peter Radstock, that's the next best thing, I suppose. He isn't the son I'd have chosen for myself either, but Jossie and I between us will soon lick him into shape.'

Ivo wondered what Sir Thomas Radstock would make of this, but he merely smiled politely. He reminded himself once more that it was none of his business.

To his relief, Jossie came back as ordered after half an hour and sat cross-legged on the floor by her father's chair. During the conversation which followed Ivo learned a lot about the Morleys. He became aware that Major Morley not only dressed his daughter like a boy, he treated her as one, forcing her to live under a Spartan regime with no concessions to her femininity. He saw that Jossie, who was by no means a mindless puppet, accepted her father's dictates without argument or question, and began to understand the origin of some of the contradictions in her character. The child was courageous and spirited enough to play the boy, loving her father so much that, to please him, she suppressed any signs of the girlishness which he so despised. She was even ashamed of it herself. Jossie Morley would continue to be the son as long as she could.

As they drove back to Danby Lodge, Ivo was unusually silent. He now understood his aunt's comments on the situation in the Morley household, and he didn't know which he felt more—anger, admiration or pity. Jossie Morley's blind acceptance of her father's decrees angered him, her courage in obeying them aroused his admiration, but perhaps most of all he was sorry for her. Whatever she did, however hard she tried, Jossie Morley was intelligent enough to know that nothing would ever make up for the fact that she could never really be the son her adored father had wanted.

Fortunately Jossie hardly noticed his preoccupation. As they came into the village they saw the housekeeper from the Hall. When Jossie stopped to speak to her she told them that Sir Thomas and his family were due back in Lyne St Michael the next day. For the rest of the journey Jossie was bubbling over with excitement and plans for outings with Peter.

Ivo found himself hoping that the other man in Jossie's life would be more worthy of her devotion than the one he had just met, and two days later he was able to judge for himself. He and his aunt were invited to tea by Lady Radstock.

* * *

The Radstocks lived in a substantial house built about forty years before. It lay among lush acres of pastures and farmland, and the house itself was surrounded by a handsomely laid-out park and garden. Evidence of prosperity and good husbandry was all around. The rooms inside the Hall were furnished with quiet good taste, and the drawing room where they were received was a spaciously elegant apartment with long windows leading on to a terrace which overlooked the garden.

Sir Thomas Radstock was a bluff country gentleman, typical of his class and breeding. He was well informed and talked sensibly of the recent wars, but his chief interest clearly lay within his own county. Bath and town life in general did not appeal to him. His wife was a gentle, delicate-looking lady with exquisite manners. She and Lady Frances were obviously old friends, and Ivo was made to feel very welcome.

'So you fought at Waterloo, Trenchard? Was that where you injured your hand? Is it permanent?' asked Sir Thomas, looking at Ivo's hand, which was now free of a sling but strapped up.

'This? No, this is nothing, Sir Thomas. I did it down here just a few days ago.'

'He was out with Jossie Morley, Sir Thomas,' said Lady Frances.

'In that case I'm willing to wager that Jossie had something to do with that,' said Sir Thomas, nodding his head at Ivo's hand.

'It was a stupid piece of carelessness on my own part,' said Ivo affably but quite firmly.

'We've seen quite a lot of her while you were away,' Lady Frances went on. 'She has been keeping Ivo entertained after he injured his hand. The poor child missed you all so much.'

'So you know Jossie, do you?' said Sir Thomas. He eyed Ivo carefully. 'What a girl she is! She leads our Peter a pretty dance, I can tell you! Still, that'll all change once they're wed. She'll settle down then.' Having made the situation clear, he sat back with a smile and accepted a cup of tea from his wife.

Ivo was amused. First Jossie's father and now Sir Thomas, each warning him off! They could both rest easy. He still found it impossible to take the idea of Jossie Morley as anyone's bride very seriously, and would never be in contention himself. What was more, their fears were quite unnecessary. It would be a brave man indeed who would interfere with Jossie's own fixed determination to marry Peter Radstock!

'I know better than to ask Sir Thomas whether he enjoyed his stay in Bath, but were you pleased with your visit, Lady Radstock?' asked Ivo's aunt.

'Very much so. And Sir Thomas took the waters, you know, so he had some benefit. We made some very pleasant acquaintances. In fact, one of them, a Mrs Cherton, may well come to stay here in Lyne St Michael when she has completed the course of treatment in Bath. She is looking for a small house in the country and I recommended our village to her. I think she and her daughter would be a welcome addition to our little society.'

'I take it she is a widow?'

'Yes, she lost her husband some years ago. We felt quite sorry for her, and took them with us once or twice to the Assembly Rooms.'

'Sir Thomas dancing? I can hardly believe it!'

'Well, you need not. Sir Thomas stayed at home, and Peter escorted all three of us ladies to the Rooms. Mrs Cherton was most touched, and her daughter was delighted. Poor child, she has had little enough amusement in her life. I think she was quite taken with Peter. But where is he now?' Lady Radstock got up to look out of the window. 'It's too bad of him. He promised to be back for tea.'

'They went to Heversham Beacon,' said Sir Thomas.

'But that is miles away! He's with Jossie, I suppose?'

'Aye, she was here before the lad was rightly up. I'm sure they'll be back soon, my dear—they set off quite early.'

Lady Radstock pursed her lips. 'He shouldn't have gone so far,' she said.

Sir Thomas gave a laugh. 'I don't suppose he had a say in it! Not when Jossie's in charge! What a girl!'

This was obviously not the most tactful of responses. Lady Frances saw that her friend was quite upset and intervened. 'Please don't be disturbed on our account—' But she came to a stop as Jossie erupted into the drawing room, followed by the errant son of the house.

Jossie gazed round and began to look guilty. Lady Radstock looked at two sets of muddy boots and wind-blown hair, gave a slight sigh, then said gently, 'Jossie, Peter, pray go and get yourselves tidied up. You know where Mrs Marston will be, Jossie. Ask her to help you. Then you can come back and join in our tea party. I am sure Lord Trenchard will be happy to wait a little longer to meet you, Peter.'

After they had left the room, she turned to Ivo. 'Lord Trenchard, I hope you'll forgive my son. Peter isn't usu-ally—'

'Please, Lady Radstock! What is there to forgive?' Ivo exerted himself to put his hostess at ease. Underneath her calmly elegant manner he sensed that she was seri-ously annoyed, and he wondered whether she was as enthusiastic as Sir Thomas about the proposed match between Jossie and her son. As the visit went on he could see why she might not be.

Peter Radstock was a handsome lad. He had inherited his colouring from his father—dark reddish-gold hair, paling to blond where the sun had caught it, frank blue eyes, and a tanned complexion. His manners were good, and he had an attractively diffident smile. But the character and strength so evident in Sir Thomas's face were lacking in that of his son. Though the boy was two or three years older than Jossie, it was clear to Ivo that Peter followed where Jossie led. Knowing as he did the girl's strength of personality, Ivo would be willing to wager a considerable sum on which of the two would rule the roost once they were married. No wonder Lady Radstock was worried!

All of which was none of his business, of course. He liked Jossie Morley, but he was not her keeper. There was no conceivable reason for him to interfere, nor did he wish to. All the evidence was that her future was fixed, and any doubts on his part about the couple's chance of happiness were simply impertinent.

But when the Radstocks produced their next bit of gossip, he forgot his conjectures on the subject of Jossie, Peter and all the rest. Unaware of the shock she was about to give her guests, Lady Radstock began, 'We met another family in Bath who might interest you, Lady Frances. Sir George Gurney was an old friend of your brother's, was he not? Well, it seems that he and his daughter have been living in Bath for over a year. Did you know that Charlotte Gurney is now married?'

'I beg your pardon?'

'Married to a man old enough to be her grandfather!' said Sir Thomas disapprovingly. 'Courtney Malcot.'

'Lord Malcot?' said Lady Frances, astonished. 'But he has been twice widowed already! Are you sure?'

'Quite sure.'

'I can hardly believe it!' said Lady Frances. 'He has *children* who are years older than Charlotte! What can Sir George have been thinking of to allow such a thing! His only daughter!'

'I dare say it's not what he would have chosen, but the girl had apparently set her heart on it. They were saying in Bath that she was ready to run off with Malcot, and her father caught them just in time. I'm surprised at Malcot—he should know better. But at the risk of shocking you, Lady Frances, it's my opinion that the girl cozened him into it. She's a sly little minx.'

'Sir Thomas, you are too severe!' exclaimed Lady Radstock. 'That poor girl! She cannot be more than twenty and he nearly fifty! Why would she do such a thing?'

'Money, my dear! Money! Malcot's as rich as a nabob. The world may look sideways at the pair, but Charlotte now has a position in Society and enough carriages and servants to satisfy the most ambitious of girls.'

'Well, well,' said Lady Frances, casting a quick glance at Ivo. 'This is a surprising bit of news. I wonder if it has reached Sudiham.'

'Surely!' said Sir Thomas.

'Oh! Er...yes, of course. Though if Sir George has been in Bath for over a year, my brother may not have heard yet. Ivo, I think you should go over to Sudiham tomorrow. This is no occasion to be bearing old grudges. Your father has had time to recover from his anger at your insistence on staying in the Army.'

'Ah! Was that what it was?' said Sir Thomas. 'We had wondered...'

*   *   *

Ivo wasted no time. He thanked his aunt for her help and hospitality during the past weeks, and set off for Sudiham the next day. He approached the house with some misgivings, but this time the doors were open and his father was waiting in the library to receive him.

'So! You've come to your senses, have you?' Lord Veryan asked gruffly. 'Come to beg pardon?'

Ivo knew his father. 'I've come to beg pardon for allowing my temper to get the better of me, Father. I should have stayed to argue my case instead of storming off as I did, and I'm sorry for it. But I have nothing else to apologise for.' There was a slightly awkward silence. Then Ivo added, 'We've been at odds for too long. I should prefer us to be friends.'

'Would you? You don't sound as if you would! Still, since you've come... Sit down, sit down! Are you staying?'

'If you will have me.'

'Of course I will! And I may as well tell you right away, before we start—' Lord Veryan shifted restlessly in his chair. 'I've decided to forgive you.'

'For what, Father?' said Ivo evenly.

'Don't look at me like that!' roared his father. 'I'm not one of your men, dammit!' He glared at his son. After a moment he said abruptly, 'I've had time, plenty of time, to think. You don't tell lies, never have, not to me. I should have accepted your word. The trouble last year was that I was too angry to think straight. It was such a shock finding you and Charlotte Gurney alone in the cottage like that! George Gurney was so sure you were guilty, and you have to admit, Ivo, the evidence was pretty damning. Then, afterwards, the arguments... losing one of my oldest friends... And then you stormed off—'

'You told me to go.'

'I know I did! But you shouldn't have gone, confound it!' Another glare. 'You ought to have known I didn't mean it.'

'I don't see how! Your words were, I believe, that you wished never to set eyes on such a villainous, un-natural monster again.'

'Yes, well, there's no need to go on about it! I dare say I was a touch out of line.' He paused. 'Oh, very well! Totally out of line. But you shouldn't have gone, all the same. It didn't take long for me to come to my senses. I still don't know who was with Charlotte Gurney that day, but I do know it can't have been you.'

Ivo was puzzled. 'But if that is the case, why didn't you tell this to me sooner?'

'I wanted to. I wanted to send for you. But Perry said you were so angry that you would probably refuse to come. I wasn't ready to risk that. He was right, wasn't he? I was sure you would come down here before you went to Belgium, but you didn't. So I tried to put you out of my mind...'

Surprise and anger kept Ivo silent. He *had* come down to Sudiham, but Perry had fended him off, had told him that his father's orders were not to admit him to the house. Any doubts Ivo might still have cherished about Perry's guilt now vanished. His anger grew as he realised that he and his father had been kept apart for all these months solely because of his brother's lies. Why had Perry done it? Had he been afraid that the truth about his affair with Charlotte would come out after all? But that was ridiculous! He *must* have realised that he couldn't keep the two of them apart forever—Ivo would surely see his father again, sooner or later! Or...Ivo grew cold. With the threat of war so close, had Perry hoped that his problems would be solved if his brother died in battle? He shook his head. No! Perry might have behaved badly, but that was something Ivo refused to believe.

Lord Veryan said, 'You're very quiet. Was I mistaken? Did Perry misrepresent you? Did Perry lie to me, Ivo?'

Ivo didn't reply, but instead asked, 'Where is Perry now?'

'He's in Derbyshire, at Arneston. He hasn't been himself for some time, so I thought a change of scene would do him good.'

Ivo made an effort to sound calm as he said, 'I'm glad to hear that. He should have gone up there years back, when you first suggested it. Does he intend to stay?'

'I don't know. He might. He seems happier away from Sudiham, and me. But then, he and I never did agree.' There was a pause, then Lord Veryan added bitterly, 'Changing the subject won't help, Ivo. I've noticed that you still haven't answered my question. But perhaps you needn't bother. It's clear enough what happened. Perry deliberately kept us apart, God knows why.'

There was a silence which Ivo found impossible to break. His father went on slowly, 'And yet...and yet, perhaps I do. Perry was afraid you would convince me of your innocence. And if that happened I would look elsewhere for the guilty party. Gurney was right, wasn't he? Someone in my family was to blame for that poor girl's seduction. But it wasn't you, it was Perry! And he was afraid you would betray him.'

Ignoring this last sentence, Ivo said scornfully. '*Poor girl?* So you haven't heard? That "poor girl", as you call her, has just married a very rich man. And Thomas Radstock believes she arranged the whole thing.'

'What's this? Who is the man?'
Ivo went on to give his father the news from Bath.

This was the last time Charlotte Gurney was mentioned between them, and by mutual consent they also avoided any further painful discussion of Perry's manipulations. It was easy enough to ignore them. Now that Charlotte was lost to him, Perry no longer found Somerset so attractive, and, to Ivo's relief, he accepted his father's suggestion that he should continue to look after the Arneston estate indefinitely.

During that year Ivo and his father lived in comparative harmony. Lord Veryan was much changed. The old fire still occasionally flashed out, but he was visibly frailer. The two were both anxious to build bridges over their separation and over the next months Ivo gradually took over a great deal of the older man's responsibilities. But he found time to visit his friends occasionally, and in May he spent a few weeks in London. He saw Adam again, and for a short while there was a danger that he might lose his heart to Kate Payne. She was so unlike any woman he had ever known before, so straightforward, so courageous, that he was strongly attracted. Kate liked him, it was clear. But fortunately, long before any serious damage was done, it became just as clear to him that she was in love with Adam Calthorpe. And it amused him to observe that Adam quickly became jealous of any undue attention paid to Kate by others, including Ivo himself. Though Kate was far from being the tame little housewife he had planned to marry, Adam Calthorpe was rapidly falling in love with the girl! Much as he would have liked to watch the progress of this intriguing love affair, Ivo decided it would be wiser to withdraw from the scene and look forward to an easy friendship in the future with Adam and his wife. And later in the year his discretion was rewarded when he was invited to their wedding.

Between Ivo's visits to London and the great deal of work he found otherwise at Sudiham, he had not had time to go back to Lyne St Michael. He occasionally thought of Jossie with a smile and wondered what tricks she had been up to since they had last met, but the girl's affairs were no longer at the forefront of his mind. When his Aunt Frances came to Sudiham for Christmas she gave him scraps of news—little seemed to have changed, though the Radstocks had begun to plan for the celebration of Peter Radstock's coming of age.

'When is that?' Ivo asked.

'Next July.'

'But that's over six months away!'

'This is a major event, I assure you. Half the county will be at the ball, to say nothing of all the feasts and so on for lesser folk. Lady Radstock is already drawing up the lists. You may assume your name will be on it, Ivo. I hope you will come.'

'I wouldn't miss it for the world! Isn't this the final culmination of Jossie's plans? The moment she and young Radstock become officially engaged?'

'Yes. I have to say the whole idea of those two getting married still seems absurd. They show no signs of settling down. I sometimes wonder if Jossie will walk up the aisle in breeches and that old coat of hers!'

'Lady Radstock would never permit it.'

There was more news of the families in Lyne St Michael at Easter. Jossie had a chaperon! Major Morley had finally given in to pressure, and a distant relative of his, a female of uncertain years, had been installed in the Morley home. What was more, Jossie was being made to wear skirts as often as the chaperon could catch her.

'I feel sorry for the poor woman, Ivo,' said Lady Frances, 'though she is something of a misery. She does her best to instil her charge with some elements of lady-like behaviour, but Jossie spends most of her time carrying on exactly as before. She ignores her chaperon's pleas not to spend so much time running wild with Peter Radstock, and as for the skirts... Halfway down the drive that wretched girl has changed, and is once more in breeches. The two of them—for Peter is as bad as Jossie—just make fun of her! They are a graceless pair, but one cannot help laughing.'

Lady Frances also told them that a Mrs Cherton had arrived in Lyne St Michael and had taken up residence in a modest house in the High Street.

'This is the lady the Radstocks met in Bath, is it not?' asked Ivo. 'Is she as much of an asset to the village as Lady Radstock seemed to think?'

Lady Frances pursed her lips. 'A very elegant lady. A beauty in her day, I imagine... She has been ill, of course, but I find her air of delicate suffering very irritating. I have frequently observed that she is seldom too ill to accept an invitation...as long as it's from the right people.' She paused, then said firmly, 'It is early days yet. I prefer to wait before giving an opinion.'

'You've just given one!' said Ivo, laughing. 'What about the daughter? Is she pretty, too?'

'Ye-es. In a quiet, ladylike way. Blonde hair, lightish blue eyes, plump cheeks, and what I believe is called a rosebud mouth. She is very much in her mother's shadow, and seldom speaks unless spoken to. She blushes a lot.'

Ivo gave another shout of laughter. 'Oh, Aunt Frances, Aunt Frances! Pray don't let your enthusiasm for the Chertons run away with you!'

'Oh, the girl is well enough. I suppose. I hardly know either of them. But Lady Radstock has been very kind to them both, particularly the girl, Rosalind.'

'Indeed?'

'She has made a great effort to introduce them to the other families in the district. Lyne St Michael has become a hive of social activity recently. You would hardly recognise it.'

'How is Jossie faring in all this social activity?'

'I think you can imagine. She hates it, and avoids it whenever she can. She is never at her best in society, Ivo.' Lady Frances started to laugh. 'But her father more than makes up for her.'

'The Major?'

'There's been the most surprising change there! He was seldom seen in public before, but now I think he is at last beginning to take his duties as Jossie's father more seriously. He accompanies her to the Radstocks, and one or two other very select neighbours. He even comes to me! I have to say his company manners are excellent. He can be most charming to the ladies, particularly the pretty ones.'

'So the Major has turned out to be a ladies' man, eh? Does it make him kinder to Jossie?'

'I do think he is trying to face the fact that he can't pretend she's a boy for much longer...' Lady Frances paused, then said, 'He has done that girl such a lot of harm! She has so many talents, so much natural vivacity that she ought to be the star of the neighbourhood. But she is completely out of her element in polite company. She hasn't the slightest idea of how to behave. If I didn't know her as well as I do, Ivo, I'd think her a true country bumpkin!'

'That is exactly what she said she wanted to be.'

'Well, it won't do!' his aunt said tartly. 'Not when there are other pretty girls in the neighbourhood, all apparently better fitted to marry the heir to the second-largest estate in this part of the county!'

'There's no danger there, Aunt Frances! Jossie would see any one of them off.'

'You may say so, Ivo, but it's time she grew up! If she is serious about marriage to Peter Radstock, then it's time she started to treat him like a lover, not a companion for pranks.'

'I'm quite certain she is serious about Peter Radstock. She talked of nothing else when I stayed with you.'

'I know. I wish...'

'What? Really, Aunt Frances, these stops and starts are most unlike you! What's wrong?'

'I had hoped you would have some influence on Jossie. Perhaps even take her mind off Peter a little. But it didn't work.'

Ivo looked at her and laughed. 'Oh, come! You must have known it wouldn't!'

'It might if you had put your mind to it... You have a great deal of address, Ivo.'

'Nothing that could compete in Jossie's eyes with Peter Radstock's perfections.'

'I was afraid it was so,' said his aunt gloomily. 'Poor Jossie!'

Chapter Five

Jossie herself would have echoed Lady Frances's sentiments. She had escaped with difficulty from her chaperon's vigilance and had ridden over to the valley where she had arranged to meet Peter, only to find that he wasn't there. It had been a morning of vexations and this was just one more of them. She shivered. Spring had come late. The track was still covered with dead leaves and on either side the muddy ground was thick with withered fronds of bracken and untidy trails of bramble. The landscape seemed to echo her own feelings of gloom.

Such a short time ago she would have laughed at herself, found something to amuse her while waiting for Peter—would have burrowed under the leaves for signs of the spring flowers, searched a hole in a tree in the hope of finding a sleepy squirrel still in residence. But now she was unable to shake off a vague but growing feeling of apprehension. Life was changing and she was changing with it, little though she liked it.

Jossie let her horse wander along the track as she considered the situation. Why had things begun to change? It could hardly have been the arrival of Cousin Martha—

her chaperon was a nonentity, not to be taken seriously by anyone. For a time, frustrating Cousin Martha's attempts to make her into a lady had even added spice to life. And while her skirts were a nuisance, she usually managed to wear her breeches when she went out with Peter. She didn't *feel* any more like a girl.

So what was wrong? Her father hadn't wanted change. True, he was mixing more in Society, but that was because he loved her and wanted to give her his support. He knew she often felt lost among the fine ladies and gentlemen and their elegant offspring at the parties that seemed to be mushrooming all over the neighbourhood. And her father wouldn't have invited Cousin Martha to come to live with them if Lady Radstock hadn't been so persistent...Lady Radstock and Mrs Cherton.

Jossie frowned as she thought of Mrs Cherton. Everyone else in Lyne St Michael, with the possible exception of Lady Frances, who had not expressed an opinion, approved of her. Lady Radstock was firmly in her favour, and Peter had said only the other day that he thought her very pleasant. Was she, Jossie, the only person in the village who was not charmed by Mrs Cherton? Even her father...

Jossie's apprehension suddenly crystallised. Her father, too, approved of Mrs Cherton. It was after an afternoon spent at the Radstocks in Mrs Cherton's company that he had seemed to change. Since then he had stopped laughing at Jossie's exploits...

Her musings were interrupted by a call from behind. 'Jossie! Jossie, old chap, wait!' It was Peter.

She turned with relief, her doubts and worries forgotten. 'Where've you been?' she asked. 'I thought we were to meet half an hour ago.'

'I'm sorry, Mama got hold of me just as I was leaving, and I couldn't get away. She had Mrs Marston in tow—'

'Your housekeeper? What on earth did your mama wish to talk about?'

'Arrangements for my party. Don't look so blank! My coming of age.'

'But that's months ahead!'

'That's what I said. But apparently there's so much to be done that it all has to be considered now. It'll be a big affair, Jossie. There's the feast for the estate workers, and the party for the children, and then there's the ball in the evening. Half the county will be invited...' He went on giving her details, taking it for granted that she would be as excited as he was.

Jossie stopped listening halfway through, boredom and resentment taking over in her mind. That damned birthday party! That was the root cause of all this desire for her to be proper, to wear skirts, to behave like a lady! For years she and Peter had planned for the day when he would come of age, what they would do after they were married, but it hadn't entered her head that there would be all this fuss, the ball, the feast, the dancing. She hadn't really ever thought about the event as a public celebration, only what it would mean to Peter and herself. She interrupted him impatiently. 'For heaven's sake, let's not talk about it any more, Peter!'

'Why ever not?'

'Parties and fêtes are boring! Anyway, it's a long time ahead, and there are other things to think about! We haven't been to Heversham Beacon since last year.'

'Heversham Beacon! That's much too far, Jossie. We'll never get back before dark.'

'Don't be such an old woman! We can do it as long as we don't waste time talking about it. Come on!'

She dug her heels into her horse and, paying little heed to the dangerous state of the path, started off up towards the high road.

'Jossie, wait! Slow down! Why are you angry? Have I said something wrong?'

Jossie ignored him. She felt a desperate need for fresh air, the wind, the feeling of freedom that a hard ride to the top of the hills would provide. Peter would follow— he always did.

As they rode swiftly over the hills the weather improved and so did her temper. The sun came out, the wind got up, and patterns of cloud and sunshine raced over the hills and valleys. Jossie laughed with relief and delight.

'This is what I want!' she cried. 'Isn't it glorious? The space, the freedom, the air! There's nothing to compare with it. Certainly not making stupid conversation with stupid people in stuffy rooms. Let's stay up here forever!'

'You don't really mean that, Jossie. You know we can't do it. Besides, I quite enjoy meeting new people, talking to them. They can be very interesting. In Bath—'

'Oh, Bath! You're surely not about to say that you *enjoyed* Bath, are you, Peter? I can't imagine any town being enjoyable. I'll race you to the top of the Beacon! Come on!'

'No!' For once Peter spoke so decisively that Jossie stopped in surprise. He went on, 'No, Jossie. I want to talk to you. Let's walk for a bit.'

The expression on his good-natured face was unusually solemn. Jossie grimaced as she felt again that shiver of apprehension, but she dismounted and they tied up the horses and set off along the path to the top.

'I know you don't like parties and such, Jossie,' he

began. 'Though I think you would enjoy them more as time went on and you got used to them. But they don't matter all that much. This coming of age—no, don't turn away! Listen to me.' He stopped and made her face him. 'I've been thinking a lot about our future and you must let me say what I have to say. This coming of age isn't just an excuse for a series of parties. It's more serious than that. It's the threshold of a new life.'

'Is that what your father said? Or was it your mother?' asked Jossie impatiently. When she saw the look of hurt on Peter's face she shook her head at herself and held out a hand. 'I'm sorry,' she said. 'That was rude of me.'

Peter took her hand and held on to it. 'You're forgiven. My mother did say something of the sort. But I agree with her, it is! And...and...these parties and things... Well, we can't go chasing round the countryside forever as if the real world doesn't exist! We have to start taking up our roles in society, Joss. I'll be one of the biggest landowners in the county when our two estates are joined, and that gives me obligations.'

'Your mother again?'

'No, my father. But I'm still in agreement. And you should be, too. We have to start growing up.'

'Of course we do! But that needn't mean we have to become part of the social scene. I hate the social scene, Peter!'

'But you can't avoid it forever! We can't bury ourselves in Lyne St Michael, it wouldn't be right. I hope we might even spend some time in London, do the season, perhaps. I'd like to see something of the great world... And Mama agrees. She thought it would—'

'In *London*! Are you mad? I'd *die* in London! Why do we need London, when there's so much here? Look round you, Peter! This is what matters—the land. *Our*

land.' When he was silent, she took his other hand and
made him look at her. 'I know you really feel the same
as I do,' she said persuasively. 'This sudden desire to
visit London isn't the real Peter Radstock. No, we shall
do what we've always planned. We shall live in our own
home country together... I thought you loved the land,
Peter?'

'I do! But I'd still like to see a bit of life—'

'Life!' she exclaimed. '*This* is life *here*! Real life! Oh,
I know your mama has always wanted you to be a gentleman of fashion, but look at you! You're handsome
enough, but you're hardly a pink of the *ton*! You would
be as uncomfortable as I would be in London Society, I
know you would. You may tell your mama that I won't
hear of our going to London.'

Peter gave in, as he always did when Jossie sounded
so fierce, but he was unusually quiet for a while, refusing
to respond to Jossie's attempts to amuse him. Finally
she gave up and said sadly, 'You're like the rest. You're
changing.'

'Oh, no! No, never that! You know I love you, Joss!
I always have. But now that...now that we're older, and
thinking of marrying, things must change—'

'But I don't want them to!' Jossie's cry came from
the heart. 'I want things to stay as they are! Forever!'

'That's nonsense! You can't mean it!' He looked at
her mutinous expression and his voice softened. 'Look,
it needn't be for the worse. We can carry on much as
we always have, if that's what you want. Cheer up, Jossie! What is worrying you now?'

She said bitterly, 'Your mother will try to make me
into a proper housewife, I know she will.'

Peter burst into laughter. 'Is that all? What a clunch
you are! We needn't listen to her!' When Jossie didn't

react he grew sober and went on anxiously, 'You...you still want to marry me, don't you?'

This time her response was instant. 'Of course I do! I can't imagine life without you, you know that. But—'

'But what?'

'I've looked forward to your coming of age for so many years. It's absurd to say that I feel I need more time. But there's *something* wrong. All this talk of celebrations...Cousin Martha's attempts to make a lady out of me...things your mother has been saying...' She looked at Peter's puzzled face and said desperately, 'Marriage makes people so...so serious! And suddenly...I don't feel ready.'

The colour in the boy's face deepened. 'Is it because you're afraid? Do you want us to...to get to know each other better? I know I would like to.'

She said in astonishment. 'Of course it's not that! What on earth are you talking about? We know each other as well as anyone could expect!'

'Not...not in the way I mean.' His flush grew even deeper as he took her hand. 'You've been the best friend a fellow could ask for, Jossie. But there's more to it than that. Will you...will you let me kiss you?'

She stared at him. 'Kiss me? What a strange notion! You've never wanted to kiss me before.'

'It was different before. We were children and I...I didn't think of you in that way. But now...I feel differently. Let me kiss you, Jossie!'

'Well, if that's what you want... Very well.' She shrugged and held up her cheek.

'No, not like that. Like this!' Peter put his arms round her and kissed her firmly on the lips. 'Oh, Jossie!' he murmured and kissed her again hard, holding her so tightly that she could scarcely move. No one had ever held her so closely, so intimately, before, and for a moment she was in a panic. She felt stifled, wanted to push him away, to escape from that suffocating embrace... But then she remembered who was kissing her. This was Peter, the man she was going to marry, and marriage, she knew, entailed closeness of body as well as of mind. If she rejected his first approach as a lover, he would be so hurt... So she willed herself to remain still, to stay passive in his arms. The kiss seemed to last forever, and the sense of relief when he released her was enormous. She looked at him apprehensively. How would he react to her lack of response...? He smiled and gave a sigh of contentment.

'Oh, Jossie! You see? Wasn't that wonderful? Things will be better than ever, don't you agree?'

Jossie bit back an exclamation. He hadn't even noticed! He thought the embrace had given her pleasure! How *could* he be so mistaken?

'Yes, yes,' she murmured. 'Of course.' Then she straightened her jacket and turned away, surreptitiously wiping her mouth on her sleeve. She found herself desperately hoping that she would learn to like such demonstrations. Or at least to accept them with more warmth.

But things did not get better, and after a while it was inevitable that Peter began to notice her reluctance. They started to quarrel, especially when Peter tried to kiss her more often.

'Why can't we enjoy each other's company without all that sentimental rubbish?' she cried one day.

Peter was hurt and angry. 'Because I love you! And you ought to *want* my kisses, Jossie!'

'Oh, fustian! All this kissing and cuddling is boring!'

'Not everyone thinks so! I could tell you of some who would welcome it!'

'Well, go and play with them, then. I'm off to Holcroft's farm.'

Of course he came with her, but there was a restraint between them that had never been there before, though they both tried to bridge it.

Jossie said pleadingly, 'I'm sorry, Peter. Don't let's quarrel any more! I hate it when we quarrel. I'll try to be…to be more like the other girls.'

His response was immediate and generous. 'I'm sorry, too. It's my fault, I'm too impatient. I forget what a strange life you've led. I can't treat you like a boy for so many years, then expect you to turn overnight into a girl, Joss. Perhaps we both need more time.'

They left it there and for the rest of that day he treated her very much as he had in the past.

The next day a message came from the Hall to say that Peter wouldn't be able to see her for a while. His mother had asked him to escort her to Bath. Apparently she needed a number of items connected with the celebrations in the summer which only Bath could provide, and Sir Thomas was busy with matters on the estate. Since one of the requirements was a new ball dress, it would be ten days to a fortnight before she and Peter would return. The note was affectionate, and full of concern. *'I wish we did not have to be apart at this time, Joss,'* he wrote. *'We used to be such good friends before my stupid lack of patience upset you. But I cannot imagine a future without you. I will wait as long as it takes, Joss. I would do anything for you, you know that!'*

Jossie was touched, but she was ashamed to admit to herself that she felt relief rather than disappointment.

This would at least give her a breathing space, time to adjust to the fact that she could no longer be Peter's 'capital fellow' and his best friend. Peter wanted something more. And since she genuinely could not imagine life without him, she must do her best to change.

The drawback was that she could not imagine how she should begin.

She spent long hours roaming about the countryside pondering this question, and after a while came to the conclusion that Peter was right. She had lived as a boy, been treated as a boy for so long, that she had forgotten how to be a girl. She must learn. Judging by some of the things he had said recently, her father would no longer object to seeing her in skirts, so she would stop resisting Cousin Martha and do as she asked. There would be no more breeches, she would wear the riding habit lying in the wardrobe, look out her mother's side saddle, and do her best to behave like a lady. Perhaps that would do the trick. It would at least be a beginning.

She occasionally sighed at the loss of the freedom her breeches had given her, but once she had made her decision she resolutely followed this plan. If Peter wanted a girl, then he would find one when he returned! But whether skirts and elegant behaviour would be enough remained to be seen. The delicate matter of her response to his embraces hovered at the back of her mind, colouring everything she did. If only there was someone who could offer her advice or help! She had never before felt so isolated. Consulting her father was obviously out of the question. The idea of Cousin Martha as a confidante was laughable! Lady Frances? Possibly. Jossie had a suspicion that the older woman was not altogether in favour of a match between Peter and herself. She might not be all that sympathetic a listener.

* * *

At this point Ivo arrived in Lyne St Michael. He had
arranged to be in London for the season, but had decided
to spend a few days with his aunt on the way. The situation she had described during her Easter visit had
aroused his interest. He was curious about the charming
widow who had come to live in Lyne St Michael, together with her nondescript daughter. And he found the
idea of Jossie in skirts even more intriguing!

He was disappointed on his arrival in Lyne St Michael, therefore, to learn from his aunt that Mrs Cherton
and her daughter had just left to spend a few days with
friends, though no one was quite sure where.

'Lady Radstock is away, too, though we do know
where she has gone. It appears that Bath is the only place
outside London that can provide a dress suitable for the
ball.'

'So I am not to see the Radstocks either? That's a
pity.'

'Sir Thomas is here. Peter volunteered to escort his
mother.'

'What about Jossie? Has she gone with them to buy
a dress, too?'

'No, Jossie is with us here in Lyne. But I haven't seen
her at all since Peter and his mother left. She has been
more elusive than ever. She's not happy, Ivo.'

'I would have thought she would be full of plans for
the summer?'

'I suspect that's half the trouble. Jossie doesn't like
the idea of all the fuss, and Peter is relishing it. I've tried
to talk to her, but she's too loyal to Peter to confide in
me. I've tried not to show it, but she knows I don't think
he's good enough for her.' She paused. 'I don't suppose
that you could do something while you're here, could
you, Ivo? She always seemed ready to talk to you.'

'I doubt very much that I could succeed where you've failed. Still, I like the child. If you think I could do something…'

'Good! The next problem is where to find her!'

'Oh, I'll find her,' said Ivo confidently. 'I know where to look.'

Jossie was where he had expected, down in the valley by the little stream. She was sitting on a rock, moodily throwing stones into the water.

'Good morning!' called Ivo, keeping his distance. He had no wish to startle Jossie when she had stones in her hand. The accident rate at their meetings had so far been too high. But all she did when he called was to look up, then turn back to the stream.

'What do you want?' she asked moodily.

Ivo came down the path and joined her. 'That's no way to talk to a man who owes you money!'

She gave him a fleeting grin. 'You never did win it all back, did you?'

'I will, one day.'

'I doubt you'll have the chance. I'm becoming respectable. A lady.'

Ivo looked at the discarded boots and stockings, the hat lying on the ground beside her, the skirts turned back to reveal bare legs and feet dangling in the water. 'I can see that,' he said.

She laughed, jumped up, and shook out her skirts. 'I have lapses,' she said. 'Sometimes it all seems too much. How are you, Ivo, and why haven't you been to Lyne St Michael before this?'

He had forgotten how direct she was, how natural her manner, how she wrinkled her nose when she laughed. She had grown, too. He liked the way her severely cut riding habit outlined her figure. One could never mistake her for a boy now...

'You're staring!' she said. 'Turn your back while I put my boots and stockings on.'

'I left my horse at the top. I'll fetch him down. Let me know when you've finished.'

He waited on the bridle path until she whistled, then led his horse down to join her. 'You've a long way to go, Jossie Morley. Ladies don't whistle! And they don't know how to dress without a maid to help them.'

'I've told you. I have lapses. Besides, I doubt you would make a very good ladies' maid. And there's no one else here.'

'Don't be so dismissive. I've had my moments—' Ivo stopped short. He had spoken without thinking. This was not the sort of thing one said to an innocent young lady! The trouble was he still half-thought of Jossie as a boy. He shook his head and said frankly, 'I'm sorry, Jossie. That slipped out, I'm afraid. Can you forget I said it?'

She regarded him speculatively. Then she said, 'So you've "had your moments", have you? I should have remembered. Everybody says you're a man of experience, though I must say I've never noticed it.'

'It's not the sort of thing I've ever wished to discuss with you,' said Ivo solemnly. He was finding it difficult not to laugh at this unexpected reply! His reputation had evoked a variety of reactions from disapproval to admiration, but never one as coolly objective as this. What was Jossie up to now?

She was still eyeing him with a look of assessment. 'I wonder if you'd do,' she said slowly. 'I know I could trust you. And if anyone could show me, you could. But would you be willing to do it?'

'I'm not sure I understand what you're talking about,

Jossie, but I don't like the sound of it. Explain, please. I'll help you if I can—without loss of limb, that is.'

'You do go on about that fox... Your hand is quite recovered, isn't it?'

'What do you want?'

Jossie looked at him, took a breath, was silent, then took another breath and began. 'I need help,' she said. 'If there was anyone else, I would speak to them about it, believe me. Lady Frances would have done, but she doesn't want me to marry Peter, so she wouldn't be very sympathetic. Besides, she's a woman.'

'I'm still waiting.'

'I would never have thought of you, before you came today. But I always felt I could talk to you about anything. And you could be perfect. I hope you don't find me unbelievably impertinent?'

'I can't find you anything until I know what the devil you're talking about!'

Ivo's impatience spurred her. 'It involves Peter. Peter and me. And I have to talk to someone!'

'Now wait! I'm not sure—'

'Oh, please, Ivo! Listen! I'm not asking you to be a mother or anything. I know about the...the processes of nature. You can't associate with farms all your life and *not* know.'

'Well, that's a relief!'

'This is more complicated.' She walked a step or two away from him and spoke without turning. 'I suppose it's natural that Peter wants...wants to kiss me, now that our marriage is not so far off. And because we've always had more freedom than many other young people, the opportunity is often there. But...but...' She put her face in her hands and her next words were muffled. 'I don't know how to say this...I dislike it!'

Ivo smiled and came over to her. 'Is that all? That's the most natural reaction in the world. Of course you're afraid. It's a new and disconcerting world you're about to enter. But if you love Peter—'

She turned round. 'I do! But it isn't *fear* that I feel. That's what he thinks, but he's wrong! I'm not afraid when he kisses me, I'm bored, impatient... I'm not nervous, I feel *stifled*. But I *am* afraid of something else.' He waited. She threw him a quick look then turned away again. 'I'm so afraid that I shall always feel like that.'

Ivo said calmly, 'I'm quite sure you won't.'

'How can you be sure? My father wanted me to be a boy and that's what I've tried to be. Perhaps all those years pretending to be a boy have...damaged me? I shall never enjoy being kissed.'

Ivo gave a shout of laughter, pulled her round and hugged her. 'My sweet, darling Jossie! No one with as kissable a mouth as yours could possibly not enjoy being kissed sooner or later.'

Her eyes shining, Jossie looked at him. 'Well, that's what I wanted to ask you, Ivo. I wondered if you could teach me how to respond.'

Chapter Six

Shock kept Ivo quiet for several seconds. In all the wide world, he thought, only Jossie Morley could have made a request such as that. So naturally, so unselfconsciously. Could he do as she asked? With almost anyone else he would have refused unhesitatingly, suspecting some sort of trap. But not with Jossie. For no one else would he have broken his cardinal rule never to become involved with an unmarried girl, but Jossie was different. She didn't want involvement, she wanted help. She had asked him as a friend, someone she could trust. Ivo did not allow himself to speculate what the request revealed of the situation between Jossie and Peter Radstock, the so-called lovers. That was none of his business. He must think only of helping Jossie.

But first he must clear the ground.

'Are you sure you're being sensible?' he said at last. 'You must have heard what they say of me.'

'Lady Frances said once you were the worst flirt in the county before you went into the Army, and she didn't suppose you had changed.'

'How very kind of her! Doesn't that put you off?'

'Of course not—it's what I want! It's no use asking

someone who doesn't know what they're doing to help me in this. I need an expert. That's what they say you are. Please, Ivo!'

If the situation had been less sensitive Ivo would have laughed. Of the many bizarre assignments given him in his career, this one must surely take the prize. But it *was* sensitive and he must do his best. Jossie's absurd fears mustn't be allowed to grow. He made up his mind.

'Let's walk a little way along the valley,' he said. 'The horses will be safe enough here.'

'I thought you were going to kiss me!'

'I am. But not yet. It's no use kissing you when you're standing like an ornamental statue waiting to have its face washed.'

Jossie burst into laughter. 'Did I really look like that?'

'The essence of an enjoyable kiss is its romance—in the beginning, at least. Come, walk with me. I'm not sure I've ever looked properly at this valley. It's quite pretty.'

As they wandered down by the side of the stream, they soon fell into their old companionship, Ivo asking questions and Jossie eagerly showing him the beauties of the place. It was obviously very special to her. Finally they came to a small waterfall. Here they paused, and after a moment Jossie fell silent. The only sounds were the wind rustling in the trees and the plashing of the water. Ivo turned her gently to face him.

'Let me look at you,' he said. 'You've changed quite a lot in the past year.' Then he smiled as she stared up at him trustingly. 'You know, I've never been sure about your eyes,' he said. 'When I first met you I thought they were blue. But sometimes they look turquoise, and sometimes they are truly green. I never know what I shall find.' He smoothed her hair back from her forehead. 'This is longer than it was.'

'I...I've been letting it g-grow. C-Cousin Martha said l-long hair was...was more s-suitable for a lady.'

'I don't know that I agree. Those short curls were very appealing.'

Jossie wasn't quite sure what was happening to her. Why was she stammering? Why, when she had not been walking at all energetically, did she feel so short of breath? The touch of Ivo's fingers was feather light, but it was burning a trail over her face, down her cheek, over her lips, under her chin....

He bent his head and kissed her. There was no feeling of compulsion, he was hardly holding her at all, just his hand under her chin... But the warmth in her face was spreading along her veins and through the rest of her body, a delicious languor was melting her bones so that she had to clutch his arms to steady herself...

He raised his head and gazed down into her eyes. 'They're purest sapphire,' he said softly. 'And so lovely.' Then he put his arms right round her, holding her close. 'Jossie!' he murmured and kissed her again. This time the kiss was more passionate, more demanding... These were altogether deeper, more dangerous waters, and Jossie felt a momentary panic, a brief wish to escape. But her trust in Ivo held. She forgot her fears and let him gather her to him. Soon she had forgotten everything but the delight of the moment. She had never before felt so gloriously exhilarated, not even on the highest hilltop. It was so easy to respond, to seek even closer contact with this body that was giving her such pleasure. She laughed in astonished joy, put her arms round his neck and pressed herself against him, her lips soft and yielding under his... With a muffled groan Ivo locked her even more closely in his arms...

Suddenly he pulled himself away. He was breathing fast. After a moment he swallowed and said, 'I think we've proved something, don't you?'

She took his hand and held it against her cheek. 'Oh, Ivo, that was...was *wonderful*! I didn't know anything could be as exciting. Is it always like that?'

He was staring at her as if she was someone he had never seen before. Then he took his hand away and Jossie felt unaccountably bereft. 'Not always,' he said. 'In fact—' He stopped and said brusquely, 'I have to get back. I'm really on my way to London. Aunt Frances will be looking for me...'

'Ivo! Have I done something wrong? Is there something else I need to learn?'

'No!' He looked at her anxious face and made a visible effort to speak naturally. 'My dear girl, you have no need to learn anything. Peter Radstock is a very fortunate man, and I wish you all the joy in the world with him.'

'But you'll be there at the ball? You'll come back from London in time? I want you there, Ivo.'

He hesitated, then, as her smile began to fade, he said, somewhat grimly, 'I'll be there.'

'Good!' They walked up to the horses, then led them on to the bridle path and mounted. When they came to the village Jossie asked him if he would like to see her father.

'Thank you, but no. I'm afraid I must hurry back. Aunt Frances is expecting me. Goodbye, Jossie.' He held out his hand.

She took it and said, 'I shall never forget what you've done for me, Ivo. For us both, Peter and me. I was so

afraid that there was something lacking in me, that I
would never be able to behave as Peter wishes. But now
I know what pleasure there can be in a kiss...' She
paused, smiling, remembering, and said softly, 'What
delight...'

Ivo made a sudden gesture, and she came down to
earth. 'I'm keeping you,' she said apologetically. 'I do
realise you have to go, though I wish you didn't. I owe
you so much, Ivo. Thank you.' She turned up the drive
to her home.

Ivo watched Jossie go, and then started off back to
his aunt's. According to Jossie he ought to have been
basking in a glow of virtue, but in fact his mood was
blacker than it had been for a long time. He must have
been mad! What had started out as a piece of kindly
indulgence had turned into a nightmare. He hoped to
heaven that Jossie Morley would never know how close
she had come to being seduced that afternoon.
Though...now he came to think of it, the reverse would
be nearer the truth. She had all but seduced him! Her
reaction to his first kiss had been sweet beyond measure.
But the second! Ivo felt the sweat breaking out on his
brow as he remembered the Herculean effort he had
needed to keep them both under control, the intensity of
his regret when they had parted. His body ached again
at the thought. She had been so innocently abandoned,
so desirable... He pulled himself together with an effort.
This would not do! The sooner he escaped to London
and away from the temptation to take over Peter Radstock's part in teaching Jossie Morley to be a woman,
the better!

He left for London the next day, resolving not to return to Somerset before July, and hoping that he would

by then have recovered his sanity. To that end he threw himself into the pleasures of the London season, and soon Ivo Trenchard was his normal self again—essential to the success of any function, a charming companion to the many ladies who sought him out, and the despair of Society's mamas. He never quite forgot the scene by the waterfall, and Jossie's eyes just occasionally haunted his sleep, but in the end he could look forward with equanimity to Peter Radstock's coming of age and Jossie's engagement.

Meanwhile in Lyne St Michael the preparations for the summer celebrations increased in intensity. Peter and his mother returned from Bath in very good humour after what had obviously been a highly successful excursion. Lady Radstock showed Jossie not one but several new dresses, and urged her to make her mind up very soon what she herself was going to wear at the ball. Jossie had not given it a thought.

'I have any number of dresses that will do,' she said carelessly. 'Most of them new. Since we've had all these dances and parties in the neighbourhood Papa has seen to it that I am always suitably dressed.'

'But Jossie, this is a very special occasion,' Lady Radstock protested.

'You mean our engagement?'

There was a little silence. 'Not quite,' said Lady Radstock. 'I think it would be better to celebrate one thing at a time, Jossie dear. And the ball in July is meant for Peter's coming of age. Let's not be hasty about anything else.' Her face was troubled. 'Has Peter spoken to you about the ball...or...or anything?'

Jossie was aware that Lady Radstock had always had reservations about her as a suitable bride for her only son. She found this completely understandable. Peter's mother placed a high value on perfect manners and an elegant appearance, and Jossie failed these two tests abysmally. But she had never been afraid that Lady Radstock's doubts would affect the outcome. Peter's mother was fond of her, in spite of her faults. Moreover, she would never refuse Peter anything he wanted. And Sir Thomas, Peter's father, was all in favour of a match between his son and the Calverton heiress. He wouldn't allow himself to be influenced by any objection Lady Radstock might raise. So she answered cheerfully enough, 'Not yet. You've been keeping him very busy since he got back, I've hardly seen him. But I expect he will soon. I need to talk to him myself.'

'See that you have a new dress, Jossie,' said Lady Radstock with unwonted urgency. 'Things seem easier when one feels one is looking one's best.'

Somewhat surprised, Jossie agreed to talk to her Cousin Martha that very day, but that was as far as her interest in the matter went. She categorically refused to go to Bath, and indeed there was hardly enough time to do so. So Cousin Martha took her to a draper's shop in the nearest small town, an establishment which was well known in the district for making clothes for the wives and daughters of prosperous farmers. The dressmaker and Cousin Martha between them decided that as Jossie had not yet formally 'come out', absolute simplicity was most suitable. The dress they produced was certainly simple, of plain white muslin and several years out of date in style. It would have suited a young girl at her confirmation. As the ball gown for the daughter of one of the richest families in the neighbourhood it was woefully inadequate. And as Jossie would never stay still long enough to have it fitted, it was not even flattering. But no one close to Jossie either knew or cared—certainly not Jossie herself.

Jossie had other things to occupy her mind. She had looked forward to Peter's return from Bath, had wanted to show him how she had changed, to prove that she was now ready to respond to more ardent embraces. But the first attempt was hardly a success. Peter seemed unsure of himself, and her own response was at the most lukewarm. A disastrous second attempt ended in stammered apologies from Peter and tears of disappointment from Jossie. After that Peter held back from further close contact. At first Jossie was puzzled, then she decided that he was trying to display the patience he had promised before he had gone to Bath, and was touched at his restraint. She told herself that things would change once they were officially engaged. They would feel easier with each other again, and she would be able to demonstrate then how much she loved him.

She saw him much less often than before. As the date of his coming of age approached, his days seem to be filled with business, interviews with the lawyers, discussions with the land agents, consultations with both his parents and all the other duties arising from his new status. The moments they spent together were often cut short by some urgent appointment which demanded Peter's presence.

Jossie found herself increasingly alone, without even the companionship of her father. Major Morley seemed to have acquired a new lease of life. Whereas in the past he had seldom left the house, and was usually prepared to play a game of piquet or whist, he was now more often out visiting in the neighbourhood. Jossie had no wish to attend dull tea parties or other social gatherings, but she was slightly hurt that he did not seem to want her to go with him.

Finally Peter's birthday arrived. It was a beautiful July morning, and Jossie got up early. The tedious months of waiting were over at last, and she was filled with excited anticipation. She dressed more carefully than usual in the prettiest of her new dresses and made her way to the little valley, surrounded by the scents and colours of high summer: dog daisies, meadow sweet, campanulas. As she walked, she gazed around her in contentment. This was the day, and this the place! Years ago she and Peter had agreed that early in the day on the morning of his twenty-first birthday they would meet by the stream. Here in this special place,- this loved, familiar valley, they would make their own vows to each other, put a seal on all their plans, everything they had lived for.

Jossie sat on the bank lost in dreams. This was all she had ever wanted, and it was so soon to be hers. Life with Peter, the love and companionship they would share through the coming years, children… She and Peter had always been true friends, and they would be true and faithful partners in marriage. That was what was important. Their recent difficulties faded into insignificance when compared with all those years of loyalty and friendship.

She sat like this for some time, until she became aware that the sun had got much higher. Where was Peter? Surely he wouldn't let his mother stop him for any reason from keeping such an important tryst? She sat for a few minutes longer, then got up and looked around. There was no sign of him. She hesitated for another few minutes, then made up her mind to go to meet him—he was sure to come along the bridle path.

But Jossie had reached the gates of the Hall before she finally met him. He was on horseback.

'There you are at last,' she cried. 'What on earth kept you?'

Peter looked startled. 'Jossie!' he exclaimed. 'What are you doing here?'

'I got tired of waiting by the stream, so I thought I'd come to meet you. Did your mother delay you?'

'Oh, my lord!' A slow tide of red mounted in Peter's cheeks. 'I...I... Jossie, I...'

'What on earth is wrong with you, Peter? You can't have forgotten. That's impossible. What happened?'

'I...I didn't forget exactly! Of course I didn't! It's just that I—' Peter stopped and slowly dismounted. Then he turned and said, 'Were you waiting long, Joss?'

'Long enough. But that doesn't matter now. You're here. Shall we go back to the valley?'

'There...there isn't time. I shall soon have to be back. I'm sorry.' Peter spoke jerkily, as if under some strain. 'Joss, I have to talk to you...Mama said...'

At the sight of Peter's discomfort Jossie forgot her own disappointment. Concerned, she asked, 'Has Lady Radstock been upsetting you? Is it because she doesn't want us to make any announcement today? That's all right, Peter! Please don't worry, she has already told me so, and I don't mind a bit. Don't fall out with your mother because of that. We can easily leave any official announcement to another time.' He appeared to be un-convinced. She went on gently, 'Dear Peter! You shouldn't worry so much! As long as we know our own minds, what can your mother do? Your father is wholly on our side. Your mother is reasonable. She'll come round in time.'

'But, Jossie, there's something else—'

Wanting only to reassure him, she said, 'Nonsense! There can't be anything else, Peter. This is your special day. You mustn't let anything spoil that! Congratulations, my dearest fellow.' She came over to him, held out her hand and after a slight hesitation offered her cheek. Peter bent forward to kiss her. 'I'm sorry, Jossie!' he said. 'I'm really sorry! I wish...' He gazed miserably at her, then turned away. 'I...I...I have to go!' He got on his horse and prepared to ride off.

'Wait!' Peter stopped a few paces away. Jossie ran up to him. 'When shall I see you?'

Without looking at her Peter said, 'I...I don't know. I shall be busy all day, Joss. We...we have so many aunts and uncles staying with us and they all want to talk to me...Mama insisted...' He looked ashamed.

'That's all right. Truly!' Jossie tried to speak cheerfully for Peter's sake. 'Till this evening, then.'

Peter nodded and rode off. Jossie watched him go. She had never before seen Peter so distressed. He was clearly suffering from conflicting loyalties. What had Lady Radstock been saying to him to upset him so on this day of all days? He had always been devoted to his mother, and on the rare occasions when she had been seriously displeased he had always been eager to make amends as soon as possible. But why was she making difficulties today? Jossie frowned. Peter's mother must disapprove of her more than she had realised.

Hurt and bewildered, trying not to feel angry, Jossie went home, changed into her breeches, collected some food from the kitchen and set off on a long ride. The day she had looked forward to for so long was rapidly turning into a disaster. If she was to rescue it, she would have to ride some of this resentment out of her system before meeting the Radstocks this evening.

* * *

She arrived back refreshed, her natural optimism and courage restored. During the ride she had faced the situation and decided that it was not incurable. It was unfortunate that Lady Radstock apparently disapproved of her so strongly. Jossie would never have guessed it from her manner. But when she saw how hard Jossie was trying to be more like the daughter-in-law she desired, she would relent, and they would all be happy again together.

Jossie had little time for further reflection. Her father seemed to think that she should have spent the day preparing for the ball, and was angry that she hadn't.

'Look at your hair!' he said. 'And your nails are a disgrace! You stink of the stables, girl!'

'I'm sorry, Papa. I know I should have been back sooner, but I was feeling rather down, and had to ride it out of my system. But I shall take pains now to make you proud of me. Wait till you see me in my new dress!'

He said impatiently, 'You haven't left much time!'

Jossie took a breath and said pleadingly, 'Please don't be cross with me, Papa! I'll do my best.' She added with a nervous little laugh, 'Isn't it strange? I've been waiting for this evening for years, and now I feel quite nervous about it! I expect it's because everyone suddenly wishes me to stop acting like a boy, and to be more like a girl instead. It's all so new! You must give me a little time to get used to it, Papa.'

Jossie took more trouble with her appearance than she had in her whole life before, and came downstairs rather pleased with herself. But when her father saw her he was not encouraging.

'I wonder if I should have consulted Madeleine Cherton on that dress? It doesn't do much for you. Why the devil didn't you take more trouble to find a decent dress-maker?'

Jossie faltered, 'Cousin Martha thought the dress was very suitable. I'm sorry you don't like it, Papa.'

'My cousin has no more taste than a scarecrow, which is what she looks like most of the time. I wish I had thought to consult Mrs Cherton. Her taste is excellent. She and her daughter always look a picture of elegance. But then they take trouble, Jossie. They know how to present themselves to advantage. That's something you'll have to learn.'

Jossie looked down. Not for the world would she show how much his words hurt her. 'I…I don't suppose anyone will look at me very much,' she said quietly. 'Lady Radstock doesn't wish any announcement about Peter and me to be made tonight.'

'What? No official betrothal? But everyone is expecting it! It's been understood for years that it would be announced on young Radstock's twenty-first! You must have done something to upset her!'

'I don't know what, Papa. I thought she liked me.'

'This is a pretty state of affairs, I must say! What will people say? I'm surprised at Lady Radstock…' He regarded his daughter and frowned. 'She probably wants to wait until you are more of a credit to Peter. It was a mistake letting you run wild for so long, wearing breeches and the rest. I should have insisted sooner that you learned how to handle skirts. Well, it's too late for this evening, but once this ball is over we shall have to see about making you into something like a lady. If Lady Radstock won't help you, Mrs Cherton might give you advice.'

'I don't think I know Mrs Cherton well enough to ask her, Papa.'

'You may not, but I believe I do. She would be an excellent mentor, and I flatter myself that she would be willing to do it as a favour to me. You should cultivate her, Jossie. She's a damned fine woman.' He looked at his daughter and frowned again. 'Now, go back upstairs and get the maid to do your hair properly. Half the pins are coming out. And that rose looks ridiculous.'

Jossie did as he asked, then came down and waited patiently in the hall while he regarded her critically and told her to give her bodice a pull here, and her skirt a twitch there. Finally, still sounding dissatisfied, he said, 'I can't do any more, we should have left a quarter of an hour ago. You know how I dislike unpunctuality, Jossie. I regard it as discourteous. Come along!'

Jossie didn't argue. Papa was not usually so critical. He must be as nervous as she was. She followed him dispiritedly into the carriage. It looked as if she would have something to prove to her father as well as to Lady Radstock at the ball tonight.

They sat in silence in the carriage, but his displeasure was patent. Jossie sighed and wondered if Ivo would keep his word and be there. He at least had seemed to approve of her. He had even found her worth kissing… Her spirits lifted a little as she thought of Ivo's kiss. He had been so kind. He had shown her a new world, a magic world, one she had badly wanted to share with Peter. Why hadn't they managed it? After all, Peter was the one she loved. It was a pity he had been so busy, they had hardly had any time at all together. But after this fuss was all over and they were back on the old footing… Jossie grew more cheerful. She knew, and Peter knew, the strength of their attachment. Nothing could break that. As the carriage bowled along to the Hall, she hugged to herself the thought of her future with Peter. It did something to dispel the chill caused by her father's words.

Chapter Seven

The ball had already started when they arrived, which was another cause for a show of displeasure from her father. He gave her no time to arrange her clothes or hair, but himself gave her cloak to the servant and ushered her in.

The rooms on the south side of the house all ran into one another, and tonight the doors between them were folded back. The evening was warm and the long windows on to the terrace were open. An orchestra was playing on a dais at one end of the room, and a set of country dances was in progress. Jossie and her father were announced and made their way to Sir Thomas and Lady Radstock, who were waiting near the door to welcome new arrivals. Most of the guests were already inside, and they were standing quite alone. Peter was nowhere to be seen.

'Major! Jossie! How nice to see you!' Lady Radstock's greeting was warm, her smile kind. No one would have guessed that Jossie was at all out of favour. She went on, 'You…you look charming, my dear. Very…very fresh, especially on such a hot night.' They exchanged a few more words, then their hostess said,

'Except for a few distant cousins of Sir Thomas, I am sure everyone here is known to you. Lady Frances has brought her nephew, Lord Trenchard. I believe you know him quite well, Jossie?' She paused.

'Yes, I do. I'd like to talk to him later.' Jossie looked round. 'But where's Peter?'

Lady Radstock's smile faltered, and she hesitated. Sir Thomas said with a laugh, 'Oh, he's dancing somewhere, but he'll be back. I dare swear he'll come looking for you as soon as he's free.' He took Jossie's hand and said with mock gravity, 'You must promise me not to play any of your tricks tonight, Jossie! It's a solemn occasion. A coming of age *and* an engagement.'

Lady Radstock said quickly, 'But, Sir Thomas, I thought we had agreed. No announcement tonight. A coming of age is quite enough.'

'So we did, so we did! But I can't claim to understand why. The sooner it's all signed and sealed the better, that's what! It's not as if the two of them don't know their own mind. Why, they've been talking about it for years! And I still think it ought to be made official tonight.'

Lady Radstock gave her husband a look. He said reluctantly, 'Whatever you say, my dear...'

It was as well, thought Jossie, that her father had wandered ahead and had not heard this exchange. He would have been more annoyed than ever. She gave the Radstocks a tentative smile and followed her father into the ballroom. He was already in conversation with a small group which included Mrs Cherton, Ivo Trenchard and one or two others.

The sight of Ivo's tall figure, a smile on his lips, his dark head bent to hear what one of the other ladies was saying, had a surprising effect on Jossie. For a moment she was filled with confusion as the memory of his kisses returned in full force. Nothing before or since could compare with the feeling of sublime happiness she had experienced in his arms... Her face burned and she moved away. She mustn't think of it. She must look for Peter.

'Aren't you going to say good evening to me, Jossie?'

From behind her came Ivo's voice, deep, drawling, with a hint of irony about it that was totally characteristic. She turned round. 'Ivo!' she exclaimed. 'I...I didn't see you!'

He raised an eyebrow. 'No?'

Jossie was too honest to persist in the lie. 'Well, I did,' she confessed. 'But I wasn't sure what to say to you.'

'That's a little unkind. I thought you were a friend. You could say perhaps, "How are you?" or, "How nice to see you again!" or, "What have you been doing since we last met?"'

This reminder of their last meeting caused Jossie to blush more deeply than ever. Ivo smiled. 'You look very pretty when you're confused, Jossie, but there's no need. Did it work?' She hesitated and he said quickly, 'No, don't tell me. It has nothing to do with me. Are you happy tonight?'

'Not...not yet. But I expect I will be.' She added nervously, 'I just have to find Peter.'

'He's dancing with Rosalind Cherton. He'll bring her back here when the music stops.'

Jossie allowed him to lead her back to the group. Ivo seemed preoccupied, but she was quite happy to stand and observe the others. Her father was in animated conversation with Mrs Cherton. What he had said was true, she thought with a pang. Mrs Cherton was perfectly groomed, from the exquisite creation on her head to the glittering buckles on her shoes. Her slender figure dressed in lilac crêpe, with pearls in her ears and a collar of pearls and diamonds round her throat, she was easily the most elegant woman in the room. It was clear that Major Morley was very taken with her. The lady was less demonstrative, but seemed quite content to accept his admiration with a smile.

The music stopped and Peter came towards the group with Miss Cherton on his arm. She was more animated than usual and smiled enchantingly at Peter as he relinquished her with a bow to her mother. The two women were remarkably alike, both slender, both beautifully groomed, both exquisitely feminine in appearance. Rosalind was slightly shorter than her mother, and more simply dressed, as befitted a young lady. But what exquisite simplicity! A plain slip of white silk, a few rosebuds sewn here and there on a net overlay, tiny cap sleeves caught up with rosebuds. A small string of pearls round a smooth white throat. Pale gold curls dressed high except for one lock which fell gracefully over her shoulder. Jossie looked down at her muslin and felt like a clumsy rustic.

'She has no wit to speak of,' said a voice in her ear. 'Playing piquet with her would be like taking candy from a child.'

Jossie looked round. Ivo was regarding her with amusement and something else in his eyes. She was not quite sure what it was, but it made her uneasy. She shook her head at him, and moved over to stand between her father and Peter who, having delivered Miss Cherton to her mother, had remained to talk. Ivo looked rueful, shrugged his shoulders and wandered through the windows on to the terrace, where Lady Frances was enjoying the fresh air.

Major Morley barely spared a glance as Jossie joined him, but Mrs Cherton turned and gave her a sweet smile.

'Have you been hurrying, Jossie? You look quite flushed, my dear,' she said, her eyes taking in every detail of the white muslin dress.

'Jossie was out all day and arrived home late,' said Major Morley with a little frown.

'Roaming the countryside again? What a girl you are for the outdoors! But there's something I've been meaning to ask for ages, my dear. Tell me, where does the name Jossie come from? It's almost like a boy's!'

'It's a family name, Mrs Cherton,' said Jossie stiffly. 'Joscelin. And it is a boy's name.'

'How odd! Have you no other, child?'

'I was christened Helena Joscelin.'

'Helena! Oh dear,' exclaimed Mrs Cherton laughing merrily. 'How unsuitable! I can quite understand why you prefer Jossie!' She ran her eye over the muslin dress once more, then turned to Jossie's father. 'I see what you mean, Major, and I'm sure I could do something. Jossie is tall, of course. But that can be an advantage, if one is taught to carry oneself well.' She turned back to Jossie. 'You poor girl, I dare swear you have sadly missed the influence of a mother.'

'Not at all, ma'am,' said Jossie stiffly. 'I have always been perfectly happy with my father.'

'Indeed, who would not be?' said Mrs Cherton. Then, raising a playfully admonitory finger, she went on, 'But I'm afraid he deserves just a little scold, all the same.'

'Mrs Cherton! What have I done? Only tell me and I shall put it right immediately!' said Major Morley gallantly.

'I am sure Jossie's upbringing has been delightfully natural, but from what I hear you have been neglecting her education, Major!'

'Oh, come, Mrs Cherton, you are being too harsh with poor Morley!' said Sir Thomas. 'Jossie is better educated than most young people round here. She rides as well as any boy, she knows more about the land than even Peter here, and she knows as much about the natural history in the neighbourhood as any professor! What's more, she can outdo me any day at reckoning.'

He smiled kindly at Jossie, who, deeply embarrassed, was trying to make herself invisible.

Mrs Cherton shook her head. With a charming smile she said, 'Forgive me, but men, of course, do not always understand what a young girl needs to learn! I am sure Jossie is enormously clever, unlike my poor Rosalind, who can hardly count! Such a dear muddlehead, she is! But I was astonished to learn from Lady Radstock that Jossie has never had proper music or dancing lessons! Not one! Now Rosalind here started before she was twelve.'

'And to wonderful effect,' said Peter, gazing in admiration at Miss Cherton. 'A perfect dancing partner.'

Sir Thomas, who had come up just in time to hear this last remark, looked disapprovingly at his son. 'I hope you're going to dance with Jossie before the evening is much older,' he said sternly. 'You haven't even said good evening to her yet.'

'I haven't had time,' Peter somewhat sulkily replied. 'She wasn't here when the ball began.'

'Well, you can put it right now, my boy. Here she is.'

'Sir Thomas!' protested Lady Radstock. 'Let the young people decide for themselves what they will do. Jossie may not wish to dance at the moment.'

'I don't expect she does,' said Peter. 'She doesn't like that sort of thing. She never has.'

'Then you can take her away and give her an ice or something,' said Sir Thomas decisively. 'Dammit, Peter, you're supposed to be marrying the girl before long. You can at least talk to her!'

'Please, Sir Thomas—' Jossie was scarlet with embarrassment, and Lady Radstock looked as annoyed as good manners allowed.

Sir Thomas seldom interfered with his wife's arrangements. He was a man who liked his comfort, and though he was not sure how she did it, Lady Radstock could make life quite uncomfortable for those who disagreed with her. But he was not stupid. He had seen the way Peter had looked at Rosalind Cherton, and hadn't liked it a bit. And now he decided to risk his wife's displeasure. The sooner Peter was officially committed to Jossie Morley the better. The two were not only ideally suited, but Jossie would bring with her a substantial dowry, to say nothing of her large future inheritance. This Cherton girl was pretty enough, and had pretty manners, too, but there was little else to recommend her. No visible fortune. Lady Radstock may say what she wished, but a prudent father would not let a prize like the Calverton Manor estate slip through his fingers just because of some scruples on the part of his wife!

So he now turned to Lady Radstock, said, 'I'm sorry, my dear, but I've changed my mind. Peter's future must be settled tonight.' He marched off purposefully towards the dais. After an anguished look at his mother, who had turned very pale, Peter hurried after him. They reached the dais together, and Peter clutched his father's arm in a desperate effort to hold him back. Sir Thomas said sternly, 'No, sir! I forbid you to say a word! My mind

is quite made up—this matter must be settled tonight.'
Then he got up on the dais, asked for a chord from the
orchestra and looked benevolently at the assembled company.

'My friends,' he began, 'we are here tonight to celebrate my son's coming of age....' He talked for some
minutes, quite amusingly, about Peter's exploits in the
past. Jossie's name quite frequently cropped up. Most of
his audience was very appreciative, and when he went
on to talk of the future, and mentioned a long-awaited
piece of news a murmur of anticipation went round the
room. It was not difficult to guess what Sir Thomas was
about to tell them. But Lady Frances, standing next to
Ivo in the window, whispered, 'Look at Peter! What's
wrong with him? And why isn't Jossie up there beside
him?'

Ivo stiffened. Peter was gazing at his father in horror,
seemingly rooted to the spot. Ivo said urgently, 'He
doesn't want to marry her! My God, Peter Radstock
doesn't want to marry her! But why the devil doesn't he
do something? Why doesn't he stop his father before it
is too late?'

But it was too late already. Sir Thomas was in full
spate. 'And now,' he said, 'it is my great pleasure to
announce that my son is to marry someone we all know
very well. It will hardly be a surprise to you that he has
asked Miss Helena Joscelin Calverton Morley to be his
wi—'

Peter found his voice at last. 'I haven't,' he cried. 'I'm
not going to marry Jossie. I know you want me to, but
I can't! I don't love her, I love Rosalind Cherton. And
she has already agreed to marry me.'

For a moment there was dead silence. Then it was
broken by a loud, shocked *'No!'* Jossie tore herself out

of Lady Radstock's restraining arms and ran up to the
dais. 'No, Peter, no! That's wrong! It must be! You don't
know what you're saying!'

'I'm sorry, Joss…' he said awkwardly. 'I wanted to
tell you, but—'

'You can't have anything to tell me. We've already
made our plans, we've known them for years! I won't
let you throw them away like that. I won't let you!' She
was whiter than her dress, frantically clutching Peter,
fighting to hold on as he tried to disengage himself.

The Radstocks' guests murmured in shocked disapproval at the scene unfolding before them. Peter Radstock had obviously behaved abominably, but this public
exposure of such raw feeling was not the way to behave!
But then Jossie Morley had never known how to conduct
herself.

Major Morley came up to them. 'Jossie! Pull yourself
together!' He turned to Peter, who was now standing
shamefacedly by his father. 'I'll see you later, sir!' he
said. 'Meanwhile—Jossie, come with me!'

'No,' she cried. 'How can you ask such a thing? It's
my life I'm fighting for! I must stay here and talk to
him. He doesn't understand. I can't let him make such
a mistake.' She turned to Sir Thomas, who was stiff with
anger and embarrassment. 'You tell him, Sir Thomas.
Peter loves *me*. I'm his friend. I've been his friend for
years. How can he love that girl? She's nothing! A nonentity. He doesn't even know her!'

Peter turned on her. 'You be quiet, Jossie!' he said
angrily. 'I do know Rosalind. We got to know each other
in Bath. She means a great deal to me.'

'She can't mean more to you than I do!'

'Well, she does! She's a proper girl! More of a girl

than you'll ever be. I want a woman for my wife, Jossie Morley, not a *friend*. I love her, I tell you!'

Jossie shook her head frantically. 'No, no! That can't be so! It can't! It's because I disappointed you. But I can make love now, Peter. I know how to kiss. Try me!' She tried to cling to him once again.

Scarlet with embarrassment, Peter dragged her arms down and pushed her away. 'Stop it! This won't do you any good! It's too late. My mind is made up.'

Major Morley looked at the crowd which had gathered round them and grew purple with rage. 'Jossie!' he said sharply. 'Come with me, I say! You're making an unforgivably disgusting exhibition of yourself!'

Lady Frances gave an involuntary exclamation at these heartless words, and came hurrying up. But the Major waved her back impatiently. 'Leave Jossie alone, ma'am! Allow me to deal with this in my own way, I know what I'm doing.' He barked, 'Jossie, I *order* you to come with me! This minute!' He took Jossie's arm and hauled her roughly away.

Jossie was distraught. She looked wildly at Peter, who was now engaged in an altercation with his father, stared at the circle of shocked faces which surrounded them, then wrenched herself out of her father's grip, and ran unseeingly past Ivo down into the garden. Ivo took a step after her, but Lady Frances held him back. 'Wait,' she said. 'You can't go yet. Her father's following her, and he's made it clear he doesn't want anyone else to interfere. We must wait. Oh, Ivo, I wish I knew what to do! That cold-hearted man doesn't know how to treat her properly. I'm very worried.'

'Damn Morley! He isn't fit to handle a dog!' Ivo looked into the room behind them. 'The Radstocks have disappeared, but they've started the music again. No one would notice if we were to leave. I'll go down into the garden and look for Jossie. She might have calmed down by now, but she can't stay here. Shall I try to talk to Morley? Offer to take Jossie back to the Lodge? You're surely the best person to look after her at the moment.'

'Do!'

Ivo moved quietly down the garden, almost as if he was in enemy country. He wanted if possible to see what was going on between the Morleys before he approached them. Persuading Jossie's father to let her go to Lady Frances might not be easy. But, far from comforting or calming his daughter, Jossie's father was still berating her, his voice trembling with rage.

'And what people must think I cannot imagine!' he was saying.

Ivo stopped in shock and listened unashamedly as the Major went on, 'You have behaved disgracefully to-night!' His voice rose. 'Disgracefully! I am utterly ashamed of you!'

Jossie's voice, full of anguish. 'But, Father...what was I to do? Peter—'

'There can be no excuse for the manner in which Peter Radstock jilted you. I was never so humiliated in my life, and I intend to have it out with him at the earliest opportunity. But I am forced to say that I cannot blame him in the slightest for preferring to marry Rosalind Cherton! She's a girl who would make any man proud to call his wife! And look at you! What man of taste would want to be tied to such a badly dressed, untidy, ungraceful hoyden? A girl who hasn't the smallest idea how to conduct herself! Believe me, my girl, not all your fortune could recommend you to any man of feeling.'

Ivo winced at the passionate entreaty in Jossie's voice as she said, 'I'll be better, Father! I'll try!'

'It's too late now! Peter Radstock's gone. He wasn't much of a fellow, but he was the best catch in the neighbourhood.' His voice rose in temper. 'Why does this have to happen to me? What have I ever done to deserve such a burden! You were never the boy I wanted, God knows, but you can't even make a decent *girl*!'

There was a cry of agony followed by a moment's shocked silence. Then Jossie's voice was almost unrecognisable as she said harshly, 'You have made me what I am, Father. And now you and Peter Radstock between you have destroyed me!'

Then Ivo saw a slim white figure speeding down the garden towards the drive, and heard the Major shouting, 'Jossie! Come back this instant! Come back, I say!'

Jossie didn't stop. Her father swore and turned back towards the house. He saw Ivo. 'That *damned* daughter of mine,' he said, shaking with fury. 'She's nothing but trouble.'

Ivo was tempted to knock the man down, or at least tell him what he thought of him, but there was no time. It was more important to find Jossie. 'I'll go after her,' he said.

'Do what you like! I've washed my hands of her. She'll come home when she's ready. Excuse me, Trenchard. I must do what I can to reassure Mrs Cherton and her daughter. This business must have distressed them very badly. I can hardly bear to think what they must be feeling. They need my support.' And Jossie's father marched up the steps and into the house.

Ivo thought briefly, then went back to Lady Frances. 'Jossie has fled. I think...I hope I know where. I'll borrow a horse and go in search of her. Can you go back to the Lodge by yourself?'

'Of course. I'll wait for you there. Take my shawl! She may be cold.'

Ivo saddled one of the horses and set off straight away. There was a full moon and it wasn't difficult to see his way. He pushed the horse as hard as he dared.

He found Jossie as he had expected in the little valley. She was sitting on the bank of the stream much as he had found her once before, slippers discarded, feet dangling in the water. There were signs that she had come over the fields, pushing her way unheeding through trees and bushes. Her dress was torn and dirty, her hair in wild disarray.

'Jossie?' he said softly. When there was no reaction he came and squatted down beside her. He took her hand. It was cold and lay limp in his grasp. 'Jossie, look at me.' Still nothing. He put out his other hand and turned her head towards him. There was no resistance, she was quite passive. But her eyes were blank. Her face was covered in streaks of blood and dirt. Though it was a warm night, she was shivering.

'Come, I'll help you out of the water. Lady Frances has sent her shawl for you. Put it on.'

Again she made no effort to resist as he lifted her up and wrapped the shawl round her. Ivo grew worried. He had come across this kind of reaction before, in men who had had some severe physical injury. This injury was to the spirit, not to the body, but the result was the same— Jossie was in a state of acute shock. She urgently needed warmth and care. He sat her down again, took off his coat, added it to the shawl and carried her, swaddled like this, up the slope to his horse. With a prayer of gratitude that he had chosen a sturdy mount, he put Jossie up, then clambered on behind. They slowly made their way to the Lodge. Jossie occasionally gave a convulsive shudder, but neither raised her eyes nor spoke.

During the next few days there were serious worries in Lady Frances's household for Jossie's state of mind. There were no tears, no outbursts of emotion. She lay perfectly passive in the bed that had been prepared for her on the night of the ball. But she never spoke. Nor did she eat anything, accepting only the occasional sip of water. After a day or two Lady Frances brought her downstairs, hoping that a change of scene might make a difference. Jossie lay on a daybed gazing out of the window, but not even Ivo could rouse her.

Ivo went back to Sudiham soon after. Lady Frances pointed out to him that it was necessary.

'This is a small village, Ivo, and there has been enough gossip already. Jossie is in no state at the moment to protect herself from further scandal, so we must do it for her. The world knows by now that you found her and brought her here on the night of the ball. It might wonder why she is not with her father.'

'With her father! I wouldn't leave a dog with that cold-hearted villain!'

'Yes, yes. We both know why Jossie is better with me. Indeed, she would be better with practically anyone other than Gerard Morley. Between them Peter Radstock and her father have very nearly destroyed that poor girl. But though the world was present when Peter Radstock treated her so cruelly, it doesn't know what happened afterwards. Indeed, I doubt anyone would believe you if you told them how inhuman her father was to her.'

'I can still hardly believe it myself.'

'I can. Just. When Gerard Morley's self-esteem is injured he is capable of anything. Jossie had let him down.'

'Let him down? But he is entirely to blame!'

'You will never convince him of that. Let us not waste our time talking of it. I mean what I said, Ivo. It is natural you feel protective towards Jossie, but you must take care. We want no excuse for speculation on the part *you* might have played in this dreadful affair.'

'What the devil do you mean by that?'

'Our neighbours are aware that Jossie frequently visited you when you were here last year. Yes, yes, I know that this was entirely innocent, and at the time I think everyone agreed. But if you spend any length of time here now, they might wonder whether Peter Radstock has some other grounds for jilting Jossie, and that is the last thing we want. Go back to Sudiham for now. It would be reasonable, I think, for you to come to enquire after her later.'

Ivo accepted her advice, though all his instincts were against it. He had been outraged by the treatment Jossie had suffered on the night of the ball from the two men she trusted most in the world. If he had had the slightest right to act on her behalf he would have seen both of them before now to demand an explanation. But he had none, and his aunt was right. To intervene would only create more scandal. But he had no intention of abandoning Jossie. He would take care not to cause gossip, but he *would* see that, from now on, she would have someone to look after her interests—even from a distance.

He found himself wondering what his friends from earlier days would have thought of this desire to protect Jossie. They might well have been astonished. Ivo Trenchard, it was well known, avoided young girls like the plague. His interest in the opposite sex was for his own pleasure, not for any altruistic motives. And it was true that in the past he had had many affairs, not all of them ending by mutual consent. But most of his amours had been ladies who had little enough heart to wound. Not one of them had been anything like as vulnerable as Jossie. Even so, he had always tried to manage the parting with grace, to minimise the hurt to their feelings or, more often, the damage to their pride. The scenes on the night of the Radstock ball, the cruelty to a girl whom he admired for her loyalty, her lack of guile, her innocent directness, had shocked him beyond measure. He did not think himself in love with Jossie. But he badly wanted to be her champion.

Chapter Eight

Ivo waited two weeks before he came back to Danby Lodge. Lady Frances met him at the door. 'Come this way, Ivo,' she said. 'I want to talk to you before you see Jossie.'

Ivo followed her into her own small sitting room, but when she gestured to him to sit down he shook his head. 'Tell me how she is,' he said.

His aunt frowned. 'She has started to eat a little—perhaps enough to keep a sparrow alive. But she still says nothing at all. I do so hope you can do something—she never stopped talking when you were here last year.'

'I'll do what I can. Is that what you wanted to say?'

'No. I want to bring you up to date on what has been happening in Lyne during the last fortnight.'

'Well?'

'The Radstocks have been doing their best to repair the damage. There's a great deal of feeling in the village about Peter's treatment of Jossie, you know.'

'You amaze me! But don't tell me that Peter has changed his mind again!'

'On no account.. He is as determined as I have ever known him to marry the Cherton girl. The Radstocks are having to put a brave face on it. Sir Thomas was bitterly disappointed, and for a while we thought there would very likely be a rift between father and son. But Lady Radstock has managed to smooth that over. To tell the truth, Ivo, it is my opinion that she is pleased rather than sorry about Peter's rejection of Jossie. She was shocked at the manner in which it was done—indeed, who could possibly approve? But Rosalind Cherton is exactly the sort of daughter-in-law she would have chosen.'

'A pretty trinket, compared with a diamond!'

'Peter and his mother may prefer trinkets. Diamonds can be very demanding to live with. Peter would always have been the weaker partner if he had married Jossie.'

'What about that wretch of a father? Has he visited his daughter?'

'He tried once, about a week ago. But Jossie refused to see him. He hasn't been near her since.' She paused. 'Major Morley has had other preoccupations.'

'Indeed?'

'He is to marry Mrs Cherton. After a suitable interval, of course.'

'Really?' said Ivo, his lip curling in scorn. 'So Peter Radstock is to marry the daughter and Major Morley the mother. How neat!'

'Neat indeed! Nor did it come about by chance! Do you know what that woman did, Ivo? I was never so shocked in my life.'

'I've met quite a few Mrs Chertons in my time,' said Ivo sardonically. 'I doubt I'll be shocked. But tell me.'

'We all knew that Lady Radstock and Peter had gone to Bath. And I for one thought nothing of it when Mrs Cherton announced that she and Rosalind had decided to visit friends for a few days. What neither I nor anyone else here knew was that they went to Bath, too. These friends of Mrs Cherton apparently reside there. Quite a coincidence, wouldn't you say?'

Ivo said cynically, 'In my experience a mother with a marriageable daughter deals in such coincidences. I can assume what happened next, I suppose?'

'She and Lady Radstock met, naturally. So did Peter and Miss Cherton. And while Lady Radstock was busy acquiring new dresses for the ball, Mrs Cherton was equally busy acquiring a rich husband for her daughter—at Jossie's expense. Those two young people were absolutely thrown together. Poor Peter hardly stood a chance.'

'One has to admire Mrs Cherton's singlemindedness, if not her ethics. From what I've seen of Radstock, I can quite believe that he found it impossible to resist both the girl and her mother!' He smiled contemptuously. 'My own opinion is that Jossie is better off without him. He's a weakling.'

'I agree with you. If it weren't for Jossie's distress, I would say that Rosalind Cherton is welcome to him. But Mrs Cherton's activities did not end there. She has now caught a husband for herself, too!'

Ivo shrugged. 'A few months ago I would have said that all women were like the Chertons. Quite ruthless in pursuit of a successful marriage—by which, of course, they mean a rich marriage. Charlotte Gurney is another such.'

'Well, Miss Cherton will be rich enough, but her mother may find she is less fortunate.'

'What do you mean?'

'Not many know what I am about to tell you, Ivo, so you will keep it to yourself, if you please.' Lady Frances smiled with malicious pleasure. 'Major Morley comes from an old family, but he has very little personal wealth. I dare say he thought he would remedy that when he married the Calverton heiress. But Sir Robert didn't altogether approve of his daughter's choice of husband, any more than I did.'

'How right you both were!'

'If Lucinda had lived longer she might have come to agree with us! But at the time she was desperately in love with Gerard Morley. Sir Robert gave in to her, as he usually did, but he was determined not to let Morley profit from the marriage. So he set up in a trust in favour of Lucinda's children. Jossie is the only child of the marriage, and she is the sole heiress. The Major has a life interest in the house and can draw a suitable income from the estate, but nothing more. On his death it will all be Jossie's.' She paused, then said delicately, 'I am not sure that Mrs Cherton is aware of this...'

Ivo started to laugh. 'Will he tell her before they marry, do you think? She would be well served if he didn't!' He stood up. 'Have you told Jossie about her father's intention to marry Mrs Cherton?'

'No. I don't want to add to her unhappiness. How can she possibly live at home with that woman as a stepmother?'

'It remains to be seen whether she can live in Lyne St Michael at all! Has she no other relatives?'

'None.'

'Can you do something? After all, you're her godmother.'

'I would love to give Jossie a home with me. So far her father has blocked anything I have tried to do for her, but I have a feeling that the situation may well have altered... I have been making great plans for her, Ivo.'

'Good! What are they?'

'When she is better I shall take her away for change

of scene. I am fairly certain that her father will now be only too glad to have her off his hands. After that, I want to fulfil a long-held ambition, one I had thought impossible before the events of last month.'

'What is it?'

'When Lucinda died and Jossie was left without a mother, I said that, when the time came, I would prepare Jossie for presentation to society. Unless Gerard Morley married again there would be no one else to do it. But then as Jossie grew older it became evident that she would marry Peter Radstock before she came out. The girl wouldn't hear of going to London. I couldn't fight Jossie as well as her father, so I had to give up the idea. But my way is now clear!'

'You would still have Jossie to fight. She would hate it! She has never wanted to live in a town, particularly not London.'

'Aha! That was before July. She may have changed her mind about living in the country now. All her ambitions for country life were focussed on Peter and her father, and that dream is at an end.' Lady Frances paused, then said briskly, 'Besides, I think she should be persuaded. She is wasted down here.'

Ivo nodded his head. 'I agree with you there. But aren't we running a little ahead of ourselves? From what you tell me, Jossie has a long way to go before she could face the world.'

'She is a *little* better, but far from herself. Come and see what you can do.' Lady Frances led the way to a sunny room at the back of the house. Jossie was by the window, gazing out as usual.

'I've brought you a visitor, Jossie.'

Ivo didn't wait for a reaction but went over to the daybed and drew up a chair to sit beside it. He sat waiting for a moment. Then he began, 'I remember you were once very scornful of me, Jossie. I believe you thought I was making a great deal of fuss about nothing. A fox bite, if you remember. Do you?'

Jossie turned her head and looked at him. Her eyes were haunted pools of dark in her thin face.

Ivo hid his shock and went on calmly, 'You didn't think much of my military knowledge, either. You couldn't imagine how anyone, least of all a serving soldier, could confuse the names of Grouchy and Ney. And as for my skill at cards...'

'You were good at cards.' Jossie's voice was low, but clear.

'You beat me too often for my own self-esteem, all the same. How much do I still owe you?'

Her interest had died. 'I don't remember...,' she said listlessly.

Ivo nodded. 'You obviously don't care, and I can't blame you for that.' He regarded her for a moment. Then he said in a different tone, 'But tell me, what has happened to all that fighting spirit you prized in yourself and others? All that wit, all that will to win? I'd like to know.' She turned her head away again, but Ivo could tell she was listening.

He went on with a touch of irony in his voice, 'I suppose the answer is that it had always been too easy for you. You had never really been tested before. You knew about Grouchy and Ney, but that was all in the mind, you had never had to fight, as I have, in a real battle. You've never had to watch while men you have known for years, some of them your best friends, are cut down in front of you. You haven't had to outwit your opponent, not to win money, but to save your life. You've never had to pick yourself up from a body blow and begin again. Not before now.' He waited. Jossie turned again to look at him.

'You're saying I'm a coward.'

'Not *yet*. You've been wounded. Badly wounded. But if you were one of my men I wouldn't let you linger many more days before you came back on duty. It's time to sit up properly and come back to life, my young soldier.'

She sat up with a jerk. 'Don't! Don't speak to me as if I was one your men! I don't want to hear about fighting and killing and battles. I'm not a soldier, or a fellow, or a good chap. And you needn't call me Jossie, either! That's a boy's name. It's an ugly name. A name for a *son*, not a daughter! From now on I'm going to be a girl, and I'll use the name my mother gave me. Helena Calverton Morley.'

Ivo smiled in relief at this return to life. He got up and bowed. 'My dear Miss Calverton Morley, I am delighted to make your acquaintance!' Then he took her hand and held it to his lips. Jossie's cure had begun.

The village of Lyne St Michael at first found it strange that Jossie Morley should stay so long with her godmother. But when it became known that Major Morley was to marry Rosalind Cherton's mother they all thought it perfectly understandable, a very good solution in fact. Indeed some of them wondered whether Jossie would ever go back to live at the Manor.

Jossie herself was faced with the same question. Till Ivo's visit she had been in a kind of limbo, hiding behind an invisible curtain that she had drawn between herself and the world in order to keep out the unbearable pain and humiliation of what had happened. She tried to be nothing, to feel nothing, to respond to nothing. The two people she had loved most in the world had rejected her. Nothing was left. At that stage she had no will to survive, so the future simply did not concern her.

But Ivo's visit had roused her from the comparative peace of that state. His deep voice, with its characteristic drawl, reminded her of the person she had been, reminded her that she had always scorned weakness or cowardice, reminded her of the uncomplicated pleasure she had had in his company, and it brought back, as perhaps no one else could have, her interest in life. From the day of his visit she started to take a more active part in the world around her, to eat with more enjoyment, to respond to Lady Frances more willingly. She was young, and she recovered her physical strength quickly enough. She was soon walking round the garden, helping Lady Frances in the stillroom, playing with the dogs. But she would not go out of the grounds. And she refused to see anyone from the village or the neighbourhood, though there were plenty who came, out of sympathy, or pity, or simple curiosity.

But with returning life came the questions. The pain, the sense of betrayal, were buried deep inside her, but the practical problems could not be ignored. What was she to do? Where was she to live? When Lady Frances told her somewhat apprehensively of Major Morley's plan to marry Mrs Cherton, Jossie showed little reaction.

'You seem to think that will distress me,' she said. 'But why should it? I cannot imagine living with my father ever again... Or that he would ever want me to.'

This was the moment Lady Frances had been waiting for. 'In that case I should like to make a suggestion,' she said. 'If your father would agree, I should like to take you away from Lyne as soon as possible. People mean well, but they will never leave you alone long enough to forget, quite apart from any…any unhappy associations of place. And next year I would hope to take you to London. I think you should be presented.'

'I have never wanted to go to London.'

'Not till now,' said Lady Frances comfortably. 'But I am hoping you will change your mind after you have had time to consider. I should love you to see London. And London to see you.' Taking a look at Jossie's face, she went on, 'However, there's time enough before we have to make any decision about that. For the present I should like to take you on a visit to my brother. Sudiham is large enough for us both to lose ourselves in if we wish! On the other hand, you may enjoy making Ivo's father's acquaintance. He is eccentric, but interesting.'

Jossie said slowly, 'I should like that. But, forgive me—I don't quite understand why you are doing this. I have no real claim on you.'

'You have a very real claim, Jossie! You are my god-daughter. I loved your mother, and have always regretted that I could not do more for her daughter. Now I can! I cannot tell you how delighted I am to have your company. Since my husband died I have often been lonely. Ivo has been very good, but he has many other commitments, and cannot always be visiting me. You will be the daughter I never had. Do you agree?'

'You are…are almost too kind,' said Jossie in a low voice. 'I have not so far been a success as a daughter. I…I hope I don't disappoint you.'

'Oh, you won't, you won't!' said Lady Frances bracingly. 'I shan't allow you to!'

Major Morley was only too glad to be rid of the daughter who had all her life given him nothing but her trust, love and admiration. To him she had merely become a burden, a source of disappointment and shame. It was not only her disgraceful behaviour at the ball which had upset him. Some of the disapproval felt among the neighbours for the Radstocks had, in his opinion, quite unjustly spilled over on to him, especially at his decision to marry Mrs Cherton. The sooner Jossie was in someone else's hands and out of Lyne St Michael the better as far as he was concerned. Little as he liked Lady Frances, she was undeniably highly respected, and Jossie's godmother, too. No one could criticise him in the least for leaving Jossie in her care, and he gave her *carte blanche* to do as she pleased with the girl.

In a very short time, therefore, Jossie and Lady Frances were on their way to Sudiham. Ivo would not be there. He had some business in London, but had promised his father he would be back as soon as he could. As they travelled Lady Frances gave Jossie some family background.

'My brother was at odds with Ivo for over a year, and he now regrets the lost time. Ivo tries to be at Sudiham as often as he can, but he is, after all, young and active, with a large number of friends whom he likes to visit, some near Bath, and many others in London. Rupert often feels lonely, especially as Peregrine, Ivo's younger brother, shows no sign of wishing to leave Derbyshire. I think we are doing him a service coming to stay. At least, that is what I shall tell him!'

Ivo had already given his father the outlines of Jossie's story. The old man had condemned Peter Radstock with characteristic robustness, and though he was careful in what he said about Major Morley, it was clear that he disapproved of him, too. Even before she came he was prepared to support Jossie in any way he could, but she had not been at Sudiham very long before she and Lord Veryan were on excellent terms.

Lady Frances was relieved. Though Jossie had come a long way since July she was still a shadow of her former self, and Lady Frances had been afraid that her brother's somewhat abrasive style might upset Jossie's hard-won equilibrium. But Jossie liked his directness and took his comments in her stride. He was inclined to be more peppery and more prejudiced than his son, but she otherwise saw quite a lot in him which reminded her of Ivo.

For a while after their arrival the weather was good, and Lord Veryan soon persuaded Jossie to come out riding with him. Here there was no risk that she would meet any former acquaintance, or see any familiar landmarks. The park was extensive, with some beautiful views to the west and no reminders of her former home, and after a few days she was happy enough to join him. The greatest difference from her previous outings was that she now always rode side saddle, using Lady Frances's old equipment. She suffered her companion's blistering criticisms of her riding style with patience and a determination to improve. Soon her seat was once again excellent. No one would have guessed that she had ever done anything other than ride as a lady should.

Lord Veryan taught Jossie backgammon and cribbage, too, and they played endlessly when the weather was poor, competing, as she had with Ivo, for imaginary stakes. At first Lord Veryan won every time for the games were new to Jossie. But she watched and learned, and after a while Lord Veryan, much to his surprise, had to work hard to win. This did not put him out in the slightest. He had always enjoyed a good fight, and was delighted to find such a worthy opponent.

'That's the way!' he would shout. 'Beat me if you can, girl! No sense in playing if you don't intend to win. Games or life, it's all the same. No sitting back. Let 'em know what you're made of! Show 'em!'

Lady Frances sat and watched her brother and Jossie becoming fast, if competitive, friends. Her plan was working better than she could have hoped.

When Ivo came back some weeks later he found Jossie apparently almost back to normal. Almost, but not quite. Some of the fearless directness which had so enchanted him, the innocent vulnerability which had in his eyes made her special, had disappeared. The new Jossie, he thought, regarded the world with reserve. She would trust no one very far. He wondered what he could do about it. He and his aunt had rescued her from the ashes of her old life, but her future would be bleak if she continued living, as she had since that disastrous day in July, with no apparent aim or goal. It was time for Jossie to wake up again.

Then news reached Sudiham that Peter Radstock had married Rosalind Cherton with great ceremony in Lyne St Michael parish church. Bride and groom had apparently looked radiant with happiness. They were at present on a simple tour of the Lakes, but were planning to spend some time in London the following year. Jossie said nothing, but spent the rest of the day in her room. When she emerged in the evening she looked paler but more resolute, as if she had come to a decision.

Ivo wondered what form it would take. He didn't have long to wait, for Jossie herself brought the subject up at dinner. They had all so far carefully avoided any reference to the events in Lyne St Michael, but she said, with something of her old directness 'I notice that none of you has mentioned Peter Radstock's marriage. I'm not sure why—it is not as if it was unexpected. And I am not upset by it.'

'That makes me very happy. When you shut yourself up in your room, I thought you *were* upset,' said Lady Frances.

'No. I think I must have been waiting for it. It has woken me up. In fact, I spent the day thinking about my own future.'

'You are welcome to stay here as long as you wish, my dear,' said Lord Veryan.

She gave him a grateful smile. 'The notion is very appealing, sir. But I can't stay here forever. And if I am to do anything with my life I must soon make other plans.'

'And those are…?' asked Ivo.

Jossie hesitated, then turned to Lady Frances. 'You once said that you would like to introduce me to society, ma'am. Are you still of the same mind?'

After a moment's surprise Lady Frances replied, 'Of course! There is nothing I would rather do!'

'Are you sure about this, Jossie?' asked Ivo.

'Oh, yes! Quite certain. Lady Frances has promised to prepare me. I shall need to learn how to behave in company—how to dress, to dance, what people talk about and so on…among other things.'

'My dear girl, of course I will! And Ivo will, too, won't you?'

'Of course.'

Lady Frances got up and threw her arms round Jossie. 'Dearest girl, this is the best news I've heard in a long time. You shall be the most perfectly prepared débutante in London! We shall have such fun, I promise you!'

'I fully intend to, Lady Frances!' Ivo looked up

sharply. His aunt seemed not to have noticed a slight undercurrent in Jossie's voice, but he was sure he had heard one. What was she up to?

They talked at length after that, but though there was nothing more that was significant in what Jossie said, or how she said it, Ivo's suspicion had been roused. Eventually Lady Frances looked at Jossie's pale face and heavy eyes and said, 'All this excitement! You look quite worn out, child. Off to bed with you! There'll be plenty of time tomorrow to talk some more. Goodnight, my dear! I think you will sleep very well tonight!'

After Jossie had left them Lord Veryan said, 'I shall be sorry to see her go, but she is absolutely right! And you'll have no difficulty in teaching her, Frances. I've seldom known such a quick mind.'

'Yes, she has. A very quick mind. And I would quite like to know what else she has in it,' said Ivo, slowly. 'Jossie Morley has never before shown the slightest interest in London, or its society.'

'I see nothing to wonder at in that!' said Lady Frances. 'She wants to make a complete break with the past. Don't be such a cynic, Ivo! You are going to help, aren't you?'

'I've said I will. Always remembering that I must tread carefully. Can you imagine the talk if I don't? You were the one to remind me how the county loves a scandal, and my reputation usually hangs me before I've done a thing!'

Lord Veryan grunted unsympathetically at the slightly bitter note in Ivo's voice. 'Don't sound so sorry for yourself, sir! You've had considerable amusement in the process of getting your damned reputation! You can't blame people for believing the worst. It's often been no more than the truth! What's more, I've never seen you worry about it before.'

'You're right, I haven't! But this is different. Aunt Frances was right! It's important that we are careful, not for my sake, but for Jossie's. We don't want any more gossip, she's had enough. Why do you think I kept away from Sudiham for so long after she arrived?'

The two older people exchanged a glance, and Lady Frances asked slowly, 'You're not by any chance falling in love with Jossie, are you, Ivo?'

He looked at her in astonishment. 'Good Lord, no! She's far too young. No, no! I regard her as a protégée...'

A sudden vision of the scene by the waterfall gave Ivo pause. The memory of how it had felt to have Jossie in his arms, Jossie responding with such innocent abandon to his kisses...the way he had felt... They were not the feelings one had towards a protégée! She had been so completely captivating, so spellbindingly seductive that he had lost all sight of how young she was... For those few moments of madness she had simply been a completely desirable woman! He stood up and walked round restlessly, oblivious to two pairs of eyes following him. Radstock was a fool! A crass idiot! Why the devil could he not appreciate what an extraordinary delight it would have been to teach Jossie the ways of love, to unlock all her sweetness, her passion...?

Ivo turned round to find his aunt and his father regarding him somewhat quizzically. He pulled himself together. 'A protégée,' he said firmly. 'That is all! But you see why I have to be careful.' He paused. 'However, I'd still like to know what she intends to do in London.'

'What an absurd question! She will meet the *ton*, of course. I fancy I still have some good friends in London who would welcome me back and receive a young friend of mine kindly. Jossie mustn't be allowed to dwindle into a disappointed spinster, and in London she might well meet someone who could persuade her to forget Peter Radstock. Between us we could introduce her to the very cream of Society. She could make an excellent match in her first season.'

Ivo did not find this notion altogether palatable. It seemed to him that his aunt was being over-hasty. Jossie would marry some time, no doubt, but he was not sure he wanted her to find a husband as quickly as all that.

'In due course, perhaps!' he said firmly. 'But not yet. I'd like her to have time to enjoy herself first. She mustn't rush into marriage with the first eligible man she meets!'

There was a little silence.

'Of course not!' said his aunt.

'Naturally not!' said his father.

Exasperated, Ivo said, 'Why the devil are you both looking at me in that absurd fashion? My interest in Jossie Morley is…is totally platonic, I assure you! I wish you would stop reading more than there is into my words!'

'All the same, it's time you thought of finding a wife, Ivo,' said his father mildly. 'Jossie would seem to me to be an excellent choice. I like the girl—and you appear to like her, too! You've known quite a few young women in your time, but I've never seen you take quite so much interest in their welfare before!'

Ivo took a deep breath and said patiently, 'You're quite right, I *do* take an interest in Jossie's welfare. She has been treated heartlessly by the very people who ought to have protected her most. I do take an interest in her welfare and will continue to do what I can to promote her happiness. Furthermore, I agree with you that she would be an excellent choice for any man lucky enough to win her. However, my own choice at present is to remain single!'

Fearing that the discussion was about to dissolve into a family altercation, Lady Frances decided to intervene. 'And I am quite sure, Rupert, that Jossie does not regard Ivo in the light of a possible husband, either. Indeed, she is in no state at the moment to think of marriage at all. Remember the extraordinary life she led before last July, dressed as a boy and behaving like one, too! Ivo is right. She must be given time to learn something of the world before she makes her choice. It is undeniable that she has the necessary looks and wealth to be highly acceptable to the *ton*.'

'Acceptable? She has the necessary spirit and originality to make herself a huge success! If that is what she wants,' said Ivo, whose mind was still half-occupied with questions about Jossie's real motives.

Chapter Nine

The weather had turned cold and frosty, and Lord Veryan declared that the ground was too hard for riding. So the next day Ivo invited Jossie for a walk in the park instead. A night's rest had not caused him to change his mind, and his curiosity about Jossie's motives was as active as ever. Why was she so full of enthusiasm for his aunt's plan? Why was she as eager now to see London, as she had been hostile to the idea in the past? Was it simply a desire for a change of scene as his aunt had suggested? He doubted it. He doubted it very much. Jossie was not a girl to be thrilled by the thought of dresses and balls and life in a big city. So why the change? A walk on a cold, frosty day seemed to provide an excellent opportunity for finding out.

'I'm delighted that you are going to London, Jossie,' he began. 'Though I never thought to see you there. I thought you disliked the place.'

She gave him a look. 'As you said yourself, I have never been there. How can I possibly judge? And since Lady Frances was prepared to be so generous I decided to go to see for myself. Who knows? I might even learn to like the company of fashionable people! They can't all be as boring as the ones I have met so far.'

This touch of the old Jossie aroused Ivo's ever-ready sense of humour, but he kept his face straight as he said reproachfully, 'How unkind of you to say so! I am generally considered to be quite entertaining. But if you are bored…'

'Oh, no! I didn't mean you!' said Jossie, immediately contrite. 'I don't think of you as a fashionable person at all!'

'Worse and worse!' said Ivo. 'A dullard, either way.'

Jossie looked at him suspiciously. 'You're laughing at me!' she said.

'My dear child,' said Ivo, giving way to his amusement, 'I think you know very little about fashionable people! You might even like some of them! But I don't believe that your sudden wish to go to London has its roots in a simple desire to see the *ton*. Why don't you tell me what is in that head of yours?'

'What do you mean?' said Jossie, looking at him wide-eyed, her eyes green as the sea. She was certainly up to something!

'Come, my girl! You know you won't succeed in pulling the wool over my eyes for very long. We've played chess too often for that. You are up to something, Jossie Morley, and I would like to know what it is!'

Jossie frowned, obviously debating what she should tell him. Then her face cleared and she smiled at him and said, almost conversationally, 'Peter said he wanted to go to London during the Season. And I expect he'll be even more determined now. He'll want to show off that new wife of his, the elegantly lovely Rosalind. He won't find it difficult to persuade her. She'll want to shine in London as she shone in Lyne St Michael. Oh, and Bath, too, of course. She shone to such good effect there. They will probably be in London next year.'

'Shine! Rosalind Cherton?'

'Rosalind Radstock.'

Ivo ignored this. 'Jossie, it's quite clear that you really do know nothing about the world! Take my word for it, whatever the girl's name is she would arouse very little interest in London. She's pretty enough, but there are a hundred prettier young women there. Her manners are elegant, but there is no lack of elegant females, either. And that is all there is to her! To be a success in London, to shine, as you call it, a woman needs something more than insipid elegance. She needs…oh, I don't know… something more special. Character. Originality.'

'Really?' asked Jossie, looking pleased. 'You don't think she would be a wild success, then?'

'I am sure she wouldn't!' Ivo was beginning to see where Jossie's thoughts were leading. He added deliberately, 'But *you* could.'

He was intrigued by the mixture of feelings in her expression. A strong touch of doubt, mixed with eagerness, certainly. But there was more. Plans were forming in that busy mind.

'That's what I want,' she said. 'And I would give anything to achieve it. But I'd have to be sure… Do you really think I could do it?'

Ivo regarded her with a small smile. 'You have no idea, have you? Jossie, you could be a sensation in London! Believe me, I know what I am saying. I've seen a good few charming women in my time, but when I first met you I was bowled over.'

Jossie forgot her schemes for a moment. 'Bowled over indeed!' she said scornfully. 'When you first met me, Ivo, you thought I was a boy!'

'Well, the second time, then. I had forgotten the pistol affair for the moment.' He shook his head. 'That first time I thought you were an impudent scamp. It was a rude shock to find you were a girl.'

'You handled me very roughly.'

'I'm surprised I didn't do worse! You had just frightened me to death! But, may I apologise now?' Ivo stopped and took her hand with a touch of gallantry. 'If I had known what an entrancing creature was disguised in those boy's garments...'

He paused. Jossie was looking at him with something of her old derision. 'Be careful, Ivo! I'm not one of your flirts!'

He laughed delightedly and hugged her. 'No, you're not. And you never will be, I promise. But I *will* be your friend. What's more, if they are what I think they are, I'll help you with these plans you are busily hatching at the moment.'

She was silent. After a pause she said in quite a different tone, 'I believe you...I trust you. Why do I have such confidence in you, when I don't seem to be able to trust anyone else?'

'What about your godmother? My father? Surely you trust them?'

'I'm fond of Lady Frances, and I like your father. I cannot say how grateful I am for what they have done. But I couldn't talk to them like this. With you it's different.' She turned away from him, and spoke in a muffled voice. 'After that ball and the...the rest, I tried to shut the world out. You know I did. But I couldn't shut *you* out. I don't know why it is, but I feel a sort of bond with you.' She stopped and said abruptly, 'I'm not sure I like it. I would prefer to be free of such ties.'

'After what has happened that's understandable,' replied Ivo. 'But no one can survive entirely alone. I'm glad you trust me.'

They walked on in silence for a little. Jossie appeared to be deep in thought. Finally she spoke.

'That kiss...' she began. 'The one by the waterfall. Was it only imagination that made it so special? Because I believed it was Peter?'

'I don't think so,' said Ivo carefully. 'But this is dangerous ground, Jossie...'

'If you kissed me again like that...would it still work? That last time the effect was magical. Even though it was only a lesson, even though you were only trying to show me how to respond to Peter, I felt for a moment that I could do anything in the world, be anything you wanted me to be! It was a glorious feeling. If you kissed me again, would it be the same?'

'I don't think...'

'I so want to feel like that again! To feel as if I could attract anyone I chose. It's not very likely, is it, when neither Peter nor my father thought me much of a woman.'

Ivo exploded. 'They were wrong! Quite wrong!'

'Were they? Peter found something in that Cherton girl that I hadn't even thought about.'

'I would say he didn't exactly *find* it so much as have it put under his nose, my dear. She and her mother between them made him aware, probably for the first time in his life, of feminine attractions!'

Jossie nodded. 'Feminine attractions,' she said thoughtfully. 'That's what we're talking about. I didn't even know they existed.' She stopped again. 'I suppose it was stupid of me not to realise... I thought friendship was enough, you see. Till then I had never...never thought about...about setting out deliberately to attract anyone. I wouldn't have known how. I suppose that's the sort of thing that woman meant.' She looked at Ivo and said with a curl of her lip, 'I mean Mrs Cherton. My father was going to ask her to teach me! I would rather have died!'

'She could have nothing to teach you, Jossie, believe me!'

She gave him a twisted smile. 'I certainly couldn't have learned anything from her. It's odd that in the end it was you who showed me something of it all. It shows how much I trusted you, even then....' The smile vanished and she added bitterly, 'But it was all too late, wasn't it? Peter had already been attracted to someone else, someone who was more of a woman than I would ever be, he said. And my father thought the same. I was not only not the boy he wanted, I couldn't even make a decent girl. That's what he said.'

Her bitterness was so unlike the Jossie he knew that Ivo said urgently, 'Don't let it affect you, Jossie! They were fools, taken in by a pretty face with nothing behind it but an ambitious and determined mother. Rosalind Cherton hasn't half your quality. Girls like her are two a penny in London. But she's been taught from the cradle to make the most of her attractions, and she used them on Peter.'

'You're saying he was trapped? Without any sort of struggle?' She thought for a moment. 'I think you're right. Now I look back I can see that he was always rather easily led.'

'To the devil with Peter! The best thing you can do is to forget him!'

'Oh no! I shan't do that. Not yet. I shan't forget either of them.' Once again her voice had the undertone which had aroused his suspicions the night before.

He put his arm around her, then lifted her chin with his finger, forcing her to look at him. 'What exactly are you up to, Jossie? Tell me!'

Her eyes were shadowed. 'I can't. I'm not yet sure I can do it. It's early days and I still have a lot to learn. How to behave, how to dress, how to dance... You know the sort of thing. But more than that I want to learn how to appeal. I want to learn the arts of attraction.' She stopped, then added, 'Except that I would prefer to call them the arts of war!'

'Take care that you don't get hurt again.'

'Hurt? You couldn't be more mistaken, my friend,' she said softly. 'I doubt anyone will ever again be near enough to *touch* me!' She stopped again, then said slowly, 'Except, perhaps, you.'

She turned and looked into his eyes. Then she moved closer to him, holding her face up to his. Ivo found it impossible to resist the unspoken invitation. He bent his head and kissed her. She responded instantly, with a mixture of passion and a desperate desire for comfort. After a while the kiss intensified, grew deeper. It was even more intoxicating than the first time...

Ivo lifted his head and gently put her away from him. 'I think that's enough,' he said softly, proud of the steadiness of his voice. 'What you need at the moment is someone to trust, Jossie. A friend, not a lover. You mustn't confuse the two. I shall try to give you all the comfort, all the reassurance, I can. But if that kiss had gone on much longer it would have been a lover's kiss.'

She turned away. 'I don't understand!' she said. 'It happened again! I felt such...such...a sense of contentment, such comfort, as if I could find the answer there in your arms. You made me feel like...like a queen among women!' She turned to him. 'I don't understand,' she said again. 'Why couldn't I feel like that with Peter?'

For a moment Ivo had a lunatic temptation to give in, to show her just how much had been missing in her relationship with Peter Radstock, to make her even more aware of her womanhood, to demonstrate how supremely appealing he found her... But he put temptation aside. He had no wish to go down such a dangerous road, for his own sake just as much as for Jossie's. It would be all too easy to find them both trapped...

She was still looking at him with bewilderment in her eyes. Ivo pulled himself together, and, putting these thoughts firmly behind him, grinned at her, saying lightly, 'Aren't you forgetting something? I'm very good at kissing—remember my reputation!'

To his relief Jossie laughed and responded in kind. 'Of course! The worst flirt in the county.'

'I don't wish to boast,' said Ivo gravely, 'but there are some who would say I'm the worst flirt in Europe!'

'Really?' said Jossie, looking impressed. She went on, 'That explains it, of course. I imagine all successful flirts must have a particular talent for kissing. I wonder where they learn it? It would hardly be at their mother's knee!'

Ivo was amused. Not one woman in a hundred would have replied as Jossie had. Some would have pretended to be shocked, others would have been sickeningly coy. But it took a Jossie Morley to enter into the spirit of his claim and manage to sound objectively interested, as if she really wished to know. As perhaps she did.

But after a moment's thought she went on, 'But perhaps you were right. I lack experience, of course, but I think you're *very* good, Ivo. I don't think we'd better try again.' She nodded. 'I'd rather have a friend.'

They walked on in silence. Ivo was a little piqued,

but at the same time relieved by Jossie's unselfconscious manner towards him. How did she manage to switch so easily, one minute behaving like a courtesan, the next like a child? She enjoyed his kisses, so much was obvious, but she seemed to be completely unconscious of any romantic resonances between them. She still regarded him as a trusted friend, nothing more.

But below his usual air of self-possession he was puzzled by his own mixture of feelings. He had been sincere when he had denied being in love with her, and equally sincere when he had sworn that he wanted only to be her friend. He liked Jossie, she amused him, he enjoyed her company. But he was not in love with her! So why did he suffer from such an inexplicably strong reaction whenever he had Jossie in his arms? When some of the most beautiful and experienced women in London could kiss him and leave him absolutely sober, why did Jossie's kisses have such an intoxicating effect?

As they made their way back along the drive he stole an occasional glance at his companion. She was such an unlikely source of temptation, about as far removed from the usual object of his desire as she possibly could be. She might wear girl's dresses now, but she still had a long way to go before her boy's coltish stride turned into the graceful steps of a young lady. She might have learned to ride side saddle, but she still had no idea how to behave the rest of the time. She was very young—in the ways of the world she was even younger, perhaps, than her years would suggest—and there was not the slightest suspicion of coquetry, not even a hint of any awareness of him as a personable male. Ivo smiled to himself. There was something surprisingly seductive in the total lack of any attempt to attract him.

He pulled himself together again. Seductive...? The

very thought was absurd! He regarded himself as a sophisticated man of the world, nearly thirty years old and
an unrepentant cynic. How could he possibly imagine
himself to be in any danger from an eighteen-year-old
innocent? Ridiculous! The child had a talent for kissing
which was unrivalled in his experience, her kisses went
to a man's head like champagne, but she knew less about
the arts of attraction than a nun in a convent! What the
devil had been *wrong* with Peter Radstock? He was supposed to have been in love with her. How could he have
known her all those years and failed to recognise the
potential passion which lay below Jossie's matter-of-fact
surface?

Or was the answer really very simple? Had the two
never truly been in love? If that were so then, in spite
of her present misery, it was possible that Jossie had had
a lucky escape. She would have been infinitely more
miserable tied for life to a country clod with little feeling
and less wit. She deserved someone more discerning,
someone who could appreciate the pure gold of her...
someone like himself.

Ivo cursed below his breath and told himself not to
be ridiculous. He had no intention of falling in love with
Jossie Morley! He wanted to help her, not seduce her!
She was too young, she didn't know the rules by which
he lived. He must remove himself from temptation before this temporary aberration got out of hand. His feelings about Jossie would soon disappear once he was
away from her—he had managed it once before, and he
would again. Indeed, in the months before he came back
to Somerset for that damned birthday celebration he had
enjoyed one or two very pleasant interludes in London
with women of experience, women who understood the
rules of flirtation. No danger there—and no thought of

Jossie either! He must remove himself to London and seek out some distractions. Then, by the time his aunt brought Jossie to London for the season, he would hope to be himself once more, able to support Jossie in the way she needed. As a friend. He would look forward to being her friend in London.

The gods were kind. The very next day they provided the excuse Ivo needed. Kate Calthorpe had given birth to a healthy baby boy a few weeks earlier than expected, and Adam had written to remind Ivo that he had volunteered to act as a sponsor to the child. No one could criticise a prospective godfather for wishing to make the acquaintance of his godson as soon as possible! He would be away from Sudiham within the week.

At dinner that night the discussion once again centred round Jossie's début. But when Ivo was consulted he said slowly, 'I'll do what I can, though I'm afraid it won't be much at the moment. I haven't had the opportunity to tell you yet, but I'm off to visit the Calthorpes before the end of the week. I learned just today that I have a new godson.'

He suffered a slight pang of conscience at Jossie's look of dismay, but she soon rallied and she and Lady Frances set about begging him for more details of the new arrival. Adam's letter had said little other than that Kate and the baby were perfectly healthy, and the baby was to be called Thomas Adam Ivo. But Ivo promised to send an answer to all of their questions as soon as he could.

When the excitement died down he said, 'About London. There is little enough I can do down here for Jossie at the moment. But I shall have a word with the Calthorpes. Kate was introduced to society just a couple of years back and had quite a time of it, encountering a number of the pitfalls on the way. I'm sure she would give any advice you wanted. Perhaps you could even stay with the Calthorpes on your way to London.'

'So when shall we see you again, Ivo?'

'I'm not sure,' he said easily. 'There are one or two people in London I want to see, so I thought I would go straight there from Calthorpe. I could easily do some business for you while I'm in town. The house in Charles Street has been shut up for years—it will need an army to put it into order before you come. And unless you take your household with you, you will need to hire servants and so on. Shall I see to some of that?'

'Thank you, Ivo. I should like you to.' Lady Frances went on, 'I intend to do this in style, with London servants, and my own carriage. Perhaps you would check the stabling.' She turned to Jossie with a smile. 'The Trenchard London house, thank goodness, is large enough for us to entertain any number and it has one of the best addresses in London. Charles Street leads directly into Berkeley Square. Thank heavens there is not the slightest necessity for economy. Everything shall be of the best!' She turned to Ivo. 'But I warn you, we shall expect more help than this after we arrive! Surely you can act as escort to your aunt and her goddaughter without arousing gossip? I know you feel a need to be circumspect, but—'

'It would be the first time in his life if he was!' said Lord Veryan tartly. 'But your aunt is right—you look after her and Jossie, my boy. Never mind the tabbies!'

Ivo nodded. 'Is there anything I can do before I go?' he asked. 'Aunt Frances? Jossie?'

'Yes, there is,' said Jossie coolly. 'These arts of attraction. I thought you were going to help me to acquire them. How can you do that if you aren't here? I hope you'll promise to show me in London! And if I wanted to be a flirt, how would I set about it?'

Lady Frances was scandalised. 'Jossie!' she protested, 'You mustn't ask things like that! And especially not so…so bluntly!'

'I haven't time to be polite, Lady Frances. Not in private. But you can teach me how to be diplomatic in public. If there is one thing I've learned recently, it is that you are judged by your shell, not by what is inside. Well, if I am to go to London, I intend to adopt a new shell! What I am inside…' She paused and for a moment her face was hard. 'What I am inside is my own business.'

Ivo left for Calthorpe soon after. At first Jossie was somewhat cast down, but she soon recovered and worked hard to learn what her godmother was teaching her. If Lady Frances had an uneasy suspicion that Jossie had more in her mind than a simple desire to be a success in London, she was too delighted at the change in her protégée's spirits to give it voice. The lassitude, the depression, were now things of the past, and Jossie was soon as active and as eager as ever, devoting her considerable energy and talents towards achieving her objective.

But as time went on Lady Frances began to wonder whether something of the old Jossie, the qualities which had made her so special—her delightful transparency, a spontaneous warmth of heart—had been lost forever on that disastrous evening in July. The new Jossie might have the appearance of openness, but was in fact considerably more reserved than before. If she hesitated now before speaking, it was not because she felt lost. She was taking time to consider the effect of what she was saying.

It had been thought that Peregrine might come home for a short time, but he sent to say that he was unable to leave Derbyshire, so Christmas and the early weeks of January passed quietly without the company of either of Lord Veryan's sons. Jossie and Lady Frances were invited to be present at the wedding of Major Morley and Mrs Cherton shortly after New Year, but not only did Lady Frances develop a bad cold, but the weather turned so severe that it would have been foolhardy for the ladies to attempt the fifteen miles along country roads to Lyne St Michael. No one was disappointed when they were forced to send their apologies.

But for Jossie the days were busy enough. She was a willing and intelligent pupil, and Lady Frances was soon delighted with the girl's progress. Her memory was excellent and she seldom needed to be told anything twice. Names, dance steps, conventions, all were quickly mastered. And, far from being a handicap, the active life she had led at Lyne now stood her in good stead, too. As her confidence in social skills increased, it was seen that she moved with natural and unconscious grace. Though her carriage was upright, it was not at all stiff or awkward. She held herself beautifully.

For a while she found it difficult to remember to limit her boyish stride to the smaller steps conventionally required of a lady of fashion, but soon that too was mastered. Lady Frances constantly gave her advice and instruction in the ways of London society.

'You mustn't think of London as a huge city,' she said one day. 'The part of it you will know is actually very limited and you will quickly learn your way about in it. Not that you will ever go out unaccompanied, Jossie. You must always, always be accompanied by a footman, or, at the very least, a maidservant. Which reminds me—we must find a suitable maid for you.'

'I promise to remember, Lady Frances, but when will you tell me the more interesting things? Rules of behaviour and the like are all very well, but they are very bor— I mean, do we really have to spend so much time on them? I want...I want...'

'What do you want, my dear?' asked Lady Frances gently.

'I want to be a great success! To fascinate them all! To show them! You all said I could, but I still don't know how!' Jossie got up and walked restlessly round the room. 'I wish Ivo were here,' she said suddenly. 'He must have known so many fascinating women. He could tell me how they do it.' She turned to Lady Frances. 'Could you?'

Lady Frances shook her head at Jossie. 'I wouldn't recommend some of the ways Ivo's ladies fascinate, Jossie!' she said a trifle austerely. 'But if we are talking of the more respectable kind... I'd say the most important thing is *not* to change, not to try to be someone different. Have the confidence to be yourself.'

Jossie instantly rejected this idea. 'Oh, no! That would never do. You know it wouldn't. Jossie Morley was an ungraceful, unappealing creature, incapable of capturing or holding any man. She liked winning arguments, not using honey words and sweet smiles. She preferred to waste her time riding over the hills, not using it to advantage in front of a mirror in her bedroom. Oh, no! Jossie Morley must be replaced! But with what? That's what I don't yet know. To learn *that* is more important to me than learning what to say or do if the Duchess of Sutherland should happen to speak to me.'

Lady Frances was firm. 'I mean what I say. You must be yourself.' She held up a hand when Jossie tried to protest. 'No, don't argue! Whatever you think, Jossie Morley was and is quite special. You must believe that.' She held Jossie's eye until Jossie shrugged and nodded. Lady Frances went on, 'Let me try to explain what I've been trying to bring about. Do you remember what you felt like last summer when you were made to attend all those balls and parties? I don't think you enjoyed them.'

'I hated them!' said Jossie with feeling. 'I had no idea what to do.'

'Exactly! So you spent your time staying in the background and wishing you were somewhere else. *Not* a way to success! But you will never have to worry again. The rules which govern behaviour in the polite world have now become second nature to you. You can walk, talk, dine, dance and perform all the other activities demanded of you as gracefully, as easily as the rest of the world. Indeed, I would say better than most. In the future, you will never wonder whether you are doing them properly. You will know that you are. They will all come instinctively.'

'I see…' said Jossie after a moment.

'Furthermore,' Lady Frances went on, 'a moderate amount of time spent in front of a mirror in the privacy of your own bedroom is *never* wasted, if it means that you can move about in company afterwards without thinking twice about how you look. Together with your maid you have done your best and you can now forget about it. There is nothing so un-fascinating as women— or men—who are forever worrying about their appearance.'

'You're talking about confidence, aren't you?'

'Yes. A woman who is quietly confident, at ease with herself, is halfway to being fascinating to others, Jossie. And when she has youth, beauty, wit and an interest in the rest of the world, she is very nearly there!'

'I'm not at all sure that I am as far along the road as you suggest, but I see what you mean. Where do we go from here?'

'Clothes!' said Lady Frances promptly. 'And I don't mean the draper's shop down the road, either!'

'Are we going to Bath?'

'Perhaps. For the less important ones. But most of your dresses will be bought in London. I wonder if Madame Rosa is still in Bruton Street? I'll write to Ivo—he'll know. Meanwhile I have some fashion journals upstairs which we shall examine tonight.'

Chapter Ten

Ivo returned briefly in March to spend Easter at Sudiham, and afterwards he escorted his aunt and Jossie to Calthorpe Court, where they were to spend some time before continuing to London. Jossie bade Lord Veryan farewell with regret, but cheered up noticeably when he promised to come to London in June to see how she was faring. Sudiham had been a safe haven for her ever since the previous summer, and though she was no longer the pitiful ghost who had come to stay then, it was still a wrench to leave it and face the world outside.

She was not altogether looking forward to staying with the Calthorpes, either. Lady Calthorpe had written everything that was kind, but Jossie was still nervous of meeting them. Thanks to Lady Frances she had come a long way in confidence, and was ready to deal with every social occasion, but she couldn't help wondering what the Calthorpes would make of her, all the same. There was even a touch of jealousy in her feelings towards them, for they were Ivo's closest friends, and she suspected that he admired Lady Calthorpe more than any other woman he had met.

But she need not have worried. Kate Calthorpe was a

warmly affectionate person, whose own great happiness spilled over everyone around her. Her lord adored her, and though she had a teasing, laughing relationship with Ivo, it was quite clear that she was very much in love with her husband. Their infant son was the centre of their existence, but he was not by any means allowed to dominate the scene. On the contrary. Lady Calthorpe took a lively interest in plans for the come out of 'Miss Calverton Morley', and spent a considerable time with her, talking of London, showing her some of her dresses, and regaling her with tales of Adam's and Ivo's exploits.

Lady Calthorpe even persuaded Kendrick, her somewhat daunting personal maid, to arrange Miss Calverton Morley's hair and give her advice on styles and colours of dress which would flatter her. Kendrick was critical of the gowns made in Bath, but unbent a little when she was assured that Jossie was to have a completely new wardrobe made in London.

It wasn't long before Jossie was invited to call Lady Calthorpe by her first name.

'Ivo is such an old friend, it seems absurd for you to be addressing me as Lady Calthorpe when we are all otherwise so informal. Do call me Kate! But what am I to call you? Helena or Jossie? Ivo has always referred to you as Jossie, but he introduced you to us as Helena. Which would you prefer?'

Jossie hesitated. Ivo had introduced her to the Calthorpes as Helena Calverton Morley at her request. In her distress after the débâcle of the ball at Lyne, she had passionately rejected the name of Jossie, along with a life she wished to forget. And she was as determined as ever to be known in London as Helena Calverton Morley. But Ivo and Lady Frances had continued to call her Jossie, and over the months she had grown used to it again, regarding it now as a nickname, a sign of affectionate intimacy. Did she wish to admit the Calthorpes to this inner circle? She looked at Kate and the warmth of Kate's smile made up her mind for her. 'I should like you to call me Jossie,' she said awkwardly.

From that moment the friendship prospered. Once she could see that Jossie was at ease with the Calthorpes, Lady Frances left her and went on ahead to London to stay with friends and vet the arrangements Ivo had made for them. Jossie was more than content to stay behind. Kate was not much older than she was, and it was a new and very pleasant experience for her to have a friend of her own age and sex to talk to. She watched and learned a good deal from Kate. Together they drove about the countryside, dined with the neighbours, danced, listened to music, played cards and had long conversations, and Jossie put into practice what she had been learning at Sudiham during the past year. Lady Frances had taught her well. Jossie knew the rules by heart and seldom put a foot wrong. But it was Kate Calthorpe who showed her how to infuse them with warmth and charm.

Ivo accompanied his aunt to London, but frequently returned to spend a few days with his friends in order, he said, to make the acquaintance of his godson. But he spent a lot more time with Jossie than with young Thomas.

It seemed to him that Jossie was improving with every visit. No doubt the attentions of Kendrick had something to do with it, but there was more than this. Jossie had always been a fast learner, and now she was learning a great deal more from his friends. He noted with amusement how closely she watched Kate, and how often touches of Kate could be seen in her manner, and in her voice.

'I approve of the new Jossie,' he said one day when they were out together for a walk in the late spring sunshine. 'But don't lose the old one completely. I should miss her.'

'Would you?' she asked, doubtfully. 'I don't think anyone else would. Besides, it's not the old Jossie who wants to go to London.' She pirouetted round and gave him a dazzling smile. 'It's Helena Calverton Morley, beautiful Helena, irresistible Helena, the feminine counterpart of the worst flirt in all Europe, Helena the breaker of hearts! Do you think she will manage it?'

Ivo looked appreciatively at the figure before him. Lady Frances had decided to wait till they were in London before dressing Jossie in style, and she was still clothed modestly enough in a grey pelisse and a simple bonnet. But the radiance of her smile and the grace of her movements were very appealing.

'I am sure she will,' he said with a smile. But he went on more seriously, 'Is that what you really want, Jossie? It can be a dangerous game for a woman.'

'I want it more than anything. And I doubt there will be any danger in it for me. But if there were I would welcome it.'

Ivo considered her carefully. That curious tone was in her voice again. He said slowly, 'There's something about it that I don't altogether like…'

'You don't think I can do it? You're afraid I shall fail?'

'I'm afraid you'll succeed! Oh, don't think I want to spoil your fun! You'll be a success, all right. I can see it getting more likely every time I come down here. You'll dazzle them. And the world owes you something after what happened last year. To be acknowledged as a beauty, to enjoy the admiration of the *ton*—yes, I can sympathise with that ambition. But a *heartbreaker*? I'm not sure I like that idea.'

'It isn't the admiration I want, Ivo,' said Jossie, suddenly fierce. 'It's the power. The power to make my father take back what he said, the power to show Peter Radstock—and Peter Radstock's mother—that he made a mistake—' She stopped abruptly.

'You surely aren't still in love with him?'

'I despise him!'

'Then don't waste your time on him!' Ivo gave her a sharp look. 'You're not planning anything so stupid as revenge on Peter Radstock, are you?' He waited and when she said nothing he gave her a slight shake. 'Are you, Jossie? If you are, then don't count on me to help you!'

'You said you would!'

'I said I would help you to enjoy London! And as long as you don't do too much damage, I'll watch with pleasure while you capture a few susceptible hearts. Capture, Jossie. Not break. But leave Peter Radstock alone!'

'Why?'

'He's married, and, what is more, he really isn't a worthy victim. I could name you two or three very presentable young men who would be a much greater challenge.'

Jossie eyed him speculatively. 'Too great a challenge?'

'Well...they've been on the town for a year or two now, and so far they've eluded all attempts to capture them. And they've left more than a few broken hearts and disappointed hopes behind them.'

'Are you one of those men?'

'Jossie! Hasn't Kate told you? I never flirt with hopeful young ladies.'

'Why not?'

'Because I have a dislike of hurting the vulnerable.'

'How very noble!' said Jossie mockingly. 'And, besides that, there's always the danger that you might get trapped into marriage, isn't there?'

'Very true! How well you know me after all!'

'So who are these young men?'

'I'll point them out when we get to London. But don't place your hopes too high.'

'You don't think I can do it!'

'It would be amusing to see you try. It's time they had a lesson. I suppose it wouldn't do you any harm to test your charms on one of them...'

'Not all three?'

'Oh, no! One mustn't look for the impossible.'

'Impossible, Ivo?' said Jossie. She gave him a slow, provocative look from sea-green eyes. 'You think it impossible?'

Ivo laughed delightedly. 'Excellent! Perfect! You've been practising!'

Jossie relaxed and grinned. 'I'm glad you like it. I thought it was rather good myself. I call it my siren look. You have no idea how long it took to get it right!' She put her arm through his and gave him another conspiratorial grin.

'Have you others?'

'Of course! There's the fresh as a daisy look, the flighty maiden look, the deeply serious look—oh, I have any number of others. But that one was the most difficult. I kept having to stop myself laughing.'

Once again Ivo found himself marvelling at the sudden changes in this girl—one minute a siren, the next a mischievous child. But he then corrected himself. Not a child any more. Jossie was unmistakably a woman, and a damned attractive one, too. He wondered how this adventure in London would turn out. It was becoming clear to him that she would need more than his help and guidance. The game she had decided to play had its dangers, dangers which she was still too innocent to see. She would need his protection. And he must see to it that she didn't rouse too much adverse gossip. That wouldn't do her any good at all... Ivo smiled inwardly. The creeping boredom which he had experienced in Brussels had recently begun to make itself evident in London. But now it looked as if that was all about to change. Boredom would be the least of his concerns!

'Well, Helena, my lovely enchantress, we'll see what you can do,' he said, adding warningly, 'But there are two men at least, whom you must leave out of your web. Peter Radstock is one.'

'Who is the other?'

'Me!'

'*You*, Ivo?' Her astonishment would have been comic, thought Ivo, if he hadn't felt just slightly piqued by it. She went on, 'I wouldn't even try to use any wiles on you. You'd see through them straight away. Besides, one doesn't use wiles on a friend. Though...'

'What?'

'You'd let me *practise* on you, wouldn't you?'

And, though he had some reservations about the wisdom of this, Ivo nodded, unable to resist the coaxing note in his protégée's voice.

In the privacy of their bedchamber Kate Calthorpe could not help speculating to her husband about Jossie and her relationship with Ivo.

'I simply don't understand it, Adam,' she said with a frown. 'From what the Leversons were telling us last week, Ivo is as much of a flirt as ever. Last month he set the *ton* by the ears with his pursuit of Lady Hartley, and before that it was Sybil Montague. They are already discussing who is to be Ivo's next.'

'What is there in that to puzzle you, my love?' asked Adam. 'I would find it strange if Ivo stopped flirting! He hasn't changed in all the years I've known him.'

'You think not?' said his wife with a glint in her eye. 'I suppose, in all those years you have known him, he has looked after any number of girls just like Jossie— just eighteen and about to make their début?'

'Well, not exactly...' said Adam.

'I suppose you will tell me that he has been scrupulously careful to avoid causing gossip about *hundreds* of young ladies, who have, like our young friend, been seen in his company?'

'He has certainly never worried about gossip,' said Adam with a reminiscent smile. 'Ivo used to keep the tabbies busy wherever he went. But I can't remember seeing him in the company of many *young* ladies at all!'

'Exactly!' said Kate, triumphant. 'So why does he spend so much time and trouble on the girl? Why is he so protective of her? Can it be possible that he has fallen in love at last?'

'In love? Ivo? With Jossie Morley? My dear Kate, you must have windmills in your head! I can't imagine Ivo in love with anyone, and certainly not with such an innocent! Ivo's inamoratas are always thoroughly experienced women. He avoids débutantes like the plague.'

'I'm not talking of that kind of love, Adam. I mean real love, commitment, marriage, even.'

Adam burst into a roar of laughter. 'Ivo Trenchard! What an absurd idea!'

In the face of his wife's silent disapproval he calmed down and said patiently, 'Have you seen anything at all romantic in his behaviour to suggest such a thing?'

'Of course I haven't! There isn't anything. That is precisely why I am so suspicious.'

'Er…' Adam was uncertain. His Kate was still capable of puzzling him on occasion. 'I am not quite sure I understand you.'

'Ivo is never "romantic" with Jossie. They are remarkably matter of fact with each other. But he watches over her like a mother hen with her chicks! He disguises it pretty well, I'll grant you that, but it is there all the same. I don't think the girl herself suspects it.'

'Is she in love with him? I hope not. Ivo is not the most constant of lovers.'

'You can really be exasperatingly stupid, Adam,' said the wife of his bosom. 'That is precisely what I have been saying. Ivo is not behaving like a lover at all! He isn't *flirting* with Jossie, he's looking after her. As for Jossie… She is not so easy to read. But I am sure the thought of falling in love with Ivo has not entered her head. Not yet.'

'Less easy to read? I find her charmingly frank and open.'

'Her manner is delightfully so, I agree. But there's something below the surface… It's quite clear to me that she has suffered a body blow of some kind. Ivo hinted as much when he came to Baby Tom's christening.'

'Do you know what it was?'

'Not exactly. Jossie herself never talks of it, and Ivo is always very discreet. But do you remember? When he visited us last July he told us a little about Jossie and said he was going to meet her again at a coming-of-age party in Lyne St Michael. He gave us the impression that she was involved with the young man whose party it was. Now neither the party nor the young man are ever mentioned. Nor the girl's family. Whatever happened to hurt Jossie, Adam, happened about that time, I am quite sure, and it was serious.'

'Why do you say that?'

'It has left her very wary of involvement. I certainly don't think she's ready for any of the more tender emotions. But she trusts Ivo. It could be a beginning.'

'You mean you'd be pleased if they made a match of it?'

'She is just what he needs! He is already used to looking after her. And she may be innocent, but she is by no means naïve. Look how quick she is at cards. It's a revelation to see how she can keep us all on our toes! It's my belief she is well up to all of Ivo's tricks—and he loves it. She keeps him amused. Moreover...' She gave her husband a mischievous look. 'She is so beautiful, and so lively, that Ivo won't have any time to flirt with anyone else—he'll be too busy fighting off the competition! Yes, I'd like them to make a match of it.'

Adam had had enough of his friend's affairs. He drew his wife to him. 'Well, dearest Kate, I'm just a simple soldier. I don't understand all these subtleties. I wish Ivo well, but just now I want to know how much *my* wife loves *me*. A little?'

'More than that, Adam,' murmured Kate and set about proving it.

Kate was still interested in Ivo's attitude towards Jossie. One night at dinner she brought up the question of how they had met.

'Ivo told us that you pursued him with a gun? Is that true, Jossie?'

Jossie shot an impish glance at Ivo. 'Perfectly true. He was trying to steal my horse.' Ivo uttered a protest, and she added, 'At least I thought he was.' She grinned. 'I've never seen a man so frightened.'

'Really?' murmured Adam. 'I always thought the Hussars were more show than go, but...*frightened*? Ivo!'

'Don't look at me like that, Adam! You'd have felt exactly the same. I saw the horse in the middle of nowhere and had merely stepped forward to take a closer look. How do you suppose I felt when I turned round to face a scabby little urchin pointing a loaded pistol straight at my head! I expected it to go off at any moment.'

'I thought he was a gipsy horse thief,' said Jossie by way of explanation.

'A gipsy horse thief! *Ivo?* Now that I find that very hard to imagine,' said Kate, eyeing the immaculately elegant figure opposite her.

'I...er...I had had rather a rough night before that. I dare say I didn't look quite my best,' said Ivo defensively.

'But how could you have thought Jossie a scabby little urchin?' asked Kate. They all looked at Jossie. The light from the candles caught the laughter in sparkling blue-green eyes, it glowed warmly on artfully arranged dark curls, and followed the beautiful curves of cheekbone and chin. The rose of Jossie's lips was echoed faintly in the delicate bloom of her cheeks. Finely moulded throat and shoulders rose from a virginally simple white silk dress. It would be difficult to conceive of a creature less like a scabby little urchin.

Kate turned for her answer, but Ivo's eyes were still resting on Jossie with an expression in them which she found difficult to interpret. Pleasure, certainly. But then Jossie was a pleasure to look at. A touch of reserve. Why? And, intriguingly, a slightly possessive pride. With every moment Kate grew more curious about the situation between her two guests. She wondered what would happen in London...

Ivo answered finally. 'She wasn't dressed like that when I first saw her.' He hesitated, and Jossie stepped in.

'I was wearing breeches,' said Jossie. 'He thought I was a boy.'

'Oh, you cannot imagine how often I have wanted to do that!' cried Kate. 'They seem so much more convenient. Did you ride astride, as well?'

When Jossie nodded she went on, 'Quite right, too! It's high time women were allowed to ride sensibly instead of the ridiculous way we have to perch at the moment!'

Adam exclaimed in horror, 'Good God! I'm married to a revolutionary!'

Ivo started to laugh. 'Don't tell me you've only just discovered it! Do you know how Adam once described his ideal woman to me, Kate? A quiet little blue-eyed blonde, affectionate, obedient—'

'Stop! Stop! What are you trying to do, ruin my marriage? Kate, don't listen to him—'

'Oh, I don't mind!' said Kate comfortably. 'I know you had a weakness for blue-eyed blondes. Julia Redshaw was your ideal, though whether she would have been either obedient or affectionate is another matter altogether!'

'Most unlikely, I'd say,' Ivo interposed. 'Do you know that the lovely Julia has persuaded Balmenny to bring her to London for the coming season? I suppose it's a reward for doing her duty and presenting the Viscount with not one but two heirs last year.'

'Julia has had twins?' asked Kate in amazement.

Ivo nodded. 'Both boys and both healthy. And since the Balmennys spent most of the months beforehand closeted in their castle in Ireland, Balmenny can be reasonably certain they are his. He's over the moon.'

Kate turned to Jossie, who was looking somewhat bewildered. 'Julia Redshaw lived next door to Adam when they were young. I rather think they were childhood sweethearts, but Julia married Viscount Balmenny almost as soon as she was out.' Kate paused, then said, 'She is very lovely, but I have to confess I never liked her. Perhaps motherhood has improved her.'

'It may, but I doubt it,' said Ivo. 'She is apparently quite happy to leave her sons behind her for three months while she enjoys the season in London.' He turned to Jossie. 'What Kate was too scrupulous to tell you, Jossie, is that Julia's husband is considerably older than she is, but very rich. Before he bore her off to Ireland she was a flirt of the first order.'

'Ivo!' said Kate scandalised. 'That may well be true, but you shouldn't say so! You ought not to prejudice Jossie against Lady Balmenny before she has even met her.'

'Oh, Jossie will not think less of Julia for being a flirt,' he said. 'Indeed, she would probably welcome her as an object for study—Viscountess Balmenny is, or was, a living embodiment of every art of attraction, Jossie!'

'But not, in the end, attractive,' said Adam. His deep voice was serious. He looked at Kate and smiled. 'I'm glad I came to my senses in time,' he said.

Kate said softly, 'So am I!' Then she turned to Ivo and said briskly, 'But tell me, Ivo, what would your ideal wife be like?'

'You mean, if I were in the market for a wife? As much like you as possible, Kate!' Ivo replied with a winning smile.

'Flummery! Save your charm for the ladies in London, my friend. I would never do for you. But seriously, I'd really like to know. What would you look for in a wife?'

Ivo thought for a moment. 'Seriously, Kate, I have no idea. I cannot imagine marrying anyone. I like my life too well as it is at present—I have no plans to change it. But I certainly wouldn't want the sort of wife who would regard my philanderings with complaisance! That could only come from indifference or timidity, and I wouldn't be content with either of those. As you know, I like women of spirit.'

'Ah!' said Adam reminiscently. 'Shades of Heloise de Leiken... What a pity she was already married!'

'Heloise de Leiken was a delightful companion but I wouldn't have wanted her for a wife!'

'Why not?' asked Kate. 'She sounds just right. What was wrong with her?'

'Oh, she was very nearly perfect. Accomplished, exquisitely beautiful, witty, elegant...you were never bored in her company. She had all the requisites for a perfect partner, except the one essential one.'

'She didn't love you?'

'I think she did, a little. In her fashion. But love is a chancy business, Kate. There are so many kinds of love.

How can anyone define it?' Ivo's eyes rested for a moment on Jossie, then he went on, 'No, what Heloise de Leiken lacked was any kind of loyalty. You may find it surprising, but I think keeping faith with one's partner is a first consideration…'

Then he laughed and shook his head. 'What a bore I am! Kate, you're asking me the wrong question. I don't know what my ideal would be. I've told you, my choice at the moment is not to marry at all!'

Adam cast a look at his wife and smiled. 'You'll change your mind when the right woman comes along, Ivo. Then it's not a question of choice. You'll find you have to marry, and marry only her. Nothing else will do. You'll see when the time comes.'

'There you are, then, Kate. Ask me again in a year.'

Kate persevered. 'What about you, Jossie? Have you dreams of an ideal husband?'

Jossie had been following the conversation with amused interest, but now the laughter faded. 'I'm like Ivo,' she said. 'I really have no interest in acquiring a partner for life.'

'You sound very sure. Isn't that the object of taking part in the season?'

'Not for me,' said Jossie with a charmingly apologetic smile.

'You must excuse my wife, Jossie,' said Adam, who had begun to think that Kate's curiosity was going too far. 'She means well. The point is, she has been so lucky in her choice of husband herself that she wants everyone to be as fortunate. I keep telling her that men like me don't grow on trees, but she still persists. And now I should like to hear that duet you two ladies have been practising. Shall we go into the saloon?'

The conversation broke up amid protests and laughter,

and Adam made sure the subject was not brought up again. However badly Kate wished to see a match between Ivo and Jossie, it seemed to him that it was most unlikely, at least for the foreseeable future. The question was best left alone.

When the time came to leave Calthorpe Jossie was filled with regret. At Sudiham she had felt safe, and had left with apprehension. Here at Calthorpe she had been reassured, able to relax for a short while, in the warmth of the Calthorpes' undemanding friendship. She had seen a truly happy marriage at work, had observed the interests, the humour, the respect, and the deep love the Calthorpes shared. And though she did not lose sight of her own aims, the memory of her time with Ivo's friends was stored away, and ultimately had a healing effect on her own damaged feelings.

Kate had one further gift for Jossie. A day or two before her departure she invited Jossie into her bedroom.

'I have been thinking of this for some time, Jossie, but you have only to say no and it shall be forgotten. I gather that you have not yet engaged a proper personal maid?'

'Lady Frances preferred to wait till we were in London before engaging any staff. But the girl I brought with me has done well, don't you think?'

'She is excellent! For the country. But in London you will need someone more experienced. Someone like Kendrick, for example. What would you say if I offered to release Kendrick? I engaged her for my own début two years ago, and she has been with me ever since. She's a first-class lady's maid, and I am very happy with her, but she's wasted down here. I know she would jump at the chance of working in London for someone like you, who was about to make her début. You would find her invaluable.'

'Do you mean it? I would love to have Kendrick, in spite of the fact that she frightens me half to death. But how would you manage?'

'I would find someone else. I don't need the high standards Kendrick imposes now, and I would really like her to have something more satisfying to do. Would you like me to speak to her?'

'Please do!'

As a result of this conversation Jossie set out for London with a maid who would have been snapped up by any one of a dozen London society ladies the minute it was known she was free. Kendrick herself was very happy. She left Lady Calthorpe with regret, but domestic bliss in the country was not what she looked for. To have such a promising candidate as Miss Calverton Morley for top honours among the débutantes in the coming season was exactly what she would have wanted. And if Kendrick knew anything of it, her new mistress would not be permitted to do anything but conquer.

They left Calthorpe early one morning, stayed the night in Hungerford with some cousins of Lord Veryan's, and by the evening of the next day they were in Charles Street in the heart of fashionable Mayfair. Jossie had never travelled so far in her life before, but Ivo's carriage was well sprung, and the journey had been enjoyable. The presence of Kendrick in the carriage precluded any very personal conversation, but Jossie had been given so much to think about that she hardly noticed. It was strange that her thoughts turned more than once to the mysterious Countess Leiken. Was she fair or dark? Had she really been so beautiful? And had she been as amusing as Ivo had said? Jossie would have given much to have the answers. It sounded as if the Countess would have been someone to use as a model. There was Julia, Viscountess Balmenny, too...but it was Heloise Leiken that Ivo had really liked...

Jossie settled herself back against the squabs and let her imagination take over. She was dancing in a large ballroom, surrounded by an admiring crowd, her father and Peter standing in amazement at one end. Two lovely ladies, both wearing coronets, one Irish, one Belgian, were standing close by, looking deeply envious as she floated past them. Her partner was holding her close, guiding her faultlessly through the steps of the waltz, his dark blue eyes smiling down into hers. She had seldom felt so secure, so happy...

But the next day, when Ivo took his two ladies for a drive through London to the park, she suddenly felt apprehensive. She looked at the stylishly gowned and coiffured ladies and immaculately dressed gentlemen passing by, listened to their drawling voices as they stopped to exchange greetings with Ivo and her godmother, endured their well-bred stares as Lady Frances introduced her. As they went along she looked at the grand houses and wide streets, was deafened by the bustle and noise, and her panic grew. What was Jossie Morley, a tomboy, a hoyden, rejected by her father as well as her childhood friend, doing in this sophisticated world? How had she thought she could possibly rival the elegance, the assurance, the style of these fashionable people? The *ton* would laugh her to scorn... She looked at Ivo in despair. How could he understand? He was more elegant, more assured, more stylish than any of them! How could she ask him to waste his time helping to launch a country nobody?

Ivo leaned forward and gave her hand an encouraging squeeze. 'Be brave,' he said softly. 'Give yourself time. I've told you. You'll dazzle them all.'

Chapter Eleven

Lady Frances wasted no time in introducing Jossie to one of London's foremost modistes. Madame Rosa of Bruton Street was as famous for the dictatorial style she adopted toward her clients as for the beautiful gowns she created for them. But no one could deny that she had a touch of genius, and most people accepted her advice without demur. Lady Frances had already been to see her for her own requirements, and had been treated with the deference due to a former valued customer. Her new wardrobe was already well on its way. Today it was Jossie's turn.

'So thees is Mademoiselle Calverton?' said Madame, circling Jossie with the predatory eye of a hawk about to swoop. Sallow, thin as a rake, with snapping black eyes and hair in a tight bun, she looked disparagingly at her new client. 'Mademoiselle is tall, hein? And thin. The figure—it is there, but it needs more emphasis. That dress is *impossible*. It 'as neither cut nor style. She needs something quite different... Walk about, *mademoiselle*!'

Jossie walked.

'Ah! She 'as grace, this one! And a good carriage. Look at me, child!'

Jossie, somewhat indignant at these peremptory commands, gave Madame Rosa a straight look.

Far from being displeased by this, Madame clapped her hands and exclaimed to her assistant, *'Mais, regardez, donc! Quels beaux yeux! Quelle couleur ravissante! Quel esprit!'* She soon recovered herself, however, and turned to Lady Frances to say condescendingly, 'I might be able to do something for your goddaughter, milady. We shall take 'er measurements, and then you may leave it with us. One week today for the fittings?'

A somewhat bewildered Jossie was led out. 'But, Godmama! Have we no say in the matter? Does Madame Rosa know what I want? All she has said so far is that I am thin!'

'She knows what you *need*, Jossie. And don't forget that she likes the colour of your eyes. And your spirit.' She gave Jossie an amused look. 'It is enough. You may trust her. And she and I have already discussed the number of dresses and all the rest you will require for your début.' When Jossie still looked rebellious she said, 'Forgive me if I'm wrong, my dear. I thought you weren't interested in clothes?'

'I'm not! But—'

'Then you may leave it to Madame Rosa and me to see that you are suitably dressed. Don't worry. She knows what she is doing.'

Though Jossie was not altogether satisfied she decided not to argue. Other questions were occupying her mind.

During that first week, while Ivo was showing his aunt and her goddaughter round London, he adopted in public an attitude of avuncular indifference towards Jossie. The last thing he wanted was to arouse any kind of speculation about his relationship with her—for his own sake as much as for hers. How the world would laugh if it were known that Lord Trenchard, the devil-may-care threat to husbands all over Europe, was personally concerned about an eighteen-year-old unknown from Somerset! No one would believe that his interest was purely platonic, even though he, his aunt and Jossie herself all knew it to be so. But it was not difficult to forestall gossip. Ivo Trenchard's views on débutantes were so well known that no one who knew him would really believe that he was taking any serious interest in the pretty young thing staying with his aunt in the family mansion. The polite world was soon persuaded that Lord Trenchard was merely showing a laudable sense of responsibility in spending so much time on Lady Frances and her young protégée, and the gossips turned their attention to the more interesting question of who would be his next amour among the ladies of Society.

Jossie herself was content to stay quietly in the background. All her study of warfare had demonstrated the importance of knowing the ground before planning an attack, and London to her was not very different from a battlefield. It was still early in the season, but she found enough to study and absorb. She soon set about winning the approval of a few important personages who held the key to acceptance in society. Her godmother was a valuable ally in this. Lady Frances had numerous influential friends who were delighted to see her again. All doors were open to her, and wherever she went Jossie accompanied her. There were even one or two older people who remembered Jossie's grandparents, Sir Robert and Lady Calverton, and who were more than pleased to make the acquaintance of their granddaughter. Soon 'Miss Helena Calverton' (Jossie quickly dropped the 'Morley') was generally held among the older members of the *ton* to be a delightful girl with a charmingly modest manner. Especially as she was widely known to be the heiress to the Calverton fortune.

Ivo soon saw through Jossie's tactics, approved of them, and derived great enjoyment from observing her at work. Previously he had always avoided afternoons and evenings spent with the more worthy members of his aunt's circle of acquaintance, dismissing them as excruciatingly boring. But now he accompanied her without hesitation. It was worth it, just to see Jossie sitting demurely next to old General Cartwright, listening to his rambling dissertation on Waterloo with all the wide-eyed admiration of an ingenue. As he knew to his cost, Jossie had the details of the battle at her fingertips, and her patience with factual errors was non-existent. But far from being subjected, as he had been, to scornful corrections, or impatient interruptions, the General was heard in admiring silence. Ivo didn't doubt that, if the old man had told her that Wellington had fought for the French, she wouldn't have blinked an eyelid!

'Charmin' girl, charmin'!' was the General's verdict. 'Not a flibbertigibbet like the rest of 'em. Sensible head on her shoulders! Knows how to listen.' And his daughter, Lady Phelps, who just happened to be one of the more influential ladies in Society, smiled favourably on Miss Calverton, and invited her to her ball the following week.

'I can see I'd have done better to be in my dotage,' said Ivo when they arrived home that night.

'Why do you say that?' asked Lady Frances, amused.

'Jossie would have treated me much more kindly two years ago. She allowed General Cartwright to talk a fine load of nonsense tonight without so much as a squeak.

No such forbearance in the past when I made any mistakes.'

'You know very well why I allowed the General to talk such nonsense, Ivo,' said Jossie calmly.

'I do, my little schemer. To win the general's daughter's approval! What are you doing? Seeing to your support group?'

'What on earth are you two talking about? What support group?' asked Lady Frances.

'We're talking tactics, Aunt Frances. Jossie here is about to launch an attack on Society, and she's making sure of her ground.'

'If you are saying that Jossie is making sure that she is accepted by the people who matter before she attempts to make her mark on the rest, then I approve. Er...are you planning anything outrageous, Jossie?'

'Oh, no! But if my new dresses are as flattering as you say they will be, I shall become...a little less... inconspicuous, shall we say? Acceptance by the people who matter is only the beginning.'

Lady Frances laughed. 'Good luck to you, my child. Enjoy yourself. Ivo and I will see that you don't come to grief.'

The new dresses were more than Jossie could have hoped for. Madame Rosa had created a wardrobe for every mood and every occasion. Floating voiles, stiff taffetas, delicate muslins, heavy silks, trimmed with lace, or edged with satin... Even Jossie, who was not a girl to rave over clothes, was enchanted with the collection. There was a preponderance of white, of course, as befitted a débutante, but no insipid pinks, washed-out blues or wan-looking yellows. Instead, Madame had taken inspiration from Jossie's indignant eyes, and the dresses were full of touches of brilliant sea-green, or dark sky-blue, and one or two glittered with hints of gold and crystal... The whole collection was full of individuality, unmistakably made for Jossie, without once overstepping what was suitable for a débutante.

'My dear Jossie! My dear! Madame has excelled herself,' cried Lady Frances. 'You must have made such an impression on her. I've never seen anything so lovely as this dress! Or this one! And just look at this one! I cannot wait to see you in it. You must wear it for your first appearance at Lady Phelps's ball. The world will be there, and this would be perfect for it.'

Even Kendrick, who was not given to enthusing over anything, was impressed. She went so far as to say that one or two of the dresses would not have disgraced Miss Payne. 'And she, miss, was the toast of London! Before she became Lady Calthorpe, that is.'

By the evening of Lady Phelps's ball Jossie had already achieved her first two goals. She had the approval of what Ivo called 'the tabbies', and she had a wardrobe of style and distinction, which was fit to impress the most demanding of critics. The Season was now getting under way, and this ball was the first of many in the social calendar. If Jossie wished to make her mark in the wider world of London society it was time to begin, and Lady Phelps's ball would be her début.

On the evening of the ball she dressed with the greatest care. Not a detail was overlooked. A coiffeur had been the day before to cut and shape her hair, and now feathers of dark curls framed her face and drew attention to the delicately lovely lines of her bone structure. Kendrick brushed and dressed the rest of her hair into a gleaming crown, then carefully finished it off with a very pretty pearl hair ornament.

'Where did that come from?' asked Jossie.

'Her ladyship sent it in, miss. A present for your début, she said.'

Jossie stared, then shook her head and swallowed hard. She wasn't used to being given presents. She waited quietly while the maid finished her work, and then, when her godmother came in, she went to her and kissed her. Jossie was not usually demonstrative, and Lady Frances looked surprised.

'Thank you for your present,' Jossie said simply. 'I can't say how touched I am. I've never had such a pretty thing before. Indeed, I can't remember ever being given such a present at all!'

'Oh, tush, child, it was nothing! I thought it would look well with these.' Lady Frances was carrying a jewel case, and she now opened it to reveal a rope of perfectly matched pearls lying on a bed of velvet. Jossie stared at them, then at her godmother. They were so beautiful, but where could they possibly have come from? Was Lady Frances proposing to lend them to her?

'They were your mother's,' Lady Frances said, as she took them out and fastened them round Jossie's neck. 'And now they are yours.' She added with a touch of satisfaction, 'I remembered to collect them from your father before we left for Calthorpe, along with the rest of Lucinda's jewels. He wasn't very pleased, but he couldn't argue. He knew they belonged to you. Your mother had a wonderful collection of jewellery, but these are the most suitable for tonight. Now let me see you!'

She held her goddaughter away from her and took a long look. Jossie was wearing a simple slip of white peau de soie. Over it was an overdress of silk gauze scattered with tiny embroidered forget-me-nots. Sleeves and bodice were held in with dark blue-green velvet rib-

bons. White gloves, and white satin slippers completed
the ensemble. The soft sheen of the pearls matched the
sheen of the silk, the deep colour of the velvet was reflected in Jossie's eyes. Lady Frances took in a deep
breath of satisfaction, then she nodded to Kendrick 'My
congratulations, Kendrick! You've done well!' Her eyes
softened as she turned back to Jossie and kissed her.
'You look beautiful, child! How proud your mother
would have been of you tonight!'

They went downstairs. Ivo was waiting in the saloon.
As they entered he held up his quizzing glass and examined Jossie. For a moment his face was quite still.

'Will I do, Ivo?' she asked nervously, impatient for
his verdict.

'Oh, you'll do, Jossie. You'll do very well,' he said
with a curiously wry smile. 'It's just a little breathtaking
to see something I foretold actually coming to life.' Then
he seemed to pull himself together and with a flourish
produced a small parcel wrapped in silver paper. 'With
my congratulations and best wishes for your début.'

Jossie looked at him in surprise. 'Another present?
What have I done to deserve all this?' She unwrapped
the packet. It was a small, exquisitely painted ivory fan.
'Ivo! It's lovely! Oh, thank you!' She smiled brilliantly
at him, then spread the fan and held it up, looking at
him provocatively.

Ivo nodded, still with that slightly wry look in his
eyes. 'A prop, Jossie. I'm sure you'll use it to devastat-
ing effect.'

In spite of this evidence of support from her friends,
Jossie was very nervous when she followed Ivo and her
godmother into the ballroom, and she maintained her air
of calm with some difficulty. Ivo looked over his shoul-

der at her. 'Go for it, my girl!' he said softly. Then he
bowed gracefully and disappeared. After a moment or
two he was back with a pleasant-faced young man, a
few years younger than himself, in tow.

'Aunt Frances, Helena, may I present Captain Fanshaw? The Captain was a subaltern in my company in
Spain, and he's relatively civilised. I think I can vouch
for him. Harry, this is my aunt, Lady Frances Danby,
and her goddaughter, Miss Calverton. You're a lucky
fellow, Harry! Miss Calverton is newly in London and
looking to be amused.'

Captain Fanshaw bowed gracefully. 'Lady Frances,
Miss Calverton...' The admiration in his eyes as he
turned to Jossie made it plain that he, too, thought himself lucky. 'Are you by any chance free to dance with
me, Miss Calverton?'

From then on Jossie's fears were forgotten. Captain
Fanshaw had several friends only too anxious to be introduced to Miss Calverton, and she was soon surrounded by a laughing group of very presentable young
men, most of them former officers known to Ivo, and
each vying for her favour.

Ivo, standing some distance away, looked on with satisfaction. Jossie's eyes were sparkling, she was smiling—she was enjoying her first ball in London. He
watched her for a while, then set off in search of amusement for himself. He soon found it, of course, and was
as charming as ever. But his partners failed to hold his
wholehearted attention. His gaze strayed more often than
he realised to where Jossie was laughing, talking, dancing with such grace, such bewitching charm. She had
wanted to shine, and that was exactly what she was doing. He remembered their first meeting and marvelled at
the change in her. The potential had always been there,

he had known it almost from the first, but it was still a revelation to see how she fitted in to the most demanding, the most exacting Society in the world. She looked as if she had been born to it. In his eyes at least, even accredited queens of society, women who had long been acknowledged as diamonds of the first water, lost some of their brilliance when put beside her. He was pleased for her, proud of her, and, though it was ridiculous, he was more than a little envious of the young men who surrounded her.

In the days that followed Jossie found herself much in demand. She rode with Captain Fanshaw, went driving in Richmond Park with Lieutenant Camden, visited Somerset House with Sir Richard Endicott... Her list of escorts was seemingly endless. And she was careful to keep it so, seeing to it that no one was more favoured than anyone else. Like Ivo, she wanted no broken hearts. Not among his friends.

If she was sometimes a little depressed that Ivo himself did not seem to have time to spend on her, she took pains to keep it to herself. After all, Ivo was well known as a flirt, and could find any number of ladies, of vastly greater experience and sophistication than Jossie Morley, eager to oblige him in this agreeable pastime. She frequently watched them doing so.

In fact, she sometimes wondered what would happen if she marched up to him and *demanded* that he should flirt with *her*! She was sure she could please him. She had watched those ladies, and was quite certain she could look as enticingly, smile as seductively, make him laugh as often as any of them. And she already knew how pleasant...how very pleasant...how *easy* it was to respond to Ivo's kisses! But in the end she knew she would never risk it. It would be useless. Ivo regarded her as his protégée, as a friend, someone he looked after somewhat in the style of a kindly uncle. He was remarkably indulgent, but he would never think of her as a candidate for any lover-like attentions. He might even laugh at her. Look at the way he had distanced himself in the past after kissing her, when she would have been perfectly prepared to continue! No, Ivo would never take her seriously, it was better not to try.

Soon, Miss Calverton was generally acknowledged to be a reigning Beauty. It became the mode to be in love with her, and many a susceptible young sprig of fashion, who had possibly not exchanged more than two sentences with the lady, claimed to have been slain by one glance from those mysterious sea-green eyes. Indeed, the exact colour of her eyes became a matter for eager debate among her admirers, some raving of sapphires and turquoises, others waxing lyrical about jade and emeralds and the like. The rooms of the house in Charles Street were filled with posies of every description, and nearly every morning brought at least one written effusion, sometimes poetic, sometimes not, and subject to Ivo's derision. Jossie was annoyed and said so.

'They mean well, Ivo. You shouldn't make fun of them.'

'I have never accepted meaning well as an excuse for poor performance. They haven't even any originality. Your name is Helena, so of course more than half of them compare you with Helen of Troy. You can't possibly enjoy such obvious bits of rubbish, or find them flattering!'

Jossie said fiercely, 'On one occasion, an occasion which I assure you I shall never forget, Mrs Cherton stood beside her exquisitely dressed daughter, and laughed at the very idea that my name was Helena. "How unsuitable!" she said. "I can quite understand why you prefer Jossie!" She didn't mean it kindly, of course. She just wanted to imply that the boy's name suited me better. You probably think so too.'

'Jossie, I—'

He was ignored. Jossie went on, 'The notes may be as badly written as you say, but I find the notion that Jossie Morley can be compared with Helen of Troy extremely agreeable! I don't believe I could possibly have too many messages like that.'

Ivo looked troubled. 'Does it still hurt so much, Jossie?' When she said nothing he went on, 'Listen to me! I do think Jossie a better name for you. For me Jossie is someone special, someone unique! There are several women in London who are just as beautiful as Helena Calverton, and could more aptly be compared with Helen of Troy—who was, when all is said and done, just a faithless wife with nothing to recommend her but her beauty!'

'Ah, but that's what you prefer, isn't it, Ivo? People like Mrs Dart, Lady Handwood, Alicia Farden. And the rest.'

Ivo started to look offended, but then he shrugged his shoulders with a laugh. 'Don't be impertinent! My *affaires* are none of your business.'

Jossie turned her head away. He waited for a moment, then he said, 'Don't waste your time making a catalogue of my *affaires*, Jossie. They are not important.'

'Then what is important to you? I'd really like to know!'

He looked at her in silence. Then he said, 'I don't

know. I'd like to see you happy, that's one thing. But for myself? I don't know.'

Lady Frances was particularly pleased with Jossie's reaction to her success.

'Jossie has always been so matter of fact,' she said to Ivo one day. 'But I am impressed how sensibly she is taking all this adulation. Any girl might easily lose her head, but from what I can see Jossie remains just the same. It is almost as if she is waiting for something.'

'She is. She's waiting for the arrival of her father and the Radstocks.'

'Of course! The poor girl wants to show them... I cannot blame her for that, Ivo.'

'Nor can I.'

'Then why are you looking so severe?'

'I hope that is all she wants to do.'

'She isn't any longer in love with Peter, if that is what you're afraid of.'

'No.' Ivo smiled. 'I dare say I'm worrying quite unnecessarily. About that, at least.'

He continued to keep a careful eye on Jossie, observed her bewitching an elderly General, or a severely critical dowager with the 'fresh as a daisy' or the 'deeply serious' look. He saw how she enchanted half a dozen young men with a sparkling smile and a look which said that she found them all as captivating as herself. But, to his relief, he had not yet seen her use what she had called the 'siren' approach. With the wrong sort of person there could be danger in it, a danger which she in her innocence would not see. He should have said so when she first used it on him at Calthorpe, of course, but he had been so entertained by it, and, yes, intrigued, that it hadn't occurred to him to warn her against using it in earnest. He must ask his aunt to say something to her. The idea of Ivo Trenchard acting as nursemaid was so absurd that he could only hope no one ever learned of it!

But more than once, indeed quite often, his decision to keep his distance from her in public seemed very difficult to maintain. Memories of how much he had enjoyed dancing with Jossie at Calthorpe kept intruding. There they had danced just with one or two other couples, to a piano played not very well by one of the doctor's daughters, but the rhythm, the grace, the rapport he had felt in Jossie had far outweighed these disadvantages. Here in London it seemed to him that most of her partners, not having had the benefit of working on the Duke of Wellington's staff, had no idea how to hold a girl in the waltz! They either grabbed her like a parcel, or held her at such a distance that the poor girl was not sure which way her partner wished to turn! His impatience grew and one evening, without quite knowing how it happened, he found himself in front of Jossie, asking her to dance the next waltz with him. She regarded him in astonishment, the colour rising in her cheeks.

'You want to dance with *me*, Ivo? Why?'

'I see that you have the tabbies' approval for the waltz. I thought it time you danced one with me,' he said, smiling charmingly down at her.

'Is it because you're trying to make someone jealous? Lady Alicia, perhaps?'

'Using you?' he asked, raising an eyebrow. 'Of course not.'

'Oh,' she said, sounding flat.

'Shall I say that I wanted to dance with the most beautiful woman in the room?' he went on, giving her a little bow.

She shot him a suspicious glance. 'You're teasing, Ivo. You've never tried before. Why now?'

'I was being circumspect, little Jossie,' he said ruefully. 'But I couldn't resist one waltz.'

When she saw that he was absolutely serious, a lovely colour rose in her cheeks. 'I'm not sure...' she stammered, looking flustered. 'I must look at my card...'

He took the card from her and put it back in her reticule. 'Don't try those tricks on me, my girl. They don't work. Will you dance or not?'

'Aren't you being a little high-handed? Here comes Lieutenant Cotter to claim me for the waltz at this very moment!'

Ivo regarded the young man benevolently. 'I'm afraid, Lieutenant, I am about to pull rank. It's one of the few compensations of age. Miss Calverton presents her apologies, but she is about to dance this waltz with me. I do beg you to excuse me. Jos...er...Helena?'

With an apologetic glance at Lieutenant Cotter, Jossie allowed Ivo to lead her on to the floor. 'Very high-handed!' she muttered as they took their places.

At first they danced in silence. Then Ivo asked, 'So how do you find the fashionable world, Jossie?'

'At the moment I like it. It wouldn't suit me forever, though.' She sighed. 'I'm not sure what would...'

'Have you had any offers yet?'

'My *affaires* are no more your business, than yours are mine, Ivo!' she said with a provocative look at him.

'Rubbish! You're too young to have *affaires*! I am considerably older and wiser than you. And I have made you my business, you know that! How many offers have you had?'

Jossie looked mutinous for a moment, then she shrugged and said, 'You know the answer, anyway... It doesn't matter how many I've had, I wouldn't accept any of them. I've told you before. I'm not looking for a husband.'

'What, never?'

She said sombrely, 'I cannot imagine ever again wanting to marry anyone.'

'Don't say that! You're too young to let that spineless fool ruin your life! You'll meet someone better than Peter Radstock, I'm sure. Why, I'd marry you myself rather than allow you to live a spinster for the rest of your life!'

'You would? And how would you persuade me to agree?'

There was a glint in his eyes as he replied. 'As long as you weren't in love with anyone else, I could persuade you—we both know that. But it wouldn't do.'

'Of course it wouldn't!' Jossie said quickly. 'But why do *you* think so?'

'I'm too old for you! Too old in every kind of way...'

'I don't want to marry, anyway! You could flirt with me, if you wished...' she said, smiling seductively at him. She had observed Lady Alicia employing just such a look earlier in the evening, and Ivo had seemed impressed with it. She was sure hers was every bit as good...

He was impressed now, but not in the way she had hoped. 'I thought Aunt Frances had told you to forget that look,' he said sternly. 'Didn't she explain?'

'Oh, she said something,' said Jossie airily. 'And I must say I was disappointed. Lady Frances is not usually so stuffy.'

Ivo regarded her coldly. He said, 'Come and sit down!'

Jossie was surprised, but allowed him to lead her to a bench in a corner of the room. 'Why are you cross with me? Is it because I suggested you might flirt with me? It would only be in fun, Ivo! It wouldn't...wouldn't mean anything.'

'I've told you. I shall never flirt with you. But that's not what I want to say. Listen to me! Aunt Frances was not being stuffy. You mustn't look at others as you've just looked at me, Jossie.'

'I don't quite understand you. How did I look?'

'You looked at me in an excessively provocative manner. You once told me you called it your siren look. I suppose between friends it's amusing. But you mustn't, you *must not*, direct it at anyone else!'

'But Lady Alicia used it on you! I don't see why I shouldn't try it.'

'Lady Alicia can look after herself. But, believe me, it could lead you into trouble.'

'What do you mean?'

Ivo took a breath. 'Jossie, I flirt. It amuses me. And Lady Alicia is experienced and well aware of what she is doing. But, surprisingly enough, I have scruples. There are plenty of men in London who have none. If you should happen to use that look on one of them, he might well regard it as an invitation to...to...the sort of... of...intimacy which you would find repugnant. Your innocence and youth would not stop him.'

'Oh, but I can take care of myself—'

'No! With such a man you couldn't! He would be quite ruthless about taking what he thought you were offering. Don't do it, Jossie!'

'Don't be absurd! I'm not a weakling, you know! I

may have learned how to be a lady, but I still remember a trick or two from my days as a boy.'

Ivo looked at her in exasperation. Then, after a pause, his expression grew enigmatic and he said gently, 'Would you care to have a walk outside, Jossie? It's warm in here and the Manchesters have a very pleasant garden.'

Jossie was suspicious, but decided to agree. They went out through the long windows which led into the garden. Lanterns had been hung on trees which bordered a path leading down into a sort of wilderness. Shrubs and early flowers scented the night air.

'Mind the step,' Ivo said, and he tucked her hand through his arm. 'It isn't too cold for you, is it? Shall we go a little further?' This was Ivo at his most charming, and even though Jossie was still wondering what he was about, she found herself walking along with him.

They reached the end of the path. Lights and the sounds of music came from the house, but here it was almost completely dark, except for a stray beam of moonlight.

'Now...' Ivo slid his arms round Jossie's waist. He drew her to him. Jossie's doubts grew. She tried to keep her distance, but Ivo's arms were too strong. She was pulled inexorably closer until they were touching breast to breast, thigh to thigh. She could feel their two bodies moulded to one another. His face was close, so close... But he looked different in the moonlight. His usual expression of lazy good humour had vanished, he looked...harder, less kind. His eyes were filled with mockery, his teeth gleaming white in a devilish smile...

Jossie panicked. 'Ivo—'

'Hush, Jossie,' he whispered. 'Let me kiss you!' He bent his head but it was her throat he kissed, then his lips moved further down... One hand came to push aside the lace of her bodice, to caress her breast. For one sudden, shameful moment Jossie was swamped by a sensation of fiercely burning desire, but then shock and outrage took over. She fought to pull back from him.

'No! How can you...? Stop this, Ivo! Let me go!'

Ivo's hand was withdrawn, but he still held her in an iron grip. She could not move. He gazed down at her grimly. 'You've had enough? Frightened, perhaps? You needn't be afraid of me. I'm not going to do another thing. I am quite sober, quite in control, and I mean you well. It was only make-believe, Jossie.'

Jossie gasped angrily. 'I don't find that sort of make-believe amusing!'

Still holding her fast, he said sternly, 'I didn't mean it to be. It was a demonstration of the very least you might expect from a man who is possibly half-drunk and certainly ruthless. If such a man accepted your invitation he wouldn't stop where I stopped.'

'But, Ivo, I can—'

'I know. You can take care of yourself. Try! Try to get away from me. I think you'll find you can't.'

Jossie tried all the tricks she knew, but Ivo's superior strength foiled her easily every time. In the end she had to admit defeat.

'Let me go. You've made your point,' she said sulkily. He set her instantly free. She added, 'But you didn't behave very gentlemanly.'

'Dammit, these are not gentlemen!'

'I could have screamed—'

'You wouldn't have been heard from here—not with all the music and chatter in the house.'

She was about to argue, but the expression on his face stopped her. For once she could see that beyond the façade of the good-humoured man of fashion, the light-hearted flirt, there lay a determined fighter, the cool but absolute authority of an officer in command. She gave in. 'Oh, very well, Ivo, you've made your point. I agree. I'll be careful in future.'

'Good! Now let me help you tidy yourself up.'

'No, thank you! I can manage,' Jossie said hastily. The thought of Ivo's fingers even tying a ribbon was too unnerving at the moment. She knew that he would take no further liberties, that was not the reason. But she could still remember that feel of his hand on her flesh, the mad, wicked moment when she would have granted him whatever he wanted... Shock, she told herself. She had been in shock. It was purely shock.

But that night in bed she lay awake, wondering what would have happened if Ivo had been serious. What would he have done next? And how did his real mistresses behave when his fingers touched them, as he had touched her that evening...?

Chapter Twelve

When Jossie came down the next morning she was relieved to hear that Ivo was out.

'In fact, I'm not altogether sure where he is,' said Lady Frances. 'It was past one o'clock when he brought us home this morning, but he went out again almost immediately afterwards. You had already disappeared upstairs, and I followed you soon after. I didn't hear him come in again.' She added carefully, 'Of course, Ivo is his own master...'

'Of course,' said Jossie. She had a sudden vision of Lady Alicia looking deliciously abandoned in a floating robe, her white and gold loveliness half-covered, half-revealed...Ivo's dark head was bent over her... Jossie jumped up.

'I'm sorry he isn't here,' she said brightly. 'I rather hoped to go for a ride in the park this morning.'

'Well, if you take your groom you should be safe enough. You're looking rather pale, a breath of air—such as it is in London—might do you good. Off you go! I propose to rest in my room and answer a few letters.'

Jossie sent a message to the stables to have her mare brought round and went upstairs to change.

In half an hour she was trotting sedately through the park gates. It was still early. Apart from servants and tradesmen few people were about. Jossie was glad. The events of the night before seemed to have removed the last veil from her understanding. The process which had begun on the night of Peter Radstock's coming of age was almost complete. She needed to think…

During her sojourn in London she had observed, she had listened, and she had learned a great deal. She was no longer the ignorant simpleton, the green girl of the year before, who hadn't thought twice about asking Ivo to show her how to kiss. She realised now how incredibly naïve she had been, isolated as she was from normal human society, brought up as a boy with a despotic father, and single-mindedly absorbed in her plans to marry Peter. The only women who had played any sort of part in her life had been Lady Radstock and her godmother, and their influence had been strictly limited. Peter's mother had confined herself to reprimanding Jossie for her careless behaviour, for being late, for looking untidy, for keeping Peter out till all hours roaming the countryside… And Lady Frances's opportunities for serious conversation had been severely restricted by what Jossie now knew to be her father's antagonism.

As a result she had been a very odd creature indeed when she had met Ivo—almost wholly ignorant of the world and its relationships, and ridiculously unaware of Ivo as a powerfully attractive male animal. The very idea of physical attraction had never occurred to her. Her childhood friendship with Peter had changed, she had thought, into love, but when Peter asked for a demonstration of that love she had been mystified and distressed. So she had turned to Ivo, who was so much older and so much more experienced, and who by that time had become a trusted friend.

What must he have thought of her? Not many men would have treated her request so seriously, so honourably as Ivo had. Now that she knew more of the world, she was astonished at his forbearance, his respect for her innocence.

And she had been so stupidly, so dangerously, innocent! Even when Ivo kissed her and she had felt for the first time the delight, the wonder, the exhilaration of desire, even then she had not recognised it for what it truly was. She had assumed that Peter's kisses would give her the same pleasure once she had got used to the idea, had thought that it was only a matter of time and patience.

Now she knew differently. She had suspected it for some time, but the events of the night before left no room for doubt. She would *never* have felt the same with Peter. Peter had held her close, but in a perfectly gentlemanly manner, he had kissed her, but gently, taking care not to frighten her. There had been no threat. But she had felt stifled in his embrace, repelled, had wanted only to escape.

Which brought her back to Ivo's treatment of her in the garden the night before. He had set out quite deliberately to frighten her, had overmastered her efforts to escape from him, had kissed her against her will, treated her with little respect, determined to prove how powerless she was in the hands of an unscrupulous and determined man. He hadn't meant it seriously, of course, he had merely intended to teach her a lesson. If his first lesson in Somerset had shown her the delights of a kiss, his second in London had been meant as a warning. None of it had affected him personally.

It was only stupid Jossie Morley who had been haunted ever since by the sudden rush of desire she had felt when he touched her. And she now recognised it as the darker side of a passion she had experienced before in Ivo's arms. Shamefully, she both feared it and longed for it again.

Worst of all, she had a suspicion that it was not Ivo, the expert in dalliance, the famed lover whose *affaires* had long been the talk of Europe, who had evoked these feelings, but Ivo the man himself. If she wasn't very, very careful, she would find herself in love with Ivo Trenchard. And if that happened, her case would be desperate. She had heard his views on love-sick débutantes often enough. If he ever believed that she thought of him as anything more than a friend and protector, he would remove himself from her life. She would lose even his friendship.

For a moment or two she felt miserable, but her natural optimism soon reasserted itself. She was no worse off than she had been before. As long as she suppressed these inconvenient feelings, as long as she kept the fears they brought with them strictly to herself, she and Ivo could continue as before. He was her friend and protector. That was all! That must be all!

Nor should she forget her main purpose in coming to London. Not to find a husband, but to show them! To show her father, Peter, Lady Radstock and the rest how wrong they had been. That had been her design from the beginning, and it was not yet fulfilled. She would concentrate on that, and forget these stupid thoughts about Ivo.

As she turned for home, she saw him in the distance.

She urged her mare to a faster trot and caught up with him just by the gate. 'Ivo! Wait!'

The gentleman turned. To her confusion she saw that she had been mistaken. This was not Ivo, but a stranger. There were resemblances, but this man was several years younger, and his features were somehow less well defined.

'I…I'm sorry,' she faltered. 'Forgive me, I thought—'

'That I was my brother?' The stranger smiled. 'I believe we are quite alike at a distance. I'm Peregrine Trenchard.'

'Oh! We thought you were in Derbyshire, sir!'

'I was till three days ago. I heard last week that my father was coming to London, so I decided to visit some old friends here and see my family at the same time.'

'You are not going to stay in Charles Street?'

'Er…no. But, please! Tell me who you are! Are you related to Lady Frances? I heard she is in London.'

'I'm her goddaughter, sir. My name is J…Helena Calverton.'

Peregrine Trenchard looked at her with a curious smile, but said merely, 'I am delighted to make your acquaintance, Miss Calverton! May I accompany you back to Charles Street?'

'Of course! But your father hasn't yet arrived, sir.'

'In that case I shall be more than pleased to escort you.'

His remark puzzled Jossie. It was said in a most amiable fashion, but, if she had understood his meaning correctly, he was not being particularly pleasant towards his parent.

'Is my brother Ivo likely to be at home?'

Jossie stayed calm, though her heart jumped. 'I'm not sure. He comes and goes a great deal,' she said with tolerable indifference. 'He wasn't in this morning when I came out.'

'Better and better,' murmured Peregrine. He saw her surprise and added, 'It means I can devote more of my time and attention to you, Miss Calverton.'

As they rode back through the London streets Jossie wondered what sort of man this was. He didn't seem to like either his father or his brother. Why had he bothered to come to London to see them?

Lady Frances was delighted to see her younger nephew, only protesting at his decision to stay in Half Moon Street with friends.

'Come, Aunt Frances! You know very well that if my father and I stayed under the same roof he would be bellowing at me before a day had gone by. It's much more comfortable for everyone if I stay elsewhere and visit you often but briefly. When is he due?'

'Any day now. But he's changed, Perry. I think Jossie has tamed him.'

'Jossie?'

Jossie blushed and said awkwardly, 'Your aunt calls me by my old name, Mr Trenchard. I used to be known as Jossie Morley.'

'Helena suits you better,' said Mr Trenchard. 'May I call you Helena? Neither Miss Morley nor Miss Calverton sounds very friendly, and if you've tamed my father you must be the best friend I have!'

Jossie smiled and gave him permission, but inwardly she was still doubtful about Peregrine Trenchard. She liked Lord Veryan, and she found his younger son altogether too frankly critical. She studied him as he chatted to Lady Frances. The resemblance to Ivo was not so marked now she was close. Peregrine's hair was as dark as Ivo's, but his eyes were a lighter blue, and, though he was equally tall, his build was slighter, less powerful. His manner was different, too. He seemed more anxious to please, less confident than his brother. Knowing Lord Veryan as she did, she could well imagine that his younger son's diffidence would irritate him.

She did not see Ivo until that evening. He had stayed out all day, and in the end it was Peregrine who escorted them to their evening engagement, a soirée with music and dancing at Crewe House. Peregrine proved to be an excellent dancer and an amusing companion, and Jossie found she liked him a great deal better than she had thought. He had a fund of amusing anecdotes, which kept Lady Frances and her friends entertained throughout the evening. The ladies were not averse to gossip, however, and the talk eventually turned to the subject of other recent arrivals in the capital.

'Of course, Mr Trenchard, you must not think you are the only newcomer. There has recently been a positive influx of visitors. I hear the Balmennys arrived yesterday, as well,' said one lady. The chill of disapproval which descended on the group at this news was almost palpable.

'I hear she is as lovely as ever,' said one. 'And as flighty. Motherhood hasn't improved her.'

'A pity,' said another dowager, and added with a significant nod, 'However, since they spent almost the whole of last year on his estate in Ireland, Balmenny can at least be sure the children are his!'

Lady Frances was shocked. 'Maria!' she said.

'Facts are facts, Frances. And it cannot be denied that Julia Redshaw was never in love with her husband. Poor Balmenny has had a devil of a time with her.'

Jossie's interest had been caught by the mention of Julia Redshaw, and she listened to this exchange with amusement. Heaven help those who offended these gently bred members of Society! They were quite ruthless in their destruction of a character—though what they were saying about the lovely Viscountess Balmenny only confirmed what she had heard from the Calthorpes. But then the ladies went on to discuss other arrivals with equal charity, and her attention wandered. She looked around the room...

On the other side, almost opposite her, was Ivo. He had clearly just arrived, and seemed to be searching for someone. When he saw Jossie and her companions he nodded and came towards them. She felt her face grow warm and turned away. To her relief he first greeted Lady Frances, then nodded to Peregrine.

'I heard you were in town,' he said. 'I'm glad to see you, Perry. How are you?'

The brothers talked for a while, thus giving Jossie time to recover. She was even able to be amused at the manner in which her godmother's friends were eyeing Ivo. They obviously felt they ought to disapprove of him, but were unable to resist his charm. He was, after all, so very handsome! Jossie was reminded that one or two of these dowagers had been famous beauties in their day, and they were smiling now as if they, too, were remembering... She cast a quick glance at Peregrine, inviting him to share her amusement, but was surprised to see that he was looking at Ivo with an expression which Jossie found hard to define. But it wasn't friendly.

Ivo's conversation with the ladies finally came to an end and he turned to Jossie. 'Will you dance?' he asked.

Jossie started to refuse, but Ivo insisted. 'Please!' She

hesitated, then gave him a nod and led the way without speaking to the ballroom.

By the time they started she had herself under control, even managing not to stiffen when he took her hand in the dance. 'I don't expect you thought you would see your brother here tonight,' she began lightly.

'On the contrary, I heard he was in town, which is why I came.'

'Oh.'

'Or rather, it's one of the reasons I came.'

Jossie took a breath and said calmly, 'There's another?'

'Two. They both concern you.'

She felt herself colouring again. 'If you mean to say anything about last night, I would rather you didn't.'

'I must. I deeply regret what I did, and I beg you to forgive me.'

Jossie managed a little laugh. 'Goodness, Ivo! Don't sound so grave! You did me a service. I am grateful to you for the warning, and intend to take it seriously. I ought to apologise to you for being such a nuisance. Looking after such an idiot can't be very amusing.'

'You're not—' He stopped abruptly. After a moment he said, 'I hope we're still friends?'

'Of course!' Ivo looked so unlike himself, so concerned, that she found it easy to reassure him. She gave him a perfectly genuine smile. 'What would I do without you to save me from further stupidities? Though I think I *am* learning more about the world. There may even come a time when I shan't need you.' He couldn't reply immediately as they were separated for a moment by the dance.

When they came together again he was frowning. It looked as if he was still annoyed with himself.

In an effort to distract him she said, 'I wish you had been here earlier. The ladies were talking about Julia Redshaw, and they were even less kind than the Calthorpes about her. They say she is in London. After all the things I've heard I can hardly wait to see her. Is she really as beautiful as they say? Was Adam really in love with her?'

'Yes, I think so. Before he joined the Army. But once he met Kate…'

'You liked Kate, too, didn't you, Ivo?'

Ivo said with some reserve, 'Yes, I liked her. I still do, very much. But I didn't allow myself to fall in love with her, if that's what you're asking. Adam's friendship was more important to me. And now they are both very good friends of mine.'

Jossie nodded. 'You're fortunate. They're very nice people. I should love to meet them again. Do you think they will come to London?'

'I'm afraid not. Not this year.' He paused, then said slowly, 'I haven't yet given you my other reason for seeking you out tonight.'

'What is it?'

'Your father is here in London.'

Jossie nearly missed a step, but rallied. 'My father?' She gave a little laugh. 'With his new wife, no doubt.'

Ivo nodded. 'Together with the Radstocks.'

'What a delightful family party!' Jossie said lightly after the briefest of pauses. She had lost colour, but her voice was under control. To a casual listener she would have sounded perfectly normal.

'Quite!'

'So Rosalind has had her way… Lady Radstock will be pleased, but I wonder what Sir Thomas makes of it? He hates towns.'

They were parted again for a moment.

Ivo, watching Jossie carefully, thought she was taking it almost too calmly. He noticed that she had not mentioned Peter. When they came together at the end of the set, she said, 'It should prove interesting. For everyone. Do you mind if we go back to Lady Frances?'

Lord Veryan arrived the next day, and the house was in something of a bustle until Lady Frances had seen to it that he was suitably installed in his own bedchamber, with his extra pillows and his special chair, and his valet in the dressing room next door.

'Don't get old, Jossie,' he said irritably. 'People always make such a fuss about your comfort. As if I can sleep anyway in this rackety place! Never liked London and never shall!'

'Then I'm all the more grateful to you for coming,' said Jossie. 'And I shall cancel my engagement for tonight.'

'What nonsense is this? I'll come with you, girl! I want to see how you're doing. Where is this engagement?'

'Oh, I won't be noticed tonight! It's at Marchant House, and the Carterets are hosting a reception for the Duke of Wellington.'

'Dammit, you mustn't miss that! Isn't he your hero?'

'The trouble is, the world and his wife all wish to be there,' said Lady Frances doubtfully. 'An invitation might be difficult to come by.'

'Carteret's an old drinking partner of mine. He'll let me in easily enough,' said Lord Veryan. 'Who else is going?'

'Ivo is one of his Grace's party. And Perry—'

'Peregrine? Is he in London?'

'Didn't you know?'

'I wouldn't be asking if I did, would I? What's the young fool doing in London?'

'He's here to meet you, sir,' said Jossie with a laugh. 'I hope you won't frighten him off!'

'Hmm. He'll be there tonight, you say?'

'Yes. He's acting as our escort,' said Lady Frances.

'You don't need him when you have me!'

'But will you be fit enough, Rupert?' his sister asked patiently. 'And, if you do come, will you promise to keep your temper with Peregrine?'

'There's no need to tell me how to behave, Fanny!' said his lordship testily. Since he knew perfectly well that Lady Frances hated to be called 'Fanny', Jossie could only assume he was being deliberately provocative. The journey had clearly upset him more than he would admit.

'Have you brought your backgammon set with you, sir?' she asked.

'Never travel without it. D'y want a game?' Jossie nodded. 'Now?'

Jossie nodded again and said, 'There's a corner in the library that is perfect. But of course you know that. Shall we go there?'

Lady Frances heaved a sigh of relief, and gave Jossie a warm smile of approval.

Others were looking forward to the reception at Marchant House. The Morleys and the Radstocks had been lucky enough to get invitations, too. It was to be the climax of the Morleys' visit to London. The Radstocks were to stay several weeks, but to his wife's chagrin, the Major could not afford to spend more than a few days in a London hotel.

'I have to say, Gerard,' said Mrs Morley in a complaining voice, 'that I think you have arranged things very badly. Surely you could have persuaded the Radstocks to invite us to stay on with them? You know I never complain, but it is very hard not to spend longer in London, now that we have finally got here. I think the Radstocks are being monstrously selfish. But you refused even to ask them!'

'Because, as I have told you more than once, my dear, Sir Thomas is not a particular friend of mine and would have been very surprised if I had. Think of the embarrassment if he had refused! Where would we have been then? We have at least been invited to dine with them while we are in London.'

'I still think you could have taken a little more trouble, Gerard! My previous husband…'

Major Morley uttered an oath, went to his own room and stared resentfully into the long mirror there. Why was he always cursed with such bad luck? Mrs Cherton had been a charming lady before she married him. Just what a man not yet past his prime had needed, especially after the fiasco of that coming-of-age ball. She had soothed his lacerated nerves and been ready to sympathise when some of the neighbours had been most unpleasant. He had been sure that in time when the world saw him with such a beautiful, elegant wife at his side, he would once again be admired and envied, instead of being pitied, or even criticised, for having such a failure of a daughter.

But the new Mrs Morley was far from being what he had expected. There had been some very awkward scenes when she learned that the Calverton fortune was not his but Jossie's, and from then on she had been much less amenable, much less inclined to minister to his feelings. And now, with increasing frequency, she had taken to comparing him unfavourably with her first husband! It was too bad! Jossie might have had her faults, but she had never criticised him! Gerard Morley looked at himself in the mirror. He looked very well in his dress uniform. What a damned shame it was that he had had to give up his career! He might well have been the guest of honour tonight, not Arthur Wellesley. But Wellesley had always had all the luck. Luck was all it needed. Just a bit of luck, and he would have given the Duke of Wellington a run for his money!

'I hope you are not going to commandeer that mirror for very much longer, Gerard,' a voice behind him said acidly. 'The one in my room is impossible!'

Marchant House was particularly suited to grand occasions. It had a huge ballroom at the back of the house, and the reception rooms in the main building were also very handsome. But even the resources of Marchant House were stretched to their limit on the night of the Carterets' reception. By the time the Duke's party arrived, the way through to the ballroom was lined with most of the polite world, all craning their necks to get a glimpse of Waterloo's hero.

The Radstocks and the Morleys had managed to find quite a good vantage point with a clear view of the procession as it made its way along.

'By Jove, look, Morley!' said Sir Thomas. 'Isn't that the Trenchard fellow? Lady Frances's nephew?'

Sir Thomas's voice was penetrating, and Ivo could hardly fail to hear it. He looked over, and bowed slightly without leaving his place behind the Duke.

'Friends of yours, Ivo?' asked the Duke in a side whisper.

'Not exactly, sir. Neighbours.'

'Don't like 'em, eh? Never mind, you needn't talk to them. I'll keep you busy.'

And the Duke was as good as his word. Ivo and his fellow officers, all former members of the Duke's Staff, were sent here and there to escort one or other of the more important personages who wished to have a word with the great man, keeping at bay the ones the Duke didn't wish to meet. But after an hour and a half even great men get bored.

'I've had enough of this,' he said. 'I've done my duty for long enough. Ivo, you usually have a line on good-looking women. I'd like to have a chat with a beautiful face for a change, and I haven't had time to find my own old friends. What about it?'

'Sir, some of the loveliest women in London would be honoured to meet you.'

'Well, get on with it, then! Is there to be any dancing? Ellington, you go and arrange it with Carteret. Duty's done, it's time for enjoyment, gentlemen!'

Ivo was nothing if not tactful. He took care to bring first ladies who were certainly good-looking, but also had some other claim to the Duke's attention, such as, for example, the Princess Lieven, Lady Cowper, and others. After that he brought one or two of his own choice. The Duke chatted with all of them, and danced with one or two.

'You're doing well, Ivo!' he said genially. 'But how about one of the younger ones now?'

Ivo smiled, looked thoughtfully round the room, and made his way through the crowds to where Lord Veryan was sitting with Jossie at his side.

'Father. I'm sorry I haven't had a chance to talk to you. My former commander has kept me busy all day.

We must have a good session tomorrow. But meanwhile, may I borrow your lady friend for a moment? His Grace wishes to meet Jossie.'

Jossie almost dropped her reticule. 'Me! Ivo, I can't!'

'Of course you can! He's as susceptible to beauty as any of us—more so, if anything. Don't keep him waiting.'

Jossie walked with Ivo up the room to where the Duke was standing and gave him a deep curtsy.

'Miss Helena Calverton, Duke,' Ivo said. 'I've warned her not to talk to you about Waterloo.'

The Duke was eyeing Jossie with approval, but at this he turned to Ivo and said, 'Why not? Does it offend her feelings to talk of battles?'

'On the contrary. It's your feelings I worry about, Duke. Miss Calverton is quite likely to correct you if your memory plays false.'

'What's this, what's this?'

'Please, your Grace, don't listen to Lord Trenchard. He talks a great deal of nonsense.'

'He does, doesn't he? Ivo, you are dismissed. Come back for Miss Calverton later.' He took Jossie's arm and led her to the floor. 'So, miss, I suppose you think I talk a great deal of nonsense as well, eh?'

Jossie shook her head and gave him an impish glance out of blue-green eyes. 'I am quite sure no one would dare tell you so, if you did, your Grace. I've heard stories of your setdowns.'

The Duke laughed delightedly and swung her on to the floor. 'Wit as well as beauty! I can see that I must tell Ivo to be on his guard.'

They passed two other dancers. Peter Radstock almost fell over. He clutched his wife's arm and said dazedly,

'That...that's Jossie! No, it can't be—I must be dreaming.'

'Where?'

'Dancing with the Duke.'

'Peter! Don't talk such nonsense. Jossie Morley? Are you mad?'

'I think I must be. But I could have sworn...'

He took Rosalind's hand and walked determinedly off the floor. When he reached his parents he interrupted their conversation to say, 'Father, that girl dancing with the Duke. Did you see her?'

'No. Why?'

'Look at her now! Does she remind you of anyone?'

They all looked. The girl did a graceful turn, then laughed up at the Duke as he said something. He was quite clearly very taken with his partner.

'It looks like... Who do you think it is?' asked Sir Thomas.

'It's Jossie!'

Mrs Morley laughed. 'Don't be absurd, Peter! That's quite out of the question. Look at the girl's style, her clothes! They are in the first stare of fashion.' Her eye rested a trifle discontentedly on her daughter. Since her marriage Rosalind had taken to wearing some very unstylish dresses. Mrs Morley blamed Peter for it.

'I don't think it can possibly be Jossie, dear,' said Lady Radstock. 'Remember how she hated to dance? That girl is unmistakably enjoying it.'

Peter turned to someone standing next to them. 'Excuse me,' he said. 'Can you tell me the name of the girl dancing with the Duke?'

'That's Helena Calverton, the latest sensation. Lovely, isn't she? The Beau always had an eye for a beautiful woman.'

'You see?' Mrs Morley was triumphant. 'I knew it couldn't be Jossie.'

'Yes, but...' Lady Radstock hesitated. 'Jossie's real name is Helena. And her mother was a Calverton.'

Ivo returned as ordered to collect Jossie at the end of the dance. The Duke was most complimentary on his choice of companion, and it took some skill to extricate her.

'Ivo, thank you!' said Jossie with a glowing look. 'What an experience! I shall never forget it!'

'I haven't finished with you yet,' said Ivo.

'What about your duties?'

'I think I've done enough for the time being. I've asked Colonel Ancroft to cover for me. Besides, the Duke is due to go into supper with the bigwigs any moment. Look! They're collecting him now. I must take you to meet someone else.'

He looked so serious, that Jossie guessed what he was going to say before he spoke. 'My father?'

'And Peter Radstock, yes. All of them, in fact. They're all here.'

Jossie stiffened. She said coolly, 'How on earth did they manage that? I thought invitations were at a premium? They were very fortunate to get any at all, let alone six!'

'I made sure they did,' said Ivo calmly.

'You? But why?'

'I wanted them to see you tonight. Having a triumph. Not very worthy of me, was it?'

Jossie regarded him with surprise and admiration. 'You clever thing!' She started to laugh. 'So you organised it all! The invitations, the dance with the Duke, all of it. And you called *me* a schemer!'

Ivo took her hand to his lips. 'You deserved any help I could give. I know what it means to you. You've worked hard and come so far in the past year, Jossie.'

Jossie's colour rose. 'Ivo,' she said nervously. 'You're not being very circumspect. People will say that you're flirting with me, if you're not careful.'

'As I've told you many times before, I will never flirt with you.'

They had reached the end of the room where the Radstocks were waiting. Jossie's father was standing to one side of them, looking furiously disbelieving.

Chapter Thirteen

The hand resting on Ivo's arm stiffened and Jossie's fingers gripped him painfully. This was the first sight she had had of her father since that dreadful confrontation in the Radstocks' garden the year before, and Ivo was not surprised that she was as tense as a coiled spring. But when he glanced down at her he could see no sign of this in her face. He was filled with admiration and pride. Jossie was showing nothing but serenely polite pleasure.

'Father,' she said, curtsying. 'How are you?' She turned to her father's wife, and curtsied again. 'Ma'am.'

Mrs Morley gave a slight nod, but her eyes were fastened on Jossie's dress. It was one of Madame Rosa's most beautiful, a masterpiece in silver and white. Tiny silver beads and drops of crystal decorated the bodice and hem of diaphanous white silk worn over an underdress of satin. A delicately wrought crescent of the same silver and crystal nestled in her dark hair, and a scarf of silver gauze was draped over her arms. The only touches of colour were found in the faint rose of her cheeks and lips, and the intensely vivid turquoise of her eyes. The effect was stunning. She looked not quite of this world—

a moon goddess. Mrs Morley's face settled further into lines of dissatisfaction.

Major Morley made no move towards his daughter. 'What's this Calverton nonsense?' he asked. 'You're called Morley. Jossie Morley. Or isn't my name good enough for you?'

Jossie gave him a wry smile. 'The last time we spoke, Father, you made it painfully clear that you didn't consider me good enough for your name! So I prefer to use "Helena Calverton"—it carries no such unfortunate memories. But don't let's spoil the occasion by disagreeing about something which happened quite a long time ago. You remember Lord Trenchard, of course?'

Her father could hardly say more in such a public place, so he gave Ivo a stiff nod. Ivo bowed but didn't speak, and moved on instead to exchange courtesies with Mrs Morley.

Jossie went on to speak to the Radstocks. 'Lady Radstock, Sir Thomas. What a surprise to see you here! Are you staying in London long?'

Lady Radstock, looking somewhat dazed, responded politely, but Sir Thomas took Jossie's hands and held them in a firm grip. 'Eh, it's wonderful to see you looking so well, Jossie girl! You look bonnier than ever and that's a fact! But what's all this? I thought you didn't like towns and suchlike any more than I do! What are you doing here?' He shot a glance at Ivo. 'Are you...'

'No, no! Lord Trenchard is merely taking me back to my godmother.'

Sir Thomas's face cleared. 'Oh, you're with Lady Frances, are you? For a moment...'

'Lord Veryan and Lady Frances are in the next room, Sir Thomas. I now live with my godmother, as I dare say you know, and she has been sponsoring my come-out in Society. I cannot tell you how kind she and Lord Veryan have been. And Lord Trenchard has been nothing more than a true friend. The best I have. Nowadays.'

Sir Thomas looked very uncomfortable. 'Yes, well… I'm sorry, lass. It was cruel of us…'

For a moment there was a flash of the old Jossie in the warmth of the smile she gave him. 'Don't say another word! *You* were never cruel.' She moved on.

Peter and his wife were next. Ivo made sure he was standing close beside her as Jossie said, 'And here are your son and daughter-in-law! You're looking very well, Peter.'

Peter flushed to the roots of his hair. He stammered, 'Jossie… You look so different. I hardly recognise you…I didn't…didn't realise—'

'That I would change? People do, you know. Sometimes overnight. But I don't believe I ever congratulated you on your marriage.' Her gaze included both the young Radstocks as she said charmingly, 'Let me wish you all the happiness you deserve.'

Ivo coughed, there was a little silence, then Jossie said, with a laugh, 'Oh dear! That isn't very tactful of me, is it? I wish you both happy—that's much better, I think.' She paused, then added, 'Kinder.'

Ivo gave her a straight look and said firmly, 'I think it's time we found the rest of our party, Jossie. They must be wondering what has happened to us.'

Lady Radstock hesitated and said, 'If your aunt has time I should very much like to see her again, Lord Trenchard. She has been much missed in Lyne St Michael.'

'I'm sure she would be delighted if you called on her,' replied Ivo. 'She's at home most afternoons. You know our direction?'

'Charles Street. Yes.'

'Excellent! She will look forward to it. Can she expect you all?'

'Unfortunately not,' said Lady Radstock, adding, with very little sign of regret, 'Major and Mrs Morley are leaving London tomorrow.'

'How sad,' said Ivo with equal sincerity. 'But my aunt would be pleased to see you and your family, at least.' He turned to Jossie. 'Come along, Jossie. Princess Lieven wishes to have a word with you, but first we must rejoin the others.' He led her away.

The Morleys and the Radstocks were left behind to wonder and conjecture.

'I would never have believed it,' said Lady Radstock, her eyes following Jossie's progress through the room. The progress was slow enough. She stopped every few paces, to curtsy to Lady Jersey, blush at a compliment from one of the Royal Dukes, or laugh with one or other of Ivo's friends. Her position as a reigning beauty was undeniable. Lady Radstock blinked. 'Tell me I'm not dreaming!'

'I've a good mind to make her come back and live with me,' frowned the Major. 'That godmother of hers had no right to take her away. We could do with someone like her at the Manor, the place hasn't been the same without her.'

Mrs Morley had no wish to see herself and her own daughter eclipsed by the return to Lyne St Michael of a wildly successful prodigal stepdaughter. 'I shouldn't if I were you, my love,' she said, sweetly. 'I doubt Helena, as she now calls herself, would come. And the village wouldn't take it too kindly if you forced her. It would only start the talk again, and you know how you hated it.'

'Well, I say, good luck to her!' said Sir Thomas. 'And good luck to the lucky man who gets her! What a girl, eh? A real beauty! Charmin', lively and with a fortune, too…' He cast a disparaging glance at his daughter-in-law.

Peter had been silent, staring at Jossie as if he still couldn't believe his eyes. But at these words he turned to his wife and said, 'Come and dance, Rosalind. I always enjoy dancing with you.' And with a defiant glance at his father he took Rosalind on to the floor.

For the rest of the evening Jossie herself put on a brave front, chatting gaily, dancing every dance, and refusing to admit how much the encounter with her father and the Radstocks had taken out of her. But after a while Lord Veryan announced that she could dance the night through if she wished, but he was going home to bed, and he advised her to do the same. So, with the exception of Ivo who, as the Duke's aide, had to stay to the end, the Charles Street party went home comparatively early.

But though Jossie excused herself and went to bed almost as soon as they got in, she found that she could not sleep. She was still taut, unable to relax. So much had happened that evening. To have danced with England's hero, the man who had saved Europe, beaten so many French generals in Spain, and ended by defeating Napoleon himself at Waterloo…! The thrill of that alone was excuse for a sleepless night.

Then there was the rest, the less glorious, but no less agitating, experience of meeting once again all the actors in the drama that had been played out on the night of Peter's coming of age. The triumph had been everything she had wanted. Because of Ivo's machinations she could not have appeared to them in a more impressive light, and she hoped and believed her performance had repaid his efforts.

But the drama seemed so long ago and so much had happened in the year since. She had both feared and looked forward to meeting her father and the others again, she had been so determined to show them. This was what had driven her for nearly a year, had made all the effort seem worthwhile. Now it was done, she was surprised to feel a sense of anticlimax, a curious sense of loss. The Jossie of those early days would have danced in the streets tonight at the discomfiture of her enemies. But somewhere along the way that girl had vanished, along with the girl who had worshipped her father and imagined herself in love with Peter. The desperate girl, who thought that her life had come to an end when they had both rejected her, simply no longer existed…

But what sort of person had taken her place?

She went to the window, quietly drew back the heavy curtains, and opened it. Her room looked on to the street, which at this hour of the morning was deserted. It was a clear night and she could see a narrow strip of sky above, brilliant with stars. The moon was still full enough to cast a faint light on the road below. She sat for a while gazing at the stars. Where was Ivo now? Was he with Lady Alicia? Or was another of his amours delighting him tonight? She realised with a pang that her success with the *ton*, her triumph over Peter and her father, would have counted for less than nothing if Ivo had not been there to share it with her. She would give up all the admiration she had seen in other men's eyes, every bit of the amazement she had seen on the Radstocks' faces tonight, if Ivo would only look at her as he looked at Lady Alicia and the others. He never would. He would never see her like that. She was his friend, his protégée. She sighed and turned to go to bed.

As she did so her eye was caught by a lone figure striding along Charles Street, in the direction of the house. It was Ivo. His head was slightly bent—he seemed to be deep in thought. Jossie drew back a little, but still watched him. He looked tired.

Then to her horror she saw another man creeping up on Ivo from behind, holding what looked like a heavy stick in his hand. Her heart gave a thump, then seemed to stop…

'Ivo!' she shouted desperately.

Ivo looked up, then, suddenly alert, turned as the thief attacked, and partially dodged the murderous blow aimed at him. If it had landed squarely it would surely have killed him. Ivo recovered his balance and promptly tackled his assailant, and a short, sharp fight ensued, which ended when the stranger broke loose and fled back down the street. Ivo stood for a moment, then made for the house again. But he staggered as he turned and had to hold on to the railings for support. He was injured! Jossie threw on a wrapper and ran down two flights of stairs at breakneck speed. She arrived at the front door just as one of the servants was opening it. Ivo almost fell into the hall.

'Don't just stand there! Help me!' she said to the servant. Between them they supported Ivo to the nearest room on the ground floor, the library. Here they helped him into a chair, where he sank back with a groan. Another servant came hurrying in, carrying the lamp from the hall.

'We shall need water and cloths,' Jossie said, carefully examining the ugly wound on the back of Ivo's head.

'And see if Lord Trenchard's man is awake. If not, rouse him. Quickly!'

'Don't wake anyone else, Foster,' said Ivo with an effort. 'I don't want my father or her ladyship alarmed. They sleep at the back, they won't have heard anything yet. And tell any other servants to go back to their beds.'

'But oughtn't we to send someone after the man who attacked you?'

'Useless! He's long gone. And fortunately he didn't get anything. You ought to go back to your bed, too, Jossie.'

'As if I could!' She turned to the man carrying a basin of water and cloths. 'Good! Put it down here, if you please. Now.'

The next few minutes were difficult. Jossie was as gentle as she could be, but Ivo's hair was matted with blood, and it took some time to clean the wound. Fortunately his manservant arrived halfway through and, after watching her in silence for a moment, he offered to take over.

'Let him, Jossie. He knows what he's doing. Kealy was with me in Spain.' Ivo tried to grin. 'He's seen worse than this! Send for some brandy and then get off to bed. I'll soon be perfectly fit.' He looked at the other servants. 'Make sure the door is locked and then you be off too. Quietly! Thank you for your help. Goodnight.'

Jossie went over to the decanter and glasses on the library table and poured out a small brandy. She brought it back and held it to Ivo's lips. His face was white, and when he reached to take the glass his hand was ice-cold.

'Ivo!' She kept hold of the brandy, made sure he drank it, then put the glass down. She put a cashmere shawl, which had been on the back of one of the chairs, over his knees, then knelt on the floor beside him and took his hands in hers.

While his man busied himself with basilicum powder and bandages, Jossie knelt close to Ivo, cradling his hands to her, giving him the warmth from her own body. She couldn't quite stop herself from thinking how like and yet how very unlike it was to what had happened just a few nights before, and when she looked up Ivo's eyes held a gleam which showed that, injured though he was, he was thinking of it, too. She smiled at him. This was different. On this occasion there was no threat, no compulsion, nothing forced or cheap about it. She was freely giving him what comfort she could through the warmth of human contact. The feeling was very precious. Ivo's eyes closed... For a few minutes there was silence in the room, except for the small noises made by the servant, as he tended Ivo.

'I think that will do, my lord,' he said finally. 'I'm pleased to say the wound is superficial. It will hardly show tomorrow.'

Ivo opened his eyes and stared at Jossie. He removed his hands from her grasp and slowly traced a line down her cheek with the tips of his fingers, ending by cupping her chin in his hand. He held it so for a moment, looking deep into her eyes, then he released her and sat up. 'Thank you, Kealy,' he said. 'Now, will you please see Miss Calverton safely to her bedchamber, then come back here and clear up the mess. With your help I think I can make it to my room.'

'But, Ivo-!'

'Do as I say, Jossie. Let Kealy take you. You mustn't be found here.' His voice was tired but determined. Jossie, feeling bereft, got to her feet and nodded. Ivo didn't want to be accused of compromising her, and he was right.

'Good night,' she said stiffly. Now that the crisis was over reaction was setting in. She could hardly speak for the ache in her throat. 'I'm glad you're not badly hurt.'

'Thanks to you. I was half-asleep as I came along that street. I couldn't have defended myself if you hadn't woken me up.'

She nodded. Kealy was holding the door, and she walked slowly out of the library and up the stairs. When she reached the door of her bedchamber she turned to Kealy. 'Don't let your master do too much,' she said.

'I wouldn't, miss. The thing is, I don't know how to stop him! But I think he'll do. This knock is nothing to what he's had in the past.'

She smiled. 'Thank you, Kealy. Good night.'

Inside her room she slowly took off her wrapper and examined it. The sleeves were stained with traces of blood. Ivo's blood. How close she had come that night to losing him altogether! She stared at the wrapper and gave a twisted smile. So much for her resolve not to fall in love with him! It was too late. She was already there. She trusted him, she was grateful to him, she respected him—all of these. But this strange mixture of loving tenderness and hungry desire, this longing to stay with him, look after him, be with him…this was different.

Deep down it had been there almost from the beginning, of course. It explained why she had responded so ardently to Ivo's kisses, and so reluctantly to Peter's, though she had been too blind, too naïve, to see it at the time. Now it was clear enough, even for her. This love of hers for Ivo Trenchard was not that of an untutored girl. She now longed for everything that love would entail, perfect harmony of body as well as of mind. And she wanted this man for her lover, her husband, her companion for the rest of her life. This man and no other. How foolish she was! How madly, stupidly foolish!

Jossie got into bed. She lay there for a while, thinking of the scene in the library, wondering what Ivo's look had meant. He had gazed at her seriously, a little sadly—almost as if he was saying goodbye… She dismissed the thought as absurd. His head had been hurting, that was all. Then she folded her hands to her, and relived the moments when she had cradled Ivo's hands to her breast, giving him life and warmth… Finally she fell asleep.

Meanwhile Ivo had made his way to his own room and removed his stained coat and shirt. Then, in spite of Kealy's protests, he sent the man to bed and sat in a chair at the window in his dressing gown. His head was aching, his body felt as if he had been in the saddle for a fortnight, but his mind was as awake as it had ever been.

He had now finished what he had set out to do for Jossie. She had been as successful in London as he had foreseen, and was now securely established in the eyes of the *ton* as someone worthy of a place in the highest echelons of society.

Furthermore, he had helped her to prove herself to those who had injured her so badly at that accursed coming-of-age ball. Her wounded spirit must have been healed by tonight's demonstration… He hoped so, at least. He had occasionally had a suspicion that Jossie wanted more than satisfaction, that she wanted revenge, but to his relief there had been no sign of that tonight. Ivo smiled involuntarily. The little minx, wishing Radstock and his wife the happiness they deserved! And the look on their faces!

His smile faded and he sighed. So what was left for him to do? Fade tactfully from the scene? Jossie would now surely forget her determination to remain single. She could marry any one of a dozen extremely eligible young men, and that was undoubtedly what she ought to do...

He sat up. No, dammit! It was not. Jossie belonged to him! He'd be hanged if he let her marry some young stripling who would never value her as he ought. Jossie might be far too young for Ivo Trenchard, but who else could possibly appreciate how very special she was? Who else would watch her as she needed to be watched, protect her from dangers she was too trusting to see?

He sank back into the chair again. He mustn't go too quickly. If Jossie was persuaded to marry him, it would mean giving up his old ways forever—the flirtations, the *affaires*, the pursuit of a new quarry.... They would all have to go. He wouldn't, he couldn't, offer her anything but complete loyalty. She had been hurt once before, she mustn't be hurt again. Not ever. The choice was simple enough—his old, very enjoyable, bachelor existence, or marriage to Jossie. There was no halfway, no compromise. Was he ready to decide between them?

He smiled ruefully. Adam had been right, after all! It wasn't a question of choice. Marriage no longer seemed a necessary duty, a trap, a limitation of his freedom. Life with Jossie offered everything he wanted, and nothing else would do.

Of course he was ready! He ought to have realised it the other night. While he was teaching Jossie her lesson in the garden at Manchester House, he had congratulated himself on managing to remain quite objective, perfectly cool. But how he had paid for it afterwards! He had been haunted by Jossie's reproachful eyes, the hurt shock in her voice, and, worse than that, he had been quite unable to forget the feel of her lissome young body under his hands... It had seemed a good idea to banish these thoughts with a visit to Lady Alicia. And what had happened? For all her charms, all her experience, the lady had never before seemed so unattractive, nor he so unable to respond. The whole visit had been a disaster. Indeed, she might never forgive him for the manner in which he had left her. And then he had walked the streets of London till dawn...

No, there wasn't much danger that he would be tempted to stray if Jossie married him. The difficulty would lie in persuading her that he was the one for her. Yes, there was one lesson he still had to teach Jossie— the most important lesson of the lot. Ivo Trenchard was the one for her, the only *possible* one to be her lover, her husband, the father of her children...

Dawn was breaking. Ivo got up, stretched and stared down at the street. He knew at last what it was he wanted from life. Now he had to work out how to achieve it. He would have to go warily. Jossie might well be willing to marry him out of gratitude, or for friendship's sake, or even to avoid loneliness. And, from the evidence of their past encounters, he could probably seduce her into marrying him, too. But it wouldn't be enough. He wanted her to come to him because she loved him in every way there was, body, heart, and soul. No other reason would do. She must love him as completely, as irreversibly, as he loved her. But with *his* reputation, how the devil was he to convince her of his sincerity?

By noon the next day, which was when everyone got up, Ivo was himself again. There was no sign, either on his person or in the library, of what had taken place the night before. Jossie raised her eyebrow as she greeted him, but he only smiled reassuringly and invited her for a drive that afternoon.

'Jossie tells me that the Radstocks wish to visit us,' said Lady Frances. 'I have no objection to receiving Sir Thomas and Lady Radstock, but I have to say I should prefer not to see Peter and his wife. But I suppose I must if they are brazen enough to call. Do you think they might come this afternoon, Ivo?'

'We didn't make any definite arrangement. However, I should imagine they would leave it a day or two.'

'Peregrine said he would visit us this afternoon. I've told Rupert he's to be kinder to the boy. He was quite short with him last night. I do wish he wouldn't always compare him with you—I could see Perry didn't like it. I hear he has done very well in Derbyshire. Why doesn't your father talk of that?' She paused. 'Mind you, Derbyshire isn't London, and last night was quite an occasion, was it not? I was very proud of you myself. It's clear that the Duke thinks highly of you.'

'You wouldn't think so if you heard what he says to me! But one of us certainly had his total approbation last night.'

'It is not to be wondered at! Jossie, you looked superb, and danced divinely! I was so proud of you! I remarked to Perry, as Ivo brought you back to us, what an impressive pair you made!'

'That will have delighted my brother,' said Ivo drily. 'You must have pleased him almost as much as my father did!'

Later, in the afternoon as she sat beside Ivo in the phaeton, Jossie asked him, 'What is it with you and Peregrine? Why are you so cool with each other?'

The lazy good humour which was Ivo's normal expression disappeared for a moment as he said abruptly, 'It's an old story, Jossie. Perry and I were good friends in the old days, but he served me a very ill turn three years ago.'

'What did he do?'

'He kept my father and me apart for over a year, including the months before Waterloo... That's something I find hard to forgive. But I'd really prefer not to talk about it.' His tone was final. 'Tell me, what did you think of the meeting with your father and the others? Were you satisfied? Do you think you ''showed'' them, as much as you wanted to?'

'More than I could have imagined! Thank you again, Ivo. I cannot say how grateful I am to you! But—'

'I don't want your gratitude, Jossie.'

'That's absurd! I owe you practically everything! But...'

'What is it?'

'Well, Sir Thomas was his usual bluff self, but the rest don't seem to be very happy, do they?'

'Good God! Do you think they ought to be?'

'I suppose not....' She paused for a moment, then said, 'It's just that in the old days I was the one Peter always looked for when he was miserable...'

'And now he has a wife,' said Ivo firmly. 'You've done what you wanted to. Now you must leave them alone!'

'Yes, of course! I know I must.' She looked away. 'In any case, he deserves to be a little unhappy, don't you think?'

This preoccupation with Peter Radstock was not at all to Ivo's liking. It seemed he had been wrong in assuming that Jossie would now be able to put her old life behind her. He said, 'What Peter Radstock feels really doesn't concern me. Nor should it concern you. It's time to move on.'

His tone disconcerted Jossie. It was so cold. 'Of course!' she said brightly. 'Do you plan to go to the Duchess of Sutherland's soirée?'

'Jossie, I—'

'Or are you accompanying us to Vauxhall? Perry has hired a boat.'

'Neither,' said Ivo with something of a snap. 'I've arranged to see Colonel Ancroft tonight. Shall we go back?'

He had decided to postpone any attempt to talk seriously to Jossie. It didn't seem to be the right moment.

When they got back to Charles Street they were surprised to find Lady Frances entertaining the Radstocks and Perry and Rosalind to tea in the saloon.

Jossie sat down next to Sir Thomas, and before long they were deep in conversation about the changes he was making on his land.

'Sir Thomas! I'm sure agriculture is the last thing Jossie—or should I call you Helena, my dear?—wants to talk about in London!' said his wife.

'She'll always be Jossie to me, Lady Radstock! And she still knows a thing or two about the land. I feel I've got something to talk about with Jossie.' His eye rested briefly on Rosalind, who was sitting, looking rather pale and subdued, next to Lady Frances. He turned back to Jossie with a sigh. 'Eh, the times we had with the two of you! I was never sure which of you would be in a scrape next, you or Peter! What a pair you were!'

Not altogether surprisingly, this led to a moment's awkward silence. It was broken by Lady Radstock, who gave her husband a severe look and said, 'Tell me the name of your modiste, Helena. That dress you were wearing last night was exquisite.'

Lady Frances eagerly picked up the topic, and the ladies talked for a while of dresses. Jossie moved over to join them, but was soon bored with the discussion. She looked around. Ivo and his father were clearly enjoying a lively conversation with Sir Thomas. Perry was sitting to one side, leaning back in his chair and quietly observing the three of them. Peter was standing by the window with his back to the room. His shoulders were drooping.

Before she could stop herself she went over to him. He turned. 'I haven't seen my father so happy since...' He paused, then went on, 'Since I came of age. He's never forgiven me, you know.'

'I'm sorry.'

Peter gave a bitter little laugh. '*You're* sorry! What a thing to say, Joss! I don't suppose you'll ever forgive me, either.'

'I already have.'

'How can you expect me to believe that? What I did was cruel! I can't even forgive myself!'

'The manner of it was cruel, I won't deny that,' said Jossie with a twisted smile. 'But I've come to see that you really did us both a service. We should never have suited.' She put her hand on his arm. 'You must forgive yourself, Peter! Be happy!'

'I...I can't,' he replied in a stifled voice.

'Why not?'

'I can't tell you here. Joss, I need to talk to you. I must talk to someone!'

'Careful! Your mother has her eye on us!'

Peter grinned fleetingly. 'That's what you always used to say in the old days. remember?'

'I remember.'

He was serious again. 'Please, Jossie, can we meet somewhere? You always helped in the past. Help me now!'

'You're asking a lot.'

'Too much?' His eyes were fixed anxiously on hers, and she was swamped in memories. She couldn't bring herself to refuse him.

'Where?'

'In the park? Tomorrow morning?'

'Very well. I often go for an early ride. We can go together. At ten?'

'At ten. I don't deserve this, Jossie, I know. But I don't know where else to turn.'

Jossie nodded. It was time to end this tête-à-tête. Lady Radstock was looking concerned. And when she looked further she saw that Peregrine Trenchard's eyes were now on them, too. Ivo still appeared to be engrossed in his conversation with Sir Thomas.

'Ten, tomorrow,' she said.

Ivo was not as unaware as he had seemed, but the failure of his attempt to talk seriously to Jossie in the park had left him at something of a loss. The expedition to Vauxhall might have offered a better opportunity to straighten things out between them, but his engagement to dine with Colonel Ancroft that evening was perfectly genuine and one he was reluctant to break. Since Waterloo he and his commanding officer had seen a fair amount of one another, first in Paris and now here in London, where they both still worked as aides to the Duke when needed. The more time Ivo spent with the

Colonel the more he liked him. By now they were reasonably at ease in each other's company, so much so that over dinner that night Colonel Ancroft was prepared to tease him about Jossie.

'I do believe you're serious at last, Ivo. I never thought to see it. But she's an enchanting creature! You'll be a lucky man if she'll have you.'

'I think so, too, sir. The devil of it is, I'm not sure I can persuade her to take me seriously.'

Colonel Ancroft laughed. 'I can see that might be difficult—but you only have yourself to blame! However, I'm sure you'll succeed. And I hope I'll still be here in London to see it.'

'You're going away?'

'Soon. I...I have things to do in the north.' Colonel Ancroft sighed and stared moodily at his wine glass. 'I can't delay much longer, much as I would wish to.'

Ivo waited, then said carefully, 'Has your journey north anything to do with the recent death of Lord Coverdale?'

'Who told you that? Or was it a lucky guess?'

'The Duke mentioned something. Are you...are you the heir, sir?'

Colonel Ancroft got up and walked restlessly round the room. 'Yes, dammit! And I wish to heaven I wasn't! But I suppose I always knew I'd have to go back one day unless Boney got me first.'

His tone was so bitter that Ivo looked for something to divert him. 'How will you travel? Not in a mule cart, I dare swear.'

'No, by heaven! That's one thing I can thank the peace for—no more Spanish mules! No, I'm taking my own carriage. And my own team of horses.'

'Surely that makes for a slower journey? More stops for resting the horses?'

'I…er…I shall have a companion. I've agreed to escort someone up north. A lady.'

'A…a friend of the family, perhaps?' said Ivo carefully.

'No, I don't know her from Adam—or should I say Eve?' his companion replied. 'I haven't yet met her. She's a widow.'

'I see,' said Ivo. 'A widow.'

Colonel Ancroft laughed. 'I thought that would intrigue you. But I'm afraid I have to disappoint you, Ivo. No intrigue there! The lady is elderly, infirm, and of a nervous disposition. I understand that she is taking her husband's ashes back to his birthplace in the north, and is convinced she will be attacked on the road.'

Ivo was astounded. 'And you've agreed to look after her?'

'To accompany her party. She has her own attendants.' When Ivo continued to look surprised he went on, 'I'm doing it to oblige a friend—someone to whom I owe a lot. He knew I was going up to Yorkshire, y'see. To take up my new responsibilities.' The Colonel looked grim. 'Yes, it means the journey will take longer, but I'm not sorry about that. My memories of the place are not happy and I'm not exactly eager to see it. Escorting this lady will give me something else to think about.'

'When do you plan to leave?'

'I'm not sure. She hasn't arrived in London yet. But I shall certainly hope to see you before I go. Meanwhile, good luck with Miss Calverton!'

Chapter Fourteen

Peter was waiting for Jossie when she arrived the next morning at the Chesterfield gate. He had clearly been there for some time—both he and his horse were restless.

'Shall we go to the far end of the park?' she asked.

'A good idea—this creature needs some activity, and so do I! But...I'd like some privacy,' he said, his eye on Jossie's groom. Jossie hesitated, then told her man to wait for them at the gate. Then she turned to Peter.

'Let's break all the rules and have a good gallop, Peter! Come on!'

She set off with all her old impulsiveness down the bridle way. They raced to the end of the path, and came to a halt on the other, unfrequented, side of the park.

Jossie sighed. 'That was glorious! But for heaven's sake don't tell a soul! I should be ruined if the tabbies got to hear of it. A sedate trot is the most that is permitted to the ladies of the *ton*.'

Peter regarded her with admiration. She was flushed, her eyes were sparkling, and she was smiling at him in the old way...

'Jossie!' he said. Her face changed.

'What is it you wish to say?' she asked, with a touch

of reserve. 'I won't listen to anything indiscreet, Peter. Nothing disloyal.'

'I don't intend to be disloyal!' he said hotly. 'I love Rosalind. Still. In spite of—' He stopped. After a short silence he went on desperately, 'I need your help, Joss! I need help to sort things out. But I do love Rosalind.'

'Good! I couldn't listen if you didn't.' Then she added, 'But why do you need *me*? Why can't you talk to *her*?'

'She's part of the problem.' He stopped again.

Jossie said impatiently, 'For goodness' sake, Peter, get on with it! We haven't all day.'

He looked hurt at her brisk tone, but pulled himself together and began. It was a sorry tale, but not uncommon. His father had never approved of his marriage, and, though not actually unkind to Rosalind, he seldom made himself agreeable to her. Lady Radstock did her best to make the girl feel part of the family, but she was hampered by the fact that Rosalind's mother spent far too much time with her daughter.

'I thought Lady Radstock liked Mrs Cherton?'

'She liked Mrs *Cherton* well enough. But Mrs Cherton is now Mrs Morley of Calverton Manor, and very ready to queen it in the neighbourhood. My mother resents it, and quite right, too!' Peter said indignantly. 'Mama has been the first lady among the neighbours ever since old Lady Calverton died. And it's not even as if your father is the real owner of the Manor!'

'No,' Jossie agreed. 'It must have been a nasty shock to Mrs Cherton to discover that. But, Peter, this all sounds rather petty. I don't believe your mother could be so upset by this that she would take it out on your wife.'

'No, but that's not all. Mrs Morley criticises me, too.

She's always hinting that I don't spend enough time with Rosalind, that I don't give her a big enough dress allowance, that…oh, everything!'

Rosalind's mother was a fool, thought Jossie drily. The one sure way to antagonise Lady Radstock, irretrievably, was to criticise her son.

'And now I'm badgered on all sides. My father can't understand why I don't spend more time on the estate. Rosalind doesn't understand why I can't spend every minute with her. My mother can't understand why I let Rosalind spend so much time with her mother. What am I to do?'

'But why are you telling *me* this? What on earth do you think I could do?'

'Oh, I don't know… Give a hint to your father, or your stepmother? Have a chat with my mother? Or even…' Peter's face brightened. 'Have a word with Rosalind. Explain to her how important it is for me to ride round the estate.'

'I know why you ride round the estate, my friend! You enjoy it! Why don't you take Rosalind with you?'

'She's not like you, Joss! She doesn't like riding rough.'

Jossie suffered a pang as she had a sudden memory of riding with Peter over the hills and fields round Lyne St Michael. She had been so happy, so unaware…the land had seemed so precious then. She had almost forgotten it in London.

She pulled herself together and said firmly, 'You must know I can't do any of that! The idea is absurd. My advice, for what it is worth, is to restore the Dower House and go to live there. You and your wife need time alone together, away from both mothers. You're not short of money—increase Rosalind's dress allowance, and take her to Bath to find some new dresses... Or, better still, buy her a few dresses while you are here. I'll introduce her to Madame Rosa, if you wish. No, I'm serious, Peter! Clothes are very important to Rosalind. It's surely worth a little time and money to keep her happy, isn't it? As for the rest... Why don't you consult Lady Frances? She is in a much better position than I am to do something.'

'I couldn't! You know what she thinks of me, especially after...'

Jossie nodded and faced the inevitable. Peter had always tried to get other people to do difficult tasks. 'Would you like me to speak to her?'

'Oh, Jossie! If you would!'

'I'll see what she has to say. Meanwhile, try talking to Rosalind while her mother is out of the way. It might be a chance to get her to listen to you.' She waited until he gave a reluctant nod. Then she said, 'I must get back to Charles Street. They'll be wondering where I am.'

His face fell. 'But we've had no chance to talk! I thought we might have a chat like old times.'

Jossie regarded him with a mixture of regret and exasperation. Why had she never before realised how childishly selfish Peter was? How blind. 'But it isn't old times, Peter,' she said impatiently. 'This isn't Lyne St Michael, and we aren't children any more. And you are married.'

He looked so disconsolate that she added more kindly, 'I'll do what I can. For old times' sake. I'll try to have a word with Lady Frances today. Perhaps I can see Madame Rosa today, too. Shall we meet tomorrow at the same time?'

'At the gate. I'll be there. And, Jossie!' She had already started off, but she stopped and looked back.

'I know I ought not to ask for your help,' Peter said, looking slightly ashamed. 'After what I did to you. But there's no one else I can turn to. I'm grateful, I really am.'

'So you've already said, but I really don't want your gratitude. In the end you did me a good turn. We should never have been happy together.' Peter looked somewhat put out at this direct reply, and Jossie wondered fleetingly whether he had, deep down, thought he could revive her old affection for him. Well, enough of it was left for her to want to help him now. But not much more.

They rode back at a more suitable pace. It was as well. Several other people were out for an early ride, among them Peregrine Trenchard. He eyed them curiously, and Jossie felt herself colouring, but she saw no reason to explain herself. She greeted him calmly, and bade Peter farewell without referring again to their next meeting. Mr Trenchard was too interested, as it was.

Indeed, Mr Trenchard *was* interested. He was so interested that he mentioned it to Ivo.

'I don't wish to interfere, Ivo, old chap,' he said later that day. 'But if I were you I'd get Aunt Frances to give a hint to young Helena. She really ought not to go riding with young men in the park, especially not without her groom. People are bound to talk.'

Ivo looked coolly at his brother. After a moment he drawled, 'I don't know why you can't mention it to Aunt Frances yourself, Perry. Or even to warn Jossie yourself. She won't bite you. If, as I suspect, what you really want is to tell me that Jossie has had a secret assignation, then why don't you come right out with it? However you try to disguise it, you're still a tale-bearer.'

Peregrine reddened but said, 'This is rich, coming from you!'

'What do you mean?'

'It can only have been you who told Father about Charlotte Gurney and the way I kept your quarrel with him going. You know he sent me to Derbyshire because of it?'

'No, I didn't. I thought you went because you had at last seen sense and got away from Sudiham. He hasn't said a word about forcing you to go. But why are you so sour? What's wrong? I thought you liked Derbyshire?'

'I do. But I didn't like being sent away like a naughty schoolboy, because of what you told him.'

'Perry, Father isn't a fool. He can work things out for himself. As a matter of fact, I didn't tell him anything at all. Not about Charlotte, nor even about your lies to keep Father and me apart. What is more, he wouldn't have liked it if I had. He doesn't like tale-bearers any more than I do. Which brings us back to the present issue. Supposing Jossie *is* meeting someone in secret— which I doubt. What do you think *I* could do about it?'

'I thought you liked her?'

Ivo regarded his brother in silence. Then he said quite pleasantly, 'I do. Very much. And I assure you, that if you tell any of your stories about her, or do her any harm, I won't waste time telling my father or anyone else. I'll break every bone in your body.'

Perry laughed nervously. 'There's no need to be unpleasant. I didn't mean any harm. But I wasn't lying. I saw them together. In the park. Helena and Peter Radstock.' He retreated hastily as his brother's face changed and he took a step forward. But whatever Ivo had intended he changed his mind. He stopped short, then, with an expression of disgust, he turned on his heel and walked out of the room. Perry breathed a sigh of relief. And smiled.

Lady Frances was not as sympathetic to Peter's difficulties as Jossie would have hoped.

'He's quite hopeless!' she said. 'A handsome face with nothing behind it. No strength of character, no determination, and not very much wit. Anyone could have foreseen that Mrs Cherton would be a difficult mother-in-law, and taken steps to protect himself against her!'

'My dearest Godmama!' said Jossie, half-laughing. 'What could poor Peter possibly do?'

'Poor Peter! You can still call him that?'

'Yes, I can,' said Jossie seriously. She went over to her godmother and took her hand. 'Thanks to you and Ivo, I'm a sane, healthy, rational being again. I bear no grudges—well, perhaps a slight remnant of one towards my father. Apart from him, I have completely forgiven all of them. I would like them all to live happily together, especially Peter and Rosalind.'

'You're not thinking of dying young, are you, Jossie?' asked Lady Frances suspiciously. 'This is far too saintly for my taste.'

'Certainly not! Why can't you believe that I am grateful to have had such a narrow escape? If nothing had happened to stop it I would have married Peter Radstock and been unhappy for the rest of my life. I might not even have realised why. I admit, that, at the time, I would have gone under if you and Ivo had not been there to rescue me. But you *were* there, and you *did* rescue me, and I shall never cease to be grateful to you both.'

'Is that all you feel for Ivo? Gratitude?'

Jossie hesitated. 'No. Not only. But without wishing

in the slightest to be rude, I don't propose to discuss what I feel for Ivo with anyone else.' She gave a wry smile. 'It's of no significance to anyone but me. Can we do anything for Peter, do you think?'

'I think you've already done something by giving him a sympathetic ear. And I agree with you—the young couple should have a home of their own. If we were in Lyne St Michael I might be able to talk to Lady Radstock, but the opportunities in London for such a talk are non-existent. Peter will have to do more for himself. He has always been very spoiled, of course. From what I've heard, he spends too much time at the races with friends, or hunting anything that moves. That can't make him much of a help to his father, nor much of a companion to his wife. He could satisfy both of them, if he would only give up a few of his own pursuits.'

'And in London, meanwhile?'

'Meanwhile, it's a good idea to persuade him to make more fuss of Rosalind while her mother isn't here to poison his efforts. By all means introduce them to Madame Rosa, though whether she will wish to make anything for Rosalind remains to be seen. She won't do it for everyone. But, Jossie...' Lady Frances looked serious. 'Be careful! If Peter's wife is feeling sensitive at the moment, she wouldn't take it kindly if she learned that he is seeing you. Make tomorrow's meeting the last time you see him alone.'

Mindful of Lady Frances's warning, Jossie remained by the gate for her meeting with Peter the next morning, and kept it brief and businesslike. She reported what her godmother had said, then went on, 'I went to see Madame Rosa yesterday, too. She is prepared to see Rosalind, and take her on as a client.'

Peter was not particularly grateful, though it had taken some hard persuasion from a valued customer to get the modiste to agree. 'Dresses! How will that help?'

'Peter, try to show a little understanding. I know clothes were never important to either of us. But they are very important to your wife, and you must try to put yourself in her place!' said Jossie patiently. 'A dress from one of the foremost mantua-makers in London would give her a great deal of pleasure—and confidence. Even I have learned that. Have you managed to talk to her yet?'

'I tried,' he said gloomily. 'She wasn't very receptive.'

'Well, try again! And ask her if she would like to see Madame Rosa. Trust me on this! I know what I'm talking about!' In an attempt to impress on Peter the importance of what she was saying, Jossie leant forward and spoke very earnestly. From a distance it looked almost as if they were touching.

Ivo saw them. He was on his way back from Tattersall's, and was passing Chesterfield Gate just at this moment. It was unfortunate. He had set out that morning with no thought of Peregrine's insinuations in his mind. Indeed, if he had remembered them, he would have taken another route back to Charles Street, in order to avoid the slightest suspicion that he might be spying on Jossie. But he did see her. And she was talking confidentially with Peter Radstock—for the second morning running, if Peregrine had been telling the truth. He spurred his horse on and passed as quickly as he could. Jossie was too preoccupied to notice him.

When he reached the house Ivo found he was trembling with rage. He had been angry before, but he had never before been so angry, so beside himself, because of a woman. No woman had ever before meant enough to him. For a while, until reason prevailed, he paced his room like a caged tiger, furious both with himself and the whole female sex. Jossie was a fool! A witless, idiotic, deceitful fool! They had been practically *kissing* each other! How could she possibly—*possibly*—want to win back Peter Radstock? Could she still not see him for what he was—a weak, spineless, dithering, spoilt, *child*? Radstock would never grow up, whatever age he lived to... Was she really prepared to nursemaid him through life? And what about his wife? Had Jossie forgotten that he was married?

Ivo started to calm down. He didn't believe it. Jossie couldn't possibly want to entice Peter Radstock away from his wife. Even if she loved him, she would still not attempt it. She was brave enough and scornful enough of convention for herself, but Radstock was neither. She must know that he would never stand the total ostracism from his own small world which would surely ensue.

But, in that case, why was she meeting him secretly in the park?

He threw himself into a chair. Was he wrong in his assumption that Jossie still felt some kindness for Radstock? He had sometimes suspected her of planning revenge. Was *that* her game? To make Radstock fall in love with her again, and then throw it back in his face?

Surely not! The Jossie he knew would not stoop so low.

Ivo got up again and poured himself a glass of brandy. Deep in thought, he stood at the window, slowly sipping his drink. Was he right to trust his instinct? The girl he had known before the previous July had been an enchanting creature, direct, original, brave and loyal. And clever. But on that night in July that girl's world had exploded in her face. It was not surprising that she had changed. Had she changed so much that she would deliberately set out to exact some kind of revenge on Radstock? He hoped not. He sincerely hoped not.

Ivo put his glass down and went slowly downstairs. The sad thing was that he was as much of a besotted fool as any of the lovers he had so despised in the past! Whether she was a witless fool, or a devious seeker for revenge, he loved Jossie Morley all the same. He was still concerned for her, still ready to protect her from any unpleasant consequences, to be her champion still. Faithful unto death like an idiotic knight in a romance! He smiled bitterly. Who would have thought that he, Ivo Trenchard, cynic, experienced campaigner, as wise as any man in the ways of women, could be so deeply in love with Jossie Morley that he was prepared to defend her, *whatever* she did. How his friends, how all the polite world, would laugh if they knew!

Ivo dismissed the reactions of the polite world. What did they matter? He would have to speak Jossie, if only to warn her. Peregrine could not be trusted. If he could make trouble he would, and others might have seen what he had seen in the park. Possibly quite harmless in itself, but dangerous in the hands of a malicious manipulator. Perry had been clever enough to see that he could hurt Ivo by hurting Jossie, and he was unscrupulous enough not to care who else might be hurt in the process. Yes, he must speak to Jossie.

Ivo found her in the library playing backgammon with his father.

'Come in, come in, Ivo! Celebrate with me! I've just trounced Jossie, and that's a rare enough event. What can we do for you?'

'Congratulations, sir. I've come to ask Jossie if she would like a walk.'

'A very good idea. She certainly wasn't on form during that game.' He leaned forward and patted Jossie's hand. 'You look pale, child. Too many balls and the like. Too many Dukes wanting to dance with you. Take some air, it'll do you good.'

He sat back comfortably, but his eyes were sharp as he watched Ivo and Jossie leaving the room.

Ivo took Jossie to Hampstead, and, leaving the carriage in the care of the coachman, they made their way on to the Heath. They walked in silence for a short while. Jossie seemed subdued, and Ivo was trying to find a way of opening a conversation which he was very reluctant to embark on.

'I saw you earlier today,' he said at length.

'Where? I didn't see you.'

'At the Chesterfield Gate. I'm not surprised you didn't notice me. You seemed very preoccupied.'

Jossie was looking wary, but she answered calmly enough, 'With Peter.'

'You're surely not still in love with him, are you?'

'That's a very big leap, Ivo! If all the people who met in the park were assumed to be in love...'

'Not many meet at ten o'clock in the morning and ride off into the distance without taking a groom with them.'

Jossie's eyes narrowed. 'We didn't do that this morning—we stayed by the gate the whole time. Peregrine has been talking to you.' She started to get angry. 'Did you send him to spy on us? And this morning you came to see for yourself, is that it?'

'No! I saw you by accident. What did he want?'

His imperious tone offended Jossie even more. She said coldly, 'I'm not sure you have a right to ask that, Ivo.'

'Of course I have a right! I've done my best to see you safely launched into the very cream of society, and I'm not having you now make a fool of yourself over Radstock! What did he want, Jossie?'

She looked at him thoughtfully for a moment, then said, 'Madame Rosa's address.'

'Dammit, this isn't a joke!'

'I'm not joking, it's perfectly true. Among other things, of course. But that's all I shall tell you.'

Ivo kicked a stone from the path, and swore under his breath. This was not going the way he had planned. He glanced at Jossie. 'I've done this badly, haven't I?' he said.

'Yes. I'm not sure why you're so annoyed.'

'When I saw you with Radstock you were practically kissing him!'

She looked at him in amazement. 'Whatever is wrong with you? You must be making that up! We never even touched. How could you think...? Look, Ivo, you don't deserve this, but I give you my word that since last July I have never even thought of Peter in that way.'

'Then why are you meeting him?' he demanded.

His tone affronted her at first. Then her expression changed and she gave him a mocking smile. 'You ought to be careful! You're beginning to sound like a jealous husband! What a reversal of role that would be for the worst flirt in Europe!'

'Stop prevaricating, Jossie! Why are you meeting him?'

She hesitated, then said firmly, 'I can't tell you. It's between Peter and me.' She stole a glance at him, and sighed when she saw that he was still frowning. 'I don't think this walk is doing either of us much good. Shall we go back?'

Ivo stood his ground. 'Not yet,' he said, pulling her round to face him. 'Listen to me, my girl! So far you've been lucky. You've managed to avoid the pitfalls there are for a beginner in society. But not everyone means you well, and any scandal could still do you real harm! If you don't wish to lose everything you've gained in the last few months, stay away from Peter Radstock!'

Jossie was so incensed by the force with which he said these last few words that she decided against telling him she had already made up her mind not to meet Peter in private again. Instead, she flashed out, 'I shan't let you dictate to me! I shall meet Peter when and where I like!'

Ivo gave her a shake. 'You exasperating little shrew! Why the devil can't you realise that I'm only trying to protect you?'

'I don't need your protection any more. I don't want your protection. Stop treating me as if I was a child!' Jossie cried angrily. 'I'm a grown woman, and I know what I'm doing. I don't need your interference any more! Leave me alone!'

Ivo was pale. Hurt and angry, he said stiffly, 'I'm sorry. I hadn't realised you regarded my natural concern as interference. Shall we go back?'

It was not a happy party which set out for Lady Porchester's ball that evening. They were only three, for Lord Veryan had decided to stay at home. Ivo was unusually silent, and Jossie's manner towards him verged on the icy. Only Lady Frances was her usual calmly cheerful self.

'I thought Perry was to accompany us tonight?' she said, as they went out to the carriage.

'He sent a message to say he was kept elsewhere. But he will see us at the Porchesters', I understand,' said Ivo briefly.

They sat in silence as they were driven at a snail's pace through the streets to Hanover Square. Lady Frances looked at each of her companions in turn. 'I haven't seen you wearing that dress before, Jossie,' she said at last. 'It suits you. Don't you agree, Ivo?'

'Very pretty,' her nephew replied in a bored voice. There was another silence.

Lady Frances tried again. 'Do you know if the Radstocks will be there tonight?' she asked.

'I believe so,' said Jossie. Ivo gave her a sharp look, which she returned defiantly, whereupon he looked away to stare out of the window. Silence fell again, and this time it lasted until they arrived. They joined a queue of carriages waiting to deposit their passengers at the door, and sat for some minutes as the line slowly moved on.

'Well,' said Lady Frances, 'The Porchesters' entertainments are notoriously dull—an evening with them is never wildly amusing. But it is going to be absolutely intolerable unless you two start talking to one another! I'm surprised at you both! Where are your company manners, Jossie? And as for you, Ivo, I cannot imagine what has got into you! Where is the polished rogue we all know and love?'

'I'm about to rediscover him, ma'am,' said Ivo, 'He was mislaid for a time while I misguidedly tried to help someone I thought needed it. But I now find the role of nursemaid beginning to pall. You may expect to see a change.'

'A welcome relief for us all,' snapped Jossie.

As they entered Lady Porchester's vast and gloomy entrance hall he said, 'I'm sorry to have disappointed you, Aunt Frances. But I see Peregrine coming this way, and the Radstocks are just beyond him. I have no doubt they will amuse you more. Both of you. Meanwhile I'll seek my own entertainment, and relieve you of the burden of my company.' With that he bowed and disappeared in the direction of the card rooms. Lady Frances gazed after him in astonishment.

'I have never, ever, seen Ivo in such a mood,' she said. 'Not even when his quarrel with Rupert was at its height. What have you done, Jossie?'

'What makes you think that he could possibly be affected by anything I could do?' asked Jossie. 'He regards me as nothing more than a troublesome child! If he is annoyed with me, it's because I won't do as I am told!'

Lady Frances looked sceptical, but was unable to comment. Peregrine was upon them, closely followed by the Radstocks.

It looked as if the younger Radstocks were feeling about as amiable towards each other as were Ivo and Jossie. Rosalind was pale and washed out, and noticeably avoided any contact with her husband. Soon after the groups had joined, Peter invited her to dance, but she turned away with a petulant toss of her head. An awkward moment followed. Peter was painfully embarrassed, grew very red, then turned defiantly to Jossie and invited her instead. After a moment's hesitation she accepted. He looked so desperately unhappy, that she simply couldn't bring herself to humiliate him further. She justified it by telling herself that it was an opportunity to find out how matters stood with Rosalind, though on the face of it the answer would not be encouraging.

As she and Peter went to the floor she saw Peregrine

stepping forward to Rosalind. Later she found it supremely ironic that she had been happy at the time, had thought that Peregrine might cheer Peter's wife up a little.

The dance with Peter was not a pleasant experience. He was full of resentment towards Rosalind.

'Your idea about Madame Rosa didn't do any good at all. Rosalind was furious when I mentioned her.'

'*Furious?* Whatever did you say?'

'That I thought she'd look a lot better if she had a dress made in London.'

'Peter! How could you be so tactless?'

'I thought I was being damned generous. She hadn't been particularly pleasant to me beforehand, you know. Most wives would have given me a kiss and thanked me. But not her!'

He clearly expected Jossie to comfort and reassure him. This was no part of her plan. Indeed, she was already ruing her decision to dance with him, when she caught sight of Ivo standing on the edge of the floor, frowning at her. She mustn't let him see how much she regretted not following his advice. She tossed her head and turned with a brilliant smile to her partner.

When the dance was over she gave an inward sigh of relief and returned gratefully to Lady Frances and the rest. Peregrine was leading Rosalind back, but they were deep in conversation, and stopped once or twice on their way. Rosalind was questioning Peregrine closely, shaking her head in disbelief, then apparently asking him to repeat what he had said. By the time they reached the corner of the room where the rest of the party was standing she was clearly in an extremely agitated state, paler than ever, eyes glittering, hands restlessly clutching her partner's sleeve. She confronted Peter, apparently oblivious to the rest of the room.

'Why didn't you tell me yourself?' she demanded.

'Tell you what?'

'Don't pretend you don't know! Never any time for me, oh, no! Never time to take *me* riding in the park, talk about dresses to *me*!' She gave a sob. 'How could you so deceive me?'

Shocked and concerned, Lady Radstock tried to intervene. 'Rosalind! My dear! Calm down! We can't have a scene here!'

Rosalind threw off her mother-in-law's restraining hand. 'I will not calm down! Wait till you hear what I have just been told, and then tell me to be calm! Your precious son has been meeting Jossie Morley secretly in the park. Early in the morning, so they will not be seen.'

'I don't believe it!' Lady Radstock turned shocked eyes on her son. 'Is this true?'

Sir Thomas said stoutly, 'Of course it isn't! Jossie would never behave in such an underhanded way, nor would Peter. The girl is raving.'

Sir Thomas's voice was loud and several of Lady Porchester's guests looked curiously in their direction.

Peter looked at his mother and said uncomfortably, 'It is true, but not the way she says it...'

'How can it be different?' cried Rosalind, now thoroughly distraught. She turned on Jossie. 'I know what it is! You think you're having some sort of revenge! You blame me for what Peter did to you, and now you're making me suffer the same fate! You've taken him back! How could you be so cruel?'

'Don't talk such rubbish, Rosalind!' said Lady Frances roundly. 'You're making a great deal out of nothing at all! Pull yourself together, girl! This is no way to behave.'

'How can I behave any other way? Don't you understand? She's not content with all these admirers of hers. She wants my husband as well!'

Jossie swallowed an angry retort, and spoke as calmly as she could. 'I assure you, you couldn't be more wrong,' she said firmly. 'Peter is yours. All yours.'

'Then why did you have to meet him in secret?'

'He wanted to—' Jossie stopped. How could she tell the girl the truth? 'Peter…Peter was worried about you,' she went on slowly. 'He wanted to give you a surprise. A new dress to cheer you up. And he asked me to recommend you to Madame Rosa. That's all. I was trying to help.' Even to her own ears this sounded rather lame, and, far from being mollified, Rosalind was even more upset.

'So it was you who told him I looked dowdy! I knew he couldn't have thought of it himself! It was you! Talking of your precious Madame Rosa… You must think I am stupid! Peter isn't interested in the way I look any more…he wouldn't think of buying any dresses. No, no! He just wanted to humiliate me. You've taken him away from me. Oh, I'm so unhappy,' she sobbed. 'I want my mama.' She cast herself on Lady Radstock's bosom.

By this time the people gathered near the Radstocks and Trenchards were looking in open curiosity. Several of them were whispering to each other in delight at the juicy scandal developing before their eyes. Miss Helena Calverton, darling of the *ton*, favourite of the tabbies, was being accused of stealing someone else's husband! Delicious!

Lady Frances gazed round frantically. A major catastrophe was rapidly unfolding, and, as far as she could tell, no one was doing anything to prevent it! Rosalind Radstock should have been removed from the scene as soon and as discreetly as possible, but her mother-in-law seemed to be paralysed, helplessly holding on to Rosalind without making the slightest effort to take her away. Sir Thomas was no better. Indifferent to the public at large, he was staring from Jossie to Peter in baffled rage. Neither of them seemed to realise how serious the situation was. Unless someone acted soon there would be a full-blown scandal which would destroy not only Jossie, but everyone else in the sorry tale. Lady Frances's eye met Ivo's in desperate appeal. He came over.

'For Heaven's sake, do something!' she whispered. 'Before we are all ruined!'

Ivo frowned, then nodded and moved to Rosalind Radstock's side. He took her from Lady Radstock and held both her hands. Then, exercising all his considerable charm, he said, 'Mrs Radstock, look at me.' Rosalind sniffed and raised her eyes. Holding her gaze, Ivo went on, 'Lady Frances was right, it is all nonsense. There is absolutely no reason for you to be so distressed. None whatsoever. The tale my brother has been telling you is quite false. It was my brother, wasn't it?'

'Yes,' said Rosalind, gazing up at him helplessly. 'I didn't know before—'

'Of course you didn't! There was really nothing to know.'

Ivo's charm was having its effect. Rosalind was calming down, though she was still unconvinced. 'Mr Trenchard said—'

'Mr Trenchard was mistaken. He saw your husband with Miss Calverton, that is perfectly true. But the rest was…a fantasy. He was wrong.'

'But how do you know?'

'I saw them myself. Miss Calverton is telling you the truth. She was trying to help an old friend, and that is all.'

'How can you be so sure?'

Ivo smiled and gently released her. He stretched out his arm and drew Jossie towards him. 'Because I know Miss Calverton better than anyone. We have no secrets. She tells me everything.' He smiled at Jossie. 'I know we hadn't intended to make it public before the end of the season, my love, but I think it would be better to let our friends know now, don't you agree?'

Jossie stammered, 'I...I...don't—'

'I think we must,' Ivo said firmly. 'You see, Mrs Radstock, Miss Calverton couldn't possibly have designs on your husband, or indeed any other man.' He cast a glance at the people surrounding them, and raised his voice a little. 'Miss Calverton and I are to be married. Quite soon.'

Chapter Fifteen

Shocked faces and critical whispers were all at once replaced with smiles of approval and cries of congratulation. In spite of his philandering ways Ivo was a popular figure, and nothing could have killed the incipient scandal more quickly than this announcement of his. No one questioned it. The world had seen how attentive Lord Trenchard had been to Miss Calverton almost throughout the season. They all nodded their heads in a knowing fashion—however he had tried to disguise his interest in his aunt's ward, they told one another, he had succeeded in deceiving no one. And now it was out! Rosalind Radstock was dismissed as an unimportant troublemaker, and she and the rest of the Radstocks were very quickly forgotten, elbowed out of the way by a crowd of eager well-wishers.

It was not every day that two of society's most prominent members announced their engagement in such a dramatic fashion, and the *ton* was amused, intrigued and, most of them, happy. Lady Balmenny was heard to remark that the girl was, of course, far too young for Lord Trenchard, but was silenced when a friend pointed out that Julia herself was at least twenty years younger than her own husband. Lady Alicia said she pitied poor Miss Calverton with all her heart, tied as she would be to a man whose affections were notoriously fickle. She did not look particularly comforted, however, when someone commented that Lord Trenchard had never before got as far as offering marriage to anyone else—not even to her... But apart from these and a few others, society looked on the match with favour, and was anxious to tell the happy couple so.

For the rest of the evening they were not allowed a single moment alone. It was quite impossible for Jossie to protest or to question Ivo's startling announcement in private, and to do so in public would have fanned the sparks of the threatened scandal into a full-blown fire. So she smiled and nodded, looked modest or flattered, walked about the crowded rooms accepting good wishes and congratulations, and was never once allowed to leave Ivo's side. There was little help to be had from Lady Frances. Whenever Jossie caught sight of her, she too was nodding and smiling, not at all modestly, but with the complacent air of a cat which is in possession of a particularly rich saucerful of cream. Her friends could have been pardoned for believing that she had known about the engagement for weeks.

It was well past midnight before they could all escape, and once in the carriage, Jossie sank back against the squabs and put her face in her hands.

'How could you! Oh, how could you!'

Ivo smiled grimly. 'There was no other way, my dear! Desperate situations need desperate remedies. You were heading for full-scale disaster.'

'He's right, Jossie,' said Lady Frances. 'That girl was bent on committing social suicide and taking you with her. To think I thought her a harmless, well-behaved mouse!'

'But what are we to do now? We're trapped!'

Ivo shook his head and said drily, 'You should moderate these ecstasies of delight at my proposal, Jossie. Who knows? I might get conceited.'

'Ivo! I didn't mean— Oh, you're teasing me! That wasn't really a proposal, you know it wasn't!'

'If it wasn't, it was a remarkably good substitute for one!' Lady Frances observed tartly. 'Half of London heard him. He might have difficulty in crying off, if you choose to hold him to it.'

'I wouldn't dream of doing such a thing! Ivo doesn't really want to marry me!'

Ivo's face was in darkness, and his voice held no expression as he asked, 'What makes you say that?'

'It's obvious! You were indulging in the very pastime I told you to abandon only today. Protecting me as if I was a child. You were right—it was stupid of me to meet Peter in the park. If I had known what would happen I would never have done so. But it was *my* mistake and I should have put it right in my own way! Now we are in a worse pickle than ever, and all because of this stupid conviction of yours that I need protection. Why don't you look after your brother instead? He was the one who stirred it all up, don't forget!'

'I haven't forgotten that. So you think I was merely protecting you? Conscience-stricken, perhaps, at my brother's ill-doing?'

'Yes, I do.'

After a slight pause Ivo said, 'Well, whatever might be my motives in the affair, I'm afraid the end result is the same. We are still committed to marry.'

'Don't be absurd! Of course we aren't!'

'I think we are.' When Jossie drew breath to argue, Ivo said with decision, 'No more, Jossie! I do not propose to argue with you here in this carriage, after a very trying evening. We are neither of us at our best.'

'Don't try to dictate to me!' said Jossie growing more agitated. 'I've told you before, I'm not one of your men! You can't announce to the world at large that I am to marry you without even consulting me first, and then expect me simply to fall in with whatever you decide! How dare you refuse to discuss it!'

Lady Frances said sharply, 'Jossie! Try for a little control. Ivo is right. This is neither the time nor the place for any argument.'

Jossie shut her mouth with a snap and stared out of the window, visibly struggling with her temper. When the carriage came to a halt she waited in silence, then got out and walked swiftly inside. Here she paused until Lady Frances and Ivo joined her. Ivo took one look at her stormy expression and said, 'The library?'

They entered in silence, and waited until the servants had withdrawn before speaking. Ivo stood by the fire, staring into its depths. Lady Frances sat in a chair nearby, frowning slightly as she watched Jossie walking restlessly about the room.

Ivo turned and said calmly, 'Now. You have made yourself painfully clear, Jossie. I'm sorry that the notion of marrying me displeases you so. Would you care to tell me why? Are you perhaps in love with someone else? Is that it?'

Jossie was tired and near to tears. She said angrily, 'Why must you think there has to be someone else? There isn't. But the sort of marriage you propose would be a disaster! You know it would! I won't marry you out of gratitude, Ivo. I have no desire to be eternally grateful, not even to you, and you would soon get bored with the role of benefactor, once you had to play it day in day out.' Lady Frances looked as if she was about to protest, but Ivo silenced her with a quick shake of the head.

Jossie went on, 'Besides, I'm not really a creature of society. I've enjoyed this season in London, and I'm grateful for what you and Lady Frances have done to make it such a success, but I'm still a country girl at heart. I don't quite know what I am to do in the future, but of one thing I am quite certain. How could we possibly be happy if you were saddled with a wife who dislikes all the things you most enjoy?'

Ivo's face was stern as he said, 'The outlook is bleak indeed. But it's a worse one for both of us if we now go back on our word. I refuse to be laughed at as a fool or condemned as a knave. Do *you* wish to be known as a jilt?' He held her by the shoulders and made her face him. 'Jossie, Society would never forgive you if you cried off now after tonight.'

Jossie's control broke. 'There must be a way out of this!' she cried in despair. 'There must! I can't marry you, Ivo! I won't!'

She tore herself free from him and ran out of the room. Lady Frances shook her head. 'Shall I try to talk to her?'

'No, Aunt Frances. Leave it,' said Ivo bitterly. 'She has made her position very clear. What the devil I am to do about it, I don't know. Is there any way of extricating ourselves gracefully from this tangle?'

Lady Frances raised her eyebrows at her nephew. 'Giving in without more of a fight, Ivo? That's not like you.'

Ivo regarded her morosely. 'It's a devil of a situation!'

he said. 'I can't really blame Jossie. She has never seen me as a possible husband. When we first met she was blinded by her infatuation with Peter Radstock, and since then I have been a sort of father figure, her rescuer and teacher. It's not surprising she can't imagine any other kind of relationship with me.'

'I refuse to believe that one of London's most notoriously attractive men couldn't persuade her to change her mind! She isn't made of stone.' Lady Frances waited a moment, then said briskly, 'This defeatism is not like you, Ivo! Pull yourself together! Falling in love for the first time in your life is no excuse for becoming a marshmallow!'

She laughed at Ivo's look of outrage, and said, 'That's more like it! You'll do!' She got up and went to the door. Here she paused and said, 'I'm very fond of you both, and, what is more, I think you are ideally suited. I'd like nothing more than to see you married. Don't let too many scruples get in the way. If necessary, remind her of what she owes you, and hold her to the engagement. You could always teach her afterwards to love you.' When Ivo shook his head she said, 'Gratitude isn't such a bad basis for marriage.'

'In this case it would be the very worst!' When she looked at him in surprise, he shrugged his shoulders and said, 'I suppose you think me absurd. But...do you remember Jossie as she was when I first met her? A free, confident, independent spirit? That's the girl I fell in love with, Aunt Frances. I don't believe in gratitude as a reason for marriage any more than Jossie does. I want Jossie to come to me of her own free will, and *only* because she loves me. After tonight I am afraid, really afraid, that that will never happen.'

* * *

The next morning Ivo decided to deal with Peregrine before seeing his father. He went over early to Perry's lodging, where he was told that his brother was not at home. With a grim smile he swept the manservant aside and strode in. Peregrine had been breakfasting, but when he saw Ivo he got up and stood behind his chair, as if seeking refuge.

'G-good morning, b-brother,' he said.

Ivo ignored this greeting. He stood frowning, pulling his riding crop through his fingers. 'Are you going to face me like a man, *brother*?' he said unpleasantly. 'Or shall I give you the thrashing you deserve?'

'No! N-Neither! I'm sorry, Ivo, I truly am! If I had known that Rosalind Radstock would make such a scene, I would never have told her a thing!'

'Don't lie to me, Perry. Face the truth for once. You're a cowardly liar.'

'I'm not! I'm not!'

'What else would you call a man who not only tried to destroy a marriage, but damned near ruined a girl who had never done him the slightest harm?'

'I didn't realise...I never intended to *ruin* anyone.' Peregrine tried to hold his brother's eye, but after a moment he said sulkily, 'I only wanted to stir up some trouble.'

Ivo regarded him in silence. 'Why?'

'I wanted to hurt *you*! You've always had everything! Everything! Charlotte Gurney laughed at me when I wanted to marry her. She wouldn't even consider it— I'm the younger son, I have nothing! You'll get the lot. And as if that wasn't enough, here in London you're the hero, Wellington's man, the favourite of all the ladies. And as for Father—' Peregrine broke off and went to the window. 'And to crown it all you were in love with

Helena Calverton, the jewel in Society's crown, the perfect bride. You had *everything*, Ivo. I wanted you to hurt, and the best way was through that girl. I tried telling you about her liaison with Radstock, but you wouldn't believe me. So I had to show you in front of the world, and Radstock's wife was the perfect weapon. I wanted you to hurt.'

Ivo cursed. He kicked the chair away and, taking hold of Peregrine's collar, pulled his brother roughly to him. His fingers round Peregrine's throat, he said softly, 'So just to hurt me you came close to ruining Jossie. And you may well have wrecked Rosalind Radstock's happiness as well. What sort of worm are you?'

'I know, I know,' Peregrine gasped, staring wildly into Ivo's menacing face. 'I...I swear that you can't say anything to me that I haven't already thought myself. When I saw how unhappy that girl was...Rosalind Radstock, I mean...I hated myself for what I had done...' He tried to pull Ivo's fingers from his throat. 'You're...you're choking me!' Ivo released him contemptuously and Perry staggered over to the window and stood there, drawing in gulps of air. After a moment he went on, 'It didn't even work. They all forgot the Radstocks when you told them you and the Calverton girl were engaged. I hadn't expected that.'

Ivo stood considering, his crop in his hands. The desire to make Perry even sorrier for his part in last night's excitement was still there. It was, after all, what he had come to do. But though it might satisfy his own feelings, it would hardly improve relations with his younger brother. He could feel his anger draining away, being replaced with the old feelings of pity and guilt.

'The Radstocks will manage. They're used to picking up Peter's pieces,' he said more calmly. 'But as for you—you'll leave London before the end of the week and you won't be back. Not while I'm here.'

'That's easy enough. I don't even like it in London. I'm happier in Derbyshire. The people there like me, they treat me as if I *am* someone.'

'Then stay there! Father says you're doing well at Arneston—he was talking of giving it to you.'

Perry's face lit up. 'Give Arneston to me? He would do that?'

'But he won't, if he hears of this latest affair.'

The change in Perry's expression was alarming. His face clouded over and he snarled, 'And that's what you'd like, isn't it? I suppose you're going to tell him!'

Ivo sighed. The charming, gentle little boy he had known years ago had vanished. Peregrine neither loved nor trusted the rest of his family. There could be no cure for his unreasonable fear of his father, nor for his childish resentment of his elder brother. And in spite of his quiet manner, he could be astonishingly ruthless when he considered he was being badly treated. The best thing for all of them would be for Peregrine to make his own life in the North, away from what he saw as a hostile world. He said wearily, 'No, I won't do that. You must leave here and make a proper life for yourself at Arneston, Perry. Go as soon as possible. I don't want to see you in London after next week.'

Peregrine looked at him suspiciously, then nodded and said with apparent humility, 'You will allow me to take my leave of Father before I go? I promise not to stay long. And I should like to make my apologies to Miss Calverton, too. Is that permitted?'

Ivo was not altogether happy at Perry's way of ex-

Lord Trenchard's Choice

pressing himself, but the request was reasonable enough. 'Of course,' he said coolly. 'You can certainly have time for that.'

It was still early when Ivo got back to Charles Street, but his father was waiting for him in the library.

'What's this I hear?' he demanded as soon as Ivo came in.

'Sir?'

'This engagement business. Is it true? Why didn't I hear of it from you?'

'How *did* you hear?'

'Never you mind. What does it all mean?'

'I've asked Jossie to marry me.'

'Good! Splendid! This is the best news I've had since you came back from Waterloo. Fetch her, fetch her, my boy!'

'Er…there's a problem. A big one.'

'Nothing that can't be overcome, I'm quite sure. She's a good girl, we're all very fond of her. And it can't be about money—you've both got more than you would ever need. So what is it? Sit down and tell me about it.'

'What have you heard about this engagement?'

'Not much. Just that it's all over the town that Ivo Trenchard has got himself engaged at last. I was hoping you would tell me more—when you got round to it, that is. What's wrong?'

'Jossie is at present refusing to carry it through.'

'Carry it through…? What d'y mean? Either you're engaged or not, there's no halfway. Is the girl mad?'

'Let me tell you what happened.' Ivo then gave his father an account of the events of the night before, leaving out only the malice behind Perry's actions.

'So… Let me just make sure—you *are* engaged? Jossie didn't deny it in public, or anything like that?'

'No. I think she was too dazed.'

'Well, then! All you have to do is to make her stick to it.'

'I thought you knew Jossie?'

'I do. And I know you.'

'I don't know why the rest of the world is so sure I can manage Jossie Morley,' said Ivo irritably. 'I'm damned uncertain myself!'

'That's not such a bad thing,' said his father, sounding pleased. 'You're usually too cocksure for your own good.'

Ivo had decided that he had had enough of his family for the time being and was on the point of taking his leave when his aunt and Jossie came into the library. They looked as if they were about to go out.

'What's this, what's this?' demanded Lord Veryan. 'No time to spare for your future father-in-law? Come here, girl!'

'I...I...' Jossie threw an anguished glance at Ivo, then said, 'Hasn't anyone told you the truth?'

'Ivo said something about it not being perfectly decided, but I took no notice. You'll marry him, of course you will. You wouldn't disappoint an old man, would you?' When Jossie looked as if she might, he went on, 'Besides, you can't cry off. You can't want to make my son look a fool!'

Jossie looked desperately at Ivo. 'I hadn't realised what it meant...but—'

Ivo came over to her and took her hands in his. 'Don't listen to him, Jossie. You mustn't do anything you don't wish. If you could bear to leave things as they are for the moment, I am sure we can find a solution to this mess before very long. But don't look so unhappy. That's the last thing I want.' He kissed one of her hands before he let it go. Then he went on in a cheerful voice, 'Where were you ladies going? Can I escort you some of the way?'

'We've decided to call on Lady Radstock, to enquire after Rosalind. And to make sure that all misunderstandings are at an end,' said Lady Frances.

'That's an excellent idea!' Ivo said. 'And it would be an even better one if I came with you! Do you agree, Jossie?'

They all waited. If Jossie agreed to Ivo's company on a visit to the Radstocks, it meant she was willing to let the engagement stand, too. When she nodded Lord Veryan and Lady Frances breathed a sigh of relief. But Ivo sounded quite matter of fact as he said, 'Good! Shall we go?' He ushered the ladies out, then, struck by a sudden thought, he excused himself and returned to the library. 'I forgot to tell you, Father. Perry has decided to go back to Derbyshire. He wishes to visit this afternoon to take his leave of you. Is it convenient? I said it would be.'

'Yes, yes! I shan't know what to say, mind you. I never do!'

'Why don't you let him know how much you approve of his management of Arneston? You might even tell him what you said to me—that it could soon be his.'

His father shot him a sharp glance. 'Still promoting Perry's interests, Ivo? I should have thought you were tired of that.'

'I promise you, I don't intend to do much more of it. But I'd be easier in my mind if Perry was happily settled in Derbyshire. Dammit, he ought to have *something*, Father!'

'Very well, very well. Leave it now. Don't keep the ladies waiting.'

* * *

Lady Radstock received them with a certain air of constraint, but thawed slowly when she realised they had come merely to enquire after her daughter-in-law's health.

'She and Peter are out, I'm afraid, but Rosalind is much better, thank you. I am sure she regrets…she is sorry—'

'Please!' said Jossie. 'Please, Lady Radstock! Rosalind may have been mistaken about my motives, but I was very thoughtless. I should never have agreed to see Peter privately. I should have realised how it might look to someone who…who—'

Ivo finished for her. 'Someone who was not fully aware of the situation between Jossie and myself,' he said smoothly.

'But I still don't perfectly understand why you had to meet Peter in such a clandestine way, Jossie. Though I cannot condone her behaviour, I can see that it was quite natural for Rosalind to come to the wrong conclusion, especially in her present state. What did you think you were doing?'

Jossie gave a wry smile. 'Trying to help an old friend.'

'Peter? How could he ask such a thing of you after—?' She stopped. Then she went on, 'But why does Peter need your help?'

Lady Frances said briskly, 'Perhaps you should ask Peter that. I am sure he would tell you if you asked him. You were always in his confidence, Eleanor. And, as Jossie said last night, their meetings were unwise, but perfectly innocent. To be frank, I really think she ought not to concern herself with the matter any further. Peter and she may have been friends in the past, but no one could suggest that he has any claim on her time now. Talk to Peter yourself, my dear!'

'Of course! Though it may no longer be necessary—today's news has made us all very happy.'

Sir Thomas came into the room at this point and heard these last words. 'So you've told them?' he said, rubbing his hands together.

'Not yet, my dear. Our guests came to enquire after Rosalind, but I haven't yet given them our news.'

'She's much better,' said Sir Thomas. 'And I'd be obliged if you'd put the fuss last night out of your minds. Least said, soonest mended. She's a sweet little thing—I'm sure she didn't mean any of it. All explained today, of course.'

Jossie stared at this sudden change of attitude, but the reason was made clear in his next words.

'My daughter-in-law is in an interesting condition,' said Sir Thomas proudly. 'I believe that's what you call it in polite society. She's breeding!' He listened complacently as Lady Frances and Jossie exclaimed, and went on, 'I hope it's a boy, of course. But even if it's a girl she'll be welcome. And brought up as a girl! Eh, Jossie?'

'It would be better, certainly,' said Jossie with a slightly bitter smile.

'Aye. Rosalind'll make a fine mother,' said Sir Thomas proudly. 'I'll get the Dower House sorted out for them as soon as we get back to Somerset. If they're starting a family they'll need a place of their own.' He chuckled. 'To think that I'll be a grandfather!' Then, as he beamed at them, he said suddenly, 'But I'm forgetting! We haven't had a chance to congratulate you on your own good news, Trenchard. You've got as fine a lass in our Jossie as you'll find anywhere. There was a time when…' He looked a touch wistfully at Jossie, then shook his head and carried on, 'But Rosalind's a good lass, a good lass. A grandfather, eh?' He chuckled again, obviously in high good humour, coming over to shake Ivo's hand. 'You make sure you take good care of Jossie,' he said. 'She deserves the best.'

Ivo took Jossie's hand. He said, 'Jossie will be as happy as I can make her, Sir Thomas. But...' he went on, looking at his aunt, 'I am sure we ought not to take up any more of Lady Radstock's time. She must have a great deal to see to.'

'We'll all be busy! We're off to Brighton in a day or two,' said Sir Thomas. 'I want to make sure Rosalind has plenty of good, fresh, sea air. Exercise, that's the thing!'

'And rest, and amusement,' said Lady Radstock gently.

'What? Oh, yes! Rest. Amusement. Of course, of course! What a girl, eh?'

Lady Frances rose and took her friend by the hand. 'I am so very glad to hear your news. And I'm sure that Brighton will work wonders for Rosalind.'

All three of them took their leave and left the Radstocks to their rejoicing.

As they were walking home, Lady Frances said, 'Well, Peter's problems seem to be sorting themselves out without anyone else's intervention. Except perhaps the difficulty with your stepmother...'

Jossie nodded. 'But he will be much happier now that his wife is accepted fully by his father. Rosalind has done the one thing which was certain to win Sir Thomas's approval.'

Ivo had been listening with growing incredulity to this conversation. 'Do you mean to say that Peter Radstock risked your reputation and his own wife's happiness, in order to ask your advice on his own, trivial, domestic problems? Family tiffs? I thought he must be desperate—I even wondered whether he wanted to declare that his love for you had returned, to ask you to run away with him!'

'I would never have listened to him if that had been the case. You know that, Ivo!'

He regarded her with a smile. 'I should have remembered. Beautiful, rich, witty...and straight as a die. But a jealous man isn't always reasonable.'

Jossie gave a sniff of disbelief. 'Jealous! You! Don't talk rubbish!'

Peregrine paid his visit, and took leave of his father. Lord Veryan, who was not always the most tactful of men, mentioned Arneston and told Perry that Ivo had interceded on his behalf.

'I'm sure my brother is very good,' said Perry coldly. 'I was not aware it was his to dispose of.'

'Of course it isn't, you ungrateful cub! But it would have been his one day! D'you want it or not, Peregrine?'

'Thank you, sir. I accept it with pleasure. It's a beautiful estate.'

'Never liked it very much,' said Lord Veryan. 'Glad to get rid of it. I'll speak to the lawyers. Have a safe journey.'

Seething with resentment Perry next looked for his aunt, or Ivo. On being informed that they were both out, and not expected back for another hour, he sought for and found Jossie sitting by herself in the little parlour.

'You seem pensive, Miss Calverton,' he said after they had exchanged greetings. 'Or is it that I have put myself beyond the pale?'

Jossie gave him a straight look. 'You have certainly caused me some distress, sir, with your over-zealous tongue.'

'I am truly, deeply sorry, ma'am. I never wished to harm or distress anyone. I merely mentioned Madame Rosa to Mrs Radstock and she wormed the rest out of me. I thought it harmless enough, believe me! I had no idea that she would react so violently, otherwise I would have been more discreet. However, I did call on Mrs Radstock this morning, and was pleased to hear that she had suffered no serious effects. I...er...I understand there is a very happy explanation for her nervous state.'

'Yes.' Jossie found herself disarmed by Perry's gentle voice and the frank contrition in his eyes. 'I suppose she did misunderstand you?'

'I assure you that she did! But mine was the fault. Were you very distressed? Surely it proved to be a happy occasion for you?'

'Why?'

'Your engagement.'

'Oh, no! Lord Trenchard ought never to have made such an announcement. An engagement is by no means planned. To tell the truth, I am in something of a quandary!'

'Why is that?'

Disarmed again by his sympathetic look, Jossie explained. 'Lord Trenchard has been a true friend and guide during the past year. He and my godmother have done so much for me! And now he has committed us to each other in front of the better part of Society—merely to save my good name! He would never otherwise think of marrying someone like myself. You know what his taste in women is like, I am sure. Not anyone like me!'

'And you are averse to the thought of marrying him?'

'In the present circumstances, yes!'

'Yet I think you love my brother, Miss Calverton?'

Jossie said after a pause, 'I cannot imagine a worse
fate than to be married to someone you love, but who
feels only friendly toleration in return. Lord Trenchard
needs a more sophisticated wife than I could ever be.
However acceptable it may be in Society, I...I know that
I could never look with complaisance at my husband's
casual amours.'

Peregrine shook his head sadly. 'His reputation would
hardly suggest that he would be faithful for long.' He
paused, then added, 'And I cannot offer much hope of
a change. He has been like this ever since I have been
old enough to notice. In fact...'

He paused and put his hand to his eyes. Jossie asked
anxiously, 'What is it, Mr Trenchard?'

He sighed and shook his head. 'It is an unhappy story,
Miss Calverton, and one I should rather forget,' he said
gravely. 'I'm afraid it does no credit to the man you say
you love.'

'You may have gathered that I am not altogether unaware of his faults, Mr Trenchard. I think you could tell
me.'

He continued to shake his head. 'There are others,
beside myself, who are involved.'

'I see. I suppose in that case I must not press you...'

'And yet...I think I will confide in you. I can be sure
of your discretion, I know.'

'Of course!'

'You see, Ivo took from me the one woman I ever
loved. Took her, and then rejected her.' He looked sor-
rowfully at Jossie. 'She was the daughter of my father's
best friend.'

'But what happened?'

'Charlotte and I were happy until Ivo came home on leave. He can be very charming, Miss Calverton, and before long Charlotte made the mistake of falling in love with him. I do not believe he was ever in love with her. When he and Charlotte were caught, *in flagrante*, in an isolated cottage on the estate, the two fathers demanded that Ivo should marry her. He refused. He and my father were estranged for over a year because of it. But of course Father eventually forgave him—he always did.'

'What happened to the girl?'

'She was in despair, naturally. She was too ashamed even to see me, though I assure you, Miss Calverton, I would have been proud to make her my wife. In the end she was taken away to Bath, and forced to marry a man old enough to be her father! I hear of her now and then. In fact, her father is at present lodged near me. I do not believe Charlotte is happy.'

Jossie was shocked, but protested, 'Mr Trenchard! That is a dreadful story! I can't believe it! I have always found your brother to be an honourable man!'

'He is! In all matters, except in his attitude to women.' He got up. 'I can understand how difficult it is for you to believe me. But would Sir George Gurney's word be enough to convince you?'

Jossie was perplexed. Peregrine had sounded sincere, but she found it quite impossible to believe his story. Ivo had his faults, but she had never heard him accused of the seduction of innocent girls. 'If it would not offend you, I should like to hear what Charlotte's father has to say. Would he talk to me?'

'I'm sure he would, if it meant that his daughter's fate was not repeated by someone else.'

'That is most unlikely as far as I am concerned, but I cannot leave it like this, nevertheless...'

'Will you be at Carlton House this evening? Sir George is certain to be there. I could arrange for you to meet him.'

'Thank you. I shall be there.'

'I shall not see you again after that, Miss Calverton. I am leaving London tomorrow.'

'So soon?'

'I am being sent off to Derbyshire. Ivo is uncomfortable in my presence. And who can blame him? Make my excuses to him if you would. I thought he would be here, but I do not feel like waiting to see him till he chooses to come.'

He collected his hat and cane and went out. Once beyond the corner, however, his demeanour changed. Drooping shoulders straightened, a lagging gait smartened up, and his expression of sorrow bravely borne changed into a complacent grin. Helena Calverton was a fool! She obviously had no idea how deeply his brother was in love with her. Peregrine himself had found it hard to believe at first, but it was certainly so. After years of philandering, Ivo was truly, seriously in love! Perry laughed. It had been a stroke of genius to think of old Gurney. Charlotte's father was still convinced it had been Ivo who had seduced his daughter. And once he had said his piece tonight Miss Calverton would be equally certain. After tonight brother Ivo was not going to find it at all easy to win the girl he loved! He might even fail altogether.

After Peregrine's departure Jossie was left a prey to conflicting doubts. She simply could not believe that Ivo had behaved as badly as Peregrine had claimed, and sincerely hoped that what Sir George said would present it in a better light. There must be some other explanation, there must be!

However, there was no evidence to the contrary in the few facts she had of Ivo's past history. She knew of his long quarrel with his father, had heard the name Charlotte Gurney in connection with it, remembered vaguely that he had been reconciled with his father after it became known that Charlotte Gurney had married in Bath... But it still seemed impossible!

Ivo's reputation was far less in dispute—almost the first thing she had heard about him was that he was the worst flirt in Europe. His attitude to her sex in general was very cynical. How many times had she heard his comments on the women he had known in Brussels and London? She had always assumed they deserved what he said of them, but how could she be sure?

On the other hand, Ivo had always been the soul of honour in his behaviour towards her—but then, as she had said, she was not really Ivo's usual taste in females. He had never flirted with her, nor had he ever regarded her as a possible wife before the previous night. His proposal had merely been an absurd extension of his curious determination to protect her, which had started after Peter's coming of age, and had now become a habit.

The change was in *her*. She had come a long way from the girl she had been then. What she now needed from any man who was to be her husband was not the milk-warm affection of a father figure, but the passion of a lover, the satisfaction of her deepest needs as a woman, a lifetime commitment from someone who would be the other half of herself...

She sighed. She had no desire to be tied to a philandering cynic, a charmer who might well be fond of her, but would betray her without a second thought once the honeymoon was over. No, whatever Sir George might tell her, she *could* not, she *would* not marry Ivo Trenchard!

Chapter Sixteen

Tormented by these and similar thoughts, Jossie found it increasingly hard to stay calm that night, to keep her smile serene and to make the right responses. Everywhere she and Ivo went their friends and acquaintances asked the date of her wedding, what she would wear, where she and Ivo would live after they were married, and a thousand other questions, all equally impossible to answer. Ivo himself was so charmingly attentive to her, so carefully *considerate*, that she felt she might scream. Even Lady Frances, usually a staunch supporter, was talking about their forthcoming marriage as an accepted fact—in private as well as in public. Jossie felt she was being slowly shepherded into a position from which she would find it impossible to escape, borne inexorably to the altar on the back of public opinion.

At Carlton House she was the object of the tabbies' constant interest, an interest which became avid every time Ivo spoke to, or even looked at, any of his former amours. He was as charming as ever to them, though, as was now usual, Jossie was often at his side. Unfortunately several of them made it very obvious, to Jossie at least, that they thought it only a matter of time before

Ivo would be back in their arms. The Prince Regent himself commented on their engagement and jokingly advised them not to make it a long one. 'Don't let him escape, Miss Calverton!' he said with a laugh. 'We all know what he is!'

During the supper interval she saw Peregrine beckoning to her. She slipped across the crowded room. Ivo had gone to collect refreshments, Lady Frances was with a friend—she would be back before either of them returned. Outside on the terrace Peregrine introduced her to Sir George, then bowed and tactfully withdrew. Jossie was at a loss. How on earth could she begin?

But, ignoring her embarrassment, Sir George said abruptly, 'That Trenchard fellow wants me to tell you about my daughter. Is that right?'

Jossie nodded. 'If you think you can, Sir George.'

'Shouldn't be here if I didn't. I don't like any of the Trenchards, and I certainly wouldn't do any favours to them! But it's only right *you* should know. I've seen you with him—the older one, I mean. The soldier. They say you're engaged. Is that right?'

Jossie said uncomfortably, 'I…we are at present, yes.'

'My advice is not to have anything to do with him. Seduced m'daughter, and then the damned fellow wouldn't do the right thing by her. Refused absolutely. I fell out with the lot of 'em over it. Veryan was m'best friend, too. Not now.'

Jossie's heart sank. So it was true. Sir George looked round. 'Is that all? I'd as soon not hang about here. Don't like talking about it much.'

She made a considerable effort and thanked him. 'Your daughter—is she happier now?' she asked hesitantly.

'Good Lord, yes. In Paris at the moment. Havin' the

time of her life. Respectably married. Luckier than she deserves. I suppose you're askin' yourself why I didn't pursue the matter with Trenchard? I wanted to preserve Charlotte's good name, d'y see, and it worked. Only Veryan and his sons know what happened in that cottage at Sudiham—and now you. No one else. The world has no idea, and it must never learn. I know I can count on you.'

Jossie nodded, curtsied and took her leave. She got back to her seat just in time, but after a short while she could bear no more of the laughter and chatter. She pleaded a nervous headache and they left Carlton House early. By the time they got back to Charles Street her headache was real, but she was determined to have no more to do with any engagement.

Ivo had been aware all evening of her growing tension. He would normally have done his best to calm her down, try to make her laugh at some of the absurd things people had said, but on this evening he was himself equally angry and disappointed. Jossie seemed to be slipping further away from him with every day that passed. Ever since their engagement, she had been on her guard against him, and the thought was surprisingly hurtful. The trusting directness which had so enchanted him had vanished, the real Jossie becoming more and more elusive. Yet he knew that the real Jossie was the girl he must find again if he was ever to persuade her to love him as he wanted. As the days passed it seemed less and less likely that he would ever succeed. Tonight, for no reason that he could see, Jossie had appeared to be more determined than ever to keep him at a distance.

When they got back to Charles Street, Jossie turned to face Ivo. 'I'd like to talk to you in the library for a moment.'

Lady Frances looked at her stormy face. 'Sleep on it, Jossie. I don't know what you want to say, but I'm sure it's better said after a night's consideration.'

'It can't wait. I need to speak to Ivo. I...I can't go on like this!'

Lady Frances looked from one to the other, then shrugged her shoulders. 'Very well. I'll be in my room if you want someone to pick up the pieces. Good night.'

Ivo saw her to the stairs, then returned to the library. Jossie was facing him. She said abruptly, 'Ivo, this has to stop. I have no intention of marrying you, and I hate the deception. It's time I went back to Somerset.'

Ivo was silent for a moment. Then, in a harsh voice quite unlike his normal deep drawl, he asked, 'And where do you propose to stay? With your father? I doubt his wife would agree. Or do you wish to take my aunt with you, away from all her friends? Aren't you being just a touch ungrateful? Or are you too selfish to see how much she's enjoying herself?'

Strangely enough, Jossie had been too preoccupied with her début to give any real thought to what she would do when the season ended. This was a rude awakening. What *would* she do? To go back to her father was out of the question. Lady Frances, Lord Veryan and...and yes, Ivo himself, had become her family during the past year. There was no one else. Suddenly there was a frightening hole in front of her. If she left London now, where could she possibly go? If Lady Frances grew tired of her, where would she live in future? She stared at Ivo, unable to think of a reply.

He went on with an unpleasant grin, 'Perhaps you could join your friends, the Radstocks, in Brighton? I daresay Peter has one or two other problems you could sort out for him. Is that what you want? To end your days as a kind of spinster companion to a spineless dolt?'

Jossie went white. 'Ivo!' she said sharply. 'Don't talk like that! Why are you saying such things? You are not usually cruel!'

'Aren't I?' Ivo's temper was getting the better of him. 'You surprise me! I thought there must be something truly awful about me! You've nowhere of your own to live, you're not apparently in love with anyone else, yet you wouldn't consider marriage to me, dear me, no! You can't even bear to stay engaged to me, not even for a few short weeks. Not even to save both our faces—' He broke off and turned to face the fire. After a moment he turned back to her. 'What have I ever done to make you dislike me so? Announced our engagement without consulting you? Is that it?'

'N-not exactly, but…'

'I can't think what else it might be! God knows, it's not as if I had claimed any of the privileges of an engaged man!'

'W-What do you mean?'

'What happened to the trust you had in me, Jossie? Do you remember how you *asked* me to teach you how to kiss? Why is it different now? Why do you stiffen every time I come near you? Do you think I haven't noticed? You're good, you're very good! You hide it well. I doubt the eyes of the curious see anything wrong. But I do! I *feel* you flinch if I pull you too close, feel your hand pull against mine if I hold it too long. Why is that? I thought we were friends as well as—' He broke off again. After a moment he asked abruptly, 'Did I frighten you the last time I kissed you? Is that it?'

'No! Yes. I don't know!'

He came across and put his arms around her. 'You

used to like my kisses, Jossie,' he said. His voice was soft, but the dark blue eyes were determined.

'Yes. Yes, I did. But please, don't do this, Ivo! Please!'

'Why not? Don't I deserve a little kindness?' His face was near her face, his lips almost touching hers.

His nearness was undermining her resolve. Thought of Charlotte Gurney faded into the background, banished by the familiar stream of excitement running through her veins, the remembered desire to be closer which only Ivo could evoke... It would be so easy to forget, she thought. To give in, just for a short while...just once.

'Jossie?' His voice was tender now and deeper than ever.

With a sob she put her arms round his neck. His eyes darkened, then he groaned and pulled her tight against him. For a moment they were still, gazing into each other's eyes. Then he murmured her name again and bent to kiss her.

Fireworks at Vauxhall, scintillating flashes of light from the crystal chandelier at Carlton House, the flames of a thousand candles...an explosion of light and power... The two figures in the library were lost in a dazzling, intoxicating swirl of feeling, never before experienced by either. The kiss this time was no lesson, no pretence, offered little comfort and certainly no safety. It was harsh, primitive, wild, quite simply a man demanding and receiving a passionate response from the woman of his choice.

They were both completely transported, and when the kiss finally came to an end they stared at each other in bewilderment and shock.

'Jossie!'

For a moment Jossie clung to Ivo as she slowly came back to earth. She would have fallen otherwise.

Ivo rocked her in his arms. 'Oh God, Jossie! Oh, my love! My life!'

Jossie swallowed. Shame was beginning to overwhelm her. How could she have been so abandoned? Ivo could have taken whatever he wanted from her during those wild moments, and she would have done nothing to stop him. Even now he was covering her face with little kisses, caressing her throat with trembling fingers, pulling her to him again... Oh heavens, the temptation was so great, but she must resist this madness, it mustn't go any further! She forced herself to be calm, to use her mind to quell her unruly emotions. Whatever he might say in the heat of the moment, Ivo was not in love with her. This was the great lover at work, the worst flirt in Europe... Remember that, Jossie! His touch was expert, but then it would have to be. He would never change, that's what Peregrine had said. Was this how Ivo delighted his other women? How he had delighted Charlotte Gurney? Was he now using his expertise to seduce *her* into doing as he wanted?

'No!' she cried, pushing him violently away from her. 'No, I will not be used!'

Ivo was suddenly still. He stood for a moment then said quietly, 'Used? How "used"? I thought we were unbelievably close, Jossie, but I don't understand you. What do you mean?'

Jossie was sobbing as she cried, 'I won't let you persuade me to marry you. You don't love me, you just want a complaisant wife, someone who is grateful enough to put up with your ways!'

Ivo laughed in relief. 'Jossie, my darling, my only

love, this is arrant rubbish! You are not yourself, you can't mean this!'

'Oh, yes, I can! I've seen you at work, I've heard what you say. You expect women to be as faithless as you are yourself! Marriage doesn't mean anything to you. You have no respect for women, married or single. I know about Charlotte Gurney, too!'

All laughter vanished from Ivo's face. 'Charlotte Gurney?' he exclaimed sharply. 'What do you know of Charlotte Gurney? Who told you about Charlotte Gurney?'

'Peregrine told me all about it! How you were caught with her and refused to marry her.'

'Peregrine!' The loathing in Ivo's voice appalled her. 'You'd listen to *him*?'

'It wasn't only your brother. Charlotte's father said so, too! Oh, Ivo, that poor girl! How could you?'

'I didn't seduce Charlotte Gurney, Jossie,' he said, his face white, his voice devoid of expression.

'I want to believe you, but how can I? Perry says you did, Sir George says you did! You and your father quarrelled when you refused to marry her. Isn't that so?'

Ivo looked as if he had just received a body blow. He turned away and put his hand on the mantelpiece. 'And I thought we were close…' he murmured. 'I thought you knew me, trusted me…' After a moment he turned to face her again. 'You seem very sure of my guilt,' he said coldly.

Jossie was trembling with distress. 'I don't wish to believe it, Ivo! Help me! Explain it!'

Ivo considered her in silence. 'No,' he said at last. 'I don't think I want to. How strange that that episode has twice ruined a relationship I thought important…' He gave her a smile as remote and as cold as the Arctic.

'I'm sorry, my dear. You'll have to ask Peregrine if you want to know any more. Meanwhile, you may safely stay in London as long as you wish. I shan't be asking you to pretend anything any further. Tell my aunt that I have moved out of Charles Street. I shall stay at my club for the present. I leave you to say what you like about our engagement.' He bowed and went swiftly out of the room.

Jossie sank to the floor and sobbed. She felt as if her heart had been torn from her body, had left with Ivo. The pain was intense. When a hand touched her shoulder she looked up wildly, thinking that he had come back, willing to talk, willing to explain. She would have thrown herself on him, begged to be forgiven for doubting him. But the hand wasn't Ivo's.

'My dear!' said Lady Frances. 'Jossie! Don't! You'll tear yourself apart! What has happened? What has Ivo done?'

Jossie could only shake her head at first, but then as the fit of sobbing abated she managed to say, 'He h-hasn't done any…anything. H-he's gone aw-away.'

'But why? What happened?'

'I s-said I c-couldn't m-marry him. Or b-be eng-engaged to h-him any…any m-more. He…he's so angry.' She lapsed into silence, as tears rolled down her cheeks.

Lady Frances looked grave. 'I rather thought that was what you wanted to tell him,' she said. 'It's not surprising he's angry. I wish you had waited as I suggested, Jossie. You were neither of you in form tonight. Tomorrow you might have been able to discuss the situation more calmly.'

Jossie said wearily, 'It wouldn't have made any difference. I won't marry him!'

'That is your decision, of course. But tell me why you are so set against the idea.'

Jossie shook her head. Badly though she wanted to confide in her godmother, she could not tell her of the business with Charlotte Gurney. That secret was not hers to tell. In any case, there was another, greater bar to marrying Ivo.

'He doesn't really love me,' she said. 'Not the way I want.'

Lady Frances shook her head. 'Well. I don't know what you want, Jossie, but I would have said that Ivo loves you as deeply, as seriously as any man could.'

'That's not so! He still thinks of me as a child, someone to protect! You've seen the way he acts.'

'Of course he wishes to protect you! It's what a man, a real man, regards as his first responsibility towards the woman he loves! But that's just the beginning.' Lady Frances leaned forward and said with great seriousness, 'I've known Ivo a long time and I have never seen him in love like this before. He loves you now in every way there is, my dear. Every way. You may take my word on that.'

Jossie gazed at Lady Frances as if she could somehow find an answer in her godmother's face. 'Why haven't you said anything before? I didn't know...' Her voice grew stronger. 'In fact, I still don't believe... He has never given the slightest indication...at least—' She stopped and coloured painfully as the memory of Ivo's last kiss returned. 'Why did you never say anything?' she whispered.

'He forbade me to.'

'But *why*?'

'Try to understand, Jossie! For years Ivo has skimmed over the surface of life, seeking and taking pleasure wherever he found it. It wasn't at all difficult. He is handsome, rich, immensely charming... Women have pursued him ever since he entered society. It was perfectly understandable that he should become somewhat blasé in his attitude towards them. He has never before felt uncertain, or inadequate, or cautious—he has never had to.' She paused, then went on, 'Then, when he is almost thirty he finds himself attracted to a naïve seventeen-year-old, as far removed from his usual world as she could possibly be. Of course he fought it! Of course he refused to acknowledge it, even to himself! And then, when he realised it was not going to go away, he was afraid. He had rescued you, given you your success— what if you married him out of a feeling of obligation? What he wanted was your love.' She smiled ironically. 'Ivo doesn't want your gratitude, my love, any more than you want to give it!'

Jossie put her face in her hands. 'Oh, my God! What have I done?' A great sob escaped her. 'What have I done?'

'What *have* you done?'

'I...I can't tell you. But I've lost Ivo forever.' Jossie was rocking herself to and fro in growing distress. Seriously worried, Lady Frances abandoned any further talk and rang for one of the servants. In a short time Jossie was in her bed, sipping a warm drink into which her godmother had put a sleeping draught. Before long she had fallen asleep. But her sleep was uneasy, broken with nightmares and an unbearable sense of loss.

Lady Frances had not really believed matters were as serious as Jossie had said. She even persuaded Jossie to stay till the end of the week in London, in the hope that matters could be mended. But the next few days proved her mistaken. Ivo did not return to the house, but stayed at his club. He acknowledged his aunt and Jossie courteously at the soirée they attended the next night, but made no effort to join them, and spent the evening with his former associates, flirting outrageously with the ladies. Society watched, nodded, and said they were not surprised. Miss Calverton was very beautiful, but holding the attention of one of London's acknowledged flirts was clearly beyond her. Jossie held her head high, and parried all enquiries with a serenity which amazed Lady Frances, who knew how much of Kendrick's skill had been needed to hide the ravages of her mistress's distress.

And so it continued. No announcement was needed. London soon assumed that Miss Calverton's short-lived engagement to Lord Trenchard was at an end, since the parties apparently never spent more than a few minutes in each other's company. Ivo's conduct only confirmed Jossie's doubts. If he had truly loved her, she told herself, loved her in the all-consuming way she wanted, he could not now appear to be so unaffected by her presence in the same room, laughing, dancing, talking with everyone, it seemed, but her. But he was if anything more carefree, more devil-may-care, more outrageously flirtatious than ever. Her godmother was wrong, very wrong. Soon the strain began to tell and she decided that she must leave London as soon as possible.

This was easier to accomplish than she had feared. Lord Veryan was tired of London. He had come to see Jossie's success, and that he had done. He had hoped to see her engaged to his son, and that had also come to pass—but not for long. Now he was tired and jaded. He wanted to be back in his own home, breathing his own fresh air.

Lady Frances, too, was ready to go. As far as she could see, there was little point in staying any longer. She had tried to talk to her nephew about his quarrel with Jossie, but he had proved so impenetrably courteous that she had finally had to give up. Though she suspected that behind it lay something more than Jossie's refusal to marry him, she had no idea what it might be. Whatever it was it had gone deep. In spite of his apparent enjoyment of life, Ivo was hurting every bit as much as Jossie, she was sure. But he remained charmingly, and adamantly, uncommunicative. At the end of the week all three of them, Lady Frances, her brother and her goddaughter, were more than ready to leave the noise and dust of London behind them for good.

They reached Lyne St Michael when the countryside was looking its best. Flowers lined the hedgerows and filled the pastures. The trees were in full foliage, but still freshly green, and the fields were lush with growing crops. The air was full of the scents of early summer.

'Ah! This is better!' Lord Veryan exclaimed as they descended from the carriage at Danby Lodge. 'Much, much better! Isn't that so, Jossie?'

Jossie looked round. Little had changed. The lodge had been well looked after during their absence, and it looked much as it had done almost a year before, when Ivo and her godmother had brought her here after Peter's coming of age. She swallowed. When would her heart stop giving that little twist of pain whenever she thought of Ivo? She smiled at Lord Veryan. 'Much better,' she said.

He frowned at her. 'Hmm. You might at least get some colour in your cheeks down here! You look like a ghost, girl!'

* * *

Later that evening the three of them walked round the garden. 'This place is very pleasant,' said Lord Veryan. 'Very pleasant indeed, Frances. But I must confess that I'll be glad to see Sudiham again. I'll be off tomorrow.'

'I thought Ivo was coming down to collect you and accompany you home,' exclaimed Lady Frances.

'Er…no. He said he will join me at Sudiham at the end of next week. He has some business in London to attend to first. No, I'm afraid you won't see him this time, my dear.' The two older people carefully avoided looking at Jossie.

'We must make some plans,' said Lady Frances brightly. 'The Radstocks are in Brighton for the rest of the summer, but there are some other neighbours to visit. Later on we could perhaps do a little travelling.'

'Will you be calling on the Morleys?' asked Lord Veryan drily.

'I should like to,' said Jossie. 'I don't expect to enjoy it, but I ought at least to call on my father and step-mama.'

'Quite right! We shall do so,' said Lady Frances with approval. She chuckled. 'I don't suppose, however, that they will enjoy it any more than we shall! Gerard Morley is not likely to have forgiven me for ensuring that his daughter was such a success. His wife even less likely! Never mind! What else shall we do?'

'If you don't mind, Lady Frances, I should like to do some exploring for myself. I could ask my father if I could borrow one of the horses. I could perhaps even have Star again.'

'Is that…wise?'

'I need to lay a few ghosts.'

Lady Frances nodded. 'If you are sure, my dear.'

* * *

Lord Veryan left for Sudiham the next day. 'I shall miss you, Jossie,' he said as he was getting into the carriage. 'Come over when you can.'

'I shall. But not—'

'I know, I know,' he said testily. 'Not when that son of mine is there. I shall never understand it, never! I would have thought you two were ideally suited. What happened? Can't you tell me? I'm pretty sure you're in love with him even now. And I know how fond he was of you.'

Jossie looked at him sadly. 'I didn't believe he loved me. And I told him I didn't trust him.'

Lord Veryan leaned out of the carriage. 'You *what*? Good God, girl, what made you say a thing like that?'

'Peregrine told me something about him. Something horrible. Ivo refused to explain. He...he hasn't spoken to me properly since.'

Lord Veryan got out of the carriage again and ushered her back into the house. He took her into the small parlour and shut the door. 'Now. Peregrine told you something. What did he tell you?'

'I...I can't say. The secret isn't mine. But it was confirmed by someone else.'

'Jossie, I know Peregrine is my son, but I wouldn't believe what he said about Ivo if it was confirmed by fourteen bishops with prayer books in their hands! He's a malicious liar! For God's sake, don't you fall into the same trap that I once did! I nearly lost Ivo over it!'

'You did?'

'Ivo's proud, d'you see? He has this devil-may-care manner, but if he loves someone it matters a lot to him what they think of him. I hurt him badly when I didn't believe what he said once.'

Jossie looked down. 'I hurt him badly, too. I can see that now. I think I may well have lost him.' She sniffed.

'Damn Peregrine and his machinations! There's always been something wrong with that boy! He seems to hate Ivo for trying to do him good!' He looked at Jossie's downcast face. 'I'll do my best with Ivo when he comes. I'll try to persuade him to come over. If I manage it, the rest will be up to you.'

Jossie visited her father. Considering the problems, she felt it passed off very well. Mrs Morley was gracious, the Major even went so far as to say that he occasionally missed his daughter. Lady Frances watched the Morleys doing their best to make as little of Jossie's success as possible, and gained her own amusement from that. Jossie found Star in the stables, and was allowed to take him away with her. She was even offered her old riding clothes, the ones she had worn as a boy. But these she refused.

'Thank you, Father, but they belong to the past. I can never go back. Thank you for Star. I've missed him.'

They left with a vague promise to see one other again. The Major watched them rather wistfully as they went down the drive. Life had been happier for him during that past which Jossie now so firmly rejected.

Jossie did as she had said she would. She visited all the haunts that she and Peter had frequented in those old, carelessly happy days—Heversham Beacon, the valleys to the west, the farms and villages round about. Knowing that the Radstocks were safely away in Brighton, she even rode round the grounds of Radstock Court. She sighed, she laughed, she reminisced, and she rid herself of any last remnants of bitterness. Peter's ghost was easily laid to rest.

But she did not go to the valley that had meant so much to her. The memories there no longer had anything to do with Peter, and were still too painful.

As time went on, any hopes she had entertained that Lord Veryan would prevail on Ivo to come to Lyne slowly faded. She would have to accept that Ivo had gone forever. So she resolved to go at last to the valley, see the waterfall, rehearse in her mind what he had said to her there, relive the dramatic scenes of their early acquaintance. And then she would do her best to forget them.

She tethered Star to that same tree not far from the stream, and wandered down the valley. She stood by the waterfall, seeing herself at seventeen, unaware, bewildered, unprepared for the demands being made on her by life. Others might have laughed at her, even taken advantage, but Ivo had been so understanding, so patient. What was it she had said to him?

'Perhaps all those years pretending to be a boy have…damaged me? I shall never enjoy being kissed.'

Ivo had given a shout of laughter, then he had pulled her round and hugged her. *'My sweet, darling Jossie! No one with as kissable a mouth as yours could possibly not enjoy being kissed sooner or later.'*

'Well, that's what I wanted to ask you, Ivo. I wondered if you could teach me how to respond.'

She had been so naïve, so innocent, making that absurd request without a second thought. And he had been scrupulous. An honourable man, Ivo Trenchard. How could she have thought him otherwise?

'*Are you sure you're being sensible? You must have heard what they say of me.*'

'*Lady Frances said once you were the worst flirt in the county before you went into the Army, and she didn't suppose you had changed.*'

'*How very kind of her! Doesn't that put you off?*'

'*Of course not—it's what I want! It's no use asking someone who doesn't know what they're doing to help me in this. I need an expert.*'

And what an expert Ivo had been! It was here, right on this spot, that she had first experienced the wonder, the rapture of Ivo's kisses. Too stupid to realise that it was Ivo himself who made the difference, she had thought the feelings transferable! Well, she knew now. The magic, the chemistry, lay between Ivo and herself. No one else would ever rouse in her that strange mixture of passion and compassion, the explosive combination of overwhelming tenderness and the demon of desire.

Jossie shivered even though the day was warm. It was all over. The desire, the tenderness, the love—all gone. She would not go under, as she had thought she might on the night of Peter's ball—that had been here, too. She would lead as contented a life as she could. But happiness was a different matter.

Sighing, she turned back up the valley. And stopped. In a strange echo of that first time Ivo was coming down the slope towards the stream, eyeing Star. Her heart gave a great leap, and she had to wait till she had enough breath. Then she cried joyously, 'You leave him alone, do you hear? Move away from my horse!'

Ivo looked over to where she stood. 'Jossie?'

She ran to him, tripping and stumbling in her hurry, sobbing his name. 'Ivo, oh, Ivo!' His arms went round her, his head was resting on hers.

'Pull yourself together, girl! You should be threatening me with a gun, not watering my jacket!'

'You came!' She looked at him with shining eyes. 'I'm so glad you came! Ivo, I'm sorry! No, no, don't stop me! I must say this. I should have known better. I don't care if forty bishops each with forty prayer books tell me that Peregrine's story is true, I still wouldn't believe him! You were right, I *do* know you! You would never do anything of the sort. Tell me you forgive me!'

'I love you, Jossie. Never, ever doubt that. With every breath of my being. There's no need for forgiveness between us. I was hurt and angry, I should have told you the truth at the time, but I was too proud. These past weeks have been torture, but I've come to my senses now.'

They gazed at each other in a happy daze. Then slowly, deliberately, Lord Trenchard drew his future bride, his love, to him and kissed her. Tenderness, protection, instruction, comfort, and a leaping passion— they all were there, but, most of all, this kiss was a pledge made to each other, a pledge of lifetime commitment, enduring loyalty, infinite love.

Lord Trenchard had made his choice.

They made their way back to the village, wrapped in a world of their own. When they reached Danby Lodge they found Lady Frances and her brother waiting for them in the drive. One look was enough to tell anyone that Ivo and Jossie had found each other, and Lord Veryan was practically dancing with pleasure.

'You told her?' he asked.

'Told me what?'

'The truth about Charlotte Gurney.'

'I didn't have to, Father. Jossie fell on my neck before I could get a word out!'

'Oh, how ungallant, sir!' said Jossie, laughing.

'It was the best moment of my life,' Ivo said, pulling her to him. 'To know that you had faith in me, loved me after all...'

'Really, Ivo! You mustn't kiss her on the drive in full view of anyone who cares to look! It isn't decent! You're not even engaged!' said Lady Frances.

'What do you mean? Of course we are!'

'In *my* day, it was considered necessary to consult the girl's father before asking her to marry you. Dare I hope that you have already talked to the Major?' said Lady Frances with mock severity.

'Aunt Frances, you are a delight! But not up to the mark every time. Yes, I called on the Major a few hours ago, and he has given a reluctant consent. Only because he couldn't think of a reasonable objection, I'm sure. The wedding will take place as soon as Jossie has her bride clothes.'

'Well, *you* may not care whether Jossie knows the truth or not, but *I* do! Come inside, both of you. We have a lot to discuss,' said Lord Veryan.

As they turned to go inside Jossie whispered, 'Ivo, how soon can the banns be called? I have enough dresses to last a lifetime. Or—couldn't we elope?'

'It wouldn't be difficult to get a special licence—not when the Great Duke himself is one of your admirers. But I wouldn't dream of eloping, Jossie. From now on the Trenchards are going to be the epitome of respectability! No more *affaires*, no more flirting. The only married woman in my life will be Lady Trenchard. And any siren looks will be for my sole pleasure. Understand?'

'Yes, my lord,' said Jossie. And gave him the best one in her repertoire.

After the first rejoicings were over, and the happy couple toasted, Lady Frances said, 'But tell us, Ivo. If you haven't yet been to Sudiham, what persuaded you to come here after all?'

'My Colonel. Who, it turns out, is the new Marquess of Coverdale—I wonder if Adam knows? Anyway, the Colonel is going north any day now, and I went to take my leave of him. He told me I was a fool to risk losing Jossie. And I found I agreed with him. So here I am!' He started to laugh.

'What is so amusing?'

'Colonel Ancroft was just leaving to keep an appointment when I called, so I walked along with him and left him at his lawyer's door.' He paused, then said, 'It's no use. I'll have to tell you the whole! You see, the Colonel has agreed to escort an elderly widow of a nervous disposition on his way north. He doesn't know her—he was to meet her for the first time that day at his lawyer's. Apparently she is taking her husband's ashes back to his birthplace—'

'There's nothing amusing about that!' said Jossie.

'No. But wait! I happened to see this elderly lady of a nervous disposition. She was getting out of her carriage as I turned to go back to Charles Street. She was just as I would have expected—rather stout, and dressed from head to toe in deepest black, including a large veil. But two things were wrong. As she stepped out of the carriage I saw the prettiest pair of ankles I've seen in a long time. They certainly didn't match the rest of her appearance. And the other was—'

'Well?' asked Lady Frances impatiently.

'A sudden gust of wind blew the veil into the air, and she was annoyed. Her voice was attractive, and the accent refined. But the word she uttered is one more commonly used in the back streets of Marseilles!'

'What was it?' demanded Jossie.

'Oh, no, my love. I'm not going to tell you—you might repeat it! But take my word for it—it shocked me! She saw me staring and before she lowered her veil she laughed and gave me a look out of the wickedest pair of green eyes I think I have ever seen.'

'Ivo! What did you do? Did you tell Colonel Ancroft?'

'I thought of it. But then I decided not to. John Ancroft is a sensible, experienced man. He won't be taken in for long. Besides, he is looking for something to take his mind off his problems. This widow of his might turn out to be just what he needs…'

* * * * *

Don't miss more romantic adventures
of soldier heroes in
Colonel Ancroft's Love
by Sylvia Andrew
available next month in
Regency High-Society Affairs, Volume 6